Praise for Gennita Low's
Virtually Hers

"...From the first page, this story will grab your imagination and not let go until the end. A third book is promised in this series and I can't wait until I can find a copy! Ms. Low is definitely a master at the cliff-hanger ending!"

~ *The Romance Studio*

"Virtually Hers is a fast-paced and exciting suspense with an ever-growing ribbon of love that you can't help but fall into. It's also joyfully recommended as a thriller."

~ *Joyfully Reviewed*

D1530251

Look for these titles by
Gennita Low

Coming Soon:

Virtually One

Virtually Hers

Gennita Low

A SAMHAIN PUBLISHING, LTD. publication.

Samhain Publishing, Ltd.
577 Mulberry Street, Suite 1520
Macon, GA 31201
www.samhainpublishing.com

Virtually Hers
Copyright © 2010 by Gennita Low
Print ISBN: 978-1-60504-798-0
Digital ISBN: 978-1-60504-802-4

Cover by Kanaxa

First Samhain Publishing, Ltd. electronic publication: October 2009
First Samhain Publishing, Ltd. print publication: August 2010

Dedication

To Mother and Father

To my Mutant Poms, my pack that echoes the wildness inside me

To Brando and Magic, Mom misses you two by her feet

To Mike, my Ranger Buddy, virtually original, my anchor and my friend

To Stash, virtually yours

Acknowledgments

My special thanks to Maria Hammon and Dee Clingman, who patiently read and reread my chapters. Their input saved my sanity.

My eternal gratefulness to Marjorie Liu, author extraordinaire, who listened as a friend, and sat down to "type" with me at the hotel lobby. And to Pamela Clare, for private confidences about *virtually* everything!

Hugs and love to my agent, Elizabeth Trupin-Pulli, the tigress who is always there for me.

To my wonderful editor, Angela James, whose insights and advice were invaluable, thank you 1000X for believing in my Super Soldier Spy series.

Thank you also to these special groups of romance readers:

1) TDD Delphites, especially Karen King, J.P., Mirmie Caraway, Katherine Lazo, Lauren Dane, Kylie "Susan" Brant, Sherrilyn Kenyon, Sandy "Sadista" Still—my lifeline, my buddies, my fellow-snarkers
2) RBL Romantica, a group of special romance lovers
3) GLow World Yahoo Readers Group, who's always there to answer my questions.

I'd also like to salute the men and women in the Special Forces and Special Operations in various agencies.

Lastly, to those who take the time to update Wikipedia on the Internet, you don't know how great your services are!

Memo
FYEO (For Your Eyes Only)

Cc: Intelligence Security Command (INSCOM), Los Alamos Task Force Unit Chief Scientist for Operation <redacted>; Armed Forces Medical Intelligence Center (AFMIC) Task Force Unit Chief Bio-Scientist for Operation Bio-Bot; Defense Intelligence Agency (DIA) Asymmetrical Strategic Counterintelligence Warfare Task Force Unit Chief for Operation <redacted>; Comptroller of Special Activities, General Accounting Office (GAO); COS COMMAND <redacted>

Past memo collected from various sources regarding human augmentation.

Re: The Virus Program

Unclassified 2003 DARPA (Defense Advanced Research Projects Agency) Report: "The human is becoming the weakest link. Sustaining and augmenting human performance will have significant impact on Defense missions and systems."[1]

Latest DARPA budget request to fulfill projects researching on:

* cracking the brain's neural codes

* manipulating complicated machinery or remote-controlled weapons by thought alone (robotics and thought manipulation divisions) (Re: MACAQUE EXPERIMENT—success in manipulation of robotic arm with implanted brain sensors in monkeys)

* more work on the exoskeletons for Human Performance Augmentation. The $40 million program is already midway through the projected six-year run, experimenting on amplification of human muscle movements through a super body suit for the average soldier.

DARPA plans for further augmentation marrying brain and muscle power are challenged by the natural boundaries of human endurance.

On the $20 million Continuous Assisted Performance program, DARPA Director Tony Tether in a statement to the House Government

---

[1] http://www.ratical.org/ratville/CAH/superSoldier.pdf

Reform Committee: "The CAP is investigating ways to prevent fatigue and enable soldiers to stay awake, alert, and effective for up to seven consecutive days without suffering any deleterious mental or physical effects and without using any of the current generation of stimulants."

DARPA's top-secret still classified bio-research and human augmentation programs are also up for more funding. Identities of all operatives in program to be held top secret.

Dr. Paul Saffo, research director at the Institute for the Future in Menlo Park, Calif., from interview, please click on link to hear entire quotation:

"Human augmentation is coming; the only question is how soon. This stuff is being worked on in all sorts of places all over the world. I'll give you three options. We can stay in it and be state of the art and deal with the moral issues. We can get out of it completely and be bystanders. Or we can do this half-assed thing in the middle. Now, of those three options, which one do you think is rational?"

Of interest to Dr. Kirkland pertaining to his questions on remote viewing: Military Applications of Post-Quantum Physics: http://www.qedcorp.com/Q/ChiaoBell.html.

Glossary for Acronyms

COS/ CCC/ Triple C/ Command
Various names for Covert-Subversive Command Center

COS Commandos
Covert subversive commandos

GEM
Independent contractors, mostly females, who are information-gathering experts. The acronym's meaning isn't shared with the public.

NOPAIN
Non-persuasive and innovative interrogation, a special GEM technique in information-gathering.

SITREP
Short for situation report

SSS
Super Soldier Spy project

TIARA
CIA's Tactical Intelligence and Related Activities, divided into task forces, one of which is headed by Ricardo Harden.

TIRVVR
Pronounced as "terror", for Totally Immersive Remote Viewing Virtual Reality, the newest in spy technology

VIRUS
A top-secret project, a prelude to SSS, in which the nine COS commandos are trained

Chapter One

Remote viewer. Supersoldier-spy. Sex maniac. Now that was some resume for a future job application when she retired from this crazy life.

Helen splashed cold water on her face. It didn't help cool her down one bit. That weird sensation was bothering her again, like invisible fingers, up and down her heated skin, barely brushing the surface of her body. It moved like an electric current, giving little shocks of awareness whenever something came into contact with her skin too long. It was as if her nerve endings were working overtime, overwhelming her senses with details that would normally be routine.

She wiped her face with a dry towel from the rack. Like this cloth. Its softness. The way it caressed like a...like a lover's hands. Like that night.

The thought evoked memories that brought a hot flush through her body. She thought of how she'd lain in bed, half-dreaming, half-coming out of an erotic dream, and feeling a hundred times more sensitive than she did now. She'd called out his name and he'd appeared—like magic—in the cover of darkness, taking her by surprise, and unhinging the last shred of control she had. His seduction and her capitulation were complete.

Dammit, dammit, dammit. Stop thinking about Hades. Stop thinking about his hands and lips.

"Okay, let's be rational about this," she said out loud, tossing the towel into the laundry basket. "You hadn't had sex in months and months and then you took this drug that suppresses your body chemistry, and during the downtime, this sexy man seduced you and gave you the best..."

No, no, no, no, no, this was exactly what she was trying to avoid thinking. The stupid night was all about him having his way with her and she had willingly let him pleasure her any damn way he pleased.

Oh, she could give an excuse or two—that she had been under the influence of the serum, that she wasn't herself that night—but it all boiled down to the fact that she hadn't fought him at all. That she'd actually *enjoyed* being under his control. Every orgasm had left her wanting more.

"Arghhhhh!" Helen shrieked out in frustration, storming out of the bathroom. The memory of her orgasms was making her insides tighten with sensitive need.

What killed her was that she still didn't know who the hell her trainer was. She was in lust with a persona she'd created in a virtual reality program.

"How lame is that, Helen Roston?" she muttered.

He was too damn clever. She had been so excited to be the winning candidate for the experimental "Super Soldier Spy" program. COS Command Center, the agency that had contracted her to win this project, had immediately prepared her for their version. The first few months were easy for her since it was all physical challenges, training that she'd already undergone as a candidate. However, the next level involved virtual reality, something that tested her physical and mental stress levels.

When she was told she had control over what her trainer would look like in virtual reality, she'd thought it was the scientists and programmers testing her. Her new trainer was going to be an avatar, a "personality" she herself imagined and created with a nano-digital program, because they didn't want any contact between the two of them while they set and synced their brainwaves.

She had rubbed her hands in glee. She couldn't resist the fun of putting together a dreamboat of a man for a personal trainer. And while she was at it, why not make him naked too? Heck, she hadn't seen a gorgeous naked man in a long time, so here was a chance to indulge herself.

Helen wanted to smack herself now for swallowing the bait. Looking back, she realized—too late—that he'd been studying her all along and looking for ways to get in under her radar. He found one. How could he not, when every single thing she'd done for the last two years was probably there for him to look at, inspect and analyze?

She sat down at the desk and turned on the computer, leaning back in her chair as she watched the screen. What was he doing now? Had she gotten Jack Cummings' location right?

She sighed. Virtual reality and remote viewing. Science and weird science, and she was the conduit. Her *trainer*, the virtual reality version, was supposed to be the monitor, someone to anchor her while she was remote viewing, making sure that she didn't stray too far into the ether.

She had a real-life monitor when she was in the CIA remote-viewing program, so she hadn't questioned about working with a virtual monitor. Trainer-monitor was a generic enough term that it'd escaped her notice that, besides training her, he was also "preparing" her mind to respond to his will. All in virtual reality, with their brainwaves synchronized.

Insidious bastard. Normal monitors use an image as a mind trigger, projecting it to the remote viewer to anchor them to the physical place. However, her damn monitor wasn't normal, not in the least. The experiment was done in virtual reality so her mind could project what she saw into her monitor's mind; he would be able to see exactly what she was seeing and thus, there would be no secondhand reports.

She should have seen it coming. A normal trigger wouldn't work because that was just a basic "knock on the door". Her mind had to be kept keenly aware of him while she was remote viewing. A sexual trigger, on the other hand, was a whole new ball game. The more aware she was of him, the more he was able to be "present" in her remote-viewing sessions, and oh, was he good at making her very aware of him with his sexual games and magic movement-inhibiting pills.

Helen gritted her teeth. Now, if it was possible that it could get any worse, something had happened to her that she hadn't imagined possible. The serum, a bio-neuro blocker, created so that the remote viewer could function without rest and under stress, had tricked her brain into overcompensating the chemical balance in her body during the downtime. Simply put, whereas under the influence of the serum, she'd been unable to feel pain and stress, now that the drug had dissipated, she was extremely sensitive to touch and feelings. Every sensation filled her with an overwhelming need that confused and even scared her.

Because she hadn't slept throughout the whole mission, everyone had expected her to immediately rest up during her downtime, except that she couldn't. It had felt like walking at the edge of a cliff. In the dark.

Until Hades surprised her with a late-night visit.

She hadn't known it, but he'd understood. Her body, injured and stressed out from the drug, and now bombarding her with too many neuro-signals, wasn't going to relent until she gave in to an outlet. It seemed that the antidote to an overload of neuro-blocker was excessive sensation that needed to be allayed. Fighting it only made it worse. The edginess wasn't going to go away by itself.

Helen pulled her hair up, one hand opening a desk drawer to get a scrunchie. Even the feel of her hair brushing against her skin was bothering her right now. *It* was definitely coming back.

She needed to concentrate on what she'd been thinking about instead of her body. Normally, she was a logical operative, able to connect unrelated things in many a puzzling situation. That ability had saved her ass many times. Her friends had called it intuition.

Whatever. Intuition or sixth sense, it was telling her now that it wasn't just the after-effect of the serum. Something *had* happened to her during the test mission when she'd gone off after the decoder. Those few minutes, while running down the stairs, she'd experienced pain to the point of blinding her. It was so bad she'd almost fallen down the stairs.

She licked her upper lip and frowned as she tried to ignore the temptation to do that again. She touched her fingers to her lips. He hadn't kissed her that night, not on the lips. How would it feel—

Helen! Stop this!

She needed to focus. She had this theory about what happened—

But the memory of the feel of his mouth on her breasts kept intruding. It was like tunnel vision, every part of her zeroing in on how it'd felt as his tongue tortured her nipples, his teeth nibbling the soft flesh around them. It'd been incredibly erotic to just lie there in the dark, unable to fight the waves of pleasure that pulsed through her, unable to see the face of her lover, as his hands and mouth explored her, giving her what her body was craving.

Helen could hear her own breathing becoming agitated. She shook her head, uselessly attempting to shut the images out, but it was difficult when her body appeared to be responding to the stimulus. Her eyes widened at the sight of her nipples straining against her shirt. Touching them with a fingertip, she gasped at their sensitivity. Pebble-hard.

She took in a long breath. Her cotton shirt scraped her skin gently as she exhaled loudly. Just as before, the more she fought, the more her body and mind demanded release. And because *he'd* planted that sexual trigger in her head, of course her brain was using thoughts of him to feed what her body was craving.

Sexual trigger. Chemistry. That and what happened at the stairwell. These were all somehow linked. If only she could stop getting distracted and overwhelmed by all these feelings...

Abruptly, she leaned forward and tapped at the keyboard, hooking into the COMCEN database and opening the program that had created the virtual reality avatar. She pulled up the original model she'd worked on, the one that became the avatar, and stared at *him* in all his naked glory.

So obvious. He'd guessed correctly that she would put in a fantasy man. Easier to bond with, right? With their brainwaves in sync and the controls at his end, her mind was ready for his stimulation. How the hell did she miss that happening to her? She'd been trained to catch these little things and he'd outwitted her. He'd even called himself Hades, the ultimate seducer to the dark side, and had played the part to her captive Persephone to perfection.

"It's always the obvious." Helen scowled, wagging her finger at the image of the blond man on the screen. She wanted to yell at someone right now but her damn trainer was a digital avatar, a naked male with a sculpted and perfect body, the kind she made up in her fantasies. Her scowl deepened. "I haven't had a serious relationship while I've been training. Two freaking years. No time. What did I do? Created a fantasy man and gave him the vehicle to seduce me. Brilliant move, Helen, just brilliant."

She'd thought it was hilarious fun to walk around in virtual reality with a deliciously sexy naked man. Why not? What could be more ridiculous than her remote viewing with a man resembling a Greek god?

She sighed, resting her chin on her hand as she kept staring at the perfect body in the screen. "Well, they don't call me Hell for nothing. Of course I have to up the ridiculous factor," she murmured. "I now get horny when my avatar wants me to."

If she weren't so pissed, she would laugh at the analysis. Something had happened to her during the mission. The serum she'd taken had an unexpected side effect. She needed to go over what happened as objectively as possible.

"From insensitive to pain to super-sensitive to touch," she muttered. Try super-super-super sensitive. She had avoided contact with anyone, managing to fall asleep finally, but somehow, in her sleep, connected to his brainwaves, she had invaded Hades' dream or vice-versa.

She shook her head. Didn't matter now. Whatever happened, he'd woken up knowing exactly what she was going through and had come for her. Super-super-super sensitive became super-super-super sensual. Helen shook her head harder. Objectivity-smojectivity.

"It's just sex," she told herself.

Yeah. With her avatar, her fantasy man. Only he'd come in human form that night, finally appearing to her in darkness. And boy, he didn't diminish her fantasy one bit with his sexual repertoire. The man knew how to touch a woman.

She reached out for the computer mouse. There was something wrong with her fantasy avatar. She just knew the reality looked nothing like this blond god she'd created. Her mind wandered idly as she clicked her mouse, moving the cursor around. Dark hair. Eyes? Dark? Black? Leaner body?

His hands. She didn't want to think of his hands, but that was what connected her to him physically. She could remember his touch—every intimate detail. He had very powerful hands; he'd shifted her body on her bed effortlessly. And talented lips and tongue. She remembered those too well.

He'd explored her in the darkness, using first his hands, then his mouth. While rubbing some kind of lotion on her injury, he'd wickedly lavished it elsewhere, using it to arouse her even more. She had almost died from pleasure when he'd settled his mouth into her heat, leisurely licking her aching need for what seemed like hours, while he massaged and caressed her body. Sensitized beyond reason, she'd finally given in to his silent persuasion, responding eagerly to his touch.

"Yes, yes, yes, yes," she'd panted out repeatedly, needing and wanting, uncaring about her loss of control. He'd been quite obliging in addressing her demands. Several times.

Helen licked her lips, feeling flushed again. That edgy feeling inside was growing exponentially. She shifted in her seat, trying to get comfortable. She closed her eyes. She desperately wanted his hands on her again, virtual or not, but he was on a mission, on a ship heading toward Russia...

"Hades," she whispered.

Water. She smelled the sea, felt the swaying motion under her. Her jaw dropped as realization dawned. She was remote viewing. How was it possible when she hadn't modulated her brainwaves yet? She didn't even feel her phantom form shoot through the ether, like she usually did while pinpointing the location.

She turned, taking in the odd-shaped walls and low ceiling. The smell of the ocean. She had a nasty suspicion about her location. There were sounds coming from the other side of the wall. Her heart thudded with anticipation as she moved toward the noise. Fighting. She cocked her head. Very intense fighting. She peered around the corner and immediately felt ridiculous. No one could see her while she was remote viewing; there was no need to be sneaky about looking.

But instinct told her there was danger for her here and she wasn't going to ignore it, especially when she'd traversed unexpectedly, without preparation. She had somehow sent herself to this place and she'd a feeling that something else was going to happen.

She saw a man lying on the floor. Dying. She felt the air thickening even as she looked harder, trying to make out the man's face. A gurgle of pain escaped from him and then...nothing. She wanted to turn away from death, but felt compelled to keep looking. Where was the other fighter? She couldn't see him.

The atmosphere felt oddly smoky, although she couldn't smell any smoke. She could make out the outline of a man as he turned toward her. Even her vision got cloudy, and she blinked hard, trying to focus. Must. Try. To. See. She took a step forward. Hard to breathe, as if the air was very thick here.

All of a sudden, her heart started to beat erratically. Something was definitely wrong. But she so wanted to get closer, to see this man...

Okay, calm down, Hell. Step back. Step away.

At the last second, Helen turned and ran. She felt herself sinking, falling into oblivion, but not before she caught a glimpse of the other man.

Silver eyes. Blue jeans.

Oh God. Not him!

It always came to this. Jed McNeil had no illusions about his role as Number Nine in the Covert Subversive (COS) commando unit.

Governments declared war—open and covert—and technology provided the instant highway, but no matter how precise artificial Intel had become, with its laser accuracy, its ability to be in places no human ear or eye could gather Intel, and its useful function of keeping danger away from operatives, there was always the one element not factored into the formula: Human beings were unpredictable, and sometimes, it was much easier to just send one man in after another.

His target was quick, making the first move, going for his throat. Jed leaped out of the way, at the same time swinging his knife upwards. The other man jumped back, wincing at the first slice of his flesh. Startled wariness entered his eyes before he gave a grim smile and resumed attacking.

There was a certain look in a man's eyes when he knew his time was up.

Jack Cummings hadn't shown any surprise when Jed appeared, knife in hand. A small nod of acknowledgment. A token, although fierce, resistance.

Cummings had some martial arts training and the hand-to-hand became a short silent dance of death, with swift punches and kicks, which Jed evaded and countered with equally lethal speed. His opponent was quick on his feet too, moving hard and fast as he jerked back and forth, looking to get Jed off-balance. He suddenly lunged forward, fist punching out forcefully.

Jed deflected the jab to his solar plexus, twisting Cummings' wrist and locking it outward. He twirled his knife into position, intending to give the final lethal blow, but the other man immediately coiled his frame around Jed's body, his other hand going for the throat. To avoid having his neck broken, Jed elbowed the ribs and rotated sideways. He rammed a fist into Cummings' jaw. Another. Then silently advanced toward the man who was holding the bloodied side of his face.

From his expression, the CIA rogue appeared to know that he wouldn't make it, even if he'd managed to scream for help, and to his credit, he hadn't. He'd seemingly been expecting someone to come after him.

Never underestimate a desperate man gambling with his life. Jed anticipated the sudden roundhouse kick, springing into a back flip. But not before he saw the flash of steel on the tip of the shoe that had barely missed his throat. Landing on his feet, he flicked his wrist and released the knife in his hand. His steel hit the mark. And it was over.

Jed slipped his bloody knife into the sheath on the back of his belt. He tapped on the tiny unit attached near the buckle, which was equipped with a GPS and coded satellite transmitter, signaling that he'd just completed his mission. He looked down at Jack Cummings' body for a moment.

To him, there was one simple truth about warfare. All the technology in the world couldn't equal hand-to-hand combat. He had seen violence from every possible angle since he was sixteen—as a street thug, an IRA lookout, a CIA trainee, an Airborne Ranger in the Army, time with the Green Berets, a covert Special Forces commando, and a few undercover stints that had him working for his enemies. It was a long resume, years spent in wars created by governments, some more secret than others.

It wasn't something he boasted or talked about, as some warriors did, comparing their adventures at one war-torn place or another, mainly because he'd seen enough in his job to learn to respect silence. Especially about death.

Mission accomplished. Not that it brought any sense of accomplishment. He had wanted to bring Jack Cummings in alive but had failed in the first attempt a few days ago. There was no other option during the second attempt. Not in the middle of the ocean, on an enemy ship.

He frowned. There was that prickle of awareness again, a feeling that someone was watching him. Years of being in his line of work had honed his senses razor-sharp; he seldom second-guessed himself.

He stepped away from Cummings' body, totally on alert, watching for the slightest movement, listening for any kind of noise that might betray the enemy. If they were any good, they would have shot him by now and not given him a chance to escape. Unless, of course, they were just watching.

In his world, there were agents assigned to just watch and report, entities his kind called "ghosts". Data-miners. Jed had caught up with a few of them in the past and was even friends with some of them. Objective information agents were useful and provided a valuable service.

But this wasn't *that* feeling of being watched. Definitely different. This was even more subtle. A light brushstroke. A soft breath on a mirror.

Jed squinted in mild amusement. He was getting poetic about his job. There was nothing at all light or soft about the bloody nature of covert warfare. The feeling persisted, although for some reason, he didn't feel threatened, just a vague nagging sensation that he wasn't alone. He circled the small room slowly and stopped in mid-stride. His gaze darted upwards and around. Nothing, but he was sure he'd felt something. There. Again.

He frowned, trying to gauge what he was feeling. It felt like...he shook his head...a vibration, and not from the ship. He didn't have time to stand here and analyze. Giving the dead man on the floor one last glance, he slipped into the shadows and headed back up to the deck.

He felt no compassion for the likes of Jack Cummings. Betrayal always had a price. Instead, he ran through the usual comprehensive profile of his target. Jack Cummings, early thirties. CIA TIARA Task Force Three, security clearance Level Four. One-half of the team who stole and tried to sell SEED—a miniature satellite encryption device, newly tested at Los Alamos. Eluded capture. Attempted escape to Russia. Information exchange/barter aggregated at ninety percent. Info risk at ninety-five percent.

Jed mentally closed the file. Operation status: target eliminated on international waters.

Helen couldn't open her eyes. They felt weighted down, as if she was in the middle of a dream and was trying to wake up. A drum thundered so loudly, it sounded as if she were listening to her iPod with its volume set way up. It took her a minute before she realized it was her own heart beating.

Her whole body felt feverish. The room was too hot. She still couldn't open her eyes. Her heartbeat grew erratic as she struggled, fighting something she couldn't see.

Wake up, Helen, wake up!

Her own scream pierced through her consciousness and her eyes flew open. She stared up at the ceiling of her living room for a few seconds as she gulped in deep breaths of air. Her heart was still racing, although that odd echoing was gone.

What the fuck was that?

She gingerly moved her arms and legs, trying to figure out what'd happened. She felt hot, as if she'd been exerting herself, but the last thing she remembered doing was sitting in front of her laptop, playing with the virtual reality avatar program.

And...

But it was no mistaking who she'd seen before everything went cuckoo. She slowly turned to the side and got on her knees. Grasping the back of the chair for support, she started to get back on her feet.

Headache. Blinding, throbbing, intensely painful headache. It struck her down like a branch hit by lightning, her knees hitting the carpeted floor.

She grasped the sides of her head, in her mind trying to loosen the imaginary band around it. Imaginary or not, the pressure was tightening to the point where she felt herself gasping for air.

Concentrate on your breathing, Hell. Concentrate.

She tried to stand but found herself unable to open her eyes more than a crack. The light coming from the tall lamp by the desk stabbed at her vision. Everything was a distorted red haze that seemed to pulse bright, then dark, with each throbbing thump in her head.

Groping around uncoordinatedly, she found the lamp stand and reached for the switch. She almost screamed her relief as the room plunged into darkness, taking some of the pain with it.

She leaned against the desk, taking deep breaths, counting to ten. The tension around her head loosened and she opened her eyes cautiously.

"Oh man, what the hell was that?" She swayed on her feet. The pain was a dull ache now. Manageable.

The computer screen illuminated the room and she reluctantly turned her eyes grimly back to the figure of the avatar. She swallowed.

No use avoiding the truth. Jed McNeil was Hades, her trainer. While trying to imagine what her avatar really looked like, she had somehow sent herself into remote-viewing mode and went in search of him instead. She knew the identity of the dead man she'd seen. After all, she'd been the one who had remote viewed and located Cummings on a ship.

"Jed McNeil," Helen said, her voice a soft hoarse. The knowledge of who Hades was would have filled her with satisfaction if her body didn't feel as if she'd gone ten rounds with someone much stronger. She felt incredibly weak and a little nauseated from the sudden migraine.

She closed the file and sent the system into hibernation. Then, slowly, she hobbled toward her bedroom. Her muscles felt stiff, contracted. She needed to sleep this off.

Stretching out on her bed, she released a sigh of frustration. She wasn't feeling like her old self yet. No use calling Dr. Kirkland; she knew he wouldn't give her a straight answer and would probably warn Jed McNeil. She didn't know exactly what she was going to do yet about confronting Mr. McNeil and demanding the truth from him, but one thing she was sure about was that she had better be one hundred percent or that man was going to eat her for dinner.

"Did you have any unforeseen problems?"

Jed thought of the odd feeling that had invaded him during the last minutes on the boat. "No," he replied. "Cummings is taken care of."

"What do you plan to do with his wife?"

"Any suggestions?" It was up to the powers-that-be, of course, what to do with a traitor who had lost her leverage, but as long as she remained at COMCEN, she could still be of use. "Besides elimination, of course."

"She might have useful Intel."

"Number Eight can extract any information that may be of use," Jed said.

"Not you?"

"I have something to do." For the first time, Jed allowed himself to think of *her.* "I'll hear all proposals in the morning."

"Must be something important."

Not something. Someone. Elena Rostova. The image of her naked under him, with her long legs open wide, came too easily. The way her rosy nipples puckered up when she was aroused. The sweet arch of her strong back in the throes of passion. Most of all, he wanted to put his mouth on the heat between her legs, playing with her till she bucked uncontrollably. Making Elena moan and come in different ways was fast becoming an erotic fantasy. The thought of doing that turned him on the most.

Jed blinked, a little surprised at his lack of concentration. How was it that the thought of this one woman could set his libido off like a rocket? He had no explanation for it, except maybe because he'd been watching her for so long, that when he now had finally had a taste of her in bed, he wanted more.

The airplane seat could be specially adjusted to any position, much like a car seat, and Jed pressed the button for it to lean back all the way. A footrest automatically popped up. Maximum comfort for any operative in need of catching up with sleep, something he hadn't had for some time, just like Elena. But, unlike her, he didn't have to remote view before going on a mission.

He closed his eyes, but his mind continued to focus on the woman in his thoughts. He wondered how she was at the moment. He had made sure she was given a few days off while he was on mission, so she would be around familiar surroundings to get that downtime she needed after the test she'd gone through. He felt the corners of his lips quirking in self-mockery. He wasn't just concerned about her well being. He didn't want Elena anywhere near his commandos, not in the state she was in. They were intrigued by the new operative in their midst too.

Elena Rostova, a.k.a. Helen Roston, GEM operative. Remote viewer—an agent trained to spy remote targets with the mind—that special covert activity that nobody wanted to talk about.

He hadn't decided whether his fascination dealt with the woman or the power she harnessed inside her. She amazed him with her calm acceptance of what she could do. For someone who had discovered her ability to remote view barely two years ago, she was remarkably well-adjusted psychologically. Most test subjects, at this stage, would experience internal conflict because remote viewing pushed the boundaries of reality and personal beliefs.

Not his Elena. He'd watched her for a long time as she underwent extreme physical and mental training, and had yet to see her crack. Even after this last mission, with the strange effect of the serum on her body, she'd fought for control every step of the way. It'd have been so easy to give in to her body's demands. After all, the mission was over and a success, and there was no need to be on guard.

Yet she hadn't.

To see that kind of control mirrored in another person had left Jed secretly amused. Fate and its twisted sense of humor. For years he'd been called a control freak and he'd shrugged it off. So that was what others felt when they were around him.

It wasn't an issue to him. He liked being the one in control. He'd been trained to manipulate, and through the years, he'd made it into a game of sorts. Mental manipulation. How many different ways were there and how far could one influence another's thoughts and actions without direct communication? He'd done it for so long that it was second nature now, and he had to stop himself sometimes from unnecessarily affecting a situation that was none of his business. He thought of the one between his friend Alex and his love interest, T., and how he had had a hand in putting them in close quarters. His lips curved wryly. Okay, so sometimes it was too much fun not to, even for a man with a busy schedule such as his.

Currently, his hands were full with a certain female operative who could remote view. The CIA remote-viewing program, Star Gate, which trained operatives to spy with their minds, had always intrigued him. He'd undergone similar mind-control training at Command Center but it was more at the level that most spies were familiar with—brainwashing, Intel-gathering, hypno-suggestions. Remote viewing was, arguably, an intangible addition to hi-tech spying, since it depended on an individual reporting, without any back-up of wire-tapping or informed sources, on something happening at some location that might or might not even be correct. And to make it even less likely for any government agency to actually be one hundred percent behind this "information", said remote viewer was, after a session, usually unavailable mentally and incapable physically to get to, or gain access of, what he saw.

There was only one known case that Jed was aware of, of the military sending in a small group of special ops personnel in a rescue mission out in the desert. The exception was made because the hostage was a four-star general, one of their own. However, they'd ultimately failed because the remote viewer had only "seen" a desert landscape with a few distinctive landmarks at which their Military Intel specialist had made an educated guess. The resulting red faces of losing men and wasting money on a mission that had depended on a remote viewer's information had all but killed the CIA ambition to integrate their secret program with Military Intel.

Jed recalled all the discussions going back and forth between departments. He'd stood by, listening, gathering the necessary information for COMCEN, and he'd privately concluded that until a remote viewer's downtime could be eliminated *and* until they could find a remote viewer whose background as an information analyst—spy—was first rate even *before* he started getting training in remote viewing, the program was dead in the water. No agency would acknowledge having anything to do with it, much less touch it with a ten-foot pole.

But he'd kept up with the research at the labs. After all, whatever they came up with, they were bound to try it out on his group of men and him sooner or later. It wasn't that long ago when the COS commandos were themselves part of an experiment.

There were plenty of theories: What if drugs were used to control the downtime, giving the remote viewer the necessary boost physically and mentally? What if each department—military and Intel—trained a candidate so he could accomplish certain missions himself, and thus eliminate guesswork? And, the ultimate question—what if they created a drug or pain-inhibitor similar to the one that had been tested on some troops, allowing them to function longer without sleep? It would put the responsibility of completing a mission solely on the remote viewer himself. Jed remembered thinking that that was a hell of a responsibility for one man and he, as his unit's leader, would never solely depend on, and blindly follow, one operative's remote viewing talents, no matter how good he was.

However, that was before TIVRRV. The lab had unfolded the possibility of him being a *participant* in the remote-viewing session. That had intrigued the hell out of him.

The new program that had trained Elena Rostova was called—tongue-in-cheek but appropriate, nonetheless—Super Soldier Spy. She was the best of a group of hand-picked candidates from different government agencies competing for the job and had just undergone the final important test to convince the other agencies that she was capable.

Not that the program would ever be fully sanctioned. Remote viewing, explained to those who weren't into psychic or unexplained phenomena, sounded like woo-woo crap, the kind of stuff that was associated with weirdoes, quack doctors and new age beliefs. Definitely *nothing* with which the Defense Department or the Army of the United States of America wanted to associate!

But remote viewing and other psy-programs had been in existence since the thirties and forties, involving top-secret scientists and para-psychologists, and administered—secretly, of course—on soldiers and civilians alike. Such things, however, were now called conspiracies.

Jed smiled. Now that was a word with which he was familiar. What was covert life without a few of them?

In twenty years, he'd seen and been involved in enough strange experiments that he hadn't questioned the validity of trusting a "remote-viewing spy" to be in his unit.

Super Soldier Spy—it was one of those controversial programs that all the agencies wanted because of the government money involved—everyone wanted to be the department that won such a highly-funded program—but only a few, he was sure, were going to actually see the project through. A few years, maybe, then let the whole crazy thing die a slow painful death, like all the other secret para-experiments, but still somehow manage to keep the government funding it. His smile turned cynical. He knew that kind of manipulation very well.

But COS Command Center's candidate had won. Jed smiled again, remembering the looks on the faces of some of the most powerful men in charge of the country's defense. And what if the least likely candidate to beat out the rest was a woman?

Helen Roston hadn't been expected to make it. After all, she was female, and there were extreme physical tests she had to train in and pass. She did that. So did most of the other candidates, who were hand-picked among the elite in their respective agencies/departments.

But it was obvious that Helen outshone all the others when it came to the CIA remote-viewing training phase. There wasn't a doubt among all the test reviewers and trainers that the woman had a particular gift that was trainable. She had zoomed past her competition and was remote viewing at a higher level before anyone else.

He remembered the buzz at COMCEN the day it was announced that their operative had taken the grand prize. But he had to admit he'd been surprised the funding committee had actually picked her. Even though he knew, from reports and personal observation, that Helen Roston should get the nomination, he also knew the bias against a woman was strong. COMCEN had taken a big risk in offering a female candidate, but then his agency had always been straight-shooters. Only the best. No exceptions. And Helen Roston was their best shot.

Jed cynically suspected that most of the agency heads voting in had probably wanted COMCEN to fail. Whatever their motives might be, now the program was his agency's, to do as they wished as long as they produced results. He had known immediately that the scientists at COMCEN wanted to try out the brain entrainment theories.

TIVRRV, pronounced "terror", stood for "Total Immersion Virtual Reality Remote Viewing". It was their pet project and now they had the perfect candidate and, most important of all, the funding. As for the female operative—she became Jed McNeil's to command.

Of course, the big brass wasn't so easily convinced. Not by a long shot.

Jed could imagine the shouting behind closed doors.

"A female?"

"Remote what?"

"Spying something with the mind? Then...going after it herself? Gentlemen, you must be out of your fucking minds!"

The idea was met with incredulity and disdain from all quarters. So they had agreed to come together for one final test on Helen Roston. If she could remote view and successfully perform the mission afterwards, then the agencies would leave Command Center alone for now.

Jed and his commandos had discussed it among themselves first. Theirs was a highly secretive outfit, and with people, no matter how highly placed, watching, there was a likelihood of making things a tad too public. Also, they had their own agenda with the remote-viewing program and COS Command Center certainly didn't want that part of it making it through the covert grapevine.

He thought of how important Helen had suddenly become.

For the last few years, COMCEN had been working on brain pattern simulation and bio-stimulants experiments, testing different drugs on their own operatives. With the addition of the CAVE, a cutting edge virtual environment, mind and body could be put in different simulated situations.

Helen Roston was the perfect addition. And she added another dimension—remote viewing. With the right handler-trainer, could they "share" what she saw in virtual reality?

That assignment, naturally, was offered to him first. His job would be to verify what she "saw" with the brain entrainment program that would sync their brainwaves during her remote-viewing sessions. In essence, if the experiment worked, he himself would be "there" with her, "seeing" what she saw, and thus, the success rate of accomplishing a difficult mission would definitely be a lot higher than a regular remote viewer's Intel.

Thinking back now, Jed understood why he'd been reluctant at first. He had had enough experience with mind-control experiments to understand the intimacy involved between subjects. Helen Roston wasn't going to be a regular "partner". Because he wasn't a remote viewer himself, he'd have to be the one "in charge" of certain parts of her mind.

From the very first time he'd observed her, he'd known there was no fucking way in hell she would've gone for that. Reasons not to accept the assignment came easily. He didn't want that kind of responsibility for a potential member of his team. Number Eight had wanted to try the serum and this experiment would be up his alley.

Those were the reasons he admitted to out loud. He didn't tell anyone that he was also very attracted to the candidate. She was the kind of woman that had always gotten his attention—sassy, bold, and full of secrets. She was also a GEM operative, so she was dangerous in many ways. And therein lay the temptation. It was hard for him to say no to the challenge of probing a dangerous woman's mind.

He knew he'd need to prep her mind for his access and to do that, he'd have to gain her trust through trickery. One couldn't be direct about it because if she'd known, Helen would have mentally fought against it.

Elena. He mouthed her name, as he sleepily recalled the challenge to slowly implant a sexual trigger in her mind. Because she was a GEM operative, trained in NOPAIN, she knew how to counter mind-control techniques. He had been careful, working slowly to get what he wanted.

First, he'd kept her off-balance by training her in the CAVE Ultimate, a ten-by-ten room that allowed multiple participants to experience immersive virtual reality, with one participant controlling the environment. He had chosen to be invisible during his training sessions with her, knowing that it would both frustrate and intrigue her.

Second, when they had advanced the training to the Portal, the VR machine controlled by the mind, he had asked Dr. Kirkland to tell her she'd been given total control in the creation of her avatar, so she could give her trainer a "face" and a "body" during their virtual interaction sessions. He'd known the idea that she could choose a face would appeal to her. He also knew she would create an avatar that would be appealing to her senses.

Third, once he had her mind and senses involved intimately with him, it was time to move into her comfort zone. And with a trained operative, he had to move in quickly and ruthlessly, before the first hint of suspicion alerted her.

Seduction of mind and body. He'd done it before without getting too emotionally involved. Just stay focused and get the job done. He wasn't chosen to be Number Nine of the COS commandos to expound on the complexities and consequences. Number Nine accomplished all operations simply and effectively.

Elena was a grown woman, a highly trained operative, who knew going into this experiment that drugs and virtual reality could affect her mind and body. So why did he feel that he needed to hurry back and make sure she was okay?

Sleep now. Elena later.

Chapter Two

One day, he would take a nice long nap, the kind that involved a hammock, a pitcher of ice tea, maybe the sound of waves rushing back and forth, with no agenda waiting for him when he opened his eyes, and if he was lucky, it would be a nap with no thought of disturbances or ambushes. Jed savored the image for a moment, imagining the warm breeze swaying his hammock. He hadn't taken a nap in twenty years, probably, and it wasn't going to be any time soon that he'd be able to enjoy a hammock by the beach.

The swaying of the elevator that led straight up to the third floor of COMCEN stopped. The first three levels of the complex were also underground and access limited. The fourth floor would be the ground floor for people entering from the front. Most of the time, his unit avoided entering and leaving the complex from there; they liked the idea that no one was ever sure they were on a mission or not.

The moment the elevator doors slid open, he was ready for the usual burst of activity that crowded his preference for silence. de Clerq was the first to meet him.

"Good job, Nine."

Jed barely nodded, striding out. Having to end a life was hardly a good job. The volume around him toned down a notch when the others became aware of his presence. His gaze swept across the room. "Does the wife know of it yet?"

"Not yet, but she isn't stupid. The moment she gave that bit of information to Heath, she knew she'd signed his death warrant."

Heath—Number Eight during operations—could be persuasive like that. He'd seen his deputy's methods of extracting information. "Let me know when you hear a decision about her."

"Of course. When will you be available for a group meeting?"

"After debriefing." They walked past the operatives monitoring activity on a series of screens around a larger one with a 3-D world map. Jed paused, half-listening to the background buzz of German,

Russian and French being spoken. He eyed the hot spot in Eastern Europe where hostage negotiations were taking place. He'd need to get hold of Flyboy for an update about that situation.

First, though, he needed to check on Elena. That would mean getting Dr. Kirkland to call her up and if she was still not feeling herself... He briefly reworked his schedule. "Strike that. Change it till tomorrow, if possible. Is T. here today?"

"Right. I'll buzz you when I check with everyone's calendar. T. isn't at HQ right now. Should I let her know you need to talk to her?"

"No." If she was undercover again, let her finish her task. He would discuss Helen's condition with her later. He stopped himself from asking de Clerq whether he'd gotten any news about Helen, pausing in mid-thought, momentarily tripped by the urgency to check up on her. Why was he so worried? He knew if he voiced his concern to de Clerq, he would be met with surprise; his ability to detach himself was legendary. Instead, he said, "I'll be at Dr. Kirkland's office."

"Sir, Admiral Madison left a message for you," a female operative told him as they strode past, handing him a file.

"Get him on the secured line for me ASAP." Jed opened the file to glance quickly through the memos as he continued walking. He tucked it under one arm and turned to de Clerq. "Madison's going to want an update about SEED and Cummings. You know if I hadn't gotten to the target, he'd send his SEALs after him."

"Yes, I know, and they'd have blown the Russian boat to pieces and we'd have an incident."

Jed smiled slightly. He'd seen the Admiral's STAR SEALs in action. "Those boys do like their fire power. Sometimes they're an asset."

"Like our ops in Southeast Asia and Macedonia."

Jed keyed in the security code to the higher security section on that floor. The doors swished open. Away from the main activity, it was quieter here.

"Yes," he agreed, "Hawk is proving that he can do solo missions when necessary."

"Oh, no doubt, even though just to play devil's advocate, I doubted they could do anything but destroy stuff, the way they eliminated a fucking bridge," de Clerq said with a wry smile and a shake of his head. "A fucking wooden bridge, at that."

"There is that," Jed conceded with a glimmer of amusement, recalling the dollar amount on the weaponry expenditure sheet for that particular joint venture. "But they completed their mission, which was to stop a certain truck."

"Does the Admiral know what SEED can do?"

Jed shrugged. "The man's smarter than the others. I'm sure he has a fair idea that SEED isn't just a password decoder. He'll be asking some interesting questions." He changed the subject. "What's its status?"

"We're working on expurgating the datagram."

"Good."

"I'll give you a buzz when I've looked at everyone's schedule." De Clerq checked his watch and gave a nod before heading off.

Jed's thoughts immediately returned to Helen as he continued his way to Dr. Kirkland's offices. As with all the departments at COMCEN, there were different levels to Medic. Underground levels dealt with experimental science and medicine. Only the highest personnel could access Level 3 and higher. Most of TIVRRV was done here. His sleeping quarters, when Helen was under sleeping observation, were here. This was where it had all began, the experiment of synchronizing brainwaves for deep immersive virtual reality.

He punched in the security code and leaned forward for the pupil scan. Who would have thought that "deep immersion" would mean that when they slept hooked to the same brain entrainment machine, they'd somehow invade each other's dreams? He wasn't sure what that meant, wasn't even sure whether he liked the idea, except that for now, it aided him to get physically and mentally closer to Helen Roston. That part, he liked. Very much.

Dr. Kirkland's office door was open. He looked up expectantly when Jed walked in.

"Were you expecting me?" Jed asked.

"No, I'm waiting for Helen."

Good. Then he didn't need to make a trip to see her. He took a seat by the desk. "I thought she's been cleared for a few days off. She should be at her place resting."

"She called an hour ago and told me that she needed to see me. She told me that her condition was back." Kirkland looked at him quizzically. "She also asked me to tell Jed McNeil that she needed to see him ASAP."

Jed waited a beat. The implication of that message was pretty clear. "Those were her words?"

"Exact words. I didn't give you away. I told her that I'd pass that message on if I saw you, adding that it was highly unlikely since I knew you were out on a mission and would be inundated with meetings when you got back. But yet, here you are." Kirkland's brows lifted enquiringly. "Did you get hurt? Have you revealed yourself to her? It sounded as if she knew who her trainer was."

Did she? Jed considered for a few moments. "She's guessing. Probably testing you too." Or maybe she'd finally seen his face in her dreams. She'd told him that she couldn't quite make out the face of the man whenever she had one of those shared dreams. "What else?"

"She said she was having problems sleeping, that her...ah...sensitivity was bothering her. Also, she had a massive migraine just before that. Being that Armando also had headaches when he was testing the serum, I told her to come in so I could give her another check-up, and that's when she said that she needed to see you ASAP." Dr. Kirkland smiled. "You haven't answered my question."

Her "sensitivity" was a polite way to put it. Jed had seen how she'd responded to his touch during her extremely "sensitive" state. She hadn't been willing to have anyone look at her injured leg because of it. Until he forced the issue, that was. He'd had to take care of her leg. And her. He doubted whether she'd forgiven him for that last part yet.

"I'm not injured, Doc." Jed debated for a moment whether to tell the doctor that he and Helen had been intimate. He probably knew already. "Did she elaborate more about her sensitivity?"

Kirkland nodded. "Extreme sensitivity to touch to the point of unbearable. That's why she hadn't wanted a physical when she first came back in from the mission. Since she wasn't limping any more, and knowing that you'd used the bio-compound on her leg the night before, I didn't give her a thorough check-up." His gaze grew more speculative. "Not that I want all the details, Jed, but if you keep giving her private visits, she's bound to discover your identity."

"You can't give deep tissue massage through virtual reality, Doc." A small wry smile formed. He liked the idea of private visitations very much. "The mind can be tricked but her injury would still be there."

"Yes, I know, and since she's as obstinate as you are, and wouldn't let anyone touch her, you took the risk and went to her yourself."

"She wasn't being obstinate," Jed said, and then conceded, "just a little, but it was mostly that she couldn't figure out why she felt the way she did. She wasn't comfortable explaining her condition."

"Even to her doctor?"

Jed shrugged. "I took care of it."

Kirkland paused briefly, studying Jed. "And now she knows you're her monitor."

"She isn't sure." He liked the idea of pushing her further. Sexual imprinting was all about manipulation, after all. "Continue to avoid giving her a direct answer. We'll see what she wants once she's here."

Want and need were two different animals. Jed knew what Helen needed. The fact that she asked about him meant she was getting closer to finding out who her monitor was, but that didn't tell him how she was going to get relief without direct confrontation. She was going to be in one hell of a mood.

His lips quirked at using her nickname as a pun. There was no halfway when it came to Helen Roston. Everyone fondly called her "Hell-on-wheels", "Hell-ery", or joked that she was a hell of a woman. Now she was hell-bent on getting his identity.

"If she insists on seeing you? You know how she can be."

"You can give her my communication number."

He'd been a little worried about her but if she was well enough to ignore a direct order to rest and instead rush here to talk Kirkland into telling her about her monitor, she couldn't be in too much need of a lengthy downtime. He couldn't decide whether to reward her or punish her for disobeying orders. He'd wait, see what she'd do first.

A strong woman like Helen would have her guard up once she found out his identity. He'd better take every advantage given him. Keeping her off-balance was one way. In her sensitive state, she was at his mercy. Surely, as a trained operative aware of having been imprinted, she'd be aware of that fact. In her condition, it'd be easy to keep her in a state of arousal for a while. It'd be interesting to see how long she would last.

Helen went through the lobby and pressed the elevator button. Dr. Kirkland was waiting for her. She wasn't in the mood to talk about anything, not really, but he was the only person from whom she might be able to get some answers. She mentally went through all the points she was going to bring up. *Focus. I need to keep focusing on the points.*

Everything was riding on her body being able to handle the serum. She'd read about the possible aftereffects, had been prepared for disorientation, pain even, but not this...this...whatever *this* was. Armando Chang had tried to warn her.

She entered the elevator. Reaching out, she realized both her hands were clenched. She sighed, unclenched them, and entered her code. She'd been trying so hard to block out her sensitivity that she hadn't noticed how tightly wound up she was. A few days' rest? What rest?

"There has to be a way out of this problem," she muttered. There had to be.

Oh, but there was, but there had to be *another* way, one that had nothing to do with *him*. Instantly, the memory of his dark shadow looming over her bed taunted her. She gritted her teeth with frustration as sensations she shouldn't be feeling while standing alone in the middle of an elevator started to bloom, making her weak in the knees.

No, she hadn't prepared herself for this at all.

She charged out of the elevator, hurrying down the corridor toward the Medic wing, trying to focus on her destination rather than her condition. If she didn't have a tight grip on herself, she'd be standing here lost in sensation. That wouldn't be good.

Hearing voices, she collected herself and slowed down before turning the corner. She came to a dead stop. Talk about the devil. Jed McNeil was standing in the hallway with two men in camouflaged fatigues, his attention on a piece of paper.

Helen stared at him. It was ridiculous how her heart rate zoomed up at the sight of him. He was dressed in black, exactly how she'd seen him in those few moments when she'd remote viewed the ship. Side by side with the other two uniformed men, he looked fighting fit, lean and dangerous, the tight black shirt molding his athletic body like a second skin.

As she headed closer toward the group, the man to Jed's right paused in the middle of a sentence and nodded at her before resuming. Jed didn't look up, continuing to read the piece of paper in his hand, as if he hadn't noticed the hesitation.

She realized then that he wasn't going to look up to acknowledge her at all. Determinedly, she walked up to them, murmuring "excuse me", as she brushed past. No reaction from Jed.

Should she greet him? Why not? "Agent McNeil."

His lashes were long and dark. A lock of hair curled over his forehead and she suddenly felt the urge to comb it with her fingers. What would it feel like?

It dawned on her that this was the first time she'd stood still long enough to really look at him. The first time she'd met the infamous Number Nine, she'd literally landed at his feet, having just fought off an attack. The next time didn't count either; she hadn't been herself.

Not that she was herself now. But if he really was her monitor...

He lifted his gaze from that piece of paper. His full attention felt like a jolt of electricity. She stared into those strange light eyes of his, trying to see whether he'd somehow betray that he was her monitor. But his gaze was cool, impersonal, curt, even.

"Agent Roston," he said. And started to walk away, followed by the two operatives.

Helen stared after him, stunned at the quick dismissal.

"Wait!" she called out.

That stopped him. He turned.

"Do you need something, Agent Roston?"

She could feel her temper rising. If that was his polite way of saying he had something important to do and she was bothering him, he failed miserably. After all, she was part of his team now. "Yes, actually I do. Can I see you in private as soon as possible?"

"Tomorrow."

Tomorrow? It had to be *today*. She had to know if he was Hades or not. "Can it be sooner?" she asked, trying to sound polite.

"Tomorrow," he reiterated softly, "will be soon enough, Agent Roston. You've been given a few days off."

What was that supposed to mean? "What if it's an emergency?"

She tried to appear cool and calm as he quietly studied her for a moment. These small silences he took were unnerving, especially with those eyes which seemed to see too much.

He cocked his head a fraction. "Well?"

"Well, what?" she asked, a frown forming.

"The emergency, Agent Roston."

She shook her head. "It's private, Agent McNeil," she said, and instantly regretted it.

A hint of amusement entered those glacial eyes. He retraced his footsteps until he stood in front of her.

"It's a *private* emergency?" His low raspy voice made the question sound even more intimate. "Is this private enough?"

He wasn't standing too close but something about him made Helen feel as if every male inch of him was pressed against her. She almost leaned closer, to see whether she was imagining the heat emanating from his body, but resisted the temptation just in time.

She stared at the black fabric spanning his chest and wondered at the solid strength it projected. What would it be like to smooth her hands over it? Immediately the palms of her hands started itching.

What the hell was the matter with her? She mentally slapped herself, lifting her gaze off his body to his face. The amusement was palpable now, even though his expression remained unreadable. She hoped he couldn't sense the highly agitated emotions that were swirling inside her.

"No," she said.

"No?" One eyebrow raised.

The other two operatives looked on with interest as Helen struggled with unfamiliar frustration. On one hand, she wanted Jed alone so she could confront him. On the other hand, she wanted to call his bluff. She had a feeling, though, that it wouldn't be an easy task to ruffle Jed McNeil.

But she wasn't nicknamed Hell for nothing. Time to be brash.

She gave him her best innocuous smile. "It isn't exactly an emergency, but it has to be now, while I'm still suff...under the effects of the serum. Since the commandos will be going on my missions, I thought I'd better test each of you for physical prowess," she drawled, "you know, see whether any of you can keep up."

She kept the smile on her face, as if she hadn't just pulled a tiger's tail. He didn't move, yet she could feel the subtle change in the air. He was holding back; she was sure of it. Besides, judging from the amused looks on the other two men, there was no way the man would back off from that kind of challenge.

"SYMBIOS 2 blocks exhaustion and pain," Jed said politely. "Do you want me to exhaust you or cause you discomfort?"

"Perhaps SYMBIOS 2 will outlast your efforts and you'll be the one left exhausted and in discomfort," she pointed out softly.

The corners of his lips quirked in that mocking way that both fascinated and irritated her. "I have three meetings today, back-to-back. I'm at your disposal any time after that." His gaze traveled down her body. "Stay comfortable, Agent Roston. All the commandos wouldn't want you suffering from the effects of the serum now, would we?"

He didn't wait for an answer, turning back to his waiting men and walking off. Helen stared after his retreating back, not at all sure who had won that round. Damn. He'd distracted her so that she hadn't asked how to get hold of him and when exactly that last meeting would end.

To her relief, Dr. Kirkland's door was open and he was alone. Right now, she didn't want his assistant or any other Medic listening in.

"Helen," he greeted her warmly. "Come on in. Close the door behind you and have a seat."

"Are we alone?" Helen asked. "No cameras, no recorders, no hidden robot under your desk?"

He smiled, shaking his head. "No, not even a robot under my desk. This will be just a doctor-patient confidential session."

"Good." Helen sat down. "It's very uncomfortable for me talking about my current problem."

"You explained it quite well when we talked the last time. The SYMBIOS serum was meant to deflect your pain receptors as well as limit certain chemicals in your brain so you could function at one hundred percent immediately after remote viewing. It certainly makes sense that as the serum wears off, your body compensates the chemicals it'd been tricked into thinking your system lacked. Hence, the over-compensating problem since they had been present all along, camouflaged from your brain."

Helen pursed her lips. Everything sounded so nicely scientific and ridiculously logical when someone in a white coat explained it. She wondered how Jed McNeil would explain it.

"Armando told me he doesn't get this feeling," she said. That was another commando she had to see soon.

"Agent Chang says he's probably had more intimate partners than you in the past two years," Dr. Kirkland pointed out.

Oh, that was just great. Her love life was the subject of conversation among them all. "Armando talked to you about me?"

"But of course. He's the only other operative who has tried the new serum, Helen. When I asked him for information that I could use to help your condition, he offered that insight. It makes sense. Messing with the brain can bring out the oddest effects and your needing sexual gratification is perhaps, for lack of a better word, a blessing."

"A blessing?" Helen asked incredulously. She leaned forward, resting her hands on the desk. The acrylic surface felt cool against her heated skin. She wanted to put her forehead down. "A blessing?"

Dr. Kirkland nodded. "It could be worse. Armando becomes blind from headaches after using the serum."

"Oh."

Put that way, her condition certainly didn't sound so serious. Why hadn't Armando just told her that? He'd made it sound like some kind of unworldly experience, the way he called it the "reckoning".

"We keep test results a secret because that's part of being an experiment." Dr. Kirkland unerringly read her mind. "Everything has to be done with a clean slate each time, so that every cause and effect are separate from the previous experiment."

"I know. It's just that I think there's more to it than chemical imbalance. This..." Helen waved her hand impatiently. "This is sensory overload. I feel out of control. If I rub a bar of soap while taking a shower, it becomes...Doc, it becomes embarrassing, okay? I forget that I'm taking a bath because my mind is on the feel of the soap suds and..."

She shrugged. No need to go into more details. She knew Dr. Kirkland wouldn't laugh or make fun of her. He was a doctor, so she was just a lab rat in his eyes, but she didn't feel like being told all she needed was sex, either.

"In every experiment, it comes down to the subject and all the things he or she has gone through and are going through in his or her daily life," he said quietly. "Control is an important part of your make-up, Helen. Loss of it is bound to affect you more psychologically. Remember too, that your brainwaves are being manipulated whenever you sleep here. We're syncing your sleep stages with that of your monitor with the theory that it'd help your remote viewing in virtual reality. That's the experiment we're monitoring, but obviously, your brain's doing other things as well that's not part of this experiment."

Like having sexual dreams that belonged to her monitor. She didn't want to go there. Dr. K would start asking her for details and the way even *thinking* about anything sensual was affecting her, she dared not imagine what *talking* about it in detail would do.

"Is there something that can be done to lessen the sensitivity?" she asked.

"I don't recommend any more drugs at this point," he replied. "It'll confuse your system even more."

Helen sighed. "I was afraid you might say that."

"You need to be examined," Dr. Kirkland said gently.

She shook her head. "Not now."

"It can be by a female physician, if you're uncomfortable. But actually, I think you already know the solution."

"I do?" she asked, startled.

Dr. Kirkland nodded. "Tell me, Helen, how bad was your condition before you left COMCEN for your downtime? You were wandering around for a long while before you finally went to bed. And then, when you finally let me examine you in the morning, you were able to walk without pain and that sensitivity had subsided. Whatever you did that night quelled your condition temporarily. It's a temporary solution until we figure out another way."

Sex. A whole night of raw sex. Helen cleared her throat. "That's why I want to see Jed McNeil," she said, avoiding a direct answer. She met Dr. Kirkland's eyes squarely, trying not to look embarrassed that the doctor might have guessed what happened the other night. "I have something to ask him. Since you can't tell me, I'm going straight to the source."

"Do you think he's the source?"

"Did you give him my message?"

Dr. Kirkland nodded. "I passed it on. Once he gets the message, he'll be expecting you, but it isn't easy getting hold of Agent McNeil. He's a busy man."

Interesting. When she'd bumped into him just now, he hadn't mentioned anything about getting a message. In fact, he'd made her ask him personally. Bastard.

"Maybe he can schedule a fifteen-minute break," Helen retorted. "You know, I'm now part of their group and I still don't know the protocol in getting hold of them or how we meet or how to call any of them! Isn't there a set of numbers I can punch into an intercom? Or am I just someone they pull out whenever they need a remote viewer?"

"It's only been a few days since you passed the test, Helen. You've barely been doing anything but training before that. Give yourself the downtime your body's asking and then you can concentrate on your new role."

Helen sighed. "You're right and I'm sorry I vented on you. But if I don't get pissed off, I get turned on. Sorry, Doc, too much information there."

Dr. Kirkland smiled. "The more you give me, the more I can help. For example, the anger comes from frustration, and the frustration comes from the fact that you aren't getting enough of what your brain's telling your body it needs. It's a vicious circle, Helen."

Hell was all for venting her frustration. And she was going to make *him* admit to her that he was her monitor.

"I want a session in the Cave," she said suddenly. Jed said he had three consecutive meetings today, didn't he? "Can you schedule one today, Dr. Kirkland? Like, as soon as possible."

He'd been testing her, pushing her. It was time to push back.

Secret CIA Testing Facility, Virginia
"Agent 51, can you hear me?"

He nodded. He was feeling a lot better but purposely kept his eyes unfocused, staring at nothing. Listen in. See what was going on. Mourn. He needed time to mourn. All those memories, stolen in seconds.

"He's been going through downtime a while now. What's wrong with him?"

"Standard. We've never given him two doses one after another before, so that's to be expected. He did better than any of the other agents and he seems to be coming out of it slowly."

"At least he isn't drooling. That's a good sign."

Fuckers. They used him to track down another remote viewer and didn't warn him that she was different. He had no proof but somehow, she'd snatched all his precious stock of memories, every single one, when he slammed through her during her remote-viewing session. He'd never heard of such a thing before, but it only made sense that if he'd found a way to capture other people's emotional memories, then some other remote viewer could have found a way to remove another remote viewer's own private stash. It made fucking perfect sense—why hadn't he thought about that possibility before? He could have maybe avoided the damn bitch.

"When do you think we can send him out again? We need to know whether they're on to us."

"We'll give him a couple more hours' rest. Then we'll have to use him sparingly for a while."

"Why? Push him, I say. We have many more to replace him if he burns out."

"You're right about that, of course, but this one's been able to stay with it successfully the last few times, so he appears to be able to control the serum's side effects. I want to use him carefully so we can get some good use out of him. He did find the location of the encryption key."

"What good is that? We didn't get it before they did. In fact, he almost got us caught, remember, screaming aloud like that in the van."

"He was in pain, Stevens. Some kind of psychic attack."

The other man snorted. "Sometimes I think you're too into this. Psychic attack." He snorted again.

Of the two men in charge of his session, he couldn't stand this one the most. He had obviously never been part of any remote-viewing program before, or he'd be more sensitive regarding subjects such as psychic phenomena and mental blocks. Every time he'd had some kind of problem, he'd noticed the same disbelieving attitude, as if his problem was just an inconvenience.

"Tell me what you need, Agent 51. It's your downtime. Would you like some coffee? Maybe a cola?"

It's not 51; it's Jonah Samson! he wanted to shout at them. He was so tired of being just a number to them. Even his chart at the end of his bed said Number 51. The white coats referred to him as 51. Now that he thought about it, he hadn't heard anyone calling him Jonah for a while now.

But that wasn't important. What was important was working with them so he could get more of the juice. He had to be smart.

"Cigarettes," he said. "Can you get me some?"

"Of course."

"Do you need me to write a report?" That was the standard operating procedure in the old days, when he was in training. But these guys seemed more interested in action than reports.

"No, this is a top secret case, no report's needed at this moment."

Just as he thought. An agenda inside the CIA. He didn't care. He just wanted access to the serum.

He felt empty inside.

He needed these fuckers as much as they needed him. Maybe more. They had the supply of the serum, the only thing more important than his lost "recordings". Without it, there would be no more emotional memories to record. So he needed to play nice for a while yet. He would be free of them one day.

Chapter Three

Jed didn't like the idea that she'd been in pain. He'd known it was a possibility, since Armando Chang had complained of blinding pain from his use of the serum. However, he'd hoped that this new version, SYMBIOS 2, would eliminate that.

Pain and paranoia. He'd seen it happening to Armando. Helen was also exhibiting an interesting side effect that Armando hadn't had. Chemicals and body chemistry, so unique when broken down in individual biological systems.

A complete spy uses everything to achieve his goals. There are no ifs, ands, or buts, once you accept that mission. Focus your mind and body on the target, Conor, and reach your goal before moving to the next one.

Jed heard his CIA mentor's calm instructions in his head, as if he were eighteen again—still cocky and brash Conor—and being scolded for getting entangled with yet another woman while working in an operation. All the right excuses had been on his side. He was eighteen, after all, with the kind of cocky charm that drew female attention too easily and an upbringing that made him protective about people for whom he cared. He was being groomed in a trade that insisted on detachment first and nobility second. It took him a few years to understand that *that* meant he couldn't engage himself one hundred percent to another human being, especially a woman, or else, somewhere along a dangerous operation, it'd be his Achilles' Heel, be it worrying about saving someone when he should be thinking of capturing his target, or being used by the enemy.

Because of his tendency to get physically, and sometimes emotionally, involved with women in his life and because women were drawn to him, instead of moving him away from operations that involved temptation, the trainers had deliberately placed him in more and more such situations, watching him modify his behavior and attitude. Jed had understood. He was one of their youngest trainees and they had plenty of time to adjust his personality. That was, if he didn't die in the process.

He'd learned sexual manipulation and what it could make him do at a very young age indeed. Since then, he'd learned to compartmentalize himself. A mission was a mission, no more, no less. If it involved sex, it was just that, no more, no less. He'd learned to keep his emotions at bay, so much so that he became proficient at seduction for information and had then graduated into the sexual imprint program at the underground CIA labs, and he did so well it'd earned him the nickname of The Ice Man there.

So what are my excuses now? He mockingly saluted his current dilemma. He was certainly not focusing on Helen Roston as if she was a mission. Not by a long shot. It'd been a long time since he'd felt like that young Conor.

He had to back off emotionally and resume control. Right now. Or this wasn't going to work. He needed to establish a sexual bond with this woman in such a way that he could harness her ability to remote view for future operations in virtual reality, an environment that required absolute control. Having feelings for her would interfere with a mission and endanger lives while he worried about her and didn't fully focus on his job.

Jed knew she'd spent her free time trying to figure out her mentor's identity. He'd watched her all these months, knew that she ran things over and over in her mind until she found an answer. He'd deliberately been a riddle for her for exactly that reason.

He had to be extra subtle because he knew she'd smell a rat and pounce on him like the wild cat he'd called her. If she'd been aware of what he was doing, there would have been no way he could have progressed so far, if at all.

Sexual imprinting was the absolute focus of mind and body on the target. No ifs, ands, or buts. No half-ways either.

Helen would ask for a session at the CAVE. Now that she thought she'd identified the man behind the avatar, she was going to turn the tables on him. Take away the avatar and she'd "see" the man in the shadows who had been training her in the CAVE. In that environment, he wouldn't be her equal because she could remote view and he wouldn't have access to what she was seeing. Also, he'd told her he had meetings most of the day—a lie—to make her think she had time to prepare herself to remote view on her own.

A very dangerous choice of action for a remote viewer who'd never done it alone, but he hadn't a doubt she would attempt it. She wasn't called Hell by her friends for playing it safe when she was out in the field. He'd anticipated it because he needed to gain the advantage by constant surprise.

Jed flipped open the small dictionary in his hand, letting his gaze fall randomly on a word. His lips curled at the synchronicity of it all.

"Trigger," he murmured. To activate, to set off, to initiate.

Well, nothing subtle about *that.*

The CAVE Ultimate—Cave Automatic Virtual Environment—had been Helen's first taste of total immersion VR. It was a ten by ten by ten room that allowed multiple participants in a simulated exercise, with one person in charge.

Many of her sessions had meant giving her trainer the ultimate control—the inability to move her physical body, for one, was still stressful for her—as he manipulated simulated situations to fit the lesson for the day. She realized now that most of these weren't just sessions on loss of control and fear management, but were also part of his mind manipulation game.

Everything he did took her a step closer to where he wanted her. He appeared to her as a shadow. He chose sexual situations that pushed her hot buttons. He ended each session by kissing her—no, *branding* her.

Helen shook her head. She'd been so caught up with the intrigue of him as she was led along down the path—touching, tasting, thinking about him—that she hadn't noticed how he'd kept her mind focused on him during their sessions. Fascination and involvement were the first basic steps in mind manipulation. And with the brain entrainment machine that connected them during the sleep sessions at Center, they were even sharing dreams now.

A plan had formed while talking to Dr. Kirkland and she'd gone for it. A session at the CAVE. It was going to be tricky, though. She would have to pretend to swallow the little pink pill, lie very still, and wait for the right moment. Usually, when she came to, the virtual program had already been activated and she'd be caught up immediately in the alternate world, undergoing her training sessions with Hades in his shadowy form. In reality, her trainer would be in another CAVE in control of the session.

Helen smiled grimly. Not this time. The key was in the timing. She'd suddenly realized, while talking to Dr. Kirkland, that she'd done something new. She'd bilocated at her house without any help. She'd never remote viewed on her own; a monitor had always been with her in her sessions, anchoring and guiding her. She wasn't sure how she'd managed to do so this morning, especially without getting herself into an altered state with a brain entrainment machine.

But she had. She'd remote viewed, or kind of, because she had definitely seen Jed McNeil. However, the experience had been different. She had trouble seeing clearly, still didn't have any explanation why she'd felt the need to turn and run, and then there was that devastating headache...

Dr. Kirkland was supposed to call her when he'd gotten hold of her trainer and set up the time. She smiled. *Take that, Jed McNeil, and see how you're going to squeeze a session with me in between your meetings.*

In the meantime, she would go to her quarters and use the brain entrainment machine. If she could fiddle with it, get to that place her brainwaves turned theta and somehow keep her mind at that state until Dr. Kirkland called her. With the darkness in the CAVE and the way Hades liked to start her out by concentrating on her senses, she might actually be able to jump into remote-viewing mode again, just like she did back home.

It was a gamble. Maybe her experience back at her place was just a fluke and it wouldn't work again this time.

Then what?

Helen swallowed. She knew exactly what Hades would do if he knew how sensitive her body was and she had no doubt at all about her response. She gritted her teeth. Already, her body was reacting to thoughts about *that*.

"I can't let him win," she whispered.

She had to risk it. Once she had proof that it was Jed McNeil, then she had a fighting chance against letting him sexually imprint her even deeper.

Jed slipped his cell phone into his pocket. Kirkland had called. He had an inkling what Elena was up to. He had years on her in the art of figuring out an opponent and hunting him down. And right now, he was her opponent, and she was his prey. It had to be this way.

The mind was like glass. It must be handled with care. Like glass, it could be molded. Like glass, it could also be broken.

He'd accepted the assignment to create a binding mental awareness between Helen and him, so that it could be the bridge for them as she remote viewed in virtual reality. The easiest and fastest way—seduction. The need for, and the sharing of, sexual release created an emotional bond between couples. Add that with the need for someone specific, and there was now a powerful mental focus. Perfect for remote viewing. Perfect for virtual reality.

Keep her focus on him.

Keep that need for release growing.

Then feed it when she remote viewed.

She would be heading for her quarters, thinking of getting her mind ready. Perfect. Gray surroundings. Brain entrainment machine on.

They used that machine to connect while they slept, syncing their brainwaves, getting ready for their virtual exercises. He planned to be at the other end while she was using it. With one exception. Usually, they would be in their own beds, going to sleep. This time, he'd be awake and focusing on her. Here was an opportunity to test the mental link they already had.

Helen took in several breaths. Her clothes were beginning to irritate her, especially her jeans. They felt too tight and bothered her so much she couldn't even concentrate on the initial state of relaxation needed to start the process. She sighed. She'd better change into something less restrictive. She got up and impatiently walked over to her dresser.

She pulled her tee shirt off and unbuttoned her jeans, inhaling sharply as the clothing scraped her hyper-sensitive skin. It wasn't as bad as the other night, but it was there, that edgy feeling, like a mild electric current.

She rummaged through the clothes in the drawer. Tights. No. Jeans. No. Exercise pants. No. Why, oh why didn't she get a pair of pajamas? She needed something that would make her comfortable enough that she wouldn't think of her stupid body. There was an oversized shirt made of cotton. That would have to do.

She sat on her bed and put on the ear buds that were connected to the brain entrainment machine. Since she hadn't done this alone before, she set its clock so that when her brainwave reached theta stage, it would buzz her, and reset itself from there. That way, if she relaxed past the theta stage and fell asleep, the buzzer would get her back on track. Once she fell into that deep alternate state, she'd test herself, see whether she could remote view Jed McNeil's location. It should be easy, since he would be at a meeting. If she succeeded, it'd prove that the experience earlier today wasn't a fluke, that she could remote view without the help of a monitor.

There was that awful headache afterwards too, though. Was that part of it? Armando Chang had complained about headaches too. She frowned. She hoped not. That was simply indescribably painful. Perhaps it had to do with the speed she'd gone into theta, causing some kind of brainwave discombobulation or something.

She laughed out loud. Fancy scientific description was never her forte.

She checked the knobs of the brain entrainment machine again. It was a risk she just had to take because she wanted—needed—to know so much. Taking a deep breath, she hit the start button.

Jed watched everything Helen did from his quarters as he put on his sensor suit. Her sensitivity must be bothering her more than she realized. First, she'd forgotten to check whether the micro-eye in her room was blinking, signaling that she was being watched. Second, she'd assumed that the brain entrainment machine couldn't be controlled from the outside.

Elena, Elena.

Putting the wireless control pad on the cart that supported the BE machine, he wheeled it to the room off the side of his office, a smaller version of the CAVE. Unlike Helen's training room, though, he had multiple control panels he could use to enhance the virtual reality experience that the CAVE provided. He even had the Portal, the VR chair that enabled immersive virtual reality, here. Whereas the CAVE was all physical, with the participants moving around, the Portal was all mental. The former prepared TIRVVR in the latter.

Jed turned on a side screen, changing the channels to Helen's quarters. He waited till she lay back and closed her eyes. Reaching for the control pad by his side, he readjusted the timer.

There will be no alarm to wake you up, Elena. Not till I say so.

He turned up the temperature in Helen's room. Then he put on the tabs and ear buds that connected him to the BE machine and flipped the synchronization button. Soon their brainwaves would be in sync as she went deeper in theta wave, the level that enabled remote viewing.

Flipping on another switch, the room plunged into deep darkness. He checked the BEM. Not quite there yet. As soon as they were close to sync, he would start the brainwave management.

He settled back, letting the sound wash over him as he relaxed. This was a new way to sexually imprint, he supposed. He'd first seduced her in virtual reality. She'd then seduced him when she invaded his dreams. After that, he'd gone to her.

He let his mind wander back to their night together. Elena naked and aroused, begging. The unique taste of her. The urgency of her release. It felt so damn good to be finally inside her instead of virtual touching.

Fucking was so much better when it was real.

Jed smiled wryly as he watched the screen. His eyes half-closed as his body relaxed. She must be feeling the warmth because she just kicked the light sheet off her, revealing beautiful bare legs. Legs that he recalled holding apart. The feminine heat between them when he'd used his mouth to pleasure her. He felt himself getting aroused.

He turned the volume higher as the brain entrainment machine continued feeding them the cycle he'd chosen, between theta and REM. That was the level she had been in when she'd unexpectedly took in the images in his dreams as her own. He hadn't been too shocked by the experience. Unconscious telepathy happened all the time among family members and lovers. The question was, in her sensitive state, would she now inadvertently take in the images and feelings of his private fantasy?

Conjuring an image of a naked Elena came easily. He'd like those strong legs around him again, this time with her moving in rhythm to his thrusts. He watched with interest as Helen's legs parted tantalizingly, seemingly responding to the sexy visual in his head.

Mental trigger had begun.

The sound waves seemed to recede into the background as Jed gave in to total relaxation, focusing on only one thing—that sexual need he'd been building up for Helen Roston. He'd always been turned on when she started undressing herself by the poolside. In response, on the screen, Helen put a restless hand on her shirt, as if it was bothering her.

Was there some kind of telepathy compounded by their brainwave syncing?

He did enjoy it so much when he'd gone to her. "But now it's your turn, Elena," Jed whispered.

Chapter Four

Helen tried to focus. It was as if she were looking at herself from the wrong end of a pair of binoculars.

Hot. Itchy hot. Thank God there's the pool nearby. It'd cool her off.

She pulled off her tee shirt impatiently. Her skin felt feverish and tender to the touch. She sat down by the side of the pool, gasping at the heat of the tiles on the back of her thighs. This was ridiculous. Even her butt was hot.

The water looked so inviting, lapping at her feet. She swore she heard it call her name.

Danger.

She looked around warily but there was no one. It was just her and the lovely swirling water. She frowned, looking down at the water again. Why was her instinct warning her?

Blue, so blue and cool looking. She was so damn hot.

She gave her surroundings another look and, seeing nothing out of the ordinary, she slid into the water.

She gasped and turned to escape but it was too late. Sensations took her prisoner, sensations that she'd rather not feel right now. Sensations from a certain night. Multiplied a hundred times.

"Ohhhh."

Just like before, she couldn't see. Hands massaging her breasts. Lips on her skin, moving down her stomach. Heat. The heat burst into flames as those lips went lower and a wicked tongue started a slow tease. The hands and lips were relentless, and so familiar.

This was a dream, reenacting a memory. She should be able to move her hands, push him away, if she wanted to. Dammit, she should be able to see him.

She opened her eyes. She couldn't move her hands. Or feet. She was chained to the bottom of the pool now, on all fours. She pulled at the iron clasps. A shadow at the periphery of her vision. She tried to turn her head to see but he was already straddling her from behind.

This wasn't possible. She'd be drowning if she were underwater. Yet she wasn't even fighting for breath.

Just a dream. It was just a dream about her faceless monitor. Immediately the image of her avatar appeared. And Hades was straddling her, pushing his erection inside her.

She gasped. Oh Lord, she had used the computer program to enlarge that part of his anatomy. Oh. Lord. She closed her eyes tightly.

This was just a dream. If she kept repeating, she might wa— She gasped as he thrust fully into her. His thighs pushed against the back of hers as he leaned forward, using his weight to push her upper body down onto the floor, forcing her legs to open wider. He thrust again. She gasped into her hand. He was deeply inside her now.

His free hand reached under her. Trapped on the tiled floor, she couldn't move as fingers found her already sensitive nub. She could feel herself getting wet. No...she was in a pool...

"It's only...a...a..." She moaned as her world zoned in on the paralyzing pleasure that took over as fingers moved in tandem with Hades' slow thrusting.

The sexual fantasy had to be the imprinter in control of the imprintee's pleasure. Jed needed Helen to want and need her avatar and monitor. Both were inclusive.

He turned on the program that projected his avatar's body likeness into his sensor suit. The weight that Helen had chosen for him. The height. He felt the heaviness of his extra-big erection. He mentally saw himself as Hades, Helen's virtual trainer.

He imagined her at the pool, taking off her clothes, showing off her curves to him. She had felt so good in his arms. Beautiful breasts. All these months, he had wanted to kiss and play with those breasts. That other night, he'd made sure he'd given them plenty of attention.

He would take her on all fours in his fantasy and if his theory were right, it'd be projected into her theta state, just as his dreams had. She would fight him, of course. Maybe he could chain her to the floor instead of giving her one of the pills. He visualized her on her knees, hands and feet pulled apart by iron clasps.

He climbed over her, positioning her panting, waiting body. He leaned his weight on one hand as he nudged her open for him. He pushed.

A hiss of sheer bliss escaped his lips. The virtual reality program felt so damn real. Determined, he focused on how good it had felt to be inside her. His whole body shook as his virtual self responded to his fantasy. He thought of making Helen come while she lay under him, with him deep inside her like this. She liked it slow that night. He'd keep it slow now too and he'd rock back and forth slowly. Like this. Till she was close to coming. Then he would—

The buzz came through, disturbing the monotony of the theta waves. Helen heard herself moaning.

"No..."

She didn't want it to stop. Not yet...

Just a dream. Why was she dreaming? She had set the alarm to stop at theta and not allow her to go to REM, rapid eye movement, the dreaming stage of relaxation.

Her whole body was on fire and she tried to kick off the sheets tangled around her feet. She gave a soft and low frustrated growl as she tried to hold on to her dream.

The sound waves were so loud. She frowned. She remembered now. She had programmed it to keep resetting itself back to theta, to keep her brainwaves constant...but why was it so loud?

She could feel her mind giving in to the sound, as she'd trained it to do so many times before. But she was supposed to stay in theta, so why was she dream...

Her lips moved in protest even as her mind let go.

"If you want it, you have to call my name, Elena," Jed whispered as he reset the BE machine.

The imprintee had to acknowledge the imprinter as the one she sexually needed. No ifs, ands, or buts.

Her moans came through loud and clear. It was happening. Somehow, with their brainwaves in sync, she was able to telepathically experience his fantasies.

There wasn't time to sit back and marvel at this phenomena. Knowing that if he started analyzing he would begin to feel uncomfortable about someone being in his head, Jed took in a deep breath, working on the relaxation techniques he'd studied. He needed to stay in control. He had to visualize himself in charge of her again. Tantalize her to come closer, to look for him.

His lips quirked wickedly. She'd asked for a session in the CAVE. He'd give her one now.

Again, he thought back to when he'd entered her room in darkness. He'd taken off her tee shirt and felt her naked skin for the first time. He'd thought about doing exactly that for months and so he'd leisurely given himself free rein of her body, his hands tracing the soft curves of her hips, then stopping to linger at her breasts.

They filled his hands perfectly. He'd kissed each nipple softly as he freed her of her clothing. He hadn't known how exactly she'd made his sexual dream part of hers, calling out his name at the crucial part, and waking him up, but he wasn't going to question it then.

Her voice calling his name—they had mostly conversed through electronic and virtual means while training—was velvety honey. Her soft little gasps aroused him even more. He'd licked her satiny skin, tasting the real Elena. Nothing virtual about that little cry coming from her lips as he licked lower, exploring and discovering parts that couldn't be conveyed virtually without real experience of the woman. He remembered how eager she'd been for him already. Wet for her lover. Aroused and ready.

The woman on his screen ran her hand down her bare stomach. She turned sideways, crossing her legs.

As if that could stop his fantasy. Not after their night together. Not after tasting the real thing. A man could bring up certain details that turned him on about a woman. He recalled how he'd tested her injured leg by draping it over his shoulder, opening her wide for...other activities.

Fantasy. How many times had he wanted to cross the line and fuck her while she lay there helpless in the CAVE? A strong woman giving control of her body willingly was a turn-on for him and as she began to trust him more each session, she'd allowed him more and more freedom with her body. But intending to feed her curiosity, he'd always held back.

He didn't need to any more. A moan came through the sound system.

"Elena. Call my name if you want me," Jed commanded softly. He closed his eyes, easily fantasizing a willing, wanton Elena needing his touch instead of fighting him.

Her whole body struggled with the tantalizing tension of withheld pleasure. She'd been so close...she opened her eyes in frustration.

Darkness. Familiar. She was in the CAVE, waiting for Hades.

She was already lying on the VR chair, the one that manipulated her movement as she trained in alternate reality. She was also naked already, which meant that the session had started because Hades sometimes liked to begin that way, to make her feel at a disadvantage.

She was used to it. It was all in the head anyway. He wanted to push her buttons, find out what made her uncomfortable.

Her whole body was burning up. She felt drunk with the need to be touched. She wanted her lover who came in the dark. She wanted his hands again. His hands and tongue. And she wanted him to make love to her like he did all night long.

She didn't care if he'd deliberately put her in this position to piss her off. She just wanted him to touch her there.

"In the dark. I don't care any more," she panted out.

She closed her eyes in relief when she felt his hands massaging her. She frowned. He was massaging her injured leg like he did last night. She wasn't hurting there any more.

Dreaming.

No, virtual reality. He was testing her in VR again...wasn't he?

Hades— she wanted to say, suddenly afraid. *Don't—*

But other words were coming out of her mouth.

"I want you," she heard herself saying instead, "to tie me up."

Helen gasped as she found herself suddenly bound spread eagle. Just like that. She shook her head. But she would never say those words!

Dream.

"Oh yes, Hades, take me," she heard herself purring, arching up for his touch.

He climbed on top of her and she caught glints of his blond hair in the semi-darkness. It was Hades, and all coherent thought disappeared as he kissed her, his big body covering her feverish one.

It was a long and erotic kiss, his tongue tangling with hers slowly, possessively, and she responded with mindless longing. His hands caressed everywhere, moving intimately over her body. The edginess inside her grew unbearable. She arched up against his heat.

"Like the other night," she whispered. "Kiss me there, Hades."

"Beg me," he commanded, in that soft Southern drawl. "Beg me and I will."

Her lips opened and the words came out of their own accord. "Please, Hades," she heard herself saying.

Dream.

If she were dreaming, she would have Hades tied up, with her torturing him. This wasn't a dream. This was VR...

"Lower," she heard herself instructing. She struggled to stop herself but it was as if she were speaking someone else's words. Her whole body throbbed with the need to have his mouth there. "Please. Lower. Yes."

She cried out. It was exactly like their night together, with that incredible mouth teasing her as she lay there, not moving, letting him build her fire higher and higher. His hands gripped under her wide open thighs as his tongue wickedly tortured her clitoris rhythmically, over and over, until she thought she'd go crazy with need. She writhed against him desperately when she felt him withdrawing.

She didn't even need any prompting. This time, on her own, she cried out, "Please, Hades, pleaassse, I want—"

A buzzing noise came through, forcing her reluctantly back to semi-consciousness. She was barely aware of her surroundings, her body silently screaming for release, her heart beating erratically. She was panting as her mind tried to will herself back to that pleasurable place.

"...want it," she groaned out softly. She was so close, so close...

She heard the sound waves and remembered the first dream, the one with her underwater. She remembered that she had set the BE machine for three cycles. The sound waves were so loud...*call my name if you want me*...her eyes closed obediently as she surrendered.

"Hades..." she whispered.

He was a bastard for setting the buzzer off. He hadn't wanted to. It took every bit of control in him to press that button. Fortunately, he hadn't been fantasizing about fucking her. He didn't think he would have been quite so willing to stop.

He was hot in his sensor suit, which was telling, as it was auto-temperature adjustable. He wanted out of it. He wanted a real live Elena in his arms, instead of a fantasy.

But he wasn't in this business to be a nice guy. Even to himself.

Elena was moving restlessly, definitely reacting to his fantasy. He wished he could see what was going on in *her* mind. The BE machine showed her to be between REM and theta and he kept it at that level as he became more engrossed in his make-believe Elena, imagining her supine and willing, saying things that he knew she wouldn't have in real life.

When he'd imagined her asking him to tie her up, stretching her arms over her head and opening her legs, he'd gone rock hard. His sensor suit with the "enhanced" feature tested every ounce of willpower he had not to go ahead and satisfy his desires.

He ruthlessly crushed his own male needs—very urgent male needs—and concentrated on the sound waves. A drop of sweat trickled down the bridge of his nose as he forced himself to relax.

"Hades..."

Her voice, a soft throaty sound laced with sexy longing coming over the intercom, tormented him to continue on, to finish this particularly erotic story in his head. He swallowed. No. Not yet.

When this was done and she'd accepted the trigger, he would act on all his fantasies. In real life, with no barriers or thought of missions and responsibility. He'd enjoy her like a man would enjoy a beautiful, sensual woman—slowly and joyfully. That was, if she didn't kill him for what he'd done.

His lips quirked into a rueful smile. He understood perfectly well that the real Elena wouldn't be as compliant and eager as his fantasy

Elena, the one that he was having so much fun with in his mind. No, she would be an angry avenging wildcat after his blood. He settled back, still smiling. He wouldn't have it any other way.

He wondered whether he could make her jealous. Jealousy was the ultimate blinding emotion. She'd now been able to react in an intimate way to his dreams and fantasies. He'd test that bond and see how her "connected" brainwaves would react to his projecting someone else into "their" fantasy. That could be the final straw to get her to take the trigger.

"Round three, Elena," he murmured. "What sexual deviant thing can I come up with that would distract you?"

His lips left a trail of fire down the side of her neck. She leaned back, silently giving him more access. His hands circled her waist firmly as he pushed her against a cool surface. He was all male heat on her; the cool against her flesh made her shiver with need for him.

Not a dream.

The warning flashed like a blinking neon sign in her head.

She turned her head and saw herself in a mirror. She was wearing a black lacy bustier with a plunging neck line. Red bowties seemed to be the only things holding the front together. That, with the extremely low neckline, pushed her cleavage together until it was almost spilling out of the top of the see-through bustier.

What the hell...I don't own such a tacky...

Understanding dawned. It was a dream, just not hers. Just like the other night. She should get used to it. She was in Hades' head again and he was somewhere sleeping and having one of his erotic dreams. About her.

Her whole body clenched as she watched his dark head dip lower to kiss the sensitive curve of her breast. Her breath came out in a hiss when she felt his tongue, wet and wicked, teasing the flesh just above her left nipple. He wrapped her right leg around his waist and she felt his hand caressing the back of her leg and bottom. She followed the hand in the mirror as it disappeared between their two bodies, and suddenly, she didn't care whether it was her dreaming or him dreaming. She just wanted to get back to that part in the other dream—she swallowed, trying to slow down her thoughts, mixed with that aching need that was pushing her over the edge.

Not a dream.

She frowned. Why was she hearing a different warning now? It was hard to concentrate. Her thoughts were a confused jumble of unfinished sentences, with odd images and thoughts interrupting.

"I know it isn't my dream," she affirmed. "I don't freaking own a bustier."

Not that the affirmation mattered. Her body was wantonly pushing against the hand exploring her intimately, her leg curling, on its own accord tightening and loosening its hold of his body. He knew exactly where to touch, inciting her into a frenzy even as he skillfully kept her right at the edge without pushing her over. She was helpless against the rising tide of heated pleasure pushing against all her nerve endings. She didn't think she could survive another interruption.

Fantasy or not, her need for him was very real. She wanted this man desperately. Now. And if she didn't make it happen soon, she knew the buzzer would wake her up again and she'd once again be left bereft, unable to get the magic release he kept promising her.

She caught an image of herself with her arms wrapped around his neck as he tilted her further back. His heat—she wanted his hot length inside her, not his fingers.

Dammit—dream or not, she was going to have him this time. That image—of her so passively supine, so willing to be led—was Hades', *not hers*. She fought with herself to ignore the urge to follow the fantasy going on in her head. She was *not* going to stay passive, dammit. She was *not* going to let him take charge.

She made herself look at the mirror. A part of her understood that it somehow represented her own mind, that she was seeing the fantasy through a mirror. Her hand felt like lead as she forced it to obey her. She reached between them, wrapping her hand around his thick length and guiding it toward her slippery heat. She stood on tiptoe, using the leg around his waist as leverage. The head of his penis nudged hard against her. She felt giddy with desire and as she slid her hand down its length, she thought she heard Hades' groan over the roar of anticipation reverberating in her ears. She smiled in triumph. At last...she swiveled her hip, undulating toward...

Nothing.

She was suddenly standing alone. She swayed on her feet. Frustration like she'd never known before spewed out violently, like water from a busted fire hydrant, and she fell on her knees. She slapped the floor in anger but barely felt any pain.

She was hot all over, flushed with some kind of sexual inflammation for which she couldn't find a cure. The sensitiveness had turned into a raging fever. Part of her was telling her to calm down, to think. The other part was keening for release, that if she didn't do something soon, she would go mad. The other part was winning.

She looked into the mirror in front of her, trying to control her breathing. The damn bustier was too tight. She grabbed at the ribbons, pulling at them till they were knotted up.

"Come back!" she screamed at her image in the mirror. "You're not going to stop this fantasy!"

She stared hard. She was still in his fantasy; dammit, she could feel his presence. Just then, she saw him, in the corner of the mirror. She reeled back, watching in shock. In rage.

He was lying on his back and a beautiful woman was sitting on top of him. She was wearing the same bustier, the top of her breasts popping out precariously as she swayed forward, teasing the man underneath her.

Helen watched as Hades reached up and slowly pulled one of the ends of the red bow. The woman pulled back, helping with the unraveling, and even in the shadows of the mirror, Helen could see the gap in front of the bustier widen.

Hades' forefinger twirled around the next ribbon's end; the woman pulled back; the gap widened into a bigger V. The woman's breasts spilled out, so white against the black lace, and Helen couldn't take her eyes away as Hades' large hands scooped under them, freeing them from the bustier.

Helen's own chest hurt. She was breathing too quickly, too deeply, and the tightness of the bustier was constricting. The lace rubbed her nipples till they puckered from the friction, causing even more sensual awareness of her body's screaming needs.

"The bastard...he's having another erotic dream about some other woman. How dare he?" She wanted to gnash her teeth. Of course he dared. A sleeping man could dream about anyone and anything he wanted. She was the intruder here, getting her jollies off someone's fantasy about her. But she was beyond logic. "He started the fantasy with me, and dammit, he's going to end it with me!"

She slapped against the mirror, pounding on the surface where she could see the image of the entwined couple. She had never felt so murderous in her life. How dare he? How dare he choose another fantasy woman other than her!

She prowled back and forth in front of the mirror, fueling her fury by sneaking angry glances at the image. She knew that her anger was irrational because this wasn't real and Hades could dream of whatever...*dammit, look at her crawling all over him*...and whomever he...*oh, be boring, dangle those stupid breasts over his face*...wished because like he'd said, she was the one invading his...*oh, hell no, you're so not going to fuck him, bitch, where's your buzzer, where's your fucking buzzer?* Helen barely registered the growl coming from her own throat.

It didn't matter that her head was telling her that she was sleeping too, that she was also dreaming.

Not a dream.

She ignored that soft repetitive voice in her head. Semantics. She was "dreaming" Hades' dream. Not a dream, but she was part of it.

She stared longingly into the mirror. Had been part of it, she corrected. She ached for his touch through and through. She choked back another cry. It was shadowy, but she could see that woman's head bobbing up and down between Hades' raised legs. *Arggggh!* That. Was. Her. Penis. She was the one who made it that size...

Oh, this was getting personal. She couldn't stay rational about it at all. All she could think about was that that woman didn't have a buzzer and she was going to get to make love to Hades. *Her* Hades, dammit. She created him and there was no way in hell she was going to allow another female tamper with *her* dream man. She would *not* be ignored for some other fantasy woman, when she, Helen Roston, was *real*.

There had to be a way to reinsert herself back into Hades' dream.

The mirror. Her mind "reflecting" his dream.

Fine. She was going to fight fantasy with fantasy. She'd just use her "mind" to interrupt his little tête-à-tête.

She walked determinedly a few feet back, gathered her strength, turned sideways, and delivered a roundhouse kick at the flat gleaming surface. The crash was strangely muted. The shattered glass imploded as if it wasn't a mirror but a doorway. She stared at it for a moment and then without a second thought, stepped inside.

Not a second too soon.

The other woman's derriere was raised up, getting into position. Hades' hands cupped the cheeks, squeezing them. The woman was moaning like some banshee. Her hand disappeared between their bodies.

"Oh, I don't think so."

Helen grabbed the back of the woman's half-loosened bustier and yanked hard, pulling her to her feet. The woman turned and brought one knee up.

Helen jumped back. Shit. What, she had to fight a fucking fantasy too?

But there wasn't any time to think as her opponent suddenly seemed to have grown into an Amazon, launching into the air and crashing into Helen like a freight train.

Helen managed to twist at the last second escaping a direct hit, but off balance, she landed hard on the floor, ending at the bottom of her attacker. She turned her head and stared at Hades for a second.

Helen blinked. The bastard was turned on by this. He was sitting up, naked, and was leisurely pulling at his erection.

She winced as her head went one direction and her hair the other, and she used her elbow for leverage as she head-butted the woman on top of her. But she couldn't budge the Amazon off her even an inch.

It became a wrestling match of strength as she grappled with arms and legs which felt like steel around hers. They rolled several times. She managed to tear off bits and pieces of bustier. She heard hers being torn too. It didn't help that her freed breasts were more sensitive than ever. Whenever her nipples unexpectedly rubbed against anything, she'd lose focus, and had to go on the defensive.

It suddenly occurred to her that her opponent wasn't hurting her too much, that the various locked positions that held her down—the one with the other woman sitting on her chest so that she had to use her legs to push up to fight off the weight, opening her thighs in a sexual way; the one where she was on top for a few seconds, her face crushed against the other woman's chest, so that to pull out of the headlock, she had to push off the floor with her hands, like a push-up, except that it was more of a butt-up—were done so for the viewing pleasure of the man watching them. The damn man was continuing his fantasy with double the fun.

Helen cursed out loud and renewed her efforts. If she had to, she would make this into a bloody nightmare. They rolled again and ended up in a sitting position, with her in front. Her opponent's legs came under and between her thighs and pushed them apart, causing Helen to lose whatever leverage she had left. Planning a headlock, she lifted and curled her arms around the back of the woman's neck. To her chagrin, her opponent countered by wrapping her arms under hers, and sharply pulled back. With her legs open and her arms off the floor, Helen found herself effectively imprisoned.

She turned to snarl at Hades. He stood up, fair-haired and golden tan, and stalked toward them. She couldn't take her eyes off his huge erection.

He squatted down in front of her and smiled.

"I like this," he said.

Helen strained against the limbs holding her so tightly. She couldn't believe that she'd lost to this...bitch... Another realization seeped in. She couldn't fight back with her usual strength because she was acting out Hades' fantasy. He was in charge. She was weaker because he wanted her to be. She finally lay there panting.

Hades leaned forward. She sucked in her breath at his touch. In contrast to her fight with her rival, he was gentle, cupping her breasts possessively with his hands. His thumbs played with her aroused nipples until she whimpered. His fingers freed the tangled ribbons and what was left of her bustier dropped away.

His lips weren't moving but she heard his voice. "Let's repeat everything. Call my name."

"Hades, you bastard," she spat out. His gaze was heavy, loaded with meaning, as it settled on her body. She started trembling as his gaze followed his hands, moving lower, sweeping the curve of her belly and hips. She made a sound of outrage as her captor's thighs opened wider, thrusting her own to do the same. There was nothing she could do except watch Hades looking down on her more intimately than any other man ever had.

"Beg me."

She opened her mouth automatically, about to obey, then suddenly remembered that she had also done so in the other dream. She bit down on her lower lip and shook her head.

He smiled. Still his lips didn't move as she heard his voice.

"It's too late, Elena."

She stared at him as he bent his head slowly, his gaze mocking as it remained fastened to hers, and she tensed as his hands splayed against the inside of her thighs, pressing down until her folds revealed the hidden pink moistness. His head dipped. She groaned even before she felt his mouth on her.

Her back arched up helplessly. His tongue was ferocious this time, mercilessly laving that most sensitive part of her with the kind of intense attention meant to bring on an orgasm. She had been so close the last few times that the edgy tension came upon her almost immediately. She gasped, straining hard again, as he sucked on her clitoris. Stars formed behind her closed eyelids as the tension stretched endlessly, drawing her to a point where she could do nothing but anticipate the coming release.

"Nooooo..." She groaned out a protest when his head lifted and he rested his chin on her pubis.

Hades shook his head. "You know what to do." That whisper came again even though his lips still didn't move. He looked so damn angelic she cursed herself for making him so beautiful. She could see his tongue snaking out and he taunted her with a torturous demonstration of how slow he could be. Each slide of his tongue went upwards for endless seconds and then he would stop and not slide down, leaving her pleasure incomplete. He repeated the upward stroking until she thought she would go crazy with need.

"Hades...please...please," she finally relented.

She suddenly found herself free and on top of him, in the exact position she'd seen Hades and the other woman in the mirror. He was looking up at her, his eyes half-closed.

"Do you want this?" that voice whispered.

Not a dream.

Helen hesitated. His fingers parted her wet folds and easily found her throbbing nub. He leisurely slid one finger up and down as he waited for her. Her eyes closed as she rocked against that finger. So close.

She turned and found herself looking at the mirror reflecting their bodies in the semi-darkness, hers so white on top of his. She saw herself leaning forward and putting her weight on her knees. Her derriere lifted. She felt Hades' hands holding each cheek, squeezing them gently. The head of his penis felt hot and ready. She pushed down. Her breath came out in small gasps as her body fought against the invasion. His size was splintering her apart but there was no escape as the hands on her ass were pushing down now too. She felt his thick length forcing its way inside her and her head fell down against his chest helplessly as she gave in.

"Do you accept it?"

"Yes," she whispered and moaned as his hips thrust up while those hands pushed. There was just no way...but this was a dream...

Not a dream...not a...

"It's inside you," Hades' voice reverberated inside her head, interrupting her warning, "but you're safe, Elena. You'll be safe with me. Here is my trigger phrase for you."

Helen frowned as she tried to understand the jumble of hushed words mixed with her own inner voice. She tried to focus but it was impossible when she was feeling like she was falling and burning at the same time. His fingers...oh God, when he flexed inside her like that...

"...trigger...you won't remember this when you wake up. Call my name again."

"Hades," she said, panting, undulating. He was deep inside and she was coming...coming...

His voice was a soft murmur over the scream of pleasure bursting in her head. "Yes, take me, baby. I'll keep you safe, I promise. Bury me deep inside like that. Can you feel me?"

He thrust up hard and she cried out against his chest. "Yes," she replied.

She turned her head, caught the image of their entwined bodies. Sound waves. So loud. She kept watching, with him locked inside her, moving, flexing. She cried out with pleasure as the tension inside snapped.

Jed barely managed to turn the knob to delta wave, letting Helen settle into deep sleep. He didn't think he could deal with her yet, not when his whole body ached for release like this. It had taken every ounce of willpower to follow through, to get her to do it.

Reshaping and remolding the mind was like handling a precious and fragile piece of art made of glass. Some were so obstinate that they'd rather be broken than be manipulated. He had to be so careful with a strong woman like Elena. He'd whispered to her, urging her to not just be part of his fantasy, but to see herself and him in a reflection. Let her shape and form her own mind.

His suggestion must have worked because as he settled into his half-dreaming state, some of the stuff happening wasn't his imagination at work. That mirror that'd shattered. The way she'd fought. Those weren't his.

He had gambled on using the presence of another "woman" to push Elena into action. It was easy enough to call up a female form and go through the motions of every teenage boy's favorite wet dream from a music video—a romp with a voluptuous woman. He hadn't needed to be so extensive, but it'd certainly added a sexual charge when he'd realized that he really had succeeded in getting Elena caught up in the action. Watching her getting so damn pissed off turned him on more than imagining a woman sexing it up with him.

He'd kept right on, fueling that jealousy, waiting for her. The moment she'd grabbed the woman, he knew his fantasy was finally not just his anymore, but that he'd gotten her to actively participate in it in her dream state. It was unexpectedly exciting. Never in his experience of implanting triggers had he ever had an encounter like this.

Helen challenged him like no one had before, pushing him to cross lines where he shouldn't have. He should have just allowed her to beat up her adversary; the triumph of winning would have served the purpose just as well since she was coming after him. But the most wicked idea had popped into his head out of nowhere.

Face it, McNeil. Two women wrestling was all about your horny libido and not much to do with trigger imprinting.

The discovery, that he could make sure she didn't hurt herself by the mere fantasy of giving his other "woman" his strength and taking away Helen's, only added to his sexual enjoyment. He didn't deny himself the pleasure of getting that sexy lithe body in various suggestive positions for his perusal. Yes, he was going to take her that way. And that way. And that way...

When he'd tasted Elena, it had felt so real. The experience had left him aching for more. She might not agree with him, but he was being tortured and teased just as much as she was.

She'd finally acknowledged him. She'd let him imbed their trigger.

"It's done," he rasped out.

She would hate him but he had her where he wanted. She would rest and then...she would come to kill him.

Chapter Five

"Where's Hell?"

Jed paused in the middle of setting up the video transmission to see who Flyboy was addressing. The tone of the question was casual but he caught the underlying tension.

"She has a couple of days off," Jed replied, returning his attention to pulling the feed from archives.

"I know that. I heard she came in yesterday and seeing that she's still at Center, I'm surprised she isn't here at this meeting."

Jed glanced up briefly. Flyboy was still looking at him intently. "This is a meeting for an undergoing COS operation in which Hell only had a tiny part," he said quietly, "so she doesn't need to be here."

"Armando wasn't actively in this project either," Flyboy pointed out.

Jed caught Armando's movement in his periphery vision. Bringing in Armando was a clever move. He hadn't given the newest commando too much to do lately.

"A failed ironist is a sad, sad man," Armando murmured.

Sullivan made a rude noise. "The weird one has spoken."

"What the hell do you mean, failed ironist?" Flyboy demanded.

"Saying one thing and meaning another, and not successfully doing both," Armando replied, with a small smile, "is a failed ironist. Now you're morphing into clueless failed ironist."

Jed was amused at the byplay. Armando might be a handful at times, but he never failed to amuse him with his oddly wry observations.

Flyboy turned back to Jed. "I don't think there's anything ironic or clueless about my question. You still haven't answered me."

The younger man had been getting more and more protective about Helen, especially since her near-escape during the test operation. "She can take care of herself, Hunter," Jed said.

"I've done as you told me to, kept an eye on her and been a friend when she has questions." Flyboy looked around the table. "I think everyone should stop keeping her at arm's length. She passed the test and successfully retrieved the SEED. If one of you guys weren't around, I'd still ask about you."

"I believe you haven't asked where Diamond is," Heath chimed in, mockery lacing his voice.

Sullivan leaned back in his chair and laughed. Even Shahrukh smiled at the dig.

"I know where Number One is," Flyboy retorted. "Easy deduction, that. He's gone after T. in Europe, what else?"

Jed hit the button that slid the middle of the briefing table open to allow the laser projection screen to activate. "Now we know who to ask when we need a SITREP of our unit," he said laconically.

"All but Hell," Heath pointed out. "He doesn't know where Hell is."

"Or whether she should or shouldn't be joining us at our meetings," Sullivan added.

"Meeting of the minds can be dangerous," Armando offered another of his cryptic remarks.

Jed paused. His men—the elite COS Commandos—were in a snippy mood today indeed. It was always interesting when someone new joined the unit—a rare thing—what with the tightly organized functions of each of the nine. He looked around...when there used to be nine, he amended. There were now just seven of them. When Shahrukh had first joined the team, his size and presence, along with his royal blood line, caused some good old-fashioned male rivalry among some of the men before he was accepted.

His gaze rested on Armando for an instant. He still wasn't one hundred percent sure whether Armando would make a good fit but he had the qualities that COS looked for. However, the Virus experimentation was taking its toll on the younger man. There was always a breaking point.

And now there was Helen Roston. How she would do in the long run remained to be seen. They hadn't yet integrated her as part of the team.

"Hell's still going through her RV downtime," Jed said. "Perhaps she's in her quarters, sleeping it off."

He'd left her sleeping. An enforced sleep, but that couldn't be helped. Much as he would prefer to spend the evening and night living out their sexual fantasies in the flesh, he had to attend to the meetings de Clerq had rescheduled for him. Perhaps later.

But right now, he had to focus on current ongoing missions, especially the one they'd been following all the way from Asia to East Europe. He activated the remote in his hand and the 360 degree-viewable screen slid into place. He did a quick test run. He rotated the map, pinpointed a spot on it, and zoomed. The map immediately enlarged, first giving the topological details, then a bird's eye view of the area, and lastly a cross section of the metropolitan.

It had the desired effect. His men turned their attention to the screen.

Jed clicked as he spoke, letting the visuals carry the weight of the operation details. With the addition of the Admiral's SEALs as well as independent contractors in the mix, his men had very little time to personally keep up with the new faces.

"Our contact in Velesta, Hawk McMillan, has gotten back to me with coordinates that could lead us to the missing explosive device. We know that the illegal shipments were dropped by the CIA in crates into Macedonia. The good news is that the device is still in one of those crates, meaning, Dilaver hasn't seen it or sold it yet. The bad news is, someone is deliberately robbing Dilaver whenever his shipments are on the road and he's getting low in funds. That means he'll be desperate to sell quickly and is antsy to get to his caches. That squeezes our time frame even more."

"Who's robbing Dilaver?" Sullivan asked. "Not that I don't approve, but I thought he was the big shot in that area. Isn't everyone either paying him or in his pocket?"

"Apparently, someone started to take advantage of Dilaver's short holiday in Asia," Jed said.

That was when the drug lord had tried to do business with the Triads and failed miserably, with some inside tinkering from Jed personally. Then, with the help of a team of SEALs doing most of the damage, COS Command had successfully shut down one of the veins that fed the heart of the illegal drug industries in that region.

Jed liked how things were going. The joint venture with the SEALs had paid off handsomely so far, enabling them to play some power games with different illegal arms dealers while looking for the missing explosive device. "Hawk told me that our Croat warlord came home to millions lost from these highway robberies. What with our taking his cache in Asia, I'd say that Dilaver is feeling the pain in his pocketbook."

Sullivan snorted. "Good. I wish we could be like the SEALs and just blow scum like him away," he said.

"We don't like to do things the easy way," Armando remarked.

"There's no easy way to kill cancer, Chang," Heath said. "You zap one cell and it keeps dividing elsewhere. The only way is to infect it from the inside."

Jed nodded. That was their way. Unlike the SEALs, who were trained to search and destroy, COS Commandos were conditioned in the Virus Program to attack like an organism. They specialized in targeting a system from within, sometimes using the enemy's own strengths to destroy it. In the case of Dilaver, with his army of mercenaries and regional warlords, their task had been to find out his strange connection to the CIA and how he came to be on the receiving end of special weapon drops. Then COMCEN could use this knowledge to trap bigger prey. Special ops, such as the SEALs, were usually not interested in insidious warfare. Which was fine with Jed; they all had their own battle zones.

"Hawk must get closer to Dilaver soon," Heath continued. "No one gets close to those caches of weapons unless he's in Dilaver's trusted circle."

"He's already been on a trip with Dilaver, so that's the first step," Jed told them and clicked on the remote to show an aerial map. "The coordinates show a large area. Several shipments, well hidden in rough mountainous terrain. Finding the exact location will take some time and with Dilaver's army of mercenaries lying in wait at checkpoints, we can't send in too large a search party."

"It's strange to be on the outside, Jed, letting some other group have the action," Sullivan said. "What's our job at this point? Take a team in there to search for the caches?"

"Sometimes it's good to study how others tackle a certain problem," Heath commented. "Look at our GEM division. If they'd taken on this stage, they'd handle the situation differently."

Jed nodded again. "Of course they would handle the operation from an entirely different angle. I've already pointed out the impracticality of using our female assets, especially with the time factor. We're dealing with a man who uses and sells young girls. It'd be very difficult to get him to confide in a woman about weapons. So inserting Hawk McMillan into Dilaver's stronghold is the best option. It frees us for the rest of Phase Three, which we'll run through right now to make sure we're all on the same page. We have a lot on our plates what with what has happened in D.C."

Ever since their team had initiated Phase Three and successfully managed to corner the CIA moles, the rats—so to speak—had been scattering back to their holes. Which was what they'd wanted. COMCEN's agenda was to follow each trail and infiltrate so they could find out more about this extensive network of spies who had been poisoning the system for so long.

It had taken them a long time to get to this point and Jed could feel a breakthrough coming. Finally—*finally*—after all these years, he would be able to crush a few enemies that had cost the lives of his friends.

"Admiral Madison is doing a great job there too, making sure that the Intelligence Committee investigates all the suspicious cases from the last ten years," Flyboy said.

"Yes, having met that man a few times, I think he should run for office," Sullivan added.

"Are you crazy, dude? That's the end of life as he knows it. He can forget about finding out traitors and getting to the bottom of this mess we're in. We don't need him running around making promises he won't keep." Flyboy scratched his nose with his pen. "No, we want him just as he is."

"True." Sullivan leaned back. "So I gather I keep on doing what I've been doing, putting together the missing weapons puzzle, right? Jed?"

Jed blinked. Part of him had been listening to the conversation, but a part of him was busy registering that strange prickly sensation at the base of his neck. He'd felt it before—when he was looking down at Cummings' body. What the hell was it?

He looked at his team. Everyone was at ease, throwing out ideas and speculations in their usual informal style. They were a tightly knit group. If anything was wrong, these men would all feel it. No, this feeling was uniquely his.

Sullivan was gazing back at him questioningly, waiting for his reply. They were used to his short pauses, so his little silence hadn't been noticed. He caught Armando's speculative gaze. Except by one. Armando was looking at him too closely. Did he have the same odd feeling too?

Jed double-clicked the remote. "Quick update. The missing weapons are showing up at odd places. The explosive device is in Macedonia. We just retrieved the SEED in Germany. What do you have for us at your end, Sullivan?"

Sullivan and Shahrukh were their weaponry and battle experts. Sullivan had connections with the West and Shahrukh, the East. The two of them worked well together, and in spite of very different demeanors, they had become very close friends, so much so that they were mocked as the twins at COMCEN.

Sullivan grinned and turned to Shahrukh. "Wait till they hear what we have."

Shahrukh responded with a mere lift of his dark eyebrow.

"First, we'll simplify each missing element," Sullivan said, counting off with his fingers. "An explosive device, practically undetectable. A decoder, one that's being designed by quantum scientists. The entire design of our newest flight simulator. A captured and still missing spy plane. That's just the big list. Shahrukh?"

"With some help from T., we've traced certain monetary movements through off-shore accounts belonging to some of our suspects," Shahrukh obligingly continued, his soft accent more pronounced than usual, betraying a little bit of his excitement. "We matched dates and events. There's an emerging pattern."

"Former KGB handlers and their leftover moles in different agencies," Sullivan interrupted triumphantly.

"It seems that the fall of the Soviet Union didn't necessarily mean the fall of the KGB powers. Through all these years, they've continued using their extensive network to collect intelligence for use to shore up their weakening base, waiting for the right time to push back," Shahrukh said.

"As shown in the current CIA nightmare," Sullivan finished up.

Jed looked from one man to the other. The "twins" made an odd couple, what with Sullivan's cowboy attitude about everything and Shahrukh's more introverted personality, but they shared an innate passion for history and old weaponry. Jed had listened to them in deep discussion about the roles of knights and the different weaponry used in ancient war. Every strategy was discussed; every role was replayed. It was interesting to see the two men challenging each other in mental warfare and reenacting battle after battle from one side, then another.

To Jed, war was war was war. To his two teammates, war was some macho form of arts and crafts. He'd often found himself marveling at how Sullivan could manage to bring in the coaching decisions of a recent football game to argue against one of Shahrukh's more esoteric theories about a famous ancient battle.

And if talking strayed into a real difference of opinion, those two had been known to reenact a one-on-one fight right there at the gym. Sullivan always started it, of course. He was competitive like that. Shahrukh, Jed suspected, went along just to amuse himself.

"So where do you think this is leading?" he asked, ignoring the twinge to look at the entrance expectantly. The others would know soon enough. "Proposals?"

"We—"

The buzzing of the exterior door interrupted Sullivan. The commandos turned to look at the monitor above to see who it was. Usually it would be one of their own—T. or Diamond—but they weren't in the country. Any other personnel, even de Clerq, would announce themselves through the intercom first.

Jed put down the remote in his hand. He already knew. It was Hell.

She pushed the interior door open, dark eyes sparkling, lips curled in a temper, all glorious raging Valkyrie.

"Excuse me, gentlemen," she paused long enough to announce, then stalked over and swung a fist at Jed.

He chose not to avoid it, only taking one step back and putting just enough distance to make sure the hit didn't break his jaw. After what he'd done to her, he owed her.

Helen shook her hand, her shoulder stinging from the direct punch. Ouch. She hadn't expected him to stay put like that.

All eyes were on her, of course. Couldn't be helped. She was that pissed and this couldn't wait. She looked at the man standing in front of her. Damn him. He wasn't even rubbing his jaw, even though she'd decked him good. She could see a slight swelling starting up already.

She looked around again and casually shrugged. They all probably knew why she'd hit Jed McNeil, and if they didn't, they would guess soon enough. Undoubtedly, they all had the same skills to seduce—she determinedly pushed away those thoughts and pulled out a chair.

"Sorry, please do continue." She clenched and unclenched her slightly numbed hand. Damn, that hurt. "Since no one stopped me from entering, I'm assuming that it's okay to be listening in on you guys."

There was a short silence. Then Flyboy spoke up, "We were just wondering where you were."

Hell held his blue eyes for a long second. Of all of them, she'd considered him her friend. Now she wasn't sure any more. How much was his friendliness an act?

"I was asleep," she told him grimly.

She wanted to pound on the table, but it wouldn't do to let them see her losing it. Not yet. Her main target was *him*. She returned her gaze to Jed McNeil, who calmly picked up a remote from the table.

Oh, he had been so damn smart, hiding behind Hades in those dreams. She wasn't sure yet how he'd managed to do that but she knew it was him. There was no mistaking those light eyes.

When she'd woken up, she'd instinctively understood what her inner voice had been telling her. She had mistaken her strange dream for what they called "lucid dreaming", that state of consciousness that she often had when she was aware that she was sleeping and dreaming at the same time. Not only that, she had wrongly assumed that she'd invaded Hades' dreams again.

Half-awake and still aroused, she'd allowed her mind to drift in search of those hands and lips, letting it wander off as she slowly surfaced. Then she'd experienced that odd dizzying sensation that she had had yesterday, catching a glimpse of dark hair and silvery eyes and this very room, before she was knocked sideways by the same blinding pain.

She knew—absolutely—bone deep, that Jed McNeil was Hades. It was too coincidental that twice now, when she'd managed to slip into remote-viewing mode while thinking of Hades, she'd seen him instead.

Fully conscious after the headache, she'd realized that it was not nighttime, which meant that she and Hades weren't doing their usual brain synchronization exercise. She'd jerked out of bed and had barely taken the time to freshen up as her mind raged, denied, processed, denied, argued, and denied. She'd rushed here without even remembering how she'd gotten there, as if she just knew where to find him, and strode through the main office past a group of operatives.

It now occurred to her that no one had stopped her. Not that it would have mattered. She had been so angry she would have fought her way in just to see whether he was really here. Punching him felt so good, she was almost too giddy to do anything but sit here and savor it.

"Proposals?" Jed asked calmly. By now, a small cut had opened at the corner of his mouth.

She had to give it to him. He was one cool cat. He was looking at Sullivan as if nothing unusual had happened.

"Umm...how about a break?" Sullivan replied drolly, rubbing his chin.

Helen noted the amused gleam in his eyes, then cast her gaze at the others. Shahrukh was looking at his notes, a tiny smile on his strong lips. Flyboy was sniffing at a pencil as if it was some fine cigar.

She relaxed—just a little. She didn't want to make things uncomfortable between herself and these men with whom she'd barely begun working. There were seven of them to her one, not counting T., and she had to figure out what the dynamics were here and learn how to work it to her advantage. Her own agency, GEM, was made up of mainly women and their *modus operandi* couldn't be more different. She had the feeling that working closely with these men was going to be eye-opening, to say the least.

"Do you need one?" Jed asked.

"Nope. But I thought you might need it to take care of that swelling before it gets too puffy. That could be problematic for the next assignment."

Helen frowned. Ooops. She hoped she hadn't caused more problems for any assignment. The fact that one of the Cummings had escaped had been her fault.

"Lucky she didn't break your nose. Puffy eyes, man. It's a major pain to sight a target from an angle."

"He could always stand sideways and look out of his good eye."

Helen felt a flash of guilt until she remembered why she'd hit him. She pursed her lips. Well, she hadn't broken his jaw or his nose, so their good-natured ribbing was for her benefit. Besides, she had the suspicion that they were trying to get her to say something, perhaps give information about why she was so angry. She looked at him grimly. Let Mr. Know-It-All explain the situation himself.

Jed cocked his head for an instant. "I'm looking at you out of the good eye right now." Helen watched as he used the remote to move a set of photos. "Resuming run-through. Gorman caught. Dragan Dilaver the subsidiary. The explosive trigger in Macedonia. The SEED in Germany. An underground network of moles inside the CIA, stealing and dispersing information. We're still in the dark about the flight simulation program and the missing Stealth. Question: Who's the hidden power behind these thefts? Agenda? Sullivan and Shahrukh, you were backtracking the list and following leads."

Helen bit down her lower lip. The cadence of his speech—it reminded her of Hades when he summarized things.

"Suggestion. We have the SEED. We can put it out in the market through Diamond. Right now, Deutsche International thinks he's nabbed it from them," Sullivan said.

"I think there is a bigger agenda than just weapons stolen. If the old KGB is involved, there is something going on behind the scenes," Heath said.

Jed nodded. "Agreed. They didn't collect information for ten years, wheeling and dealing weapons, just for profit alone." He clicked on the remote and two maps came up side by side. "On the left is Velesta. On the right is Frankfurt. Both these cities are on opposite ends of the economic scale. We need to find out three things. One, who is Dilaver's contact? Two, why is Deutsche International, a think-tank, buying a decoder from a double-agent? Three," Jed paused for a moment, then added, "we need to find out what Hell bumped into when she was in the stairwell at Deutsche. These CIA hostiles were after the decoder *and* her, since they tranqued her instead of using live ammo."

Helen straightened up at the mention of her name. He called her "Hell", though. Hades liked to call her Elena.

"Wait, we don't know if they were really after the decoder," Flyboy pointed out.

"You don't think it's coincidental that they showed up right after Hell finished her mission? Why couldn't they have just nabbed her when she was entering Deutsche?" Jed countered.

"Point taken, but if it was related to Hell, then it has something to do with the Supersoldier program and not the mission itself," Flyboy said.

"Why would the CIA want me?" Helen asked, puzzled. "They trained me themselves."

"We're talking about the faction inside the CIA that's been infested with moles," Flyboy told her. "We've been working on zeroing in on their identities the past two years while you were in training. Many of them disappeared underground when we caught CIA Deputy Director Gorman."

"Cummings and his wife were two of them," Helen guessed.

Flyboy nodded. "A few of them took off with some important documentation. The SEED is one of the most important items that disappeared." He gave her one of his trademark devastating smiles, flashing teeth and dimples. "You finding and retrieving it before it was sold and distributed was tantamount to a miracle. Gorman could only provide a list of names and we have a special task force at the CIA working on matching up possible leaks and weapon drop-offs from the past ten years. It was taking forever."

Helen smiled back. "Why do I get the feeling that no one had much hope that I'd get it done?"

"Not true. You think COMCEN's going to waste all that money on something it hadn't run through Eight Ball for success/failure percentages? You should know better than that by now, Hell," Flyboy chided.

Eight Ball was the Center's supercomputer. Helen liked its quirky personality. Its programmer obviously enjoyed tinkering with it, what with the computer's knack at finding odd catch-phrases and using them at the strangest moments.

"What was Eight Ball's percentages for my performance?" she asked curiously.

"Heath, any information coming from Mrs. Cummings?" Jed asked, interrupting them.

Helen looked at him and thought she saw a glint in his eyes. Was there finally a reaction to her punch? She glanced back at Flyboy who gave her a small shrug.

She turned her attention to Heath, sitting next to her. A few days ago, she'd thought he could be Hades. In comparison to Flyboy, there was something very dark and very still about Heath, like a deep lagoon. When she'd asked about his role within the unit, she'd been told it was "retrieval". "Retrieval" appeared to include interrogation of prisoners.

"I'm working on it," Heath said. "She gave up her husband for a reason and I'll get a name sooner or later."

"Make it sooner," Jed said softly. "I've a feeling there is a time schedule behind all this. We have to find the connection between the trigger and the decoder, between Dilaver in Macedonia and the think-tank in Germany. Something's brewing."

"If we retrieve both items, we stop it. Helen's helped us with one, why not let her try to get the other?" Shahrukh suggested.

"You mean, remote view it?" Helen asked.

"Couldn't you pinpoint where the explosive is?"

"No," Jed said.

"Why not?" Flyboy asked.

"Because remote viewing doesn't work like that. From what we know, the crates are somewhere in the hills in Macedonia. If it's there, Helen would see the same mountainous surroundings unless there's a specific landmark, which we don't have. Isn't that right, Hell?"

She nodded. "Yes, that's right. Locating objects or persons in a vast area isn't easy for a remote viewer. We sense the surroundings and describe them, but we don't really know the exact spot."

"Not understanding," Sullivan said. "How did you manage to get the exact location of the SEED during the test then?"

"I described what I saw to my monitor," Helen explained, staring hard at Jed, "and he appeared to recognize enough elements of my visual to narrow down the options. Then, he directed me to certain landmarks he knew would pinpoint the exact location. It appeared my monitor was picked specifically because he had inside knowledge of a number of places that are off-limits to outsiders."

"It sounds like guessing to me," Sullivan muttered.

"Unless immersive virtual reality's more than just the monitor listening in on her remote-viewing sessions, Sullivan, but you'll have to ask Hell about that," Armando said and slyly added with a wink at Hell, "which helps you, Hell, to eliminate one more man off your list, hmm?"

Helen had to stop a grin from forming. Armando knew she'd been trying desperately to figure out which of them was Hades. He had been one of the prime suspects, actually, until he'd kissed her and then backed off. Something had told her that the real person behind Hades wouldn't have done that in real life; he'd have kept pushing, just as he always did in virtual reality.

"It takes time to eliminate a man off my list," Helen drawled, sitting back and studying them, "and definitely more than a few questions about my remote viewing skills. I like being thoroughly sure, but I don't think any of you would like me inside your mind that long, would you?"

She almost chuckled at the predictable "no fucking way" expression in their eyes. A couple of them looked intrigued. One in particular was looking at her too intently. She knew whom she was after but it didn't hurt to let them all know that she was after their asses too for having played a part in not telling her what was going on. Each of them had been testing her, wondering about her skill, and trying to see how far they could push. She was enjoying turning the tables, letting them think she could get into their secrets if she chose.

Ha, take that. Her chin tilted up just a tiny bit when her gaze encountered Jed's, which seemed to have the ability to make her spine tingle. The trickle of dried blood at the side of those masculine lips made him look even more dangerous. A bruise was starting to show.

"I wouldn't mind it at all," Heath said quietly. "It might be an interesting experience, having you in my mind."

"I suggest you make the appointment later and keep your mind on breaking Mrs. Cummings for now," Jed said.

Heath smiled slowly, as if what Jed suggested was child's play. "I'll hurry up the time table," he promised softly. "Helen and I would make a good team, don't you think?"

"Yes, don't you, Jed?" Helen asked, smiling too.

Icy silver eyes met hers. Those eyes had been watching her all these months. "We'll see. You'll need to catch up on the Cummings files now that you've passed the test the other agencies demanded. De Clerq will give you the relevant passwords later so you can download from Eight Ball."

The person she was trying to provoke wasn't taking the bait. She felt frustrated. Cheated. Damn him, he was determined to be the one to set the tone and the pace of their relationship.

She quickly averted her eyes. Where the hell had that come from? They didn't have any relationship. "Partnership," she mumbled to herself, her mind scurrying to find another choice for whatever it was they had between them. "Collaboration. Dammit." None of the synonyms fit.

"Did you say something?" Jed asked.

She shook her head. "It's nothing." That she wanted to share out loud anyway.

"Then let's wrap it up. The old alliance within the KGB theory sounds interesting. I'm going to call up some old contacts. You all do the same. We have to find a way for us to infiltrate."

With a few parting instructions, Jed turned and headed for the door. Helen frowned. Wait a minute. He wasn't going to just leave again without talking to her, was he?

But he most definitely was. As the others got up, gathering their files and folders, Helen pushed her chair back and took several long strides after Jed. All she saw was the back of him, nicely molded in a pair of jeans, and the door shut.

"Do you think she's going to hit him again?" Someone mockingly asked, followed by male laughter, as she slipped through the door.

Chapter Six

"Wait!"

Jed kept walking. He hadn't planned on Elena getting up so soon. She was supposed to be resting. Usually, it took quiet time for the subconscious to absorb a hypnotic suggestion. Had he failed? It sometimes took a few sessions to embed successfully, but he'd thought he'd managed to lead Elena along to the right point.

He frowned. For selfish reasons he hadn't exercised his usual patience with her. And that odd sensation that told him when she was near—what was that? His frown deepened. He'd felt it earlier while on the ship too, but she wasn't anywhere near that location.

He ignored the open curiosity from the others in the office area at the sight of them. No doubt the swelling on his face had something to do with it. He pushed his tongue against the inside of his cheek. Elena packed quite a punch in her swing.

"I'm getting tired of going after you. Are you such a fucking coward," she demanded, as she fell into step beside him, "that you won't face me and answer my questions?"

His lips quirked. But he did want her to chase him around. He'd wanted her to keep thinking about him. "I thought we had an appointment, which you missed," he reminded her. He had other things in mind besides talking, of course. "Now I have two more meetings today."

"That was before...before what you did." She grabbed his arm hard, then deliberately stepped in front of him, halting his progress toward the elevator. "I want to talk now."

Her words told him a lot. First, that she knew and comprehended what had happened besides their sexual encounter. He wasn't surprised that she'd caught on because she was a strong woman mentally—one of the strongest he'd met, actually—and had continually resisted him.

It wasn't until the breakthrough with the brain entrainment machine, when she'd somehow entered his dreams, that he'd found a chink in her armor. He would use that subconscious desire to seek him out even in her sleep against her. It was new territory for a jaded operative like him. Seduction had never been this intriguing. Now, he wondered whether he'd possibly not pushed hard enough. Sexual imprinting, after all, meant sexually bonding with a target repeatedly, and he had just started.

He almost smiled again. Not hard enough? The growing constriction in his pants reminded him how hard she'd gotten, and was now making, him. *Without even trying.* Damn, but he wanted her.

He moved to the side. She countered, blocking his path again.

He considered the idea of pushing her through one of the adjoining doors in the hallway and showing her exactly what he had in mind. Talk wasn't the top priority. His session with her had left him hard and wanting, needing the real touch of her instead of all that virtual shit floating in his head. But his job had to come first.

Even now, standing inches away from him, the faint scent of her fragrance teased him with thoughts of using his tongue to find its source. He hadn't been so easily aroused in a long time.

He studied her angry eyes. Some things one couldn't find out in virtual reality—her eyes changed to a muted green when she was emotional. Would they change color when he was buried inside her?

That thought made him even more aroused. This sexual need for her. Maybe he'd mistakenly imprinted himself instead. His lips finally quirked with suppressed humor.

"It's not funny!"

Her other hand reached up to shove him. At that moment the elevator door opened. Jed neatly caught the free hand, twisted his body sideways and pulled her along with him into the empty carriage. He pressed the floor he wanted and the doors slid shut. Noting that she wasn't putting up much of a fight, he typed the code onto the pad, deactivating the micro-eye. He supposed he could test whether his *hard* work paid off.

Her eyes widened when he moved her captured hand down to the bulge in front of his pants.

"Five minutes," he said, then pressed forward, pushing her against the wall, holding her hand tightly as she reflexively cupped him. She gasped as he bit her neck. "Starting now. I'll just show you your answers."

He had to be quick, knock her off her feet before she realized what was happening. Her free hand slammed up against his chest in warning.

"What the hell are you—"

He easily unzipped her pants. He liked this latest style of low-riding hip huggers. Made access easy. Especially when the woman hadn't bothered with panties.

He buried his face in her neck, ignoring the slight discomfort of his bruised face, and used his weight to trap her. He was counting on her still having that strange sexual sensitivity she'd somehow gotten from the use of the serum. Two years' worth of imbalance for him to take advantage of.

"Stop it," she whispered, the tone of her voice hushed and urgent.

"Make me," he challenged.

But she was already wet and ready, her body limp and willing, allowing him to easily knee her legs further apart. His fingers fit tightly inside those hip huggers. He slid them downward. Then up. She let out a familiar throaty sound. There. Found the right spot.

"Wherever I want. However I please," he whispered. She gasped, her hand no longer pushing him away. That was a good sign. "Isn't this what you're after?"

"No...!"

"So why aren't you stopping me? Admit it. You want this more than you want to beat me up."

"I want to see the real Hades. Then I'll beat you up."

"Maybe you got the wrong guy," he challenged softly. He teased the wet entrance with his middle finger, probing the top of the sensitive slit, pushing in slightly against her natural feminine resistance. "What if I'm not him?"

She shuddered at his intimate caress. "I'm still going to beat you up." Her voice was strained.

He laughed. "Greedy. I like that in a woman. You want more than just to see Hades."

He looked at her flushed face as he continued to pleasure her. He had his answer about her eyes; they were definitely getting greener. Why couldn't she have continued sleeping so he could wake her up the way he'd planned? Now he had to keep her focused on him for the next few hours.

"You want Hades inside you. Admit it." He leaned on her harder so his hand could get better access. Deeper. Wet and hot. He jammed her hand cupping his cock between their thighs, so he could use his to yank the waistband of her pants lower. Like that. Nudge her free leg wider. Like that. He just loved these pants.

Decision came swiftly. He couldn't let her on her own yet. He had a feeling she would spend all that time trying to find a way to undo what he'd done and thus, blocking it from sinking deeper into her subconscious.

"Only if you'd admit to me that you're Hades," she panted. "Then I might let you fuck me. But I don't think you're him anyway. Five minutes? Hades can do a lot better."

Jed smiled slowly. She was bargaining with him while letting him win this fight. It was a classic NOPAIN move. He expected no less from a GEM operative. She wasn't going to win today, though.

That smile sent her heartbeat into warp speed. She'd never seen a smile so sinfully sensuous, oozing unspoken sexual promises that made her toes curl in her shoes. His eyes, that strange light color, held a male heat, frank and assessing, and she found herself unable to look away, unable to stop him from doing whatever he wanted. And the hard bulge nudging into her hand left no doubt what he had in mind.

What was wrong with her? She couldn't form a single coherent thought as he pulled her pants further down her hips. All that resonated were the waves of pleasure pulsing from between her legs as she let him bring her closer and closer to climax. If he wasn't holding her against the wall, she was going to slide down onto the floor.

She needed this. Ever since last night, she'd wanted this feeling again. It was as if she couldn't get enough of this man. His fantasies fueled her desire. And knowing that he desired her, dreamed about sex with her, turned her on. Deviant. Maybe she was warped too, because she just couldn't find a way to stop her body from betraying her. And the more she let him take control, the less she wanted to fight it.

His erection pushed boldly against her hand that was trapped between their bodies. God, she wanted to look at him. Not some computer-generated avatar. Just him and her, with nothing between them.

There was no lingering doubt left. Jed was indeed Hades. No one but Hades would be this audacious. That night, when he'd came to her in the dark—he'd bit her the same way as he was doing now, marking her neck on the same delicious erogenous spot. He knew now, as he'd discovered then, how doing so rendered her helpless with desire. The way her stupid body was out of control now, every single sensation was doubled. She closed her eyes. She shuddered as she concentrated on a finger wickedly making tiny circles. *That* tripled the pleasure.

But she wanted him to tell her himself that he was Hades. It wouldn't make this surrender any easier but it would ease her mind if he admitted it to her face.

She forced her eyes open. He was still looking at her with the same hungry passion. His nostrils were flared. His eyes glittered in his tanned face. The kind of sexual teasing in which they'd been engaged went both ways; the man had to be just as turned on as she was. Testing her theory, she squeezed his arousal. His retaliation was devastatingly effective. His fingers pushed inside her and started stroking with a determined rhythm. At the same time, his other hand slid up under her shirt. She cried out as he gently pulled at her tender nipple, her whole body jerking forward and upward. She curled one leg around his. She was so close...right at the razor edge of pleasure...

"One more minute," his voice was silky smooth, his breath teasing her ears. "Didn't you say five minutes wouldn't be enough?"

"No..." she protested, knowing instinctively what he was going to do. She pulled at his shirt fiercely. "Damn you...I know you're him. Just...tell me."

"I thought I've been showing you," he mocked. "Thirty seconds. I don't think you're going to make it. Uh, uh, uh, no words...you're going to waste these last twenty seconds."

He nipped wickedly at her neck again, the slide of his fingers slowing down. She gurgled some helpless nonsense as he counted in her ear, dragging each number out. "Ten...nine...so wet...seven...six..."

She was getting faint from holding her breath. He had her so close to coming, her heart rate roaring like a freight train, her whole consciousness zeroing in on the silken glide that was moving in slow motion, a chaotic mixture of pleasure and panic. She whimpered, straining to reach...no, not yet...he stopped. For one frozen second, she stood at the knife's edge of climax. Her breath whooshed out in total shock and disappointment.

"And one. I guess I'll just have to show you more later."

Her humiliation was complete as she stood there in helpless anger. She couldn't believe he'd leave her in the lurch like this. Not like this! She watched silently as he adjusted her clothes. Zipped her pants back up. Released his hold of her.

He stepped back and unhurriedly licked his fingers, the sexual hunger in his eyes reflecting her own tumultuous feelings. Then, as if he turned a switch off, the look was gone. In its place was the cool, emotionless commando look she was beginning to recognize. How did he do that? The shuttered expression stopped every word hanging fiercely on her lips. She struggled to look equally unruffled, knowing damn well that was impossible with her mussed-up hair and smeared lipstick.

He ran his card through the security slot. The doors slid open. He cocked an eyebrow at her. "Coming?"

"So what's the decision?"

Jonah continued studying the menu, pretending an interest in different choices of main entrees. He hadn't eaten out in ages and he wanted to eat everything. But he wasn't stupid. He knew they weren't giving him a treat because they felt sorry for him.

"We aren't needed in Velesta. They have activated a cell."

"Is that right...how interesting."

"I think they don't want to chance using another weapon."

"We'd have fucking gotten the SEED if 51 here had been quicker locating the COS candidate."

Jonah turned the page and stared blankly at the choices of desserts available. He should have known the fatter one would put the blame of losing the decoder on him. He wanted to say something to defend himself, wanted to point out that without him, they wouldn't have known that the SEED was in Frankfurt, that he wasn't the one who had failed to capture that remote viewer. In fact, he'd been the only one who had done everything right and had been quietly sitting inside the vehicle watching them fuck up. It wasn't *his* fault that they couldn't get inside a building themselves. Hell, those other agents did.

He frowned. He didn't want to think about those moments when he was remote viewing that building. He didn't want to remember the loss of his precious cache.

He snapped the menu shut. All his wonderful sex-filled recordings that he'd carefully collected and stored for his viewing enjoyment. They were his comfort in this stupid medical place. Now nothing to fill that empty void. Remote viewing was no fun without that serum. Just another fucking task to help these idiots get their reward. 51 go here. 51 look for that. What about his reward?

"So you've decided what you want to order, 51?"

"It's Five-One," he corrected with slow emphasis. If they were going to use him, they needed to at least call his special handle correctly. "It's Five-One, not Fifty-One."

He stared back at the man studying him. He heard the fat one snorting impatiently. The first agent put up his hand to stall his partner's sarcastic remark.

"Of course, if it's important to you," the agent said mildly. "I didn't know that's the correct way to address you."

Which told him that these two weren't ever involved with the original CIA programs. There was a reason why the numbers were called out individually instead of as an entity. Five-One would have told a knowledgeable agent the division and experience. There were very few with the experience level he had and that was why it irritated him to be treated like a useless experiment by these assholes.

"Fifty-One makes it sound like I'm just a number down a long line of experimental remote viewers. I'm not. I've been handpicked for very special assignments, including for part of the supersoldier-spy program."

"Which you failed almost immediately," the other agent sneered.

Jonah refused to acknowledge that he was considered a failure. He was more than an experiment; in fact, he was a success for a long time. Why the fuck would climbing a rope or running for miles be so damn important anyway?

He shrugged. "I've never been in the army. I didn't know they were expecting me to train like some athlete."

"The serum, Five-One, was supposed to help you through that phase. Anyway, let's get back to ordering food. We aren't here to discuss the success of the program or the serum."

Jonah reopened his menu, restlessly looking at the items again. Of course, they didn't know how successful he really was with that serum that they'd fed him. Not only was he more clear-minded, not only was he able to function physically without the usual downtime after a remote-viewing session, but he'd discovered that he could pull and absorb certain energy from those he was covertly watching.

He'd gone after the pretty ones, the ones with their sexy late night romps still lingering around their aura. He wasn't stupid. He put his life on the line for their covert games every time they shot him up with the juice, so he should have a few perks too. He'd kept his new power a secret. No harm done.

Payback was a bitch, though. The longer downtime and the headaches took him out for days. But his cache of recordings was worth it. In those hours of pain and darkness, he could retreat into himself and let all that sexy energy wash over him. He would replay them over and over and no one knew because he was left alone to rest.

But his treasure was all gone now. He felt that rage inside him growing again. He wasn't enjoying his downtime at all. He needed the serum in his system soon. He had to get out there in the ether and get his fix, or break down like a lunatic. A fix, that was all. Just to tide him over till he found that bitch who stole his cache.

"I want the house steak, rare, with spicy potato wedges," he said, "and afterwards, a banana split, with everything on top. Can I have coffee too?"

Caffeine and nicotine were no-nos during prep time for remote viewers. He had snuck a couple of cigarettes in past sessions. Unlike their tests, he found that the nicotine calmed him down. No one was regularly checking his blood pressure anyway. Besides, it wasn't as if they were right about their serum. He couldn't do what that bitch did.

"No caffeine, sorry, Five-One, but everything else is fine."

"Am I remote viewing again so soon?" He hid a surge of hope.

"I haven't gotten the green light yet but I've put in the suggestion to use your ability to find the missing explosive device in Macedonia," his monitor said.

"So, we should be prepared in case the higher-ups give the thumbs-up."

"Is it like the last assignment, when we were looking for the data converter device?" That was what the SEED had appeared to him when he was looking at it through remote viewing. It was used by some operative to retrieve some kind of codes from the computer. "And are we working against that other team we bumped into in Frankfurt?"

"Yes to the first question, not sure to the second, although the location's a bit trickier this time. We have the basic location but it's a lot bigger than a building. But let's not get into the details right now."

"Okay."

"Think you can locate it this time?"

He looked at the fat one. He wished they would give him their names but they were so damn secretive. So, Fat One and Thin One.

"I located the SEED for you all," he calmly pointed out. "I wasn't the one who failed to get that woman."

"You were supposed to get information on which exit she was using," Fat One growled back.

"I did!"

"Not till too late. You went into some stupid panic mode and got all crazy. Look, if you'd done your job, I would have no problem tranquing and hauling her into our vehicle before her people even knew there was anyone after them. You fucked up and my partner here had to waste time calming you down. Precious seconds that we could have used to get us to that entrance. But no, he had to talk to you to get the garbled information out of you. So don't sit there looking all snotty just because you could do this remote-viewing shit. As far as I'm concerned, you're a loser, just like the rest of the ward..."

"Okay, okay, we're going to calm down right now and have dinner." His monitor gave his partner a warning look. "Enough. We aren't going to make a scene. We'll concentrate on Macedonia when the right time comes. Five-One, let's eat and enjoy your night off."

Jonah nodded. He was pissed. The rest of the ward...what did they think he was, some kind of lunatic? And were they idiots? His night off wouldn't ever include two CIA clowns. But he would play their game right now. He needed them just as much as they needed him.

Catching sight of a beautiful couple entering the restaurant behind their table, he pretended to drop his menu onto the floor. He bent down to pick it up, covertly watching those two longingly. They had had sex that day, he was sure of it. Who wouldn't want to fuck that beautiful woman? If he were on the serum, he would dip into their energy and record everything. Especially her, all naked and writhing for her man.

He sat back up, taking a deep breath. Fuck, fuck, fuck. What had he done to deserve eating dinner with these two?

Chapter Seven

Jed could feel her bristling as she walked beside him. She was well and truly furious now. Good. Keep that focus on him and let the subconscious do its work.

He tongued the inside of his bruised cheek, which was throbbing like a toothache. Fighting mad. He deserved everything she was going to dole out. The key now was not to push her so far that she'd hate him afterwards. He needed her willing cooperation. To a point. He suppressed the urge to smile. That would probably start her swinging at him again and he'd prefer to do that in private.

He hadn't wanted to keep her hanging just now, but she'd challenged him with the five minutes comment. It had been a long time since he'd let a woman get under his skin enough that he'd considered all out sex in an elevator. He wanted her badly enough that he questioned himself about it, something unusual in itself.

Usually, he could step back and detach. With Elena, he found himself wanting more.

He blamed it on yesterday's events. He always needed an outlet after finishing a mission. In his job, facing an opponent and taking care of business usually meant ending a life. He'd learned to be unemotional about it, to put his reaction on hold, and then, when the time was right, to channel all that energy into something more positive.

He'd wanted to come to Elena in a better mood, but instead, she'd come to him when he was at his most detached. Had to be, because he was getting ready to dissect the situation for debriefing and discuss the operation with his teammates. Not the time to get emotional about anything.

Elena showing up and challenging him was an easy excuse to make her the outlet for that tightly controlled coil of tension inside him that was patiently waiting for release. He could have put her off till he was in a less edgy mood, but her prickliness had pushed him When she'd confronted him, he could sense her discomfort and knew without being told that her "problem" was still bothering her. The thing was, thinking about her "problem" made him hard just like that, especially now that he knew just how wild she was in bed.

He clamped down on his straying thoughts of coming inside her and turned back to the next meeting on his schedule. So much at stake and he couldn't get sex out of his mind. Sex with one woman, that was.

But what was she thinking now?

He'd known what she was up to yesterday, with that request for a session in the CAVE. He'd easily guessed her plans in her quarters. Sabotaging them was too much of a temptation to resist.

Karma was a bitch, though. He wanted to get to his own climax with this woman and he couldn't. Not possible. It would be selfish to find release when she wasn't cognizant of what their time together meant.

He wanted to be as honest as he could. He gave himself a mental shake of the head. That was something new—being honest and trying to sexually imprint another operative. When did he ever have the dilemma of his conscience tugging at him?

Jed glanced to his right. She was too quiet, a murderous look in her eyes, as she kept in step. A sudden urge to soothe her arose from nowhere, but he knew Elena well enough that words wouldn't mean much at this point. He was used to pulling back and reacting later; she wasn't.

"After the next two meetings," he told her, "I'm all yours."

Her hazel eyes flashed back at him. Still a little green in them, he noted.

"You mean you'll answer all my questions?"

"Perhaps." Never make a full promise to any dangerous woman.

"Will you at least let me hurt you the way you deserve?"

He ran his tongue against the inside of his cheek again, regarding her for a moment. The woman did have quite a punch. Her raised eyebrow amused him.

"That depends on how long you propose to have me sit there passively while you're at it." A deliciously devious image of her taking charge in his bedroom filled his mind.

Her brow rose higher. "Oh, I don't care if you fight back," she retorted. "I'm still going to hurt you."

"Done," he said, privately amused. A little aggression in bed could be exciting foreplay.

She was looking at him, her eyes narrowing as she studied the bruised side of his face. Her face was flushed and he knew she was thinking of other things besides injuring him. For an instant, he wondered whether she'd somehow caught the erotic image in his head. But they weren't sleeping or hooked together by the BE machine. She looked away.

"Just answer this and I'll wait till later," she said. "Are you responsible for what I'm going through right now? Was the strange sensation in the stairway in Frankfurt your doing?"

He realized that it was important to her that he wasn't the cause of her inability to fight what her body craved. Fortunately, he didn't have to lie.

"I have nothing to do with that," he assured her. "I don't know what happened there. That's why I brought it up at the meeting. We have to find out whether it's just you or something more. Dr. Kirkland's theory makes sense. I do understand that withdrawing from the serum caused this chemical imbalance in your body but it's accelerated, so you're feeling two years' worth of need, if you want to call it that, instead of a normal dose of healthy sexuality."

"Ouch." She grimaced. "Do you always sound so matter-of-fact?"

He inclined his head. "It makes the discussion less emotional for you," he pointed out. His voice went a notch lower. "In the privacy of bedrooms and fantasies, however, we can talk as dirty as you want without you being conscious about how it's making you feel."

"It makes me feel nothing," she declared.

"Liar." He supposed he could be a gentleman and not bring it back up. He chose ruthlessness to push his point. It would keep her aware of him while he couldn't fully focus on her. "You know you're going to think about my hand in your pants every time I look at you there."

Her face flushed but she still refused to meet his gaze. "I never had a chance, did I?" she asked, her voice low.

Jed paused to look at her. He would have gone after her even if she hadn't been assigned to him. That was how much he'd wanted her. But covert life meant unexpected twists, even in one's personal life. He'd just have to do everything backwards. Fuck her crazy first. Woo her later.

"No."

She should be angry. She wasn't.

She should be plotting murder. Instead she was a mass of confusion, following this man around just because…just because. He was like a new found flavor, something she couldn't decide whether she liked or not. And that aura of danger around him reminded her of those lost childhood days when she ran alone in the streets, not knowing whether there's menace lurking around the corner.

Those pauses he made would drive a woman crazy. Did he deliberate about every single thing he was going to say?

No, he said. Arrogant devil. The look he gave her was frank and sexual, making her stomach churn, and then it was replaced by that cool, assessing gaze again, all business.

It was fascinating how the man could shut off just like that. The lighting in the elevator had accentuated the angles and planes of his face, making those strange eyes of his glitter even more against his tan. There was nothing subtle about him, not in the way he'd touched her, not in the way he'd looked at her. In those few minutes, he'd shown desire so palpitatingly raw, it'd kept her frozen in place, every part of her connected to that need in him. And with a bite, he'd turned her on even more.

She felt her insides clench at the memory. Ordinarily, she would sit down, think everything through, and come up with a game plan. But she'd better toss that strategy out of the window when it came to Jed McNeil. He'd successfully foiled and thwarted every one of her plans. Hard as it was to admit it, he'd kept her off-balance since...had it been only yesterday since her "freelance" remote viewing? God, it felt like days.

It paid to remember that this was Number Nine with whom she was dealing, the one who finished each mission. He ultimately dealt with death. That accounted for the dangerous air that she sensed cloaking him all the time.

Her eyes narrowed. Dealing with him wasn't going to be like the way she'd beaten the other males against whom she'd trained these past two years. Jed McNeil, she suspected, was an entirely different species altogether. He'd yet to acknowledge her blow to his face. That dried trickle of blood on his chin was still there. It was all deliberate, of course, because *now* it was like a mockery, daring her to do her worst.

Her shoulders straightened. Dammit, she wasn't going to slink away to lick her wounds. Deep down, she was still that orphan running wild in the slums in Russia, a stray who wouldn't join any of the gangs, and she *had* survived those times, so this was nothing. Like everything else since, this was nothing compared to those dark days.

No stomping off right now. She had to understand what was happening to her before working out her next steps. And this feeling...she had to get it under control somehow. Because right now, without being connected to him with machines or virtual reality, she was actually seeing the two of them in bed, with her on top and doing naughty things that an angry woman shouldn't be doing. And the thoughts weren't helping her overdriven libido at all.

She was overwhelmingly conscious of his eyes settling on her briefly again. "I'm not the one invading dreams, Elena," he said, in that low tone of voice that forced one to pay attention. "For what it's worth to you, it's unsettling to me too."

Unsettling? She choked back her laugh. What she was thinking of right now was unsettling. "You aren't walking around with a sexual trigger in your head," she pointed out bitterly. "You aren't the one who's going through this body chemistry overcompensation that makes me want to...want to..."

She wasn't going to finish that sentence. She shrugged.

"You signed the Human Use Agreement Form. You were aware that in doing so, you put your life in a government experiment," he said.

She glared at him. "I'm perfectly aware of what I signed. I'm also perfectly aware of what you're doing."

"If I'd told you, would you have gone along?"

"Of course not!" She'd seen the effect of mental triggers embedded in assassins. No way.

They turned the corner and stopped in front of a door. "I thought not." His gaze warmed. "You want to be asked? Okay. May I seduce you, Elena?"

His voice was oh, so damn polite. His question, oh, so double-edged. An invitation and a challenge, the question was worded to throw her off-kilter. This was seduction at its best.

"Not answering?" he chided.

Study your opponent. She had to understand Jed McNeil, and to do so, she had to play his mind games.

She chose the challenge. "No, you can't seduce me," she declared.

Jed slid his card into the security slot. His eyes never left hers as he tapped on the keypad. "Give me time," he said softly.

She wanted to say something sarcastic to counter such display of supreme male ego, she really did. But it was hard when her own body was betraying her. Her gaze lowered and admired the supreme male ass in the snug blue jeans and she gave a mental sigh as she followed him inside.

The first thing she registered when they entered was that the room was oval shaped. There were monitors and electronic maps on the walls that surrounded a large oddly shaped table, which was half-circular on one side, with extended arms at zero degrees and one hundred and eighty degrees that protruded outwards about six feet. There was a chair in the empty space in the middle; whoever was sitting there would be surrounded by more computers, monitors, and electronic gadgets than she'd ever seen in one room, outside a computer store.

"What room is this?"

"Debriefing," Jed said as he coded in something on a pad in the wall. "You'll be given access to this room once you run missions regularly."

"I thought debriefing was, like, sitting in front of a bunch of balding old men answering their questions," Helen drawled, looking around, intrigued by all the gadgets. Some of the screens on the walls were in different languages. One appeared to be showing weather updates around the world.

"That's standard debriefing, which is still done, but COS commandos and operatives have many different tasks and operations, with many different assets involved who need to be present during the debriefing. Some of them are in different countries. Some of them are underground and don't want to be tracked. In this room, all the relevant participants can function as a group."

It made sense, except for one thing. "I'm assuming that a satellite is hooking all this up," Helen observed. "So, wouldn't the signals be easily tracked by outsiders?"

"Scrambled," Jed explained.

"Ah."

"Signal diffusion technology. Electronic encryption. Quantum..."

"All right, all right. I get it. Security's taken care of." Helen wasn't giving up, though. She cocked her head, adding slyly, "What about remote viewing? They might send someone like me to spy in here."

His lips quirked. Taking her by the hand, he led her to one side of the oval room where, inside a glass-protected portion of the wall, similar to a fish tank, out of the way of busy hands, some kind of weird instrument was glowing with electric-like sparks inside a dome.

Very conscious of her hand in his, Helen studied it for a few seconds. "What the heck is that?"

"It's an improved version of the Tesla coil. It's used to repel mind spies like remote viewers."

Helen turned and stared at the man beside her. "You're kidding me, right? I thought the government didn't believe in the stuff. Is it like the energy alarm ring T. gave me to wear?"

"No, but they're probably similar technology." Jed studied her for a moment. "Covert bases aren't as inflexible. You'll discover that there are secrets within secrets inside our government branches that are extremely well guarded."

Helen waved at the room behind her. "Like what goes on in here?" Obviously, paranoid people ran this place.

"What goes on in here can sometimes be an amalgam of different groups of people working covert missions within missions."

Hell moved closer to the protected panel. Could that thing really stop remote viewing? During training, she'd been told of the existence of certain devices but had never seen them.

"Double agents," she guessed.

He nodded. "COMCEN has operatives who are different personas in different groups. In this room, he or she can perform their communications effectively and give SITREPs of their assignments without confusing the various departments. It's very streamlined and effective. And Eight Ball takes care of what information goes where."

Then Eight Ball, the crazy computer, was even more powerful than she'd thought. She arched her brows in mockery. "You trust a computer that masquerades as a surfer dude with all that information? Does he use that same persona when he's giving the situation reports to the higher-ups?" *That* she wanted to see, some big brass's face when Eight Ball addressed him with "Dude, here are the SITREPs for the day."

Jed's lips quirked in amusement. "I think he programmed himself to add 'sir' after his 'dude' just to be respectful."

Helen chuckled. She talked to Eight Ball a lot but hadn't really seen him in his full capacity. She looked over her shoulder again. "He must be quite the supercomputer if he's the one with all the data that runs this place."

Wow. She was standing in the heart of COMCEN. And Jed had said she would have personal access to it one of these days. The fact that he'd brought her in here couldn't just be coincidental.

"Eight Ball is actually only a program within a Mother Eight Ball. There are different versions of Eight Ball running this place. A supercomputer for a supersoldier-spy," Jed said softly.

She turned back to him. Once again, he'd managed to read her thoughts even though they weren't in virtual reality. "Why am I here? To watch you get debriefed?"

His hold tightened slightly. "I need your trust in me," he said simply. "Making you aware of what's going on will build that foundation. Letting you see the many intertwining projects will give you a quicker understanding than reading situation reports and files."

But the message in his light eyes wasn't as simple. He was giving her that look again, the one that somehow managed to make her feel naked. His gaze swept lower and settled on her jeans.

Helen breathed in sharply. Dammit, he was right. Every time he looked at her there, she started to think about his hand. And his hand was connected to how he'd stimulated her, not just in the elevator, but during their virtual reality sessions. He knew he could affect her this way, especially now. She wanted to hitch up her jeans and run away.

"I think it's a little too late to gain my full trust," she said tightly, refusing to shift her stance. Her eyes challenged him as she pulled her hand out of his. "Information is nice. Knowing all the details of what's going on is helpful. But that won't make me any more agreeable to the trigger."

He lifted his gaze. "But it'll reinforce it."

Her eyes widened. "What will?"

"The information. The details. You want to know what's going on, you said. So I'm going to show it to you with fair warning. Knowledge will reinforce that trigger."

She frowned. "How so?"

His debriefing couldn't possibly do that. She didn't like the way he smiled, like the Cheshire Cat who knew too much and not sharing.

"You can't have it both ways, Elena. You want answers, you'll have to stay with me. Spending more time with me means giving me the opportunity to strengthen that trigger. By staying now, you're consciously giving me permission to reinforce it."

"I'm not going to play your mind games," Helen told him grimly. He'd called her *Elena*. "What if I choose to leave now?"

He nodded. "Of course you can leave. We can have our appointment later."

"Then why are you telling me this?"

"Because I want you to trust me."

"That's the most ridiculous way to get it!"

His direct gaze was unsettling, as if he could see right inside her. She had never felt so self-conscious with any male before.

"Is it?" he asked softly. "There's no reason for me lie to you now. If I can't tell you, I'll just say so. That way, you'll always know where you stand with me."

"Right," she drawled sarcastically, wrapping her arms across her chest. "If you think I'm going to take your word about anything you tell right now, there's a bridge I have for sale."

"I don't expect immediate capitulation," he told her.

"There, you see? Capitulation is not a word that would make me trustful of you, Mr. McNeil."

His eyes gleamed with sudden amusement. He'd known she'd jump all over that word, dammit. Instead of answering, he moved from her. She watched his back, frustrated.

It would feel damn good to throw his bait in his face and walk out of—she looked around again—and sighed. He knew damn well she wouldn't. This was the Bat Cave, for heaven's sakes. He knew she was dying to see everything he could show her. Questions hung in the air between them.

Yes, she was now connected to him in ways she couldn't explain to anyone. Yes, he was manipulating her deliberately, getting behind her defenses and planning God only knew what else about her operative status. Yes, she was turned on by him; there was no denying *that*. And finally, yes, she was really his supersoldier-spy.

Hell couldn't say no to him. "Where do you want me to sit?" she asked quietly.

He walked to the space behind the oddly shaped table in the middle of the room. "If you sit there," he said, pointing to a small desk she hadn't noticed, "you'll be able to see most of the screens I'm using. I'll turn on the monitor to your right. There's several earphones connected to the module. Use the one blinking each time I switch."

"Each time you switch?" she asked, nonplussed.

"Each time I switch channel," he explained. "You'll see what I mean when it's happening. And Elena, no interruptions, please. You can question later."

She resisted the urge to stick a tongue out at him. Barely. She turned to the desk he'd pointed to.

"Yes, Master," she replied, affecting a lisp, shuffling her feet in imitation of Marty Feldman's famous role of Igor as she limped toward the desk.

Jed didn't see her act since his back was toward her. She watched him fiddling with the control panels from where she sat. Her turn to study him. Her turn to figure out what made him tick.

"Dude, I thought you'd never turn on the voice control so I could speak," Eight Ball's "voice" suddenly filled the room. "You guys are no fun."

"Exactly," Jed said. "Operation updates, please."

Screens started turning on left and right. There were whirrs of activity in different parts of the room. From where she was, Hell figured out several satellite calls being made and fax machines coming alive.

"Tsk. Hunger and sexual tension make two very frustrated human beings. High probability of—"

"Eight Ball, operation updates for now." Jed reached over and touched the screen to his right. "We want to let Hell see the business side of you, don't we?"

Several maps lit up on the electronic wall. The screens at her desk started flashing messages and Helen checked where they were coming from. All over the world, it seemed.

"Of course, sir." Eight Ball's voice turned into a snotty uppity British butler accent. "We will indeed show the vast project being undertaken by COS Command in an orderly fashion. They're already waiting for your report, sire."

"I'm ready."

Immediately a few other screens came on, one showing a man, and another a woman. Both looked to be in their mid-forties. Helen didn't recognize them.

"They've already contacted us on Cummings, confirming his death," the man said immediately, without greeting.

Helen watched as Jed appeared to connect something to his wristwatch. "I took pictures of the sailing vessel for the file. Eight Ball?"

"Downloading them, sir. Analysis within the hour."

The woman smiled. "I see we've got Lord Eight Ball with us today."

"That's supposed to be the business side of him," Jed said dryly. "Better not give him a title. He might get ideas."

"*Pshaw*," the computer said, followed by a sniff that gave Helen an image of some dour-looking balding British actor on some British TV show.

The man on the screen shook his head. "Retrieving the SEED was important but we're now worried about what Deutsche International was trying to decode when Helen Roston showed up."

Helen sat up straighter at the sound of her name. That was her first assignment; retrieving the SEED was the first test of her remote-viewing abilities and the serum. She'd had no problem locating the decoding device. With Hades' help in virtual reality, she added. She looked at the back of the dark head in front. Jed, she amended.

"Agent Roston destroyed the laptop they were using and T. is still in there. She might find out something," Jed said. "It *is* strange for a think-tank that's associated with peace foundations to buy a hot market item like the SEED and use it. I agree we should try to find out what they're after."

"Is that your next avenue of action?" the woman asked.

"No. It's more important right now to locate and retrieve the different missing weapons and devices."

"Jed, we're pleased that you finally caught up with Jack Cummings. It wouldn't have been good for us if he had been successfully smuggled into Russia," the man said. "He'd have gotten very wealthy by selling everything he knew to the highest bidder."

"His price wasn't that different from his wife's," Jed said. "Freedom."

"Yes, but they didn't choose to steal Intel and weapons for freedom, Agent McNeil. This network was deliberately set up to stay in place for a long time so that their agents could work themselves high in our system," the woman said. "In fact, they'd created their own Virus System, infecting parts of our government from the inside."

"Yes, they've taken various facets of the Virus program but with a big difference. They're after our technology and secrets. They sustain themselves through profiting from what they can steal."

"Point taken, Agent McNeil," the man said, "but the problem remains. They're in our system. The only thing going for us is that we've caught on and are trying to eliminate the problem."

"But the damage done is tremendous," the woman added. "Stopping Agent Cummings took a little pressure off. He had very high clearance. His quick disappearance, along with other key personnel, after Washington's scandal came into light has surely warned their shadowy counterparts to move faster, don't you agree, Jed?"

"Yes," Jed said.

"It was fortunate then that Miss Roston was able to locate Agent Cummings, wasn't it?" she continued.

Helen stiffened at her name being mentioned again. It had been her fault, of course, that Jack Cummings had managed to escape the first time, during the initial operation in Frankfurt. Jed had used up some precious time to help her out. She bit her lower lip.

"I didn't have any doubt that she wouldn't," Jed said.

"From reviewing the video feeds, she should have canceled the man instead of tying him up," the man said, his voice getting a bit sharper. "Then you wouldn't have had to go down there and finish the job for her. Have you and the other commandos addressed this problem internally?"

Helen chewed on her lip some more. Uh, no, since she'd sucker punched Number Nine and had distracted everybody instead.

"We didn't have any problem with her decision," Jed replied enigmatically.

Helen frowned. They didn't? Or was her monitor just being protective of her?

"You should assess the damage at your end," Jed continued.

"All damage control is our business, Jed," the woman said smoothly, "even yours."

"There's nothing going on at my end that's of any danger to my people," Jed said. "As long as you can keep those eight other departments off our backs, we'll find those weapons. I'm not comfortable about their being constantly updated on the operations."

"They all have a hand in creating your supersoldier-spy, Agent McNeil," the man pointed out. "A little feedback can't hurt."

"It irks them that they lost." He paused. "To a woman. And it irks them that she belongs to me."

"To COS Command," the woman corrected. There was another pause, then the woman pressed, "She's COS Command's, right?"

"She's an independent contractor," Jed said, "who's agreed to work with the Viruses. I'm her monitor and trainer. Therefore, she's mine."

"That's a very strange way of looking at it since she signed the contract with COS Command," the woman pointed out.

"Read the contract," Jed said softly.

"I think I will."

Helen looked on with interest. She wasn't sure what was happening but her being at CCC looked to be more interesting than a mere contract job. Now she wanted to reread her contract too.

"Macedonia for you next, then," the man said, changing the subject.

Jed nodded. "Yes." He leaned forward and pressed some buttons on the panel. "Listen to this uplink from Hawk McMillan, our asset there."

One of the earphones started blinking and Helen picked them up and inserted the buds into her ears.

"It's partly in Serbian," Jed's voice came on over the channel. "He's talking to Dragan Dilaver. Eight Ball is providing the translated transcript on your screen now. Read the highlighted parts as you listen to the conversation."

Helen looked at the screen to her left as a word processing document appeared. Without waiting, she used the mouse to click on the start window prompter. She was getting the hang of this debriefing business.

Two men were speaking in the recording, sometimes in English, sometimes in Serbian. She knew that Dragan Dilaver was a notorious drug- and human-trafficker in Macedonia. It was easy to pick out his gravelly voice as he spoke with the undercover American. She wasn't particularly good at Serbian, but it was similar enough to Russian in parts that she caught the gist of the conversation. Weapons, women, dangerous liaisons. She followed the scrolling text on the screen, reading the parts that were highlighted as she listened in.

"Your government's sneaky, Hawk. They negotiated to have the KLA take over what's left of Yugoslavia and they make drops in big crates called 'Relief Aid'. Some of these crates are actually filled with weapons and they're dropped at specific locations for me."

"How did they choose you? Do you have a direct line to the U.S. Armory? Come on, Dilaver. Don't tell me you're an agent for the American government."

"No, you have it backwards. I have an agent in the United States..." Male laughter.

"Your aunt?"

"She's high level, got the authority to approve shipments or something... She said there's some problem moving the weapons from her end right now and she might need my help. What do you say, Hawk? Help me out?"

Eight Ball interrupted in the ear phone, "End of snippet One."

Helen pulled out the buds and returned her attention to the big overhead screens. The man appeared to be talking to someone off-screen with his mic off. The woman was taking notes. Jed remained silent, apparently waiting.

While he waited, Helen mulled over the recorded conversation. That was probably the operation the commandos had been talking about in the meeting she'd interrupted. From what she could gather, there was a list somewhere with some big important weapons that were missing. Jed and his men's task was to find and retrieve them. One of them was the decoder she'd helped locate recently. The other was this shipment in Macedonia. She frowned. Dropped by the CIA themselves? Whoa. She'd missed that part while watching the nightly news.

The man shifted his gaze back to the camera. "We'll work on the identity of the female relative."

Jed nodded. "Affirmative. Easier at your end. Get Ricardo Harden from TIARA in on it. He has resources inside the CIA."

"I know he's your friend and that he's a major part of Admiral Madison's investigative council, but can we fully trust him?" the woman interjected. "He's still CIA."

"Once a bureaucrat, always a bureaucrat," the man observed.

"Harden wasn't always a bureaucrat," Jed said. "Besides, this is personal to him. His wife, GEM operative Nikki Harden, was a victim of the CIA moles."

"All right, McNeil. I'll update you on any conversations with him."

"In your opinion, is the Virus unit still overextended, now that you have Admiral Madison's SEALs to help you out?"

Helen frowned. She knew, from T.'s briefing and some reading, that the COS commandos—the original nine—had undergone an intensive experimental training program called Virus, so this "Virus unit" must be referring to *her* team. There were seven of them now, excluding her. Like her, two of the others, Armando Chang and Shahrukh Kingsley, were relatively new additions. It'd never occurred to her till now why there was the sudden merger between certain parts of CCC and GEM. She'd figured the need to avenge for lost teammates came into it but, in this room, she saw that the merger was more than that. The big explosion that had killed a few of the COS Commandos and her sister operatives so many years ago had effectively shut down many ongoing operations and pushed CCC to the limit.

So now they were back to eight, if they counted her. She rubbed her nose. She wondered what "number" she'd be assigned. The thought made her roll her eyes. Why couldn't men be more creative and use gems and jewelry instead of stupid numbers?

She looked thoughtfully over at Number "so-I-can-still-freak-you-out" Nine. He projected the aura of a man who very seldom failed. How galling it must have been for him to see his men die, to acknowledge that he'd failed them. His job was to close a mission. It suddenly dawned on her that he'd never "finished" that particular one. Her eyes narrowed. She didn't know where the feeling came from, but she'd bet a whole week of coffee that Number Nine had been working toward some end game he wasn't revealing to whoever these two debriefing him were.

So many layers to this man. Could she ever have the time to peel him apart like he did her?

Chapter Eight

Secret test facility, Virginia

"Five-One, are you ready?"

Of course he was ready. He was beyond ready. When he'd been told about the test run, he'd wanted to kiss his so-called monitor in gratitude.

"Yes," he said crisply. "No alcohol or caffeine in my bloodstream. No contaminants. I'm fully rested."

So that was a white lie. He'd managed to bum some cigarettes from the few patients he'd befriended because he needed a buzz. They were so lucky not to be in any program that cut off their goodies. Downtime had been the pits. He hadn't been able to sleep well at all, not with the headaches and nothing to soothe him.

His heart was beating so loudly in anticipation that he was afraid his monitor could hear it. He so, so wanted this, needed this. But he had to be careful and not let the bastards see what the serum was like for him. If they knew, they would probably use the knowledge against him.

And this was perfect. They were going to look in on the bitch and now he could retrieve his cache. He'd been thinking of how she'd done it, hadn't quite figured that part out yet, but since she took from him, he couldn't see why he couldn't take from her too.

"Now you know what your assignment is, right, Five-One?" his monitor prompted him, holding up a sealed envelope.

"Yes, the universal agreement is to go immediately to where the winner of the supersoldier-spy program is and make sure she isn't in Macedonia. That way we'll be sure she isn't in our way this time when we're there."

"Yes, that's right. Do the best you can to describe what you see, and then come back immediately because we're going to need all your strength for the next assignment. It's going to be a tough one and we'll need you one hundred percent."

One thing he had to say about his monitor, whatever his name was—Thin One, as he called him—he was very succinct in his instructions and knew how to keep him focused. If it had been Fat One, things would have gone disastrously wrong from the get-go. He couldn't focus when there was such impatience and ridicule around him.

He glanced at Fat One. Maybe that was why he was sitting across the room this time and not taking up so much of his personal space. Maybe Thin One told his friend to shut up for once.

"Not a problem," he told his monitor. "I'll focus on her and make sure she's nowhere in Macedonia, or going there."

If he could, he'd make damn sure she would feel as lost as he was right now.

"Good. Take a deep breath. Focus on the soundwaves while I inject the serum into you. There you go. Five-One, think of the envelope and tell me when you're where you're supposed to be. Details, please."

He did as he was told. Remote viewing wasn't a complicated process for him any more. Once his brainwaves went to theta, he could bilocate—go to the agreed universal location—without even being conscious about it.

The heat of the serum. Oh, God, the rush, the rush. He felt his head go back as the heady feeling spread inside him. Trigger code...

Switch to channel three. Set programming time. Set channel.

Timer on. Record.

"I feel the coordinates," he announced.

"Bilocate," his monitor ordered.

He hoped he wasn't shouting his joy as power surged through him. *Fast forward! Fast forward!*

And there the bitch was, right in front of him.

Jed beckoned to Helen with a slight shake of his head. He was done. He quelled the amusement that rose up as he watched her affecting an exaggerated shuffle, dragging one foot behind her while holding one hand against her chest as if she was disfigured, and awkwardly swinging the other hand, in such perfect imitation of a hunchback that there was no mistaking who she was impersonating.

She was something else. No woman who knew him here would dare make fun of him in quite that way. The bold ones flirted. The married ones gossiped. Those who disagreed with him were still careful with words and actions. No one had ever pretended to be the classic Igor to mock him.

"Your leg must be hurting you more again," he commented. "I must not have taken care of it enough the other night."

He enjoyed the way her eyes narrowed, the way her lips curled down into that sinfully sexy pout. She had no idea what she did to him every time she came close. In fact, neither had he anticipated it, since all he'd ever done was watch her on-screen and interact with her through virtual reality.

Meeting Helen Roston in real life was like watching HDTV for the first time. Everything about her was more vibrant, taking his breath away. He'd never get tired of looking at her. Of wanting her. His desire was like a freight train. One could see it coming; one could even brace for it; but there was no avoiding the oncoming collision.

Also, her sassy and quirky humor made him see something in a different light. Like now, for instance. What woman would mock herself as Igor to his Frankenstein?

"Who are those two?" she asked.

"Checks and balances." He keyed the door open and they both exited.

She frowned. "What does that mean?"

"Show any deficit or overextension, and someone somewhere will find a reason to put you more behind."

"I mean their names," she said.

He glanced at her. "They change faces, so it's easier to just remember them as checks and balances. You'll see what I mean the more you deal with them." He glanced at his watch. "One more appointment."

"Can we first pick up some food? I'm starving."

So was he. But then he'd never liked to eat much after finishing an assignment.

"We'll be eating with Admiral Madison," he told her, watching the surprise in her eyes. "So that should take care of that problem."

"The same admiral from the group of department heads watching me during the test run? The one with the nice voice."

Amusement filled him again. He'd bet the admiral—a tall, distinguished man, with medals hanging out his ass, and whose valor on the field earned him the nickname "Mad Dog"—had never been recognized for just his "nice" voice before. "Yes. The SEALs we're conducting the joint venture with are his boys."

"Ah. Makes sense now. Do I just show up with you? How does one dress for a meal with an admiral, anyway? Not that it's going to matter, since I don't have any change of clothes at Center other than workout and casual."

Jed glanced at her again. She was talking quickly. There was a faint blush on her cheeks, as if she was aware that she'd given herself away.

"It's coming back again," he observed. "Our time in the elevator alleviated your condition for a while, but it wasn't enough to stop it."

Her cheeks went even pinker. "You're making it sound as if you did that to help me out," she muttered. "I'd feel a lot better if I didn't feel so helpless against it. It makes it impossible for me to think, and you're using it against me."

"Yes," he acknowledged.

"I should've seen it coming," she continued. "I knew you were up to something but I kept getting distracted by all that techy stuff."

He could tell that she wasn't really talking to him, that she was trying to distract herself now. He frowned. He didn't want her to suffer. After feeling a little bit of what she was going through while they were connected in VR, he understood her distress. The inability to control one's impulses would frustrate him too.

He put a finger under her chin, tilting her head up. "Everything's going to be all right. We'll fix this." He frowned. Her eyes were dilated. "What's the matter?"

"I'm not sure," she breathed. She touched her forehead tentatively. "Tension."

"Tension? As in headache?"

She nodded, then shook her head, as if she couldn't decide. She jerked her head out of his hold, sweeping her surroundings. Her body language was tense. Jed looked around too. Nothing.

Channel three. Zoom in.

That was her! He was sure of it. Tall. Long brown hair. Pretty eyes. She was quite an attractive woman, which was surprising. He'd thought she'd look like some big biker chick, considering that she could climb ropes and wrestle with those fucking special ops trainers. Those assholes were mean fighters.

So his image of her was totally one-eighty. She looked a lot softer from this distance. He gazed at her body appreciatively. And nice curves. He ignored the man by her side as he reached out with his senses. No thoughts of Macedonia. No plans. He took one step closer to her, mentally opening all his channels, and almost moaned out loud.

Holy shit. His dick instantly went hard, stopping him in his tracks. Holy. Shit. She was emanating sexual energy like he'd never felt before. That was her, all right, with *his* cache and what was more, she had been sexing it up with that man beside her. Even from here, he could feel the combined sexual energy between them, waiting, waiting for him to taste, to bathe in.

Erotic need blanketed his mind as he probed the energy field. This was a first for him, to actually feel so much from this far away. Usually, he just "saw" the energy and had learned to recognize certain types as sexual afterglow.

His own need rose hungrily, eagerly. She had had plenty of sex recently. Her energy was heavy with desire, as if she was still in a sexual state. Those two must have just had it in this hallway and he'd missed it, dammit. He would have loved to have been there, watching them. No matter, soon he would get her memories and watch those moments for himself.

A mental picture of her on her knees slammed into his senses. He felt his erection stretched so painfully, he couldn't think at all. This was going to be so good.

He had to have it all. Had to take what was his back and more. Her energy was delicious, so strong that he just wanted to stand there and jack off.

"Agent Five-One? Details."

He cursed silently, trying to concentrate. "Yeah, hang on. I see the target. I have to get closer, though, to sense."

"Go ahead."

Like he fucking needed permission. He took another step closer, uncaring, releasing all his channels. *Record. Record it all.* There was white noise interrupting him. He turned and looked to his right. Some guy in black walking quickly toward him. If he turned the corner, he would see the couple. He didn't sense anything unusual about him. No thoughts of Macedonia...something urgent, though. What the fuck was this white noise? He couldn't filter the thoughts from the noise.

No time. His woman was walking down the hallway toward him, a frown on her face. Could she feel his presence? Of course not. No, no, she was listening to the other man's footsteps and telling her companion that someone was coming.

He mentally shrugged. Who cared what they were up to? He was going to drop in on her aura and wrap her energy around him and happily feed. She owed him.

"I'm almost there," he told his monitor, trying to curb the excitement in his voice. "Wait while I search for information."

"Affirmative, Five-One."

He smiled. Hello, supersoldier-spy. So what sexy thing have you been up to with your boyfriend lately? I want it all, bitch.

He started toward her. *Record. Full speed.*

"What's wrong?" Jed asked again. Something was bothering her and it wasn't just her sensitized state.

"Danger," she whispered. She gripped his upper arm. "Can't explain it. I just sense this feeling."

"Now?" Jed asked, looking around again.

"Suddenly. I get this warning...it's..."

She raked her hair restlessly. She started walking, heading toward where the corridor split to the left and right. Jed reached out, wanting to tell her to stay back behind him. She put up her hand to signal stop, her head cocked, listening.

Footsteps approached. He was about to step in front of Helen when Armando appeared in their left corridor, with his boots clicking noisily. He was in a hurry, as if he was late for something. His eyes widened at the sight of them.

"Timing is very important in an illusion," he said, his strides gathering speed as he broke into a run toward them.

Before Jed could say anything to stop him, Armando crashed into Helen, bringing her down. As one part of his mind registered that Helen didn't attempt to avoid Armando at all, falling onto the carpeted floor without a fight or a gasp, another part, trained from years of instinctive reaction, instantly pushed his own body forward into a defensive stance, to face whatever it was that prompted one of his team to rush them like that.

A few seconds went by. Not a sound. Nothing came from around either corner. From behind him, he sensed Armando and Helen moving on the floor, getting up.

"What were you running from, Armando?" Jed asked, still looking at the empty corridor ahead.

What the fuck? That man in black was running. The stupid Asian was going to run through him while he had all his channels on record! All that white noise! Oh fuck!

No time! He couldn't command and pull back all the channels at once. He mentally pushed his shadow self down the corridor, going for the woman, focusing only on her. No way any man could go faster than a bilocated remote viewer. Only ten feet or so separated him from his beloved treasure.

He sped forward and yelled in agony as his whole being smacked into some kind of invisible wall in front of the couple. He felt his insides crumple into dark swirls, as if he had a lit candle there and it was rapidly melting, coating everything in hot wax. It was horrible. His heartbeat churned and echoed. His eyeballs burned. Melted. He couldn't move quickly. Fear engulfed him. What was happening?

He screamed. It felt like he'd been sliced in half. The running man, who had been way behind him, caught up, and ran right through his shadow self at top speed. His remaining open channels...recording... This wasn't possible. A remote viewer could pass through anything...

"What the hell? Five-One, what's happening? Why are you screaming?"

He couldn't answer his monitor. The serum, the acceleration of which he'd been so addicted to, was pulling in everything from the man who'd just passed through him. Pain. The agony dropped him to his knees. Couldn't breathe. Couldn't get up. The gooey mass that had stopped him before had now penetrated into his "body", blocking sight, blocking air. He fought for breath. Gasped for help.

"Five-One! Five-One! Calm down! Listen to my voice. Disengage. Change channel, disengage and return here. Do you hear me?"

Disengage. Change channel. Yes, yes, yes, disengage! His monitor's use of his trigger released the mass that was holding him captive.

"Disengage," he whimpered, pushing with his hands, trying to crawl backwards from all that white noise, that invading thickness in his head. "Change channels." Change all the fucking channels.

He opened his eyes. He was curled into a ball. He screamed when someone touched him.

"What's wrong, Five-One? What happened there?" his monitor's voice asked in the distance.

"He's fucking losing it," another voice said.

He squeezed his eyes shut. He couldn't explain to these morons about recording energies, that he was after their precious super spy's sexual aura. He couldn't explain what had just happened. He didn't know what had caught hold of him and squeezed the life out of him like that. He had had every available channel open on record and he'd absorbed the running man's energy as he went through him. Pain and shame. Amplified dozens of times.

He curled tighter into a ball. And wept.

"She can't stand up properly," Armando said.

After making sure no one was coming around both corners, Jed turned to look behind him. Armando was on his feet, trying to help Helen up. She looked pale.

Jed checked the corridors again and tapped at the intercom by the wall. "Eight Ball," he said. "There was no warning of any intruders. Are you sure the micro-eyes haven't been compromised?"

"Nothing's compromised, dude. I saw everything. There were no hostiles involved except for Armando running toward you guys," the computer reported back. "Checking all entranceways. Every known body one hundred percent accounted for. Nice leap, Bruce Lee-style, dude, with all that killer hair flying around."

Jed relaxed just a little. If Eight Ball had seen what happened, then the signals hadn't been switched. If so, then what was that all about? Just before it happened, Helen had felt something...but she wasn't herself today. "Make copies of the whole incident for review," he ordered.

"Done, dude."

He turned back to Armando and Helen. She was leaning on Armando for support.

"I think I reinjured my leg when I fell," she explained. "It's just feeling a bit tender."

Jed gave her a quick look-over. Other than her favoring one leg, she seemed okay. He wanted to know more about what preceded Armando charging them, but first things first.

"Why did you run toward Helen like that, Armando?" he asked quietly. The man had acted as if he knew Helen was in danger. "Were you looking for her?"

"I was chasing the Cheshire Cat," Armando said solemnly, "and he led me here."

"I don't have time for puzzles right now, Chang," Jed warned. He wasn't chancing anything happening to Helen.

Armando shrugged. "I'm explaining it the only way that could be understood. I'm always after the Cheshire Cat. I see parts of something and I want to see the rest. This time, the Cat's tail ran ahead and I felt danger, so I decided to chase him. And there you two were at the end of my tunnel."

"But there was no danger," Jed pointed out. Except Helen had said she felt danger...

"I felt something was wrong too," Helen said, echoing his thoughts.

"That you could see," Armando chimed in at the same time. He flicked his hair back and shrugged. "I don't know any other analogy to explain what was happening to me."

"So you two sensed danger and somehow crossed paths right here," Jed said, eyeing both of them speculatively. Was it coincidental that these two, who had used the latest version of the serum, had sensed something that wasn't there? "Simultaneously? Eight Ball, track back to the earliest shot of Armando in the hallway."

"Program initiated," Eight Ball replied. "Location?"

"Where were you exactly?" Jed asked.

Armando shrugged again in answer and hooked a thumb in his black leather belt, bracing his weight so Helen could lean on his arm. "I was having one of my weird blind attacks while I was walking on the floor above this one. I didn't have far to run. What about you two? Why were you here at this time?"

"Just done with debriefing," Jed replied, studying Armando closely. Blind attacks meant the younger man was in pain. "I thought the attacks were getting rarer."

Armando ignored his comment, and instead cocked a dark eyebrow at Helen. "Debriefing with Hell? Fascinating."

Jed said nothing, waiting for Eight Ball as well as Armando, staring intently at the younger man, looking for clues. Armando was in one of his moods. It was in the bored tone of his voice, the little furrow in his brow, which he knew appeared when the younger man had another migraine attack. When his own schedule was a little lighter, he was going to resume training him, but for now, it was up to Heath. Right at this moment, he just wanted to get to the bottom of what just happened. He watched as Armando took Helen's hand in his, looking deeply into her eyes.

"How's the chosen one's hypothalamus doing?" Armando continued.

Most people paused, smiled politely, looked puzzled, or frowned whenever Armando asked one of his offbeat questions. But Helen wasn't anyone. Jed had had many months of looking into those eyes on the screen and knew every nuance in their expression. He had seen that barely discernible calculating look entering those hazel eyes before, many times, while being tested during training. He blinked. She was in GEM mode.

"It's functioning," she said. "How's yours?"

"Mine hasn't been tricked by drugs lately," Armando mocked. "My neuro-hormones haven't been overproducing but all this sexy talk might start the process."

"I'm beginning to realize that certain drugs have a habit of tricking the user for longer than they think, Armando," Helen said, the careless casualness in her voice catching Jed's attention. For two people who had just collided with the floor, these two were acting way too calmly. "Are you so sure there's nothing wrong with your limbic system?"

She'd obviously paid attention to all the doctors and scientists at the group debriefings, Jed noted, slightly amused such mundane talk would include the hypothalamus and brain stem. During the ones he'd attended when the first version of the SYMBIOS serum was introduced, he'd sat through hours of lectures about how the drug could, would, and should affect the hypothalamus, the part of the brain in control of body temperature, hunger, thirst, emotions, and—he slid another glance at Helen—sexual activity.

Nothing new. Except he didn't like the way those two were standing so closely together, as if they were having a private communication. He pushed away the sudden urge to interrupt. Something else was happening here and he wasn't going to let his personal feelings come between him and finding the answer.

Jed looked at Armando again. Helen's problem had been pinpointed.

Sort of. But what about Armando? The man admitted to migraines and periods of blindness that lasted up to an hour. None of the scientists and doctors had come up with an explanation. Almost the same drug, but different effect. What else wasn't he telling them?

"Location confirmed, yo," Eight Ball's surfer lingo added another odd touch to the ongoing conversation. "Agent Chang's location was exactly right above where you and Hell were standing four feet back from your current location. Using Agent Sullivan's words, dudes, woo-woo simpatico shit."

Armando looked surprised for a moment, then burst out laughing. Helen grinned.

"Thank you for your diagnosis, Eight Ball," Jed said wryly. He needed to talk to the COMCEN supercomputer programmer one of these days about Eight Ball's choice of persona...when he found a slot of free time. "Make two copies of both recordings and send one to my quarters and the other to Dr. Kirkland's. Send a message to him that we need him at his office now."

"Affirmative."

"What if he isn't there?" Helen asked. "Aren't we supposed to be going to eat with the admiral?"

"You're limping," Jed pointed out, "and I thought we'd all compare our hypothalamuses and limbic systems at Dr. Kirkland's office. I'll just have to cancel my meeting with the admiral till later."

"But I'm hungry," Helen said.

"Brains for food. Yum," Armando murmured. "I think I should carry her the rest of the way, Jed, what do you think?"

Jed looked at the younger man. The inscrutable Asian face was firmly on, revealing nothing, but a male challenge was universal. He could say no and therefore show his hand, that Helen was his weakness.

He looked at Helen. She was still too quiet. Either she was still processing what had happened or she was using NOPAIN to nettle him. It didn't matter. There were other ways to win a pissing contest.

His gaze traveled lower on her body and he knew from the slight twitch of her leg that she was affected by it. His gaze slid back up leisurely to meet hers.

"By all means," he said softly.

Chapter Nine

How bizarre, how bizarre. That phrase from some long ago song popped into Helen's head. That about summed up the last twenty-four hours.

The familiar tingle that always warned her of imminent danger had disappeared. She trusted that instinct in her; following it had saved her life before. However, this time, nothing had happened. Eight Ball had confirmed that there had been no intruder, nothing out of the ordinary.

The only strange thing linking it all was the man carrying her, Armando Chang. He'd sensed something was wrong, she was sure of it, and his strange explanation had caught her attention. He'd told them that he was chasing the Cheshire Cat, something she'd just used in her head in reference to Jed McNeil.

Which brought her thoughts back to the man walking a little ahead of her and Armando. Jed had a headset on, seemingly absorbed in a conversation with Admiral Madison, barely paying attention to the people who stared at them as they passed by their offices and desks.

That was an act, she realized it now. Jed McNeil was the master of multitasking. He seemed able to hold meetings, reschedule an appointment with an admiral, and make snap decisions about this operation or that operation, all while being interrupted by operatives at the same time. When one or two stopped him to ask questions, he'd pause and give her one of those looks that made her shiver inside. *And the man could still seduce without words.*

"But can he chew gum and whistle?" Armando said softly into her ear.

Helen looked at the man carrying her. "Is mind-reading one of the many COS commando talents?" she asked teasingly.

"A combination of good timing and lucky guessing," Armando told her, a small smile on his lips.

"Oh yeah, we must put all that good timing and lucky guessing to good use and play the lottery some time," Helen said, watching as Jed walked a little further ahead of them with de Clerq, who had joined them.

"You're only given a certain number of opportunities," Armando said. "If I'd used my limbic talents on the numbers game, then it wouldn't have directed me to you. So actually, you owe me a meal rather than with McNeil. We have so much more in common than you and he."

"Is that right?" Helen asked, keeping her eyes on the man ahead, catching phrases here and there.

The dark smoothness of Jed's voice was strangely soothing and at odds with the commotion that surrounded him. Armando didn't seem to care that he could listen in if he chose to, even though he was talking to three or four people at the same time. "Yes, Miss Roston, we do," he said, his hand under her giving her side a small squeeze. "Lost in a maze. Unfamiliar feelings. Stranger in a strange land. Speaking in tongues."

Helen arched an eyebrow at him. "You're the one speaking in tongues, Armando. Everyone can understand me fine."

"Do you think blaming everything on the hypothalamus is a normal everyday topic?" he countered mockingly.

Helen conceded with a shake of her head. He had her there. Everyone was giving her scientific explanations and Armando was pointing out the obvious. No matter how they explained away the effect of the serum on her system, they couldn't deny that there was something else happening, something that only she could feel. Her gaze caught Armando's sardonic one. No, him too.

Dr. Kirkland and his assistant Derek, were looking at the recording Eight Ball had sent them when they arrived. Dr. Kirkland looked up, his eyes assessing, looking for injuries.

"How bad?" he asked.

"It's just the same leg that was injured," Helen told him. "I can't put my weight on it right now, but I'm sure it's nothing serious."

"It's serious enough that you can't walk on it," Jed pointed out.

Armando put her down on the examining table. "My fault," he said.

"No, really, I like being carried around by commandos," Helen said airily. "Why, a few days ago, Flyboy carried me to the restroom. Then Heath carried my useless tranqued body up to Medic. When is it your turn, Jed?"

She swore the man had no sense of humor at all. Everyone else was grinning at her attempt at humor. Hadn't he ever tried laughing when something serious was going on? Apparently not. The darn man just stood there like a block of ice.

"That leap was awesome!" Derek said to Armando, then flushed. "Ooops, sorry, Dr. Kirkland."

Dr. Kirkland just shook his head and turned to Helen. "If nothing's broken, we'll examine the leg afterwards. Let's talk about what happened. Pull the two monitors forward, Derek. Let's rewatch."

Everyone gathered closer around Helen as Derek positioned the screens. Helen sat up and watched curiously, eager to see whether the micro eyes captured anything out of the ordinary.

The replay was exactly how she remembered it. They were walking down the hallway from the debriefing room. Sitting at debriefing for so long and just watching and studying Jed had made her clothes uncomfortable again and she'd tried to distract herself by talking as she tried to ignore the odd tension in the pit of her stomach. It took a few seconds but she'd suddenly become aware that not all of that strange tingling was caused by Jed's nearness.

In the video, she saw herself suddenly give a start, the way a body reacted to a sudden jab or needle prick. She pursed her lips as she watched Jed caress her lower lip with his thumb. No one said anything but oh, what she wouldn't give to read their thoughts at that moment.

The screen divided into four at this point, showing footage from around the corners of the corridor. Nothing.

"Now watch this as a whole scene with the video of Armando upstairs," Kirkland said, using the remote in his hand. "The clock at the corner of the screen is especially interesting."

Helen watched, going back and forth on the side-by-side screens. She could feel Armando's tension as he leaned closer to the screen. In the video, the microeye was directly above him as he walked past. He suddenly grabbed the back of his head and stumbled, one hand reaching out for the wall. Kirkland paused the feed, clicked a couple of buttons and the screen divided into half, one showing Helen's location, the other, Armando's.

Helen brought up the obvious. "The clock. On both videos, the point where I jerked and where Armando held his head was the same," she said. She turned to Armando. "What did you feel?"

He paused, his hand rubbing the back of his head. "Pain," he said. "Extreme pain."

"Is it similar to the headaches you complain about?" Kirkland asked.

Armando shook his head. "No. This time I could see." He turned to Helen. "When I get my headaches, I become blind. In this instance, I was knocked down by the suddenness of it and then I became angry and got up and just ran downstairs."

111

"Angry?" Jed interrupted. He pointed at the screen. "You were down with pain and then you just got up and ran? Not just the clock. I think if we use a site map, we can confirm Eight Ball's report that Armando was right above Helen and me. Unpause it, Dr. K."

Dr. Kirkland clicked on the remote. The video showed Armando holding on to his head with both hands for a few seconds. His eyes opened. Even on film, Helen caught the anger in his dark eyes. And then he started running. The video blinked as the next micro eye took over, recording Armando disappearing through the exit door.

Both screen clocks mirrored each other on the screens as they showed the simultaneous actions of what happened next, first from Helen's location, and then from Armando's, splitting the screen when they were only divided by the corridor wall. One thing was screamingly obvious. There wasn't anyone else shown, just Jed, Armando, and Helen.

When the video reached the part when Armando was leaping in the air toward her, Helen tapped Jed's elbow, remembering something. "I thought I heard something right then," she said softly, thoughtfully. "Not from Armando. I thought I heard a scream. It sounded strange, though, like an echo."

"I didn't hear anything. Did you?" Jed addressed Armando.

"No."

"What about your headache? Do you have one now?"

"Disappeared. The moment I landed on Hell, in fact." Armando snapped his fingers. "Like magic."

Helen sat back against the pillow. "I give up. I have no idea what that was all about." She waved at the screen. "Nothing was captured on video except Armando charging at me like he knew something bad was going to happen, and now he's saying he just had a headache and decided to go for a run. Right to where Jed and I were standing, funny, that. Meanwhile Jed didn't see or hear anything. I didn't see anything. And the microeyes didn't pick up anything. So, if it were just *my* imagination, why did you decide to run downstairs to where I was?"

Everyone turned their attention on Armando, who shrugged. "I can't explain the unexplainable. All I know is that I was very angry and I just ran in the direction of—" he paused, slowly finishing his sentence, as if it'd just occurred to him, "—the anger."

"The anger?" Helen repeated, really puzzled now. "Well, that explains everything clearly."

Armando shrugged at her sarcasm.

Jed walked to the glass window that looked out into the next room and lifted one of the plastic shutters with his finger, peering through it. "Everything's all about feelings," he said softly. "SYMBIOS 2. Synthetic biochemistry. Armando's headaches. Pain. Elena has sexual sensitivity. Both experienced their problems at the same time. Armando rushed toward what he felt was anger. Elena walked toward what she felt was danger. Both collide. Headache gone. Sense of anger and pain gone."

Armando nudged Helen. "Sexual sensitivity?" he murmured.

"Hey, you called it the 'reckoning,'" Helen reminded him dryly. She really had to talk to the man about privacy. Talking about her *sexual sensitivity* in front of four other males, even though two of them were in some measure her doctors, was a little too much information.

A part of her, however, was busy admiring yet again how Jed McNeil could pull apart a complex situation. Right now, even as her mind was busy trying to put together what he'd broken down, he was already turning toward the screens, snatching the remote from Dr. Kirkland's hands. He replayed the scene one more time, slowing down the film frame by frame. He paused at the one where Armando was in mid-air.

"There. Helen wasn't looking at Armando. Her gaze was in this general direction." He pointed at a spot in front of where he stood in the video, then clicked the remote. "Eight Ball, use the trajectory and pinpoint the exact spot Helen was looking."

Geometrical lines aligned and separated on the screens as Eight Ball started his program. "Trajectory is ninety-eight percent accurate. The angle of Hell's eyes falls right about a foot in front of Jed McNeil. The arc of sight goes from there to five feet beyond you to the wall, dude."

"Something definitely caught your attention, scream or no," Kirkland said as he studied the different angles the super computer had drawn on the stilled frame.

Jed turned from the screen and looked directly at Armando standing by her. His voice was calm. "Two things. You used a dose of the serum about the same time Helen did. I want to know why." Then he turned to Helen, his eyes gleaming, "There was another presence on site."

"Huh? How did you get to that conclusion? The microeyes are showing noth—oh." Helen blinked. The experience in the stairwell in Frankfurt...

Jed nodded. "It seems that, for some reason, those who have taken SYMBIOS 2 have some kind of sense of another remote viewer."

"I did think about that incident in similar lines yesterday morning," Helen admitted, frowning, "that I crashed into the remote viewer. But Jed, it's impossible to feel another remote viewer's presence."

"You were wearing the energy alarm ring," Jed said. "Where is it?"

"T. took it back to the labs. Probably to test what happened at the stairwell." When she was at the CIA, she'd been told about energy alarms, which agencies used to detect the presence of remote viewers in a small area. She'd never seen one till T. had given her a ring to wear when Helen had been about to go for the test set by the agencies. It seemed her chief had been suspicious herself. She rubbed her bare finger thoughtfully. "According to T., the energy alarm shouldn't have affected me at all. It sets off a warning at the lab and I wouldn't know till someone contacts me about it."

"It didn't happen that way. Something set it off and you knew because you reported that you almost fell down the stairs," Dr. Kirkland said.

"Well, that still doesn't explain why Armando feels it."

"He took the serum," Jed said, an icy edge to his voice again. "Didn't you?"

Armando didn't show any emotion. "Guilty."

"Why?"

"I needed to stop the pain."

"How?"

"When everyone had gone off to the dog-and-pony show with Hell. Kirkland and Derek left everything easily accessible."

Helen remembered how everyone had been eager to start the test. Almost the whole Medic department had left so they could be on hand if the serum had a negative effect on her. Of course, the few personnel that were left wouldn't question a COS commando walking into the clinic.

"We're going to talk later," Jed said. He turned to Helen, his eyes raking her up and down, as if he was considering whether she was up to it. Apparently he thought she was, because he added softly, "Get ready for a remote-view session."

"But her leg—" Dr. Kirkland protested.

"A quick check-up, but we must hurry. If there really was a remote viewer here at COMCEN, I want to know where he is right now."

"But she's barely got the serum out of her system, Jed."

"We aren't using the serum," Jed said, his eyes never leaving Helen. "She can handle it."

Of course she could. She'd been trained to be pushed to the limits, and one limping leg wasn't going to be a problem. However, the feminine part of her was just a tad miffed that he looked at her as only some kind of extension to his spy games. They had been planning to go have a meal with an admiral before the incident, for crying out loud. And then afterwards...he'd promised her afterwards... This supersoldier-spy thing was really getting in the way of her love life.

Helen squinted, pretending to consider the idea of refusing him. "I'm still starving," she announced. "If you bring me something from the cafeteria, I'll work for food."

"Done," Jed said. He looked around. "Get started. Armando, you'll stay in the next room and get thoroughly checked out. Thoroughly. Brainwaves, Kirkland, and a drug test. You'll stay till it's all completed, do you hear me, Chang?"

Armando hooked his thumb on his belt. "Time out, I suppose."

"More like a spanking," Helen said. What did he mean when he said that he injected the serum to stop the pain? Was his "reckoning" this pain that he kept having?

"Chang? I didn't hear your answer."

"Yes, I'll be in the next room." Armando exchanged a glance with Helen as he pulled open the door by the examination bed. "This is my reward for saving damsels in distress."

She grinned. She couldn't help it. He was probably in serious trouble but he didn't seem at all remorseful. Dr. Kirkland ordered Derek to move the tables with the monitors out of the way, as he headed to the medical cabinets.

It was a familiar procedure. Helen returned her attention to Jed.

"If he's going to draw blood from me, I'm going to need food. Send up some," she hinted again. "Then I'll see your fake ass in virtual reality, Hades."

Jed walked to the examining table and paused to look down at her. Something indefinable flickered in his light eyes. He said nothing, simply locked his fist in her hair and pulled her head back. His mouth came down on hers hard. He angled her chin just so. His tongue tangled with hers for a brief moment.

It happened so quickly, she didn't think Dr. Kirkland, intent on measuring meds, even noticed. Derek had his back to them.

"That," he said softly, "wasn't Hades kissing you."

A smile touched his lips before he turned and strode out. Stunned, Helen stared after him. She touched her lips. The freaking man had a sense of humor after all.

Kevin Kirkland shut the cabinet door. There was a mirror on the inside of the door that Derek had recently hung there.

In all his years monitoring Jed McNeil in the Virus Program, Kirkland had never seen the man kiss any woman in public, not even Nikki Taylor, an injured GEM operative Jed had rescued and with whom he'd had a relationship a long time ago.

Such a long time ago, Kirkland reminded himself, that his head of hair wasn't salt and pepper then. Before Jed brought her to GEM. Before she got her memory back. She was Nikki Harden now.

He considered Jed a friend. He'd started out as he was doing now with Helen, just charting vitals and making scientific observations on the subjects for the Virus Project, but over the years, the doctor-subject relationship had morphed into something closer. It had to, since Jed McNeil had to trust him when it came to things he had no control over, such as drugs and medical needs.

It wasn't exactly a communicative kind of friendship. Jed wasn't much of a talker when it came to his personal thoughts. An excellent communicator when it came to being a leader; a great conversationalist when it came to philosophy, music and sports; a remarkable chess player; even an excellent cook; but not exactly very sharing about his past or his beliefs.

Even after all these years, Kirkland had trouble getting him to talk about his past whenever the chance came up. He had learned to listen for clues and had pieced together some background information.

Other than a childhood in Dublin, Ireland, it seemed that Jed McNeil had pretty much been a CIA protégée for most of his life. He'd been sent into the Special Forces and Rangers school for training and warfare experience, had been through one covert program and another, all at the behest of the CIA.

Kirkland still wasn't sure exactly how Jed had parted ways with the CIA and become a COS Commando. COMCEN and CIA weren't exactly great friends these days, yet he still had ties in the latter agency, giving him a lot more access to covert information than most operatives.

One thing was clear, though. Jed McNeil was a very powerful person and many people listened to him when he did communicate. Kirkland had personally seen how his wishes overrode a few powerful names, some of them generals and department heads, and other than voiced outrage and threats, there didn't seem to be any repercussions. It was a simple rule: what Jed McNeil wanted, Jed McNeil got.

And from that kiss he'd just witnessed, Jed McNeil wanted Helen Roston. The act itself—a kiss—was telling. During times when he was in his element, when he was figuring out all the different variations of a spy scheme, Jed had always been unemotional, almost robotic, as his mind worked out the next best step.

It was part of the Virus Project training, the compartmentalization of emotions. In his personal file given to Kirkland in the beginning, there had been a small notation that had caught his attention. There were little things the attending doctor and a scientist must take into consideration when it came to his test subject. In Jed McNeil's case, it was noted that his primary mentor had mentioned that the young subject had shown an inordinate capacity to sacrifice himself when it came to protecting someone close to him. Case in point, the notation went on, was Kitty. That was all Kirkland had, nothing else that would tell him what or who "Kitty" was. He did get to ask Jed about it a few years later, showing him the file.

The silence that had followed was telling. He'd learned that Jed liked to think over whether his replies would take him to places he didn't want to go.

"She was my wife."

It'd shocked him because Jed was the last person he'd thought would be married. "What does it mean by 'inordinate capacity to sacrifice' in the file?" he asked. "It's important I know, Jed."

Jed had just shaken his head. "No, it isn't," he'd told him. "Kitty's dead. It was a long time ago, when I was barely a man. Not everything in the file about me is true, Doc, and not everything psychologically explained about my personality is correct either. I've been in this game twenty-odd years. Do you think a woman who's been dead for that long could affect me now?"

As a scientist with just the facts, no. But as an observer doctor and friend, he'd watched Jed McNeil in and out of COMCEN, in and out of relationships, moving through countless women as assignments and moving on with nary an emotional exchange. He seemed to like to end things before they truly started.

Nikki Taylor came to mind again.

Kirkland turned to study Helen Roston, still lying on the examining table. She was yawning.

"Boy, this place is no five-star hotel, for sure, Derek," she complained. "Lousy food service and horrible bed. Jed had better show up with food soon or he won't get a tip."

"The cafeteria food isn't bad."

Helen wrinkled her nose. "Yeah, but you hadn't been planning on dining with an admiral," she said.

Kirkland smiled. So there had been plans.

Yes, all signs pointed to Jed McNeil wanting Helen Roston. He'd always suspected it, of course, what with Jed's obsession with watching the woman on camera, studying her even while she slept in her quarters.

He'd keep an eye on this to see where it was going. Usually, once an assignment was over, Jed would disengage himself without a problem.

A knock at the door. Someone appeared with a tray of food.

"I was told to bring this up for Agent Roston," the young man said, looking at Helen. "That would be you, right?"

"Duh. You just won the lottery." Helen sniffed the air. "I have a suspicion that Jed sent you because he's too cowardly to bring it to me himself. Is it that bad?"

The man set the tray at the foot of the bed. "Edible."

"Personal opinion, of course."

"Thanks, anyway." She reached for the food. After he left, she turned to Kirkland and growled, "I still think he's a coward. I wish I had time to play with the VR avatar program. I'd make him dickless. It's what he deserves."

Kirkland couldn't help smiling at the thought. "I'm going to get everything ready. Be right back," he said. "Derek, prepare the Portal program."

Outside the room, in spite of himself, Kirkland's smile widened into a grin. He had a feeling that it wouldn't be easy for Jed to disengage himself from Helen Roston.

Chapter Ten

Jed didn't like it that he had to put Elena through virtual reality so soon after Frankfurt. This was supposed to be her downtime and she hadn't actually been resting, dammit. He had plans—

He tamped down his sudden burst of irritation. Everyone had plans. His job was to make sure he was in control, no matter how the plans changed. He should have thought of the CIA's hand in this matter; after all, he'd practically grown up within its many programs. They didn't let go of their children easily. Not even him, who'd been one of their own before the transfer.

Helen must have impressed them during her training in their remote-viewing program, so much so that they were sending in their own remote viewers to check up on her. Probably because of what happened in Frankfurt too. She was the only remote viewer who had ever successfully RVed, pinpointed a location, *and* completed an operation without canvassing an avalanche of red tape, reviews, generals, interdepartmental consent, and body count.

Jed wasn't surprised about the covert meddling. The CIA had been known to ignore interagency agreements before. The SSS program was supposedly koshered by all the department heads and everyone had agreed to leave the chosen candidate and her winning agency alone for at least a year. They had agreed to come to COMCEN if they needed to use the supersoldier-spy for their individual cloaked activities. That was why the candidate was so damn important and why everyone worked so hard to win. The winning agency had dibs to special allocated funds and certain power over the other agencies' agendas.

This definitely had the smelly smell of the CIA.

Jed nodded cursorily at a passing operative's greeting as he reached the set of elevators that would take him to the secured levels. Several conclusions came to mind. A, the CIA was either trying to understand what they did with Elena that was different. Or B, the rogue CIA rats needed information, which meant that COMCEN was doing its job, slowly cutting off the many heads of the serpent, and with Jack Cummings and his wife their latest casualties, they must be desperate. Or C, they were experimenting with their own version of the supersoldier-spy and coming to COMCEN for information.

His gut pointed to conclusion B. The events in Frankfurt suggested it. If they had wanted Elena, they could have had a better chance with a surprise attack at the beginning of the operation, before they'd entered Deutsche International. But they appeared to know about Cummings already and knew that Elena was after the device, and deliberately waited till after she'd located and retrieved it.

Jed needed answers and he needed them quickly. He had no choice but to get Elena into TIVRRV again. She would be out of it afterwards for sure. He was going to have to get hold of T. ASAP. She needed to know what was happening. There was no way he was going to allow any of their enemies to slip away. Not when COMCEN and GEM were this close to achieving their goal.

He slid his security card in the slot and keyed in his code. As the scanner took his thumb print, he activated the screen so he could check up on Elena at Medic. One of the perks of high security clearance in this place, he thought dispassionately, then smiled at what he saw. She was licking her fingers like a kid while Kirkland was taking blood from one arm. She didn't seem tired. Yes, she was chomping at the bit to meet him in VR again.

Out of habit, he changed the view to see what was taking the elevator so damn long to reach him. His eyebrows shot up.

"Speak of the devil," he murmured. It was T. Cornered by Alex. Usually his friend was smart enough to use his own secured code to deactivate access, but he was obviously too distracted at the moment.

Jed executed a few more access codes and inserted his earpiece. A slow smile formed on his lips as he listened in. "And how are you going to escape him this time, dearest T.?"

"I heard Nikki Harden's pregnant," Alex's voice came through.

Jed frowned. Somehow he hadn't gotten that news.

"Yes, she is," T. said, her eyes trained on the lights above the elevator door.

"Will she be taking time off soon?"

"I don't know. I haven't talked to her."

"If I were Rick Harden, she'd be."

Jed watched Alex reach out toward the elevator control panel. Probably remembering now about overriding the microeyes. *Sorry, pal, I got to you first.* A man had to be entertained sometimes. Besides, he wanted to hear more about Nikki's pregnancy. Jed keyed a command to Eight Ball to zoom in.

"What are you doing?" T.'s voice sounded husky and unsure.

"I was thinking of you pregnant with my baby."

Jed blinked in surprise. From T.'s frozen expression, she must be as astonished as he was. This must be the first time the operating chief of GEM was rendered speechless.

"It isn't going to happen," she finally said. Alex took a step toward her. "Don't come any closer."

"That's going to stop a Virus, T.," Jed murmured, amused. As if he heard him, Alex took another step.

"You agreed if I transferred back you'd keep your distance," T. reminded him tensely.

"I changed my mind."

They were whispering, but COMCEN micro-mics were state of the art and Jed was also an excellent lip-reader.

He watched T. move her hand, jamming one finger on the red button. The alarm started. COMCEN elevators were also self-programmed to restart when they detected no problem.

"That's going to stop a Virus," Jed repeated, smiling now.

Oblivious to the shrill alarm, Alex crowded her against the corner of the elevator, obscuring Jed's view. His hands braced against both sides of the walls, trapping T., as he leaned into her. Jed couldn't see their expressions now but he would bet that T. wasn't a happy camper at the moment. Perhaps he should save her. He needed her in a good mood.

"Unchange it." Her demand was muffled.

Was that the best she could do? Jed shook his head. He fingered the pad next to the elevator.

"But I like the thought of you pregnant," Alex murmured.

The elevator door opened. Jed walked in.

"Go take another elevator," Alex said, not turning around.

"Don't mind me," Jed said, "I'm just the service man. By the way, don't you think you two should at least use the places where the microeyes aren't trained on you? T., I need to talk to you later. Important mission stuff."

With an indiscernible reply, T. gave Alex a push and he stepped back, giving her room to get away. They walked out of the elevator, leaving Jed.

Jed pressed his floor and then turned and looked dead straight at the microeye. He pulled out his ear piece. "Triple-C, I'm ashamed of you," he mocked quietly, "letting me listen in on them like that."

"Dude," the computer's voice mimicked his voice to perfection. "Information is everything."

"Erase that from file." Jed gave the password for the command.

"Password received. File erased."

Nikki pregnant. He released a soft sigh. He was happy for her.

Helen looked up at the sound of the knock. It was Flyboy. He was giving her the kind of smile that made a girl spontaneously smile back, but she was supposed to be angry at him, so she schooled her expression.

"Can I come in?"

"I've been ordered to digest my food before my VR session. I suppose I can talk while that's happening," she said dryly.

She couldn't help but lie back and admire appreciatively as he bent over to pick the tray of food out of the chair, moving it to the table by the window. She eyed the back view equally appreciatively.

Flyboy was gorgeous with a capital G. Of all the commandos, he had been the friendliest and most accessible, but now she wasn't sure whether that was an act or not.

"Why are you here?" she asked.

"Armando called me, said he's in trouble and needed to talk to me. He gave a quick version of what had happened. I'm just checking to make sure that you're okay before I see him."

"Huh, good to know I'm more important than Armando," Helen said, with a smile. "He won't be happy about that."

Flyboy sat down by her. His deep blue eyes slid over her body. "He'll get over it. You haven't answered my question. How are you?"

"Besides re-injuring my leg, I'm okay. Jed thinks a remote viewer was invading our territory and somehow Armando and I felt his presence." Helen shrugged. "Too science fiction to explain."

"But you're buying it."

Her eyes met his. "I'm a remote viewer. I've also experienced several very strange happenings lately." And she didn't mean just the incident in the stairwell. Her stare hardened. "I hardly have any room to be skeptical at this point."

He studied her for a second then sighed. "Okay, so I'm guilty of knowing who your trainer was. I was ordered not to reveal his identity till he said so."

"So our friendship was just a game?" Helen crossed her arms. "I'm just an assignment, right? You were to be my 'friendly companion', so you could watch over me."

He smiled, shaking his head. "No, not a game, Hell. But yes, I was told to keep an eye on you, make sure you have someone to talk to."

He leaned closer. "I wasn't pretending to like you, if that's what's making you mad."

"No, no, no, what I'm mad at is that you, and the rest of the guys, were doing your best to confuse me enough not to figure out which of you is my trainer," Hell said, with a sniff. "That's typical male behavior, covering the ass of one of your own while he does his nefarious deeds."

"You mean women don't cover their female friends' nefarious deeds?" Flyboy countered reasonably.

She chose to ignore that. She had every right to be angry and wasn't going to let the man get off with reasoned arguments. "You and the others went along with him against me, the newest member of your team. How's that supposed to make me feel?"

"Every one of us is tested in different ways."

"Yeah, you guys get into pissing contests, get to see whose dick is bigger, but when a woman comes along, all of you get together to trick her so she's in the dark."

"So, you want to compare dicks?" Flyboy asked with a straight face. "We can compare dicks. You whip yours out and I'll do the same."

She tried to stop it but found herself grinning back at that infectious dimple. "I'm very good at enlarging dicks," she reminded him, airily.

"Oh, I know. I saw you giving your Hades a particularly ridiculous embellishment."

It was just too darn easy to banter with this man. In spite of his incredibly good looks, he had a boyishness about him that was very appealing. Helen narrowed her eyes. "That's your job within the ranks, isn't it? You're the one who gets to play the guy next door. That's why you're the one friendly with me."

His eyes rounded innocently, but there was a tiny twinkle in one of them. "Heath's friendly too. And from what I can tell, Jed and Armando are friendly with you."

"Ha. No, let me rephrase that. Ha, ha, ha," Helen mocked disbelievingly. "Can you see Jed playing the boy next door in an assignment? People volunteering information to him without him either threatening or seducing them? No, he's Number Nine because he's scary and can kill someone in a hundred ways. Armando's idea of friendliness is behaving like the cryptic Yoda. All that gothy gloom and doom. Then there's Heath, the one who interrogates and retrieves, remember? That's little Jed McNeil there."

She had to stop there because Flyboy was laughing so hard, he was making her join in.

"Oh my God, Hell. Yoda," he chuckled. "Little Jed McNeil."

He broke out laughing again, a sexy male sound that hit her gut, reminding her she wasn't exactly immune to charming men at the moment. And this particular commando had charm dripping like chocolate syrup on ice cream. She sighed. She wished she had that for dinner instead.

Flyboy wiped his tears from his eyes. "I don't think I've had such a good laugh for a while," he told her, still smiling. "Look, yeah, you have your teammates pinned down with your description of our...skills, shall we call it...but it's all part of the outfit. We are Viruses."

"And you're trained to be insidious, like one. But not to one of your teammates, right?" she pressed on.

"You're wrong there. We challenge ourselves constantly, but that's beside the point. Back when it became obvious that we were going to gain a new member, someone who has a different kind of *insidious* talent, it became our immediate problem to protect you while you were still learning the program. I admit it, I'm attracted to you." His blue eyes turned bluer. "I'm a man and you're one hell of a challenge and a beautiful woman to boot. I flirted with you not because I had to, but because I like you. Was it that bad, going out with me, and having a nice chat or two? I answered the questions that worried you as best as I could and if you had asked the right question, who knows, I might even have told you. But you didn't. You wanted to test all of us back. Admit it, Hell. You're all 'I'm woman, hear me roar' sometimes."

Helen stared back at him. His male logic was amazingly crazy, yet he somehow managed to hit a few home truths her way. She had dug around on her own. Had kept her suspicions to herself.

"I didn't trust most of you," she finally admitted grudgingly, but quickly added, "and rightly so! You knew what Hades was meant to be to me."

Flyboy would be smart enough to know that anything with Jed would mean more than just trainer. Intimacy and more would be part of their "partnership".

He shrugged in reply. "I don't know what to say to that, Hell. I don't know anything about RV. Just the virtual reality part. You'll have to talk to Jed."

"And you claim that you're attracted to me?" she scolded him softly. "What kind of man lets another man seduce his girl?"

He shook his head, a small smile forming. "I tried my damnedest, girl, but you were already into your trainer like white on rice. Sorry, you aren't going to blame me for that." He lowered his voice. "But I'm here. Not just for friendship. When you're over with him, I'd like more. But most important, I'm here if you need someone to talk to. He isn't the easiest man to communicate with."

"But?"

"I'd trust him with my life," Flyboy said simply. He stood. "I've to go to Armando before he decides to disappear. Are we cool?"

She narrowed her eyes at him. He dimpled at her. Damn that smile. A girl would forgive murder with that smile.

"You're on probation," she told him. "Maybe after you've shown me your collection of *Carol Burnett Show* episodes."

He looked momentarily surprised that she remembered that he was an avid Carol Burnett fan. Her heart did a slow flip at the boyish delight in his face.

"You're on," he said and touched her shoulder briefly, hesitated, then appeared to change his mind. His blue eyes, though, held hers for a few seconds, telling her what he'd wanted to do. He winked at her before opening the connecting door to the next room.

Helen smiled and stretched on her bed. Viruses, if handled properly, could be controlled.

The Portal in his quarters was similar to the one Elena would be using, except that the controls were on his side. He could change the preprogrammed scenery within the virtual reality program with a voice command or a tap of his finger.

It was good he had most of the commands memorized because once their brainwaves were in sync, he usually found himself so immersed with Elena that he'd forget he wasn't in a virtual bodysuit.

He could sense her thoughts. It was amazing. They hadn't anticipated that when they'd planned to add the synchronized brainwave experiment as part of TIVRRV.

Totally immersive indeed. He still couldn't decide whether it was a fair exchange, that he was able to remote view through her, sense her experience through her, and she, on the other hand, was able to move into his subconscious and participate in his dreams. And he was aware that his dreams betrayed his feelings more than anything else, because every dream he had when he sensed her presence was about his desire for her.

It was not enough, though. He didn't want just the virtual part of her, or dream-fucking her, or watching her romp around the pool naked. He wanted to be alone with her—man and woman—in a bedroom, all to himself, with no technology or serum enhancing the experience.

His lips twisted. *Too late for that, McNeil.* Everything, as usual, was ass backwards.

One day he would get back to normal.

Jed looked at the control panels in front of him and a rueful smile crept onto his lips. Getting back to normal? With a woman who could spy with her mind? With a woman who joined in his sexual fantasies when they were asleep? He shook his head, slightly bemused by his own thoughts. What was he thinking?

He had been having some strange ideas lately. When emotions got in the way, he did what he did best—compartmentalize.

If he stopped viewing his assignment as part of his job, there would be more complications than it would be worth. Lives could be put at risk. He'd learned that lesson a few times in this lifetime.

In comparison, in many ways, Elena was a fledgling in the cloak-and-dagger world. Her two years away from field experience had also made her vulnerable emotionally. Killer instinct was usually the first to go. He had to be careful and not give her too many choices, especially in the beginning.

Sexual desire was an important part of an intimate bond, but so was trust. It surprised him that she wasn't fighting him as hard as he'd thought she would. One punch. Probably more coming later. But there was no deep hatred or hysteria, powerful emotions that could weaken any imprinting process.

Elena definitely wasn't acting revolted or disgusted. That meant what they'd intimately shared didn't revolt or disgust her. He found that oddly pleasing.

"Activate program," he instructed softly.

Chapter Eleven

It was like standing in a huge spotlight on center stage. Except there wasn't an audience waiting for her performance. She stood there, waiting.

And on cue, he suddenly appeared, timing impeccable. Hades.

Helen grinned. She couldn't help it. When a delicious naked man, sleek and sensuous, sauntered toward a girl, and he was all hers in that place and time, there was just so much self-control a healthy female had. Her libido didn't seem to care that said male was also a computer-generated avatar.

She went up to him, eyeing his body appreciatively. One would think that now that she knew the face behind the avatar, it would be less exciting to watch a naked man. Not so. It made everything brand new, more exciting, even. The real man behind the controls was far, far more intriguing.

They met in the middle somewhere, still in that spotlight. The few times they'd done this, he had activated different scenes, once using the virtual image of a room that looked the same as the VR room in which she'd learned remote viewing, and the last time, he'd recreated her quarters to the last detail, reminding her how he'd come to her that one memorable night.

She knew him well enough by now to understand what he was trying to do. He wanted her to anticipate his next move, to wonder, and thus keep her mind on him. It was essential because of the brainwave synchronization going on.

She cocked her head. *"Hades or Jed?"*

"Does it matter?"

The man before her was a blond god, created by the newest virtual programming technology. She had had a hand it. At first, Derek had produced a really buffed up version of the caveman type, and that wasn't anything like the way she'd envisioned the perfect male, so she'd fiddled with the program and *voila!* A dream man, virtually hers.

Did it matter what she called him? *"No. Yes."*

"You sound undecided."

She changed the subject. *"Shouldn't we get started?"* She looked around her. *"Where's the scenery?"*

"We have time while our brainwaves get in sync." He stepped closer. *"Do we really need any scenery?"*

She cocked her head to one side. *"Do you think, now that I know what you're up to, that I'd let you seduce me so easily?"*

"Yes."

"What, you just snap your fingers and my body will magically obey?"

His smile indicated an arrogance used to compliance. Her eyes narrowed.

"You're asking for another punch," she warned, *"and that's not going to help with the brainwave syncing going on, what with me in a mood to kick your ass. Unless, I can make you pissed off too?"*

Jed McNeil pissed off? Every time she'd seen him, he was downright cold-blooded. Did the man even feel anything?

But he did. Her mind mocked her with a sexy memory of him pushing deep inside her as he climaxed. He'd growled out something and had kissed her till she was breathless. His heart beating rapidly against hers as he lay on top of her. His soft words spoken against her ear, words that had turned her on.

"I want more of you," he'd told her before starting all over again.

She shivered at the heat of that memory. She turned away from the naked avatar.

"I want more. It's all been virtual or in darkness or some kind of mind meld sex," she said. It was everything a woman like her should abhor. But there was no denying that he had used it to intrigue her and she'd found it seductive. Defensively, she tossed a shrug, and said over her shoulder, *"What, don't you think the real thing with me would live up to your fantasies? You know, there can't be any real bonding without real intimacy. And no, the other night doesn't count because you came to me when I wasn't ready."*

"You were ready," he drawled in that lazy Southern voice that she'd given him. *"And it was me in the dark, not your fantasy of a blond Adonis. You responded to me, not some visual sex candy."*

She should have thought about making him look like some hairy ogre with Darth Vader's voice. He laughed softly, reminding her that he was able to catch images of her thoughts.

"What makes you think that would stop me from touching you?" he asked.

"But I wouldn't be turned on," she retorted.

"Tsk. Shallow."

She shrugged. The bait had been giving her the power to create an image. She'd taken it and created something she'd personally find attractive.

"I'm not into ogres," she said. *"If I were, then you wouldn't look so pretty right now. What I'm saying is, had I known, I wouldn't have fiddled with that program, and you would still look like Derek's version of Tarzan of the Big Man Boobs."*

He laughed again. Her own lips curved up reluctantly and she added, *"I know, I know. This is a ridiculous conversation."*

He came up behind her. *"You forgot something."*

"What?"

"That I'm turned on by you." His hands settled on her shoulders, squeezing gently. *"That I'm dreaming of having sex with you. There's nothing virtual or Hades about that."*

Helen blinked in surprise. She hadn't had time to process what was happening to her to think of all the possibilities. She had been too busy nursing her bruised ego at having been tricked.

But her subconscious hadn't been. In fact, it had somehow sought out the culprit and tried to tell her, at every possible turn, who was behind the avatar. Only, she'd been too busy with the physical aspects that she'd ignored her strength—her instinct.

He wanted her. Not just as someone to seduce, because people didn't dream about doing erotic, sexy stuff to someone if they weren't turned on by that someone in the first place. Dammit, it felt good to that bruised ego to know that she could turn him on too.

"You do turn me on, Elena. In my sleep, I dream of doing you in every way imaginable. But you already know that, don't you? I know you want more, and I was going to let you have your way with me tonight before we were interrupted. So you'll just have to make do with another virtual date."

She felt his hand slide over her breast and sucked in her stomach at the sudden heat of his touch on her bare flesh. She frowned and looked down. Her eyes widened at the sight of a familiar red bustier. The very same one that she'd seen earlier while she was trying to remote view on her own. Her breasts strained against the neatly tied bows. The thong was a mere scrap of cloth, not much protection from his hand.

She made a sound of disgust. *"I thought that stupid garment was torn to pieces! You can't use the same cheap slut suit on me twice!"*

Before she even finished her sentence, the red bustier had morphed. She was now wearing a hot pink number, the décolletage so low and tightly held together, her breasts were in danger of popping out. In fact, she could see her nipples... Glitter caught her eye. She shrieked.

"Tassels! You...gave me tassels!"

"You said slut suit," he reminded her, laughter tingeing his voice.

Helen struggled half-heartedly, distracted by his amusement and the sight of his tanned hand sliding lower. She reached behind her and circled his arousal. It was hard and ready. There were a few moments of silence as their hands imitated each other's teasing.

"When we're into each other like this is when we're most in sync. We don't need any setting. Just you and me, giving each other pleasure, thinking of what we're doing to each other."

Thinking? There was no thinking at this point. All she could do was emit a groan. She widened her stance.

"Swivel your hips for me like you were doing," he whispered in her head. *"Slowly."*

"I'm not. Swiveling. My hips. Ooooh!"

He'd simply pulled the strip of thong aside. His intimate touch was unerringly on target.

Helen bit down on her lower lip. She could feel herself getting wet and she couldn't help but wonder if in real life, her panties were getting wet too.

Couldn't think. Not when those fingers traced slow circles that were driving her crazy, making her unconsciously grind her hips, trying to make him go faster. A part of her—a tiny, tiny part that was left of her ability to think—noted that every time she tried to analyze her situation, he made sure to stop her from doing so.

"I don't like the ribbons," he murmured. *"In my way. I want your breasts free from clothing. Yeah, like that. I like the tassels. I like the way they sway every time you swivel your hips."*

Parts of her clothing disappeared and rearranged before Helen's eyes, like one of those crazy supernatural movies with lots of CGI. Her corset became some sort of push-up contraption, giving her a view of her own nipples like never before, then the tassels reappeared and she shrieked again. This time they were weighted, their swaying pulling heavily at her nipples.

Hades' legs widened her stance and he pushed her forward, his fingers relentlessly chasing her pleasure. She gasped as his erection slid between her legs and he undulated. He slid a wet finger inside her.

Helen closed her eyes. His fingers. His hips moving hers back and forth. The swaying of the weighted tassels massaging her nipples. The pleasure was sharp. Focused. She could hear her heartbeat thundering, and in the background, the soft echo of his following hers. The slide of his fingers slowed down; the pleasure building inside her spreading like wildfire. She swiveled her hips and moaned softly at the feel of his penis probing her tantalizing heat.

"It's time to go to our intruder's hideout, Elena. Checkered flag."

She could only moan her protest when she heard his soft command. She'd known it was coming—the trigger code that started the RV process when their brainwaves hit simultaneous theta.

"Don't stop..."

"I feel your pleasure, Elena. Your body is soft and pliant against mine right now. So wet I want to turn you over and spread your legs—"

Not knowing whether he was carrying out his promises never failed to push the excitement ratio way up. She had never known a man who could undo her like that, just with words.

Helen felt a delicious shudder through her body as his fingers brought her ever closer to orgasm, her need to come locking his consciousness to hers as her mind obeyed the embedded trigger and hurtled into the ether.

It surprised Jed how quickly he was growing used to her. The real Elena was funny, quirky, and spontaneous—something he wasn't—and he'd thought that she'd find it difficult to be in a controlled environment with him. Yet she'd adapted quickly. Not without a fight, and he was sure, not without future retaliation, but she had come along once she'd figured out what was going on.

She was amazing.

It also surprised him how easily she turned him on. His response wasn't, like he'd thought, just visceral or sexual. Not any more, anyway. He was attracted by the woman herself. Plus, being able to remote view along with her was exciting. Twenty years in this business and there had been some crazy advances in spy technology, and he was hooked to this remote viewer.

As she bilocated—the moment the mind was said to disengage from the physical plane—he experienced that floating sensation, similar to skydiving. There were random colors and shapes floating around, as if his mind was moving through time and space before settling on the agreed targeted coordinates.

And then they were there—wherever that was. Did she even understand how amazing it was to be able to do that?

It was difficult to explain even to himself how he was there, and yet not. His brain wasn't confused at all, though. With his eyes open, there was Elena in his arms, suspended in virtual reality. With his eyes closed, there he was seeing another place through Elena's mind.

During their first session, when he'd first experienced this, it had taken him a few minutes to adjust mentally and physically. He'd prepared himself but it was still difficult to suspend the initial mental disbelief that it was happening, and even as he told himself to not think about what was happening, to just experience it for what it was, his mind refused to stop analyzing.

Perception was oddly uncontrolled, for instance. That made it even more difficult to adjust. It was all somebody else's viewpoint. It was a strange thing to turn his head and still see the same angles. His brain initially rebelled against the "logic", and he had to stop the urge to open his eyes.

He'd since learned to control the urge to fight it. Like watching a movie, right? Observe. Take it in. Then, and only then, analyze. It made it easier to let go.

He heard the roar of the race car engine. That meant Elena's consciousness had started the remote-viewing process. Some remote-viewing programs taught their trainees to use a "vehicle" to control the way they gather information. This helped, especially the beginners, to not be overwhelmed by the senses. He'd been told that one could wander around in the ether without a "vehicle", but there was less control, and the viewer wouldn't remember as much.

From his studies of the subject, the most used mode of observation was usually an electronic vehicle, such as a camera or a digital recorder, something with which the viewer was familiar. He'd smiled when he'd learned that hers was a race car. Perfect. Elena and high speed went hand in hand.

Through her eyes, he looked at the cockpit of her "car". They told him that as the viewer became more experienced, their vehicle became more "real" to them, with their subconscious adding little details that only the owner would do. A fuzzy pair of purple rabbit's feet dangled from the rearview mirror. Purple rabbit's feet as décor? He curbed the urge to ask her about it. Not the time. But he was sure there was a story behind that if Elena felt so strongly that she brought them into her subconscious.

What was Elena needing luck for? From his observation of her all these months, she'd rarely displayed any fear in all her challenges. The real woman underneath all that muscle and cockiness held secrets that he wanted to explore, but to do that, he had to find time outside the mission.

Elena's voice interrupted his train of thought. *"We're here,"* she announced. *"Are you with me?"*

A small smile curved his lips. She was always challenging him. She knew damn well he was with her. He could *feel* her awareness of him, her need and desire fueling that mental connection. She was frustrated, still reeling from wanting to come, and mad that even in the ether, she wanted him to continue caressing her.

He would never tell her but her feelings tortured him too. It was so tempting to just let go and let their mutual attraction take them to the ultimate conclusion, but he knew if they did that the mission wouldn't be completed for a long, long time because they would just be having one long bout of virtual sex. Not that he wasn't interested in exploring *that* with her.

But the urgency of finding the mystery intruder reminded Jed to always put the job first. The danger the intruder represented was real. He knew there was a correlation there with Elena's problem, but he hadn't been able to connect the dots yet, and he was determined to. Something told him that if he didn't, the problem was going to get bigger than just a need for sexual gratification as a side effect for Elena down the road.

So, no climax for them both till he had more control of himself. He could just imagine how absorbed they would be in each other's senses that he would put their safety at risk.

"I hate it when you're silent like that," Elena interrupted again. *"Stop teasing!"*

Jed sensed her thinking about his hand inside that scrap of thong, wondering whether he was still playing with her.

Teasing Elena was becoming a habit. *"I'm changing the program over here,"* he told her, *"so when you come back, you'll be bent over in a special chair and I'll be inside you, fucking you senseless."*

Her response was spontaneous. Intense. The sensation of being turned over and taken from behind...he realized immediately that he was catching her visual thought and her excitement made him hard as a rock. And in that instant of joint mental concentration, his inner vision "opened" and he began to clearly see her surroundings, what she was looking at.

The first sense was the smell of antiseptic in the air.

"Bastard. One day, I'm going to tie you up and make you my love slave for a week." She sounded breathless. *"But I can feel your connection, like you're part of me."*

Another interesting development. She hadn't said that before. *"I'm more or less having the same experience as before."* Except that he really wanted to make love to her even more so than before. *"Antiseptic, Elena?"*

"Yeah. I'm getting out of the car. Moving down this long tunnel. Corridor, not tunnel. Doors on left and right. Okay, antiseptic smell is definitely everywhere. Medical place?"

Here she was in charge. He could only follow her. He could only absorb everything she saw and felt, and nothing more. It was both exhilarating and frustrating.

"*Look to the left and right so I can examine the walls and doors,*" he told her. They were so new at this that she was forgetting that he was there as another pair of eyes, to see whether he could recognize places, faces, and objects. Walls might hold no interest to a remote viewer who was immersed in the experience—and in his position, he understood the compelling need to be an explorer in a different world because he, too, wanted to do just that—but he mustn't lose sight that he was also here to protect her and they had come to this place, wherever they were, because the intruder was here.

Walls could tell him a lot. A well-decorated wall, for instance, would suggest some place entirely different from a bare white one. If this was a medical facility, there would be clues.

"*The walls? Why...oh, okay, never mind, got you.*"

Jed examined the walls through her eyes. Bare so far. Some wood paneling, but nothing ornate. Nothing to clue one in about their whereabouts. Light in the far corner. There was a window at the end of the hall.

"*Let's look outside,*" she said. "*Maybe there'll be more clues. All building corridors look alike to me.*"

Slow down, Elena. But he chose not to say that. "*All right, but keep looking at the walls.*"

"*Yes, sir.*" Her voice was lightly mocking. "*You know, I could just say, Oh look, surveillance cameras! But I figure that's not a problem for us.*"

He smiled inwardly. "*I can feel your sarcasm.*" Along with a bunch of other interesting feelings. He was beginning to discern the different layers of her emotions.

"*Oh, yeah? Then tell me why I don't like the feel of this place. Can you sense that?*"

He could tell she was curious. He tried to explain it to her in words. "*Elena, I'm awash with all your emotions. I can't help but sense what you're feeling, but it's more complicated than that. For example, when you mentioned 'tunnel', I was sensing the same thing almost instantaneously, and so I have to wait for your conclusion that we're in a corridor of sorts before I actually 'feel' that too.*"

"*In other words, you have to wait for me to make sense of my senses.*"

Satisfaction seeped into his consciousness. Not his. Hers. He smiled again. "*Right. So, I can feel your discomfort but it's mixed up with your physical discomfort too. You have to direct me, Elena, or I'm going to be just as lost as you are.*"

"*Interesting. You must really hate it then, not being in control.*"

He'd learned to be very, very careful when practicing NOPAIN on a GEM operative. They fought right back with the same stuff. "*Slight correction. You mean, not being totally in control. I still have you comfortably arranged under me right now, as a matter of consideration."* He so enjoyed the way they kept each other on their toes. *"Elena, your holding your breath like that makes me dizzy."*

"I don't know why I bother talking to you. You're always trying to manipulate me."

"And you want to test me," he pointed out, amused. Like a puppy. But he'd better not bring up that comparison or that would really get her going. *"You're in charge of where to go right now. Take us to the window. Let's see what's out there."*

"Enough about the silly blank walls, huh? Here we are. I see lots of green. Wow. Nice yard, mamma."

Jed sucked in his breath. *"Look around more. Can we go through the window and float outside?"*

It couldn't be. He caught a panoramic visual of the "yard" as Elena scanned the area. Something went very still inside of him. Not a yard. He had been here before. Twenty years ago, he'd stood right next to that fountain and had taken a photo in front of it.

Chapter Twelve

Remote viewing was all about the senses. No matter how they tried to scientifically explain the process, with their "theta waves" and "bilocation", there was no description that Helen knew of that would do justice to the strange and wondrous mix of perceptions of the remote viewer.

The first sensation of disengagement, when in that altered state of consciousness, another part of her arose from deep inside. She could feel it like a door opening and her walking through it.

And then...yeah. Bilocation. Whatever.

That one word didn't describe the bloom of colors rushing past as the world seemed to melt and reform. There was no sense of space and time. If there was such a thing as going into another dimension, this would be it.

Then, everything slowed down and she'd suddenly be aware that she was at the agreed target location. Not physically, no, but her essence was there. Her former instructors at the CIA had called it "phantom form". Fancy name. But it still didn't accurately describe this feeling. More like, self-projection. A mixture of falling, floating, and flying. The colors. Oh man, the brilliant colors that slowly took shape into the location.

Then there was the physical freedom in movement. One could be as "solid" in the ether as one wanted, or one could just pass through objects like a ghost. Her race car was her thought-vehicle; she could use it to speed or slow down, giving her the ability to see certain events in slow motion. That was dynamite cool, especially in the midst of striking colors.

The sensations were powerfully addictive. Floating through air, rushing from the top of a mountain to its foot, trying to distinguish all the colors and smells as they first formed—all these experiences tempted Helen to try doing new things. Like hovering outside a window fifty, sixty feet from the ground. It didn't even take more than a mental effort and she was learning how to do it quickly and efficiently.

Much better than looking at walls. She understood Hades' point in doing it, but they were using her eyes and she wanted to look out the window. In some ways, it was tough "sharing" senses. He couldn't see without her seeing for him. She saw nothing but walls, and had no idea whether he saw anything different. Besides, it became boring looking at the blankness when the sunlight beckoned. She didn't like the vibes emanating from these walls at all, if walls could have vibes.

"Well? Do you see anything familiar?" Helen asked. The sunlight was strong but not too warm. The yard below looked well manicured, the kind that took a maintenance crew to take care of it. *"It's nice out here. Doesn't feel like a residence, though."*

"It's not a residence."

Helen frowned. Was there a slight tension in his voice? It was impossible to tell when the conversation was being held in one's head. Nonetheless, she felt an edginess that didn't come from her.

"Je...Hades?"

That silence again. She reached for him inwardly. Blankity-blank. She sniffed. Really, why couldn't she read his mind like he could hers? It would make communication with this man so much simpler.

"Actually, I'd imagine it would complicate it even more, what with you arguing and analyzing my thoughts and me doing the same with yours."

There was no mistaking his lazy amusement. Helen stuck her tongue out and bit back a quick rebuttal. The two of them having sex and anticipating each other's needs...nope, not going to go there. Still, she was sure he felt the thrill of pleasure that went through her at *that* particular thought, even though he didn't say anything this time.

The fountain kept drawing her attention, so she followed her impulse, willing her shadow form to stand in front of it. The splash of the water became louder and the surface shimmered with gleaming shadow and reflected sunlight.

"Why did you choose to stand at this spot?"

"I don't know. It was calling to me."

Another pause.

"That's a strange way to put it. Is there a reason why it called to you?"

Helen shrugged. The man asked impossible-to-answer questions. *"I depend on my senses a lot when I remote view, remember? I think I get pulled to a certain location because it's important to the universal agreement, which is, in this particular case, the location of our intruder. Perhaps he was just standing here. Or perhaps something happened here that was very important to him and I locked on to it, it's hard to say."*

"Something happened here that was very important...interesting."

His voice was a soft murmur, as if his mind was somewhere else. Again, she felt that slight tension—imperceptible, but because it wasn't hers, she caught it—and then, a distancing, as if two bubbles floated together, touched, and then parted in opposite directions. The feelings were fleeting, but definitely powerful enough to seep into her consciousness.

"I think the intruder is very attached to this spot," Helen said, looking around at the beautiful yard. *"This place means something to him."*

"Do you think so?"

She frowned. How come he wasn't giving her directions to look at? He hadn't shown any recognition of the place when they were in that corridor, but out here, he hadn't even attempted to check out the landmarks, or look back at the building.

"Hades?" She cocked her head. *"Do you know this place?"*

"Turn around. Look at the building straight on," he told her. After a pause, he added, *"Now scan it slowly from left to right so I can see the entire place."*

She did so. The main structure was magnificent, with four columns in the front that stood at least two stories high. Its architecture gave its façade a Greek look, with ivy climbing all the way up on parts of its walls. She looked at the roofline, then let her eyes travel from left to right.

"That's why I didn't recognize it," Hades said quietly.

"So you know this place?"

"Yes. Where we came from must be a new wing. Look at the newer structure to the right. It's an addition."

Helen studied the building. Yeah, that part had cleaner lines and looked different from the rest of it.

"I agree. The roof shingles are different. They look like a different brand," she noted. Another wave of amusement slid subtly through her and she briefly closed her eyes to savor the maleness in it. When she focused intently like that, she found that she could discern feelings that weren't hers. This was too cool. *"What's so funny?"*

"And since when did you become an expert in roof tiles? I didn't know GEM operatives were assigned roofing jobs. Did you have to translate for some roofers' treaty?"

The amusement became more pronounced at each question. Helen grinned back.

"*You mean you guys didn't have to learn roofing and carpentry during spy training? Tsk. COMCEN's spy courses need revamping.*" She looked at the roof line again. "*My next-door neighbor did his roof one summer and it just so happened that I was on vacation, so I helped him. He's a contractor, so I got to learn a couple of things about building.*" She patted her hair airily, and added, "*Just call me supersoldier-spy builder.*"

"*What about race cars? Flyboy tells me you know quite a bit about them. Another vacation friendship?*"

Now it was her turn to be amused. "*Hades,*" she said teasingly, "*are you probing me? You know T. has taught me better than that. You'll have to be a bit more subtle.*"

Had he been asking Flyboy about her? Or was Flyboy reporting back to him? There was a difference. And why did he bring this up in the middle of their RV session?

"*I just find your tidbits about your past fascinating, that's all. But back to our current mission, yes, I do know the location of this place. I've been here before the addition of that new wing where we came from. Since our universal agreement brought us inside that building, I'm assuming that our intruder comes from there.*"

"*You going to tell me where this place is?*" Helen scanned around again. "*No one around. The antiseptic smell from that wing suggests that it's a medical center of some sort but it seems an awfully quiet place to be one.*"

"*It was a different kind of medical center when I last saw it. I'd call it a place for convalescing. I'll give you more details later. Just to make sure, go through the front. It's probably going to be different from the way I remember it but the layout should look familiar.*"

"*All right.*"

The entranceway looked like someone's grand mansion, its brick façade laid in a geometrical design. The double doors, however, seemed out of place, made of glass and with the modern look that reminded her of a bank. Her phantom form floated through. The inside was very pretty, decorated in warm colors, with plush sofas and chairs scattered around. She noticed a huge fireplace and even a piano. There was no one there.

"*Convalescing, huh?*" She glanced around curiously. "*It's a very nice peaceful scene, but how come I feel constricted and even...hmm...pain? I don't like it.*"

"*You feel pain?*" Surprise tinged his voice. "*Interesting. The place looks more or less the same. Different furniture. There used to be a counter there to check in visitors but that's gone now. Look to your right. There should be a wall at the far end. Tell me what you see.*"

Gennita Low

She was getting very curious about the place. Hades seemed to know a lot about it. She had questions, but decided to leave them till later. In remote viewing, a monitor guided for information, not questions, and it was her job not to contaminate her perception with too many personal details. If done incorrectly, the remote viewer would muddle up what she was viewing with what she thought her monitor wanted her to see.

The wall was there, just as he'd told her. A fleeting sensation invaded her, too vague to define. Again, she had the feeling that it wasn't hers.

"I see pictures. Photos of various sizes. Let me focus on them." The wall was filled with numerous photo frames, too many to really take it all in. Mostly men standing around what she assumed were various rooms in this building. Some were taken outside.

"Way to the right, about tenth row, around there. What do you see?"

Helen obediently counted. The frames weren't arranged in neat rows, so she stopped about where she thought the ninth or tenth row was, then looked carefully at each photo in that area. Her hand flew to her mouth. Her eyes widened as she drew closer to a black and white photo.

"Holy batshit. Is that you?" The silence that followed was telling. Helen cocked her head, all her attention on the photo, taking in the fountain, the familiar tall hedge in the background. The *young boy* standing in front of it, with another older man. She momentarily forgot their little role playing game, her voice a mere whisper. *"Jed?"*

The silence was maddening. That feeling that wasn't quite hers slid through her being again, like the smooth side of velvet, just enough to tease but not enough to discern exactly what it was. She just knew it was not her feeling it, that she had invaded some private space.

Tough. He'd better get used to it. He certainly had no qualms doing it to her. *Her* tidbits about her past fascinating? Well, ditto his tidbits.

She put her hands on her hips and glared at the picture, as if that would convey her irritation to the man she was addressing. *"You're not going to say that's not you, because I'm not believing that. Brother? Cousin? Son?"*

"That's me. Go back to the first place we started at. I'm curious now what it's for."

Oh, wait a minute. He wasn't going to leave it just like that, was he? No explanation of this photo at all? *"Jed..."*

"Not now. We're looking for an intruder, Elena, not taking a tour."

140

She bristled at his sudden coolness. He had mentally shut a door and she *felt* him doing it. It was like a slap to her face. She considered going somewhere else in this building to look for answers to the new questions in her head. Like, what is this place to Jed McNeil? That it was the same place the intruder was at made it doubly tempting. Was Jed—

A gasp escaped her lips as a sudden image loomed up in her mind; she was lying on her back in her quarters at Center. She saw a pair of male hands tear the thong she was wearing and her legs were firmly parted. She was seeing herself through his eyes.

She heard him say something softly and the sudden swift kick of desire overtook her senses. How was this possible?

Can't. Think. His hands were gentle but insistent, his fingers enjoying the slick feel of her. She tumbled against the wall as pleasure spiraled uncontrollably. He was deliberately letting her see what he was doing to her.

What did he say before that? What did he say? Some part of her urged her to try to remember. But she couldn't focus.

"All I have to do is open my eyes, Elena, and do this to get your attention back to me. I need this connection. Every time you start analyzing, I lose focus here." His voice in her head took on a silky edge. *"We're still new at this. It's the only way I know to make you stop thinking."*

The sensations were all hers now. Every shudder of pleasure. She couldn't tell whether he was just sending her one of his fantasies or if he was really doing this in virtual reality. It didn't matter. Her concentration came back to him, to his hands and lips, everything.

"I want to be inside you, but I can't. Not now or we'll both be mind-fucking. Take us back to the first building, Elena. Open your eyes."

His voice was seductive, like a man with sex on his mind. She knew better. Yet her body shivered in delight at the thought of mind-fucking... The smell of antiseptic overwhelmed her. She opened her eyes. They were back at that other place. She wrinkled her nose. Nothing like antiseptic to stop a good mind-fuck.

"Happy now?" she growled, angry and frustrated. *What did he say?* that inner voice repeated urgently.

Helen shook her head. Too many damn voices in her head.

"Not really, not where it counts. Does it make you feel better if I apologize? I'm sorry I have to use our sexual desire to get you to do what I want."

"But you're not going to stop," Helen said, rubbing the sides of her arms, trying to stop the tightness in her lower body that had nothing to do with remote viewing.

"No. Not if it means you going off without taking me with you."

141

"My mind isn't yours, Jed!"

"Not all the time. Just now. Want another demonstration? With my apologies first, of course."

Helen wanted to scream. She was spitting mad and turned on at the same time. She turned around abruptly, ignoring his chuckle in her head. She was going to find that damn intruder. Then she was going back to virtual reality and kicking his virtual ass. Then kick his real one after that. It would double the satisfaction.

Jed ruthlessly strangled his own sexual thoughts as he focused in on Elena's senses. The fact that he could feel her desire too wasn't helping his own raging need to go away that easily.

He'd done what he did out of reflex. He told himself that it was necessary, but a part of him regretted that he had to. He pushed the feeling away. Careful. Elena was beginning to get wisps of his thoughts too. This brainwave entrainment experiment was unpredictable; no one knew exactly how she or he was going to be affected with prolonged synchronization.

Capturing each other's thought-images as a side effect was logical. If he'd been doing it to her, it was also logical that she would probably be able to do it to him too. His lips quirked. So far, it was fortunate that they didn't actually read each other's minds. He didn't think that would be possible, seeing that the brain generated a multitude of random thoughts and sensations in a second.

Jed shook off the analysis. Later. Questions and analysis would make them inattentive and put Elena in danger. He concentrated on Elena's perception of this new wing of Stratter's Pointe. He shouldn't be surprised that the old building had been renovated and added on to. After all, it'd been twenty years or longer.

This new section looked nothing like the rest of the place. Very clinical, like a hospital. Stratter's hadn't had a medical wing when he was there.

"There are bars on the inside of windows on this floor, Hades."

"Yes, I'm seeing them." Jed frowned. Prisoners in need of medical attention? At Stratter's? Things had changed.

"There's a reason why I bilocated here, Hades. Our intruder is somewhere in this place with bars in the windows that smells of antiseptic. I'm going to go check out a few of the rooms."

"Your attacker, Elena. Be careful."

The intruder somehow had managed to do something to Elena. In Jed's book, that made him dangerous. That they had to deal with something as yet unknown, someone who could possibly hurt Elena while in remote-viewing state, didn't sit well with him. It was difficult to protect someone from the unknown and it was his job to make sure she remained safe.

"*I hear something. Follow it?*"

"*Yes.*"

Jed let go of his thoughts about his past and concentrated on Elena. He knew, from previous experience, if he just kept quiet and let her work instinctively, she would relax enough to allow their thoughts to immerse even more, thus projecting her experience on him naturally. When Elena wasn't concentrating too much on being tied to him, he'd found that her thought-images even projected themselves into the virtual reality environment, that he could see her surroundings with his eyes open. It was as if he'd bilocated with her. It didn't happen often because they were both controlling persons by nature; sooner or later their self-consciousness intruded and he would find himself blinking away the sudden double vision.

He saw four people in a room. One of them was curled in a fetal position on the bed. He was drawing deep, sobbing breaths, as if he was in pain. A doctor was attending him. The others, in suits, were doing most of the talking. Their words, murmurs in the background, became more comprehensible as Elena focused in. Jed emptied his mind, letting the whole scene immerse like a movie into his consciousness, listening to the conversation taking place.

"*The doctor said to let him rest up for a few days. Maybe we should.*"

"*He can rest on the plane. Bring the doctor, in case he needs more drugs to calm down, that's all. Right, Doc?*"

The doctor looked up from his patient. "*His BP is back to normal, but he's suffering from some kind of mental trauma. Something happened to him out there in the ether and...*" He looked down and shrugged before adding, "*I've been told it happens more often than we know. Personally, I think these out-of-body experiences overwhelm the brain and it gets fried, so to speak.*"

"*Oh, like the drug doesn't have anything to do with it?*"

That was from the stockier of the two men in suits. He wore a sneer on his face as he, too, looked at the curled-up man on the bed.

"*Like I said, I think it's information overload for the brain.*"

"*Yeah, you said 'fried'. Is it truly fried, like some of the others?*"

The doctor shook his head. "*No, I think he's going to be fine. He's coherent, although in shock. He just needs rest. I need to question him again when he's less emotional, perhaps learn what set it off.*"

The other man spoke up. "*Perhaps we can try another patient.*" He studied the man on the bed thoughtfully. "*He has been the most useful*

143

thus far, though, actually able to penetrate through COMCEN's security net. Most of the others could barely function after five minutes. If we can get him calmed down enough I can ask him about the weapons and Macedonia. It's crucial we find out whether they're going to the summit."

Jed stiffened. Summit? The mention of Macedonia and summit was too coincidental.

"We already have confirmation that the trigger pickup was on schedule, so we don't really need him around. They aren't good at locating things, remember?"

"Hades," Hell interrupted. *"I'm guessing that man's a remote viewer."*

Her wonder and curiosity brushed against his consciousness. *"Agreed,"* Jed said. *"Do you think he's the one who was spying on us at Center?"* After a moment, he added, *"Perhaps even the same one who might have run into you during the mission a few days ago?"*

"He looks injured and in pain. If he were the one, not only do I want to know how, because my CIA trainers told me it was impossible, but also why he attacked me at COMCEN. What was he after? And why is he hurt anyway? This place's giving me the creeps. The smell, the vibes, everything feels negative, Hades."

"I think if we find out what his handlers are after, the rest of the answers will come."

"Yeah. They mentioned something about a summit in Macedonia. How's that connected to our last mission in Germany?"

Jed thought about it a moment. *"We were seeking out one of the lost weapons on the DC list as part of an experiment to prove your importance to the different departments. This place belongs to the CIA, by the way, so I'm thinking our men here are connected to the moles within the CIA."* The DC list was a top secret document of all the weapons that a CIA director who had been caught recently had sold through the years. Of that list, there was another top priority list of sensitive weapons and high-tech Intel that had to be found ASAP. COMCEN, with their inner links to so many underground weapon dealers, had been given that list. *"Remember the missing weapons we were talking about at the meeting earlier? One of the weapons, a unique explosive trigger device, has been changing hands in the black markets. With the help of the SEALs, we've traced its move from Asia to Macedonia. The mention of Macedonia and the summit is troubling."*

"Why?"

"Can't say. We'll discuss this later. Do you think you can remote view if the universal agreement is changed?"

"What do you mean?"

Jed looked at the scene in the room again, considering their options. The man on the bed let out a soft moan and turned around, still in a semi-fetal position. Helen's quick intake of breath interrupted his thoughts.

"*What is it?*" he asked.

"*I recognize that dude on the bed. He was in several of the beginning training classes.*"

Jed checked out the patient again. "*The Super Soldier Spy tests?*" he asked, just to make sure. He didn't recognize the face, so this man couldn't have lasted too long. "*Did he remote view with you?*"

"*We were divided into different groups. He wasn't in my group but in the few experiments that we participated in together, he was one of the fastest to finish and I heard his accuracy ratio was pretty high. But he disappeared.*"

"*Did you ask why?*"

"*No, not really. We were competing for a job and I just assumed he didn't pass some test. It wasn't unusual for the training classes to get smaller and smaller as time went by, Hades.*"

Until one was left standing, Jed added to himself. And Elena was probably the least expected to get the coveted Super Soldier Spy funding. It suddenly became very clear that the moles were inside so deep within the CIA that they'd view the Super Soldier Spy program, and hence, the winner, as a weapon that was worth selling. He looked at the man on the bed again. And perhaps, they were trying to create their own version.

"*Yo, monitor darling, you've gone all quiet again. Am I supposed to be twiddling my thumbs while you solve the problem of world hunger here? Are we forgetting the focus thing? You know, that me on you and you on me mantra, babe, or we lose connection?*"

Her sarcasm amused him. She was right, of course.

"*Touché,*" he said. "*I was letting myself get distracted.*"

"*Not you!*"

He hadn't been teased like this in a long time and he was enjoying it too much. He changed the subject because there wasn't a lot of time left.

"*About the universal agreement, can we change it?*"

"*How so? What are we looking for now?*"

"*Our initial object was to look for the intruder. Just now, one of those men said it was crucial to find out whether the weapon's going to the summit. That's the explosive device and it's supposed to be in Macedonia, but nowhere near the summit.*"

"*So you want to find out if the device is...where?*"

Jed paused, wondering if the information would contaminate the remote viewing process. She already knew what the weapon was, but locating anything through RV was tricky. A mere suggestion could send the viewer on a wild goose chase, looking for something that wasn't there. He had to be extra careful here.

"Elena, I need you to just concentrate on the missing weapon because I can't project what I know on you."

"Hmm. I see your problem." There were a few moments of silence and Jed could feel her weighing different options. He couldn't get the thoughts but he saw random images—the man on the bed, the quick flash of the device that she'd seen from the video during the meeting, then back to the people in the room. *"I'm going to guess that one of these men is our patient's handler and monitor. How about I concentrate on what that man over there said, about finding the weapons and Macedonia? We can shift the universal agreement to that man's next remote view point."*

Jed smiled internally. She'd managed to surprise him at her quick, innovative ideas. She always found a way.

"Can you do it? Two universal agreements, one after another. You're going to be totally exhausted when we're finished."

"I'm doing my job."

He smiled again. She was in outright mocking mode all right, sarcastically paraphrasing his oft-used words. The woman was still angry at him for what he'd done.

"I'm ready when you are. We have to both mentally think of the agreement at the same time," she told him. *"I remember his name, so it'll be easier. I'm pretty sure it's Jonah."*

"Let's do it," Jed said.

"What about this place? And them?"

"They're after what we'll be finding out next. So we're one step ahead." Which would be very good indeed. The international summit in Skopje was going to be attended by some world leaders, some of whom had a few enemies for balking the old Russian system.

He looked around one more time before he closed his eyes to merge his thoughts with Helen's. This place might look new, but it was also attached to a very familiar old system. Things on the outside might have changed, but old spies and their world didn't die easily.

Chapter Thirteen

During Elena's remote-viewing training, the concept of going somewhere using the mind didn't quite click into place until she found the "vehicle" of choice, her race car, which she'd nicknamed "The Rocket Ship". Breathing control, check. Relaxation and reaching an altered state, check. Consciously groping for some unknown destination identified only as a universal address—half the class had failed that exercise. Describing the target successfully, whether it was a bag of marbles on top of a building or the inside of a cave filled with bats, tested her senses and belief system. And yeah, half of the class had failed that one.

Those who were left—Elena included—started advanced training under the care of two operatives from the CIA's Directorate of Science and Technology. She was introduced to "long-distance remote viewing", a program focusing solely on operation-based objectives, moving from Point A and B with minimal guidance, the use of a mental trigger, and, most important of all, moving from Point B to A without losing control or information.

The use of a familiar travel or observation device was just a means to an end. To escape the grueling internal war with the belief system, it also became a comfort zone, or an escape hatch, should the surroundings or sensations start to overwhelm. Now, the mental leap of jumping into her vehicle and taking off was a natural extension to her remote-viewing process.

Change gear. Speed up. Focus on the universal agreement.

The mental toll exacted a heavy price. Seventy-five percent of her "class" didn't complete the course.

Having seen firsthand how a few of those who failed had to deal with the stress, Elena was very aware of the danger of overextending her remote-viewing session. One universal agreement was usually it. She'd never done two, and an unspoken universal agreement that was somebody else's at that.

She stepped on the gas, adrenaline fueling her excitement. That feeling that had haunted her during and after completing her training—that she was in some state of "becoming"—filled her again, pungent as the sweet smell of strawberries, her senses unfurling in some kind of need that she couldn't even explain. She stuck out her tongue as if she could taste it.

"Elena."

Hades' Southern drawl made her shiver. Strawberry and a chocolaty mudslide. Oh, man.

"Elena, Dr. Kirkland's reporting a spike in your readings. Are you feeling okay? If you don't feel right, we won't continue."

She smiled, her eyes looking at the speeding space and colors zipping past her race car. Was he showing some concern? *"I'm fine. The colors seem brighter this time. Can you see it?"*

There was a pause. *"No. I can feel your excitement. And I taste strawberries."*

Elena grinned. It struck her as funny how her feelings could be transferred, just like that. She didn't even understand why strawberries were invading her senses, so how was she going to convey to him what was happening to her?

"It's my excitement," she offered an explanation.

"Your excitement tastes like strawberries?"

Even there, in the middle of mind space, she could hear that slight twang in his voice, his amusement slipping through. *"I feel...amazing. Like I can go faster and faster."*

"Concentrate on the universal agreement, Elena."

That was definitely the monitor exerting his control. She made a face. The temptation to put her foot on the pedal and just go where the flying colors would take her was very strong. But Hades was right. This was unchartered territory for her and she must be careful. She closed her eyes, extending her will over the unknown universal agreement.

"A bag of marbles for him would still be a bag of marbles for any other remote viewer. Therefore, I'll go to his bag of marbles," she mumbled.

She opened her eyes as the floating sensation slowed. And *voila!* she mouthed silently. *Here we are, wherever this is.*

She exited The Rocket Ship with a thought, concentrating hard as the usual jumble of sensations poured over her consciousness. The key was to pick one thread, one sensation, and focus on it. Her CIA mentor had likened it to finding the end of a rope and using it as a guide in a maze.

It was pitch black and everything around her was shaking. She could hear labored breathing and jostling. Someone was speaking urgently, but his words were muffled and coming from above.

"*I'm totally disoriented,*" Helen said. "*It's hard to figure out where I am. I'm trying to crawl forward but I can't.*"

"*Stand up?*"

"*Can't either. Definitely someone upstairs trying to come down here.*"

"*How do you know it's upstairs?*"

Helen frowned. "*Well, his voice is coming from above me, but not directly, so I'm assuming it's upstairs. For some reason, my senses are telling me that I can't move, Hades.*" She gasped as her head spun, as if there was an earthquake. "*I think...I think I just toppled over.*"

There were several loud thuds and a very distinctive American voice came through.

"Ah, fuck! My foot! Fuck, fuck, fuck!"

The voice grew less distinctive, but it wasn't too hard to guess that each staccato-like enunciation was the same cuss word over and over.

"*I'm seeing it through your eyes now,*" Hades said. "*Total darkness. It's cramped.*

"*Tell me something I don't know,*" she said, dryly. "*I feel heavy. Like, if I were here in person, things would be on top of me. Maybe I'm buried.*"

"*Do you think you're in a coffin?*"

Oh, shit. She hadn't thought of that. Ugh. Coffin equals dead body. On top of her. Her mental self recoiled as if snake-bit. She started gagging. She thought of the confined space holding her prisoner. No air. Immediately she started hyperventilating. Her hands automatically reached out to claw at her containment, but there was nothing there. She began to choke, flailing around.

"*Elena! Calm down.*" He gave the order tersely, anticipating her panic, speaking with a measured steeliness, as if he could impose calm into her by sheer force of will.

But it was difficult to concentrate when one was fighting for one's life. Helen could feel her rising panic stifling the reasonable voice in her head. She was buried and her mind was telling—ordering—her to get out of there. Now.

He continued calmly. Firmly. "*Remember what you told me. It's like the illusion of drowning when you're underwater. Your mind thinks you can't breathe because it seems so real, but it's an illusion. You aren't there. You're here, with me, in my arms. Think of me, Elena, not in that coffin, but with me, in our VR space. You're holding your breath here, and you need to take in air now. Now, Elena.*"

Helen squeezed her eyes closed, paying attention to his voice even as fear threatened to overpower her. She wasn't buried. Deep breath. She concentrated on Hades but couldn't call his face up. The enveloping darkness seemed to have taken away all her senses.

"No, I'm still here. I'm seeing the same darkness too. Your fear is so real to you, you've projected it into our VR space. I'm actually seeing your remote-viewing target in virtual reality, Elena. Take another breath." There was a pause and she could feel his curiosity of what was happening at his end. The cool remoteness that was so uniquely Jed seeped through her fear.

Jed. Not Hades and that sinfully sexy body she'd designed. What Helen needed now was the man behind the program, Jed McNeil himself. The man with that calmness that took in every emergency and deflected them like a shield. She mentally reached for that iron stillness and wrapped it around her. The sense of safety enveloping her was immediate and exactly what she needed. And behind that watchfulness, she felt his concern and his preparation to end the session.

"No," Helen said, taking several breaths. *"Don't activate the trigger, Jed. I'm okay. Just give me a few moments. I need to really concentrate on that voice up there, that's all."*

"Maybe he's trying to open this coffin you're in. There's a reason why you remote viewed here, Elena."

Helen jerked. Of course. *"Hades, they're tracking the same list we have from a few months back. This is the location of the first weapon there, the most recent one. The explosive trigger or whatchamacallit,"* she breathed. *"Wait a minute, wait a minute. They didn't bury the weapons...you told me the CIA airdropped them, right? In crates. Crates that were marked as U.N. aid. I'm in a crate."*

That explained why she felt that she couldn't stand up or move around. And the sensation of things piled up. She was under a cache of weapons. No dead body. She breathed out a sigh of relief. Somehow a crate was so much easier to deal with than a coffin.

"A crate can be a coffin."

"Oh stop being so darn matter-of-fact," she snarled, embarrassed now that she wasn't that afraid any more. She didn't like the idea of him knowing that she had given in to fear. *"I panicked, so I'm sorry about that. It won't happen again."*

"There's nothing to be sorry about. Normal reaction, Elena. It's my job to anchor you, remember? Now you have a job to do."

She scowled. He was a manipulative bastard, getting her defensive to distract her and succeeding with just that snotty tone. She turned her attention back to the voice outside the crate, grounding herself.

"Yes, I feel that we are exactly where one of the weapons is," she said. *"It's in this crate. Someone outside is pushing on it very hard. It's someone speaking English and because he's cussing like a pro, I'm guessing he isn't Macedonian. Or we aren't in Macedonia. Can't verify, Hades. I can't go through the crate and not change the universal*

agreement. If I do, we lose trail of all the other weapons those guys were trying to locate through their remote viewer."

Location was so hard to pinpoint. In the first experiments, her monitor, who usually knew the universal agreement, guided her "tours", making her describe the target area in detail. She never knew the location till she was back from the ether. They'd hand her the envelope that had the universal agreement written inside and then they'd wait for the "outbounder", the person outside the loop, to call back to verify and confirm what she saw. As she advanced, she learned that the universal agreement was just that—there really wasn't any need for an envelope containing coordinates or names—and just focusing on one would get her to the agreed target. When she finally became the lone viewer left in the supersoldier-spy program, they'd tested her with further targets, some top secret, that couldn't be verified except by satellite photos.

All those earlier assignments seemed so easy compared to what she and Hades must now accomplish. Her monitor was as blind as she was, and without an outbounder, she had to depend on his experience to find a way to verify. It was hard, very hard. But she sat there in the dark, biting her tongue, ignoring the impulse to escape the feeling of confinement, and waited for further instructions.

"Is that man on the outside still shouting and trying to move the crate? Is he really trying to open it?" Hades asked.

Helen tried to gauge the different muffled sounds. *"He did turn the crate over before he started cursing non-stop. He sounds a bit calmer, actually. I'd guess he's talking to someone but I can't hear any other voices."* She paused as her surroundings started shaking, and like earlier before, her head began to spin dizzily, reacting to the sensation of freefalling upside down in total darkness. She fiercely reminded herself that the sensation wasn't real, shaking off the urge to escape outside.

Following instinct, she pushed her senses outward, reaching for God knew what. Ever since she was a kid, there was a part of her who could "sense" things, a part inside her that somehow manifested itself into a voice that would warn her if she was near danger. She had long ago stopped questioning the feeling, trusting the voice when it ordered her to move out of the way, or to run the other way, or to pay attention to what appeared to be harmless. It was just a voice in her head, nothing more, until now. She'd never consciously tried to exert the sense before, didn't even know she could do it.

Then, without warning, something inside burst out and there was a loud popping, like air pressure in one's ears when a plane took off. It happened so suddenly that she couldn't think of anything for a minute. It was no longer dark, yet she knew she wasn't outside the crate. She didn't know what had just happened, but she could *feel* what she couldn't see, the outside of the crate. She let out a long breath of awe. *"Hades—"*

"Shhh. I'm feeling it. Whatever it is, I'm feeling it." And there was wonder in his voice. He paused, and she could feel his curiosity and his will combating it. *"Later. We'll talk about this after the session. I don't know if you realize that you're not wholly in the crate right now, Elena."*

Duh. Since she was the one here in the ether, shouldn't it be her explaining the phenomena?

"Care to explain where I am then, Mr. Know-it-all?" she asked, and refused to admit that she was doing so because she wasn't truly sure herself, even though she suspected the answer. *"What did you see from your end?"*

"I felt you trying very hard to stay inside the crate. Usually, when you reach a target, you're free to move out and about, to explore for details, but to do so now would break the universal agreement because those men were after more than one weapon. There was a floating sensation that expanded and then you moved forward—or I felt you move forward because it was dark and I was about to say the trigger code to get you back into the race car—but you were too fast and then suddenly, you stopped. You stopped just before you were out there, Elena. You're actually, for lack of a better explanation, stuck in one side of the crate."

Helen reached up and patted her face. She felt about the same. His explanation sounded so ridiculous she couldn't help saying something ridiculous back. *"You know, I don't think I've ever heard you string so many sentences together. You should talk to crates more often."*

His quiet chuckle made her laugh out loud. It was, she knew, a sort of hysterical reaction to this new sensation, of being and not-quite being. When she'd gone through "solid" things before—doors, walls, even steel—she hadn't stopped in the middle of the "thought". Those acts were done without the thought of ever being "stuck" inside because it'd been instilled in her during training that she, her physical body, wasn't in the ether. It was her projection of what she was "seeing", a way her brain was trying to understand the experience. She'd accepted the explanation. But now, she wondered whether there was actually more to the "phantom body" being her brain's projection. Because she could actually feel her crateness, the flatness of the surface, the dimension. She could—

"Hades? I sense the writing on my...the crate's sides." She concentrated on reading the strange letters, taking a few seconds before realizing that it was Cyrillic. It was awkward, as if she were reading something written on a tee shirt she was wearing, that was

how real it felt to being part of that crate. She said each letter out loud, trying to make sense from her angle.

"*Serbian and Croatian. Food Aid,*" Hades translated for her. "*This is what Hawk's looking for. One down. You ready to leave?*"

Best words she'd heard all trip. "*Yeah. We have to hurry. Whoever is out there has found something to pry the crate open. If I tumbled out, that's the end of our little trip.*"

"*Checkered flag, Elena. Go back to the race car and continue to the next weapon those CIA agents were after.*"

Helen saw the checkered flag the moment he mentioned it. It served as her guide post, the mental trigger a monitor assigned to his remote viewer to get her back to her physical self. Without it, a novice remote viewer could easily get confused or lost in the ether. She moved toward it and there was a sucking sound, like she was a suction cup stuck to a surface. She felt slightly giddy, her mind still reeling at the realization of what she'd just done, as she felt herself departing the location. She stumbled in the direction of her waiting car, still feeling the pull of the crammed space behind her.

A soft, thready moan. A creak. "*Cam...Cameron?*"

Helen froze at the whisper, her hand on the car door. There was so much fear in that voice. That kind of total darkness could drive a person mad.

"*Get in and go, Elena. Checkered flag.*" His order was quiet but firm.

"*Did you hear that? There's someone in that crate,*" Helen breathed. "*A woman.*"

"*And someone's trying to open it. He'll help her. Get inside the car, Elena. You can't do anything. Checkered flag.*"

Helen reluctantly obeyed. Who was in there? How did she get in a CIA-dropped crate? She gave a sigh as she started the car up and put it into gear. She hated leaving unsolved mysteries just when they got interesting.

Chapter Fourteen

Time to bring her back. Jed readjusted the controls. It'd taken longer than he'd thought. Those CIA bastards were really pushing their remote viewer, giving him such a broad universal agreement. Following it had taken Helen and him, as the passenger, on the trail of more weapons than he'd anticipated. He had better get more vigilant in his care of his remote viewer, or she might suffer whatever was hurting that other one at Stratter's.

He opened his eyes, making a quick check on her vitals. Although she hadn't mentioned it, she was getting tired. The mind could only take in so much and Elena's had been absorbing a lot. He did a mental countdown of all the extraordinary experiences. Some form of psychic attack. "Borrowing" some other universal agreement and basically getting a free ride. That strange experience in the crate, whatever that was. He had no words for it right now and hadn't had the time to mull over it. Elena needed his fullest attention as she wasn't done with her joyride yet. Then the unexpected mother lode of them all—the discovery of some of the other missing weapons on the list.

The CIA moles were definitely trying to recuperate their losses from the last few months. They must be desperate. Usually, when the top-ranked moles were exposed and the fallout was still happening, many of them would lay low, waiting for the next lull in carelessness. There must be something very important, some projected plan that must be done at a certain timetable, for them to risk their being found out. Desperation often led to desperate acts.

Excitement and triumph pushed at his concentration, the need to dissect and analyze contesting the need to focus on the job at hand. Closing his eyes, Jed willed himself to "listen" in on Elena's feelings and impressions. Their connection was still strong, but exhaustion could play a part in breaking that. He could feel the mental stress like a buzzing distress signal between them. One mistake, loss of concentration, and they'd no longer be in sync and she'd be out there alone. He wasn't going to let that happen.

His job was to keep her alert, to reassure her, and to engage her sexual interest so they didn't lose their mental connection. Sharing pleasure with a woman like Elena was easy. She was responsive and seductive at the same time, and their minds opened to each other in recognition of their natural attraction.

Therein lay the danger. Because of what happened earlier—in that dark space, when she'd thought she was running out of air—she'd shared her fear with him and he'd almost forgotten his role. He'd wanted to reach out to protect her instead of calm her down with words. In the darkness, so merged with her mind and her fear, he'd momentarily fallen into the trap that he was there with her and could physically help her. That couldn't happen again, he told himself. He must remember that he had to take her out of any danger with words, not with action, when it came to remote viewing.

He turned up the volume of the brain entrainment machine, the biofeedback sounding loud and echoey. With her gone into altered state for so long, he wanted to be very sure that he brought her out of it slowly. The mental image from Stratter's, of that man curled up and obviously in pain, bothered him more than he cared to admit. He didn't ever want to see Elena like that.

"*Checkered flag, Elena,*" he said, fascinated, as always, at how her whole body reacted to the mental trigger. Over here, in his arms, he could feel her physically tensing; in his mind, he felt the swirl of jumbled thoughts, some of which he caught, most of which scattered like so much dust. There was a part of her that fought his order, a reflex, he suspected, that was uniquely her. Relatively speaking, from experience, this type of mental trigger was very mild in comparison with others he'd witnessed. That was why he'd resisted being her trainer at first. He knew he'd have to do more. There was an independent streak in her, as well as her having been trained in NOPAIN, that would take more than a mental trigger to manage.

He smiled ruefully. Not that he'd resisted being her trainer that hard. He hadn't figured out exactly why or what yet, but something about Elena Rostov made it more than the usual challenge for him. Her resistance was to be expected. It was his own response that surprised him.

"*Hades, can you see them?*"

He blinked away his thoughts. "*See what?*"

"*The colors. They're so beautiful. Can't you see them? I don't even have names for some of the shades.*"

He frowned. He couldn't see any colors. She'd mentioned something similar before. Moving from bilocation back to the self felt like a rapid descent from a great height to him, nothing more. There were streaks of light here and there and if he concentrated too hard, it made him slightly dizzy because of the loss of sense of direction.

"No, I can't see anything."

"They call out to me, Hades. They make me want to stay and explore."

A dreamy sensation invaded Jed's senses. Not his. He didn't like it at all.

"Elena, checkered flag," he said, firmly. He caught her reluctance, a pulling away from him. She should be seeing the checkered flag in her vehicle and following it back to him. But what if she wasn't looking? What if she was too busy looking at those damn colors?

"Elena? What are you feeling?"

"Like a sunset. The colors are just gorgeous and I'm in the middle of the magic!"

He didn't feel good about this at all. She was definitely pulling away. He could feel it. Quickly, he opened his eyes and deliberately changed the virtual reality scenario. Something shocking to her system. Something to outrage her. Something to get her connected back to him. He was glad now that he had other ways to achieve this besides a stupid and inefficient mental trigger.

Sunset, she said. He'd better hope that their sexual attraction for each other would rival a magical sunset.

He pressed the controls, readjusting temperature and scenery. Unlike her one program of him as the blond and naked Hades, he'd a lot more freedom on his side. His virtual Elena could wear many different costumes. Or go naked, just as she'd made him. He'd created the programs mostly for himself since the idea of the virtual Hades was to give Elena a measure of control, but he'd discovered that snatching back that control when she least expected it—like when he showed her his fantasy of her wearing that gaudy piece with the tassels during the beginning phase of their session—caused the kind of outrage that got her attention solely back on him. And her response always made him push her a little further, which also completed the circle, requiring him to give his full attention in pleasuring her.

Virtual space changed into an exotic stage effect. She was naked, gloriously so, the way he saw her when she stripped down to nothing before swimming, the way he'd like to keep her for the next few days, if he ever had a few days to himself. Heat mingled with desire. He took her in his arms and kissed her.

It was strange how it felt so real. The times when he'd tried with others in virtual reality, he had been clinically disengaged, part of him always gauging his mental and physical reaction. With Elena, he could recall her taste and scent so intimately that the real woman appeared to be in his arms.

She was so beautiful. He buried his nose in her neck, inhaling her sweetness, breathing the words in her ear that they'd agreed would catch her sexual attention. As if in answer, her body gave a little tremor. If he really had her for a few days to himself, he would do this. And this. And this.

"...I want. Did you hear me? That's our secret password. Now turn away from that sunset and come back to me."

But the colors... Helen didn't even know how long she'd been staring at the floating colors. She didn't want to turn back.

She shuddered at the teasing arousal calling at her. She'd heard his order, her attention brought back by a need to obey—she could never catch those important trigger words but they had the ability to make everything else unimportant. It was as if a switch had been turned on and she could feel all that male attention focused on her and her needs, bringing her secret desires to life. What woman could resist that?

"Elena, if you can hear me, put your hand between your legs and show me. That's right. Like that. Are you wet? Close your eyes and feel how wet you are for me."

But the colors... If she closed her eyes, she wouldn't be able to see them. She hiccupped. Could one's phantom body hiccup?

"Show me how you pleasure yourself, darling. Close your eyes and touch yourself. Open your legs a bit more. Can you feel the vibration? That's right, wider. Think of this and the checkered flag, sweetheart. You have to come back to me."

Helen moaned, feeling a deep vibration penetrating her. What was he doing to her? She couldn't quite see...got to concentrate... Fingers. Pressure. Floating. Every sensation was jumbled. Her phantom body fell, spread-eagled, spinning, so close to orgasm.

"So wet. Everyone in the audience can see how wet you are."

Audience? What the—her eyes snapped open and met chocolate brown ones. Part of her struggled because she understood that she was back in the Portal. She wanted to go back to the colors. But she was back in Hades' arms. And coming.

"No..." she whispered, weakly. Not in front of an audience.

"Yes. It'll go back to soft vibrate for a minute before starting again. You'll come for them till you're back here. And I've reset that vibrator till you obey me when I tell you to come back. Till you call me master."

Outrage poured out of her and she struggled to beat him off her. Call him what? How dare he? How dare he bring an audience in to humiliate her? She would not...

"Your minute is up again. Can you feel it?"

She gasped. It felt so good against her clitoris. She screamed, unable to stop her orgasm. Her whole body convulsed as waves of pleasure took over. Panted. Horrified. People watching. Hate him, hate him.

"Say it. Master, I'm back here with you." His voice was mockingly soft, his hands like steel bands around her. *"Ooops, your minute's up again. Feel it moving against you, exactly where you want it. Look, everyone is gathering close. I love to show them how you come for me, Elena."*

She shook as the vibrator kicked up again, stimulating her already sensitive flesh. She couldn't think, couldn't fight, as all her muscles tensed in excruciating pleasure-pain at coming so hard a third time. She could feel the eyes on her. No, she couldn't take them coming closer...

"Master, I'm back...with you," she gritted out, acknowledging his power over her, opening her eyes to glare at him.

Immediately, the feeling of being watched disappeared. There was no one. No vibrator. She looked down and saw her own hand between her legs. Oh God. She had been the one doing herself. She jerked her eyes up to meet Hades'. There was a tender curve to his lips and his hand stroked the hair away from her face. He had put the whole thing in her head. He knew she would be pissed off at having to call him master. And in front of an audience, as the final outrage. He'd manipulated her to come back.

"I hate the power you have over my mind," she told him, in between small pants. *"In fact, I hate you right now."*

"Hate, love, lust. I need all your strong emotions tied to me," he replied grimly. *"I won't lose you out there in the ether. You'll obey me in this. Once we're back in reality, you can punch me again, if you like. In here, you're mine. The more you accept this, the less dangerous it'll be for you when we're pushing the unknown in immersive remote viewing. Get it?"*

She was too damn tired to argue right now. She closed her eyes. *"Well, get me out there right now so I can fucking punch the daylights out of you, then."* Her threat was as weak and useless as her mind and body. She wasn't feeling very energetic right now.

Her eyes were half-closed. She felt his kiss, soft and promising. *"Unfortunately, supersoldier-spy, you're going to have to sleep off a lot of your RV jetlag first."* She stuck out a tongue and her eyes closed fully on their own. She thought she heard him add, *"I'm sorry."*

"Yeah, but you'll still do it again," she mumbled.

His reply sounded from far away. *"Affirmative. Especially if I can get you to perform like that for me in real life. Disengage from VR mode, Dr. Kirkland."*

Helen yawned.

Chapter Fifteen

It took Jed longer than usual to peel off his sensor suit. His legs felt wobbly and he had to hold on to the back of a chair till the lightheadedness passed. He reached for a bottle of water and took one long gulp, taking a few minutes to gather his thoughts.

He cracked his neck. Normally, he would wait for Dr. Kirkland, but he wanted to go to Elena quickly to see how she was. Dr. Kirkland would probably want to run a battery of tests, but what she needed was complete rest right now.

He wasn't feeling exactly perky himself. Absolute focus took its toll on mind and body. As Elena's monitor, he'd discovered that he needed to be several steps ahead all the time as he switched his attention back and forth from Elena-in-the-ether to Elena-in-the-Portal. What she could do—what they could do together—was so incredible that it sometimes distracted him. He'd listened in on remote-viewing exercises before, learning from experienced monitors how to guide and what to expect. They hadn't prepared him for immersive remote viewing.

He downed the rest of the water and grabbed the towel set neatly beside his clothes. He felt clumsy and awkward moving about, as if he was slightly inebriated. He was just about ready to leave his quarters when a buzz sounded from the intercom. That would be Kirkland, checking on him.

Jed frowned. In his hurry, he'd forgotten to type the requisite code after logging off the Portal control pad, which was a signal to let Dr. Kirkland's crew know that all was well at his end. He picked up the call.

"I'm all right and I'm on the way," he said crisply. "How's she doing?"

"Vitals are fine, but not normal. She's barely coming out of REM. Aren't you going to be at your quarters?"

"No, I'm coming over right now. She's still in the sleep-dreaming state because she's exhausted. I'll explain more when I'm there."

Jed rolled his shoulders discreetly while he was in the elevator, trying to rid himself of the knots bunching his muscles. If he were feeling out of it, she must be a hundred times worse. He wanted to be there for her. Besides, she was likely to be looking for a fight when she regained her strength and would insist on looking for him again, just as she did earlier. Even if she had to crawl. The corners of his lips lifted at that image.

He paused for a moment at the entrance, surprised and yet, not, at the sight that greeted him. This was one of the highly classified areas and usually, those who had access didn't congregate in one room unless something important had happened. *Elena.* He was at her bedside in a few strides.

"What's wrong?" he asked quietly. Her face was pale, her eyes closed.

"She's fine, Jed," Dr. Kirkland reassured him. "She's just a bit out of REM, but she's drifting in and out of consciousness. She was aware of her surroundings but needed help to get off the Portal."

He touched her cheek with the back of his hand. Her eyes fluttered, then opened. "Goodie," she mumbled. "All the boys are here."

Indeed. Jed finally turned around to acknowledge the presence of most of his team. They were watching and no one seemed in any particular hurry to leave. He looked at them questioningly, lifting his eyebrows a fraction.

"Is there a reason why all of you are assembled down here?"

"Eight Ball sent a message to me that Hell wasn't breathing," Flyboy said. "I've asked the computer to let me know if anything went wrong during a session."

"I was with him when he took off." Shahrukh shrugged. "We were in the middle of discussing something so I came along."

Not breathing. That was probably when she was in a panic. Flyboy was the friendliest with Elena so Jed wasn't surprised he'd be down here.

"Your vitals were also alarmingly out of control, Jed," Dr. Kirkland chimed in, "and I was about to shut the thing down when you signaled that you were aware and doing something about the situation."

He remembered how his mind had been so immersed with Elena's consciousness that he'd felt all her panic and fear at the idea of being buried alive. It'd taken him by surprise how real the sensation was and he'd undergone a few long seconds of sheer panic before his own logic broke through. He recalled his hand reaching out to curl around the emergency handle—if he'd pulled it, Dr. Kirkland would know something was very wrong; if he pushed it forward, that would mean that he wasn't able to talk right now but was functioning. There were other buttons on it to help communicate any problems he couldn't express but he hadn't had the time while talking Elena out of her panic and had trusted Dr. Kirkland not to panic at his end too. He turned his attention to Alex. So that was why Number One and Tess were here together. His lips quirked. And not quarrelling. Chain of command was priority. If anything had happened to him, Alex would take over this particular mission.

Tess's eyes narrowed. "It couldn't have been that bad if you can still make snide remarks with your eyes."

Jed didn't allow his smile to surface. Tess, as usual, was testing him, using her own way to assess his condition. "I'm never snide," he said. He nodded toward Elena. "She's okay, but we had the interesting experience of finding ourselves inside a crate. Not knowing our exact location and with the cramped space, the first conclusion was that it was a coffin or something buried."

Understanding dawned in Tess's and Alex's eyes. A soft whistle came from one of the others and a few cusses.

"You mean—"

"Full-blown panic?" Alex asked, at the same time.

"And you experienced it too," Tess finished. "That's why your readings were going nuts."

Jed nodded. "It took a minute for me to realize that I wasn't actually buried and wasn't unable to breathe. It was Helen experiencing it."

"Wait a minute. From what I've been reading, remote viewing is like watching something from a distance. The person I talked to said it's similar to seeing the reflection of an event. So how is it that her experiences are so real that she literally can't breathe?" Flyboy asked, a frown forming.

"I think the most interesting question is why would her choking affect you?" Armando said from the corner of the room. His dark eyes met Jed's. "You're the monitor, not the remote viewer. Synced brainwaves can't be that intimate, can they?"

Jed flicked his attention back on Elena. "My concern now is giving Hell some rest. Don't wake her up, Doc. Believe me, she went through a lot."

"Interesting non-answer," Armando commented softly. "Isn't that right, T. darling?"

"He's looking a bit off himself, I think," Tess murmured. "If nothing's too urgent, questions later."

"I have verification of a number of the locations," Jed announced quietly.

There was a stunned silence.

"On the list?"

"Not all of them, but yes," Jed confirmed. He absently massaged the stiffness in his neck. "I wouldn't say it's not urgent, but we have some time. I need a half hour to make some notes. Maybe an hour."

"He needs sleep," Elena interrupted, her eyes still closed. She yawned, then turned on her stomach. "Hey, if he can know I'm exhausted, and you guys believe him, then it stands that I can know he's just as exhausted."

"You should be resting," Jed told her.

"Can't. Too many people talking."

He signaled for the others to leave. "Meeting in three hours," he said, looking around. "Where are Sully and Heath?"

"Sully's spending the night at his tree house. Heath's somewhere in the complex," Flyboy said, his eyes still on Elena. He didn't look happy. "Are you okay, Hell?"

"Umm," Elena replied.

Jed studied the little group around Hell. He reminded himself that they weren't here to talk to him. Not counting Tess, who was Elena's chief, in their own way, his men were worried and protective about the newest member of their group. They had all arrived here the moment they found out that Elena was in danger.

"She's fine, Hunter," he said, reaching out to flick Elena's hair out of her eyes. "She's just done the equivalent of several somersaults in a fighter jet, that's all. There were some anomalies but she did great."

"If the meeting's not absolutely urgent, at least five hours of total rest for you," Dr. Kirkland said firmly. "Then you can have your meeting. Your body can only take so much, Jed. At least five hours and that's the doctor's orders."

He had to be at the summit in three days. There was some time to rest up and prepare. Not much, but enough to afford taking a few hours to recharge himself.

"Go make your notes and rest up," Alex said. "I'll let you know if anything urgent comes through."

Jed nodded. What he really wanted was to stay with Elena. She was peeking at them through her lashes, trying to stay awake. No, he would just be a distraction if he stayed. Knowing her, she wouldn't want him around when she was vulnerable and would fight complete rest. He caressed her cheek again and felt the small quiver.

"Go to sleep. I'll be in my quarters." He turned abruptly, adding over his shoulder, "I'll see you all in five hours."

By the time he'd reached the elevators, he'd already started to compartmentalize his worries and feelings about Elena. He told himself that she was more comfortable without him hanging around anyway. Now that he'd given himself five hours instead of three, he could take care of some other paperwork and a few calls, especially one to an old friend. First, though, he needed to make quick notes of all he'd seen. Outline the idea he had with targets and retrieval. He knew the others would have plenty of questions, some of which he wasn't prepared to answer.

"Five hours? I thought he said three."

"Old man needs his sleep."

Eyes closed but still aware of the quiet conversation around her, Helen could hear them leaving the room. She made an effort to wave at the few who addressed her.

"Hey, see you later, Sleeping Beauty," Flyboy said.

"Sweet dreams." That was pure Armando.

"You'll feel a little prick. We're going to make sure everything is being monitored while you sleep," Dr. Kirkland said.

Try as she could, she just couldn't keep her eyes open. She was simply wiped out by the remote-viewing session. She hadn't thought it possible to RV so many different locations, one after another. During her training, her instructors had told her that there had been previous experiments but most of the remote viewers had gotten confused about locations—going from one apparently distorted spatial awareness to another. After a while, there was also the weariness factor.

But none of them had a Hades to anchor them, she thought sleepily. None of them shared the remote-viewing session in such a way that one could monitor directly.

"*Viva la* brainwaves," Helen murmured in self-mockery, then added, "I know you're still here, T."

"Just making sure."

T. didn't sound worried, but Helen knew that her spiked readings were serious enough to warrant the presence of so many commandos and her operations chief at her side. She was aware that she had stopped breathing at one point.

"Got y'all scared, huh?" Helen said wryly. "I'm sorry, I can't think at the moment. It was quite a session."

"I know. Do you have anything to tell me before I leave?"

"Yeah. Make sure Jed tells you about the girl in the crate. I'm worried about her. I'll feel guilty if they find her body because she's alive right now."

There was a pause. "Okay, I'll do that."

"T.? Tell Dr. Kirkland to administer a dose of the serum if, in five hours, I can't get up. I want to be able to make that meeting."

"Hell—"

"It's important that I'm with the team all the way, T. And it's important I get the mission deets firsthand from Jed. I want to be sitting there and be part of the operation and not just some crazy experiment they pull out of bed when it suits them." She sighed. Seeing that other remote viewer all curled up had really gotten to her. "That came out bitter, didn't it?"

She felt T. move closer and a hand touching her forehead. "Well, no fever, so you're lucid. What brought that on?"

Helen turned over on her back. She could barely stay awake now. She wondered whether Jed was asleep already. She wondered what it would feel like to curl up next to him, both of them sleeping soundly.

"I want to be at the meeting so I can ask Jed about Stratter's," she told T. "What is that place? And who are those people?"

"Okay, you're definitely no longer making sense to me. Sleep. I'll take care of everything. I'll make sure you're wide awake for the meeting."

That was all the reassurance Helen needed to hear. She'd intrigued T. enough to make sure her operations chief get her there. She drifted off.

"Five-One, can you hear me? If you can't continue, let me know. We'll let you rest up, but you have to be honest with me. Can you continue? Our mission is very important and we need all the help we can get."

The soft persuasion in his monitor's voice didn't reassure him. Liar. At least his partner was more honest about their intentions. He understood the veiled threats, even though they weren't addressed to him.

"Why don't you just tell him that if he fucks up one more time, we'll just let his ass rot in a windowless cell instead of here? I don't even know why you're so damn nice to him. You weren't so friendly with the last one we had."

"This one has more potential. He's gone further than the others and could have even beaten COMCEN's remote viewer if not for the physical exercises. Have you checked his file?"

"Not interested. I care only to get our operation done."

"Then you'd better look after our boy here, don't you think? Unless you want to go look at the others we have and hope we find another who's not so into the serum that he'd be lost within a day or two."

"Fuck. I don't trust him."

"I'm sure he doesn't trust us either, but we have what he wants and he can give us what we want. And you will, won't you, Five-One?

You know it's important we get to the weapons before they do. The more successful we are, the more of the juice for you. Right? Nod if you understand me, please."

He nodded. His monitor, bastard that he was, understood how to get his attention. From listening to their conversation, all the other remote viewers they had tried were all hooked on the high that came with the drug. He was too, in a way, but it was different for him. He wasn't hooked like a junkie; he just wanted to seek out those secret sexual details from the people he encountered. They looked so damn prim and proper, but what walking storages of sexual energy they were indeed. Whatever happened just now was an anomaly. COMCEN was a fucking weird place, anyway. It didn't feel "natural" to him, not like when he was remote viewing other locations. He remembered how difficult it was for him to focus, as if there was some kind of other energy interrupting his concentration. And then there was that bitch who was enjoying his collection of energy, and making more for herself. There had to be a way to get it back.

If he just stayed strong, just kept in control, the serum would give him what he needed. These CIA handlers mustn't know what he could do, or they would use it against him. They forgot he was a smart man, and like them, trained in covert activities too. An asset, that was what he was. That was what he needed to remain. To stay an asset, he needed to give them something back.

He nodded again. "All I know is I didn't go to Macedonia. It had to be COMCEN and that place had certain blockers. I don't know what they are but they make it hard for remote viewers to stay long there." He swallowed, trying to stop his body's shivering. "While I was there, I did record that they weren't planning on retrieving any more weapons."

"That's impossible. They've been making a list of all the weapons that have gone missing all these years. I know they're going to be looking for the bomb trigger next. It's the next logical part after their success in retrieving the decoder at Munich."

Jonah finally opened his eyes. Were they actually having a conversation with him? Usually, the insults came first before they started questioning his findings. For once, the fat one stood there without a sneer on his face. Should he show them that he was, at least, able to understand what they were trying to accomplish? Better not.

He cleared his throat. "These weapons are on a list, you said. I think I recorded a list but they don't know where they are either. Remote viewing for locations takes time. The last mission was a lucky one because they had the Deutsche International logo on everything at that place. If, let's say, the next bomb device you're talking about is in Macedonia, and they don't know it, it'll take them a lot longer because

I know that region speaks a mixture of Serbian and Croatian, so to pinpoint the exact location would really take a lot of sleuthing." He gestured to the globe in the middle of the room. "If you know where it is, we're ahead of the game already. All you need is to tell me and I'll verify the location."

"We want to know for sure who has it," his handler said, handing him a glass of water. "Our head contact knows it was dropped off in a CIA crate not long ago in KLA territory and that's controlled by Dragan Dilaver. What we need for you to verify is whether the trigger is in his possession yet. Our sources told us Dragan has been out of the country, so we're worried he's already sold the device, which would complicate things."

Time to show that he knew a thing or two. "From my little time in decoding, I know the CIA has an off-record relationship with Dilaver, that is, we won't touch his drug activities if he takes care of certain business for us. So why can't you guys just give him a call? Ask him whether he has the device?"

Jonah noted the way his two handlers exchanged glances. That told him a lot. The CIA's inside contact to Dilaver must not be with the CIA anymore. Or maybe Dilaver had changed sides and that was why they needed to retrieve this bomb trigger. Or maybe they were no longer friends with Dilaver. One could never tell with the CIA agenda. One minute they were on one side, and the next, they were playing on the other. Political ping-pong, the intricacies of CIA games. He knew, from the start, that if he were to go up the CIA ladder, he was to do his assignments without too many questions. But that didn't stop him from conjecturing.

It excited him that he was actually in the middle of a CIA mission. Most of the time, his work had been mainly at the tail end, working in the dark rooms, decoding stupid data. Signing up for the top-secret experiment had been his one shot to move up. Remote-viewing experiment? Sure, bring it on. And through that, he'd discovered his new unique talent, the special ability that these goons didn't have. If only he'd won that damn competition, taken out all those other test agents, he'd be living the high life right now. Like that bitch. The thought brought back sensations that he didn't want to recall right now. The ear-splitting white noise. That sense of overwhelming pain. He shuddered. He didn't want to go back to COMCEN if he could help it.

He took in a deep breath and released it slowly. What he wouldn't give for a cigarette right now. "I need some downtime," he said. *Give them something so they'd think he was an asset.* "Look, I already found out that those people aren't in Macedonia. I can do this. My brain isn't fried because I know my limits. The juice helps me to withstand the stress after remote viewing, but something happened back there. That place has something—I can't explain it—that seems to affect me."

His monitor nodded thoughtfully. "That might explain the other two viewers we had who couldn't breach their security." He turned to his partner. "The Russians used a similar system. We'll just have to add that to our report."

"That might get us off his shit list for losing the decoder in the last job," the other man grumbled. "He wouldn't be surprised that COMCEN has some Russian secrets, though."

Who was this "he" they were referring to? Jonah lay back in the bed. He was feeling nauseous again. Every time he thought of COMCEN, that pain shocked his psyche like a live current. So much pain. Why did he feel as if the weight of the world was on him? He hadn't done anything wrong.

"Take a break, Five-One. We have to get this particular weapon ASAP. We'll be back in a few hours. Do you think that's enough time?"

"Nothing another dose won't cure," Jonah told them quietly.

He winced as he tried to relax. This pain made him want to cry as if he'd lost something very important. It disturbed him. He couldn't figure out why he was feeling like this. He thought about the lost cache with all those wonderful sexual memories that were his to play with till that woman stole it. Ah. The familiar anger was back. He closed his eyes and prayed for sleep.

"It's been quite some time since I've seen your number on my caller ID, Conor."

The voice was raspier than he remembered, but Joe McGuy always greeted him as Conor when it wasn't business between them. Through the years, Jed had approached his mentor both for and outside business reasons. It was a friendship built from a promise that one man kept and the other never forgot.

"I wouldn't want you to think I'm checking up on you in your old age," he said easily, the Irish lilt of his growing years threading through his words as easy as ivy climbing up a wall.

"Harsh on an old man. What's the world coming to?"

Joe might be retired and he might be up there in age, but old wouldn't describe him. He still ran and finished the Boston Marathon every other year. Someone told Jed that he skydived on his birthday this year.

"Can't be too harsh with your granddaughter's wedding coming up," Jed said, leaning back in his chair, relaxing for the first time since he sat down to do paperwork.

"Ah, that's the fruit of my labor and I'm enjoying every minute of my retirement. When's Trouble getting married anyway? She's around the right age, isn't she? I haven't seen her for a while now either."

Jed smiled. Joe had a special spot for Grace, his daughter, even though he hadn't seen her a lot as a grown woman. It all had to do with that long-ago promise.

"She's still young and wild. I don't think she's going to be tied down by a husband for a long, long time, my old friend."

"Don't be too sure, my old friend. DC has a lot of young men."

Jed frowned. Had Joe been keeping an eye on Grace after all? "She's there for an internship. Please don't tell me she's in trouble already."

Joe gave a raspy chuckle. "Your daughter has your genes, remember? And her mother's. Which means, she's in and out of trouble a lot, God help her."

He supposed if it was anything to be really concerned about, Joe wouldn't be teasing him. "I'm assuming she's managing on her own, since she would be calling me if it gets out of control. She knows how to get hold of me."

This time, Joe snorted. "Jed," he chided, using his other namesake now, "that daughter of yours thinks trouble is fun. She's also at the age when they all think they're invincible. As for that internship, I think you should ask what her job entails exactly, if you care to call her more than once in a while."

It was Joe who had taught him how to be a father. But his training had also taught him to distance himself from those he loved. Grace and he had a different father-daughter relationship. In many ways, she had turned out a lot like him. Except for that devil-may-care look in her eyes. That was all Kitty's.

"Perhaps I'll find out more about what's happening at her end," he said.

"Do it soon," the older man advised. "Now, what is it you need from me?"

They slid from personal to business like well-oiled parts that had worked with familiar intimacy. Jed had always appreciated how Joe could drop the mantle of friendship and assume his old role of mentor without a change in appearance or inflection.

"Stratter's," he said.

"Stratter's Pointe? All the way to the beginning?"

"Yes. Do you still have connections there?"

169

"Of course. A few of the old colleagues have gone there, just as you did."

"Are you sure it still functions the same? It's been two decades, Joe. Maybe it's more now."

"I wouldn't doubt it," Joe said, curiosity entering his voice now. "And what is that to you?"

"You know that COMCEN won the funds for the SSS project." Catching the flicker of lights out of the corner of his eyes, Jed leaned forward to check the screen to his right. T. had just punched the codes to his quarters.

"Oh, yes. Super Soldier Spy. That's causing quite a stir among us old farts in the know. It's too super secret for us, really, so we don't like to talk about it much. What's that got to do with Stratter's?"

Jed punched the code to allow T. to access his floor. "The CIA has their remote-viewing program. I've been given partial access to it. What I want to know is, since when has Stratter's become a medical ward with bars in their windows?"

"Sometimes we have political prisoners who are injured, Jed."

Jed used his remote to unlock the front door. T. hadn't even attempted to knock; she'd known he'd be expecting her. He waved her in.

"They're using it as a medical lock-up for remote viewers there now?" Jed asked, his gaze catching Tess's interested one. "Are they prisoners, then? If they aren't, I'm sure they would be among the usual operatives on the other floors that don't have bars in the windows."

There was a short pause. Jed watched T. as she sat down on the chair on the other side of his desk. She folded her hands primly on the edge of the desk, then rested her chin on them, effectively looking thoughtful and bored at the same time. It was also a good way to conceal her eyes from him, so he couldn't read her.

"I'll find out what I can and call you back," Joe finally said.

"If it's possible, I'd like to send in one of my own." Jed caught the little flicker of T.'s eyelashes, signaling that she was listening very closely. "As a political prisoner in need of healing time. Paperwork and a few calls. And privileged visiting hours, if that still exists there. That way, one of us can 'interrogate' him."

"That kind of string I can pull. I'll let you know the details ASAP."

"Thank you. I must go now, but we'll talk again soon, old friend."

"I hear your accent disappearing. You must have company. This late, it couldn't be for business. Wait a minute, I'm losing it. It's Jed McNeil I'm talking to." The mockery in Joe's voice was unmistakable. "It's always business. Goodnight, son."

Jed hung up.

"Hope you're not sending Hell in. She'd make a lousy political prisoner."

Jed sat back comfortably, his arms relaxing on the armrests. "Is Alex allowing you up here alone?" he baited. "I'm surprised he isn't frantically hunting you down."

T. frowned, her lips pursing mulishly for a fraction of a second. It was enough to let him know that Alex hadn't let down on his determined chase since T. had relented and came back as part of the team when Helen was unexpectedly chosen as the winner of the Super Soldier Spy project. She couldn't just let one of her GEM operatives flounder in COMCEN alone, so she'd signed transfer papers and returned, even though that had meant working side by side with Alex Diamond again. It was one of the few things Jed liked to rile T. about, a weakness that he enjoyed poking.

"Alex doesn't care where I am as long as I'm at COMCEN, at his beck and call," she said, a little too coolly, as she sat back up. She ran her forefinger over the smooth oak of his desk. "And you're changing the subject. Hell mentioned a place named Stratter's. And someone locked inside a crate."

Jed rubbed his chin. Elena wasn't going to let him off easy, was she. And how the hell did she know—of course, she caught that name off his thoughts, like he sometimes caught hers. He really didn't want to talk much about Stratter's. "Stratter's I can explain later during the meeting. The crate I can try to explain, but whether I'll make sense is another matter entirely. I might need some time to think it over."

"Okay, I can wait. She was in danger this time and you were affected. Care to explain that instead?"

"She thought she couldn't breathe when I suggested— thoughtlessly, I might add—that she might be in a coffin. Which she wasn't. But the idea, as you might suspect, induced normal fear and panic, enough so that it affected me because I was so immersed in her experience."

"Immersed," T. repeated, her gaze questioning now. "How immersed are you two, exactly? I have a feeling both of you are keeping some things from me. When you see what she's seeing, are you experiencing everything she is too? Because that's not in the Remote Viewer Handbook, you know. Armando asked the correct question just now. Why was her choking affecting you?"

"We're capturing glimpses of each other's feelings and thoughts," Jed told her off-handedly. "Bound to happen, with our brainwaves in sync and spending more and more time together. It's called bonding."

"And are you two...bonding?"

Jed studied T. through half-closed eyes. GEM had secrets that they didn't share with anyone, even their relatively new partners. He wondered whether Helen knew her operations chief wasn't telling her everything.

"We're learning to trust each other," he said, "if that's what you mean."

"You know that's not all I meant."

"And you know by getting me involved as her monitor, what that entails."

"I was hoping you'd be gentle. I would hate to see her feelings hurt."

Jed arched his brows. "Sleeping with Alex is making you soft, darling," he mocked. "Elena's feelings have never been your number-one priority before. You, or rather your higher-ups, wanted to see the extent of her gifts and abilities, and wanted someone with whom she could get personally involved. Bonding, I believe you yourself called it. Care to cut the bullshit and tell me what's at stake here? Besides the supersoldier-spy part, of course. I know that's important, but there's something more that you aren't willing to tell."

T.'s eyes widened, a triumphant gleam entering the golden brown depths. "You have feelings for her," she breathed. "I'm pleased."

Jed didn't deny it. No need to. He acknowledged a certain mix of possessiveness and yearning for Elena Rostova, feelings that he was willing to explore a bit more if only he had some time.

"I'll give you that. Now your turn," he said. There was a silent agreement between T. and him. Give a little, take a little. That way they both could walk away winners.

T. combed her hand through her blonde hair, a small satisfied smile settling on her perfectly shaped lips. "While working on the ring-alarm, I've come across something that confirmed something else I've been working on. There'll come a time when Helen might need someone she can trust." Her expression suddenly turned serious. "She could reject my friendship with her, thinking I've betrayed her. It's good to know she'd have you by her side."

"You're making me more curious than ever," Jed murmured. "Are you betraying her?"

"No. I've been having certain suspicions about certain GEM inner circle things and have some of them confirmed, but not enough to really say anything. I have no solid evidence. It's big, Jed. When it blows, all GEM operatives will need to take cover. As for Helen—" Tess paused. She shook her head. "I'm not willing to bring it up before its time. There's a list of dangerous weapons to take care of first. Like you love to say. Do the job. Everything else will take care of its own."

Everything she'd told him so far was both nothing and yet, something. NOPAIN at its best. She was right, though. "I'll stick to Helen," he assured her, then leaned forward to wickedly add, "like your man's sticking to you. Seems like you've got to learn to trust your feelings, T. Go for it. Give in to him. Let yourself trust him."

T. shrugged. "You forget. He doesn't trust me," she said.

"Well, then, aren't we both in the same hot water?"

"Helen will trust you eventually, darling. She'll figure out that you're a softie inside," T. said smugly.

"And so will Alex trust you eventually, darling," Jed drawled. "He'll figure out that you're not totally heartless."

T. stared at him, then started to laugh. Her beeper went off.

"I bet I know who's looking for you," Jed mocked.

T. smiled. "Goodnight, Jed. I actually like you when you're tired. You're less guarded."

"Using NOPAIN on a tired man is very amateurish, T." He was tired, but knew she was just baiting him too. Another Jed and T. unspoken rule: Always leave with the last word, if possible. "Ooops, is that Alex down there staring into my micro-eye? I believe it is. How is a tired operative ever going to get his beauty sleep?"

T. made a face and turned around, clicking the door shut behind her without another word. Jed noted that she never answered her beeper or checked the video screen. He would have found that amusing if he hadn't understood the urge to check on someone sleeping too damn far away at this moment.

He secured all the codes, set the alarm, stood up and stretched. Was she dreaming about him tonight? Or would he dream about her instead? He rubbed a hand over his eyes. Either way, it just wasn't going to be the same without them dreaming together.

Chapter Sixteen

"Miss Roston, wake up!"

Helen grunted, trying to crawl back into the dark fog of sleep, but the shaking was persistent.

"Miss...Hell, Miss Montgomery said you wanted to be awakened early enough to go to a meeting. Would you rather sleep?"

Oh, yes, sleep. That was what she'd rather do.

"You can stop shaking her, Derek. She should just stay in bed. I can fill her in about the meeting later when everyone's gone off."

Her eyes snapped open at the sound of another familiar voice. Heath Cliffe was standing beside Derek, Dr. Kirkland's assistant, his arms crossed in front of him. Amusement filled his eyes, as if he knew she would react to his statement.

"Good morning," he greeted. "T. sent me down here to make sure you get up. She told me you have some interesting questions to ask our Number Nine."

Good old T. That was Heath's main job—asking questions. He was The Interrogator, the one who could break the obstinate ones. T. knew she would pique his interest if she brought up questioning Jed McNeil. After all, what interrogator would want to miss Jed McNeil avoiding questions? Besides that, Heath was the only one among the commandos interested in using the new serum. He would like to watch her as it entered her system. Drugs, questions, personality changes— these were subjects dear to Number Eight's heart.

"Are you awake, or are you remote viewing?"

"Funny," Helen managed to whisper, then groaned. "I feel like shit."

When she'd first experienced downtime—the aftereffect of a long RV session—she had likened it to being drunk. It wasn't unpleasant, because she mostly slept. The following days, her mind felt drained and her concentration was shot. She and the others in the program weren't allowed to drive afterwards.

However, the prolonged session with Hades had packed a wallop. She felt like she'd been in an Iron Man contest. Last night, she'd done something that someone her level shouldn't have been able to—gone off using two universal agreements and popping up all over the ether. *And she'd almost not come back.*

"You're staring into space again," Heath said quietly. "What do you want to do, Hell? Get up? Sleep? Your choice. Jed would want you to rest, of course, after what you've been through last night, but he's already up and about, all bright-eyed and bushy-tailed."

Hell's eyes widened sardonically at the "bright-eyed and bushy-tailed" remark. "That's the best you can do to get my competitive juices up?" Her voice sounded a little stronger. "Is he really up already? Ugh. Hey, Dr. K. Got my morning juice?"

Dr. Kirkland nodded, looking at her charts. "Everything was normal while you slept and everything looks good now. I'll let you take half the dosage this time. We'll see how your body adjusts to that."

"No late night hot tubbing in your near future," Heath said, a teasing reminder of their private encounter.

He really had the sexiest, meltiest puppy dog eyes. Helen pulled her sheet up to her chin, remembering the last time she'd made the mistake of getting into the hot tub in the training rooms naked, thinking no one was around at that late hour. Heath had shown up and almost trapped her there.

The glint in his eyes turned mischievous as he continued to watch her squirm. "It was getting too hot for you anyhow. I wonder whether you'll feel the same aftereffects the second time using the serum. What do you think, Dr. Kirkland?"

She sincerely hoped not, but there was no way to find out till afterwards. Dr. Kirkland obviously didn't know that Heath knew about her "problem" that came with using the new serum as he proceeded with the usual explanation.

"The serum's a bio-blocker, similar to what had been tested on certain pilots. It effectively removes the exhaustion that comes after remote viewing by manipulating one's chemical balance. You can look at the 'before and after' charts, if you like," he said. "When Helen is on it, she won't feel sleepy or tired. Remember she didn't feel any pain when she hurt her leg during the mission."

Thank God Dr. Kirkland omitted the fact that once the serum wore off, her body had reacted by overreacting. Whatever she'd been lacking in her chemical makeup, her body had decided to overcompensate. And she suspected that Heath already knew what her body was overcompensating because of their encounter in the hot tub. It took all her concentration not to cross her legs under the sheets.

"I'm ready, Dr. K.," she cut in, just in case Dr. Kirkland continued with too much information, keeping her eyes on Heath. She arched her brows at his knowing smile. "Give me enough so that I can stand up, brush my teeth, and make an intelligent report to my team, please. Also give me enough so my eyes are bright and my tail bushy too."

Dr. Kirkland and Derek laughed at her sarcastic joke. Heath just pulled up a chair and sat down, his attention intently on Dr. Kirkland now.

"That's what you should do to your avatar," Derek said, with an evil grin, as he pulled the IV tray to Helen's bedside. "Make Hades a squirrel."

Helen blinked at the sudden ludicrous image that popped up in her mind and then laughed. "That," she said, punching her pillow, "is a great idea. A giant squirrel yelling at me in virtual reality."

"Does he yell?" Heath asked, his head cocked.

She extended her arm out to Dr. Kirkland. "Well, I guess not," she replied. Yelling would make Jed McNeil human. "It's supposed to be funny, Heath, you know...a joke. Jed McNeil as a loud quarrelsome squirrel. Come on, lighten up."

"When the serum enters your system, do you find jokes like that funny?"

"What do you mean?"

"It's supposed to stop your feeling fatigue and pain. Does it stop you from laughing? Would the laughing Hell become all serious and boring?" Heath fingered the IV bag. "This stuff is supposed to be so potent, it's given to those on the war field to make them super soldiers."

"It blocks fatigue and pain, but I certainly didn't feel like I was the Terminator robot or something when I was on it." Helen tried to explain it, then shrugged. "It's a neuro-blocker, so it's deceptive. For example, it made me forget to drink liquids because I didn't feel thirsty, but that didn't mean my body wasn't thirsting for water. Alex was the one who brought that to my attention."

"I see."

The serum going in felt cold, then tingly. She felt it working. Already, the heavy tiredness was lifting. "You knew that, right, Heath? Didn't you try the first serum?"

A few of the commandos had been tested with the first version of the bio-serum, but Helen didn't know more than what Flyboy had told her. He had used it to test its effect on pilots, and he'd said he hadn't felt more than a rush.

"No, I didn't volunteer," Heath answered.

"Heath was allergic to a synthetic element in that serum," Dr. Kirkland explained, as he checked her pulse. He clicked on a little flashlight and Helen obediently lifted her head and looked up so he could shine the light into each eye. "Everything looks good. Now, remember your leg's still hurting from yesterday's incident even though you aren't feeling the pain. Please don't run and jump about and destroy all the work I put into getting it healed, Helen."

"Yes, Dr. K.," Helen said meekly. "It's only a meeting, all sitting around and talking."

"I heard there was a punching incident at a meeting yesterday," Dr. Kirkland said. "Maybe I should amend that to 'no wrestling matches' during meetings."

Helen turned to a grinning Derek. "Maybe I'll have Dr. K. stand beside me to protect me from the big bad squirrels in there."

Dr. Kirkland shook his head. "How am I ever going to get that image out of my head today?"

"It's going to be one big bad squirrel you have to worry about. He knows you're going to be there, all juiced-up," Heath reminded her, his dark eyes still assessing her. "I've a feeling he might want to know why you aren't resting."

Helen lifted her chin. "Let him try being a sexist at a team meeting," she announced. She felt wonderful, awake and ready for a fight. "Now let me get to my quarters and have a shower and some breakfast. We'll see who's bright-eyed and bushy-tailed then."

Of course, it wasn't quite fair that she needed some stupid bio-serum in her to be able to get out of bed and function like a normal human being, but she wasn't going to go into trivial details like that. The rush of energy this second time gave her an unexpected urge to do some spontaneous cartwheels, something she liked doing when she was an over-energetic child. She snuck a glance at the doctor...okay, she'd better not run or jump around. She needed her leg to work properly when she was off the serum.

"Crazy juice," she muttered, as she untangled her long legs from the sheets. It was already subtly working its odd magic. Usually, she'd stay under the covers till at least the room was clear of a few of the men. Right now, she didn't care. The serum made modesty feel unnecessary.

Heath got out of his chair. "Interesting to watch," he said, extending a hand to help her. "Now I'll have to be there when Armando uses the serum, see whether there's a difference."

Helen didn't make any objections. It was useless to point out that had she been a man, he wouldn't even have entertained the thought of her needing his help to hop out of bed. These dudes were just going to have to get used to having a woman doing field work with them.

Unlike Jed, Heath emanated a subtle strength. Whenever she was by Jed, she always felt a bit wary, as if a wild animal were somewhere inside him, waiting to eat her up. With those smiling eyes, Heath appeared like a helpful choir boy. But, she reminded herself, he was the trained interrogator. It was noteworthy how the serum was expanding her analytical skills.

"News travels fast around here. Does everyone know Armando secretly used the serum?"

"Only those who need to know," Heath said.

"Is he going to be punished?" she asked, curious. Jed hadn't seemed particularly angry when he confronted Armando yesterday. But he did give very specific orders about staying at Medic to be tested.

"Punishment?" Heath finally smiled. "We aren't in school, Hell. We don't punish bad behavior. Endangering one's team through bad decisions is the only thing that makes us lose our temper a little. No one wants to die from carelessness around here."

The man made jokes with subtle threats. Helen mentally shook her head. On one hand, she knew her normal self would be making a sarcastic remark right now. Instead, her mind was busy computing and analyzing Heath as if he was a target. Dang if the serum wasn't curbing her inner snark bunny.

Jed didn't look up. He sensed the moment Elena entered the conference room. She hadn't said a word, but he knew she was there. When he'd found out this morning that she was going to use the bio-serum, his initial reaction had been to countermand her decision. He'd stopped himself just in time, not only because he realized how extraordinary that move would seem to anyone, even to Dr. Kirkland, but also because his wanting to do so stemmed from personal reasons.

Preventing an operative from doing his or her job was alien to his nature. What Elena had decided to do made perfect sense as a responsible operative. The serum was to be used to alleviate the effects of remote viewing so she could perform her job at optimal capacity. She was the prime mover in their assignment; it was her right to be here to give a summary of what she'd seen during the remote-viewing session.

That he himself didn't like the idea of her using the serum so soon after the first dosage shouldn't be a reason to question her decision. But the image of that other remote viewer at Stratter's haunted him. While Elena had been watching the curled-up man on the bed, he'd scanned the room, noting the medical trays and the IV bags. The set-up looked awfully familiar. He didn't doubt that the CIA and other agencies had been testing their versions of a serum on their remote viewers; science and technology didn't remain a secret for long, especially with the speed of email and spying technology these days.

Those agencies were looking for their own super spy, and from this one instance, at least one remote viewer was negatively affected. Jed couldn't prove whether it was the serum, the strange encounter with Elena and Armando, or some other outside interference, but that man didn't look well at all.

He waited till she'd chosen her seat, listening for clues as he heard her greeting the others. She sounded pleasantly normal, but was she? He, as Number Nine, couldn't countermand another operative just because he was worried for her welfare now, could he?

"How are you feeling?" he asked, still writing.

"Bright-eyed and bushy-tailed."

Something inside Jed relaxed. That was a typical Elena smart-ass reply. He put down the pen and finally glanced up. He waited for the familiar thrum of desire that always kicked in whenever he looked at her. Having her around him in real life had only kicked up that in-the-gut feeling a notch.

There was something appealing to him about the way she always had messy hair. Even tied up, little wisps would escape, framing her face, hinting at the rebellious nature underneath. Right now it looked damp and spiky, as if she had been in a hurry.

She looked rested. The serum had also probably taken away the pain from her leg. There was a faint challenge in her body language, although her gaze was searching his coolly. He could think of several reasons, all of which were understandable, why she wanted to be here in person. She didn't want to be some member of a team only good at one thing. She was curious to hear his explanation of what had happened in the crate. She'd brought up Stratter's to T. because of the photo. He still wondered why he'd guided her to look for it on the wall. Maybe it was his perverse way of giving her a part of himself. His history at Stratter's Pointe wasn't something he shared with anyone.

The serum, he noted, had taken the edge off her anger. Knowing her, she should be frustrated by his manipulation of her mind and body all yesterday. Not that he had any regrets. He was honest enough to admit that he enjoyed every side of her. He had meant what he told her too, that in virtual reality, she was his, that he had to be the one in control. Last night, out there, when she was either hallucinating or seeing some kind of strange colors, he hadn't seen anything out of the ordinary. He must be careful not to push too much because Elena pushed herself hard enough. His hand curled tightly around his pen.

He'd nearly lost her. The force of the emotions that came with that thought shocked him.

"Hell, tell them the weapons you saw and each location, please."

Helen couldn't stop looking at him. In a room full of men, she was drawn to him and him only, and they hadn't even greeted each other yet. The idea that it might all be that trigger he'd put in her head nagged her.

She'd been prepared for some arrogant display from him, perhaps ordering her back to rest. Once again, he had surprised her by giving her center stage. His light eyes looked back at her coldly, his face stern and unsmiling. He was always light and playful when he was Hades, but out here, no such luck. Number Nine was all about work. She wasn't deceived. He wasn't happy she wasn't resting, even though he was choosing not to say anything about it.

"You experienced it firsthand," he continued, misreading her hesitance. "I'm here to confirm what was seen as well as point out the clues that pinpointed the locations."

He clicked on a small remote pad by his side. Each of their computer screens lit up. Helen looked at the images carefully.

"We saw a few on this list last night," she confirmed quietly, still a bit wary that he was letting her run the show. "We tried changing the universal agreement midway during the RV session, and it worked."

"Do we really have the exact locations?" Sullivan asked, impressed. He took a large swallow from the largest coffee cup she'd ever seen.

Helen shook her head in answer. She'd only been to two of these debriefings. She wasn't sure how much these guys—her team, she corrected—understood about the ins-and-outs of remote viewing.

They've all been testing you in their own way these past months, Hell. They knew about RV and all experiments you and Jed were undergoing.

"Sully, your caffeine's not working. Exact isn't a term used in remote viewing," Flyboy said.

"We were pretty good the last mission," Sullivan pointed out. "I mean, Hell was. Heck, she made every one of those department heads sit up when she gave the exact location *and* proved them right by coming back with the decoder."

"I think it might have made a few of them determined to get the same results at their agencies," Jed said. "Continue, Hell."

She was slightly amused that he'd never called her Hell except during a meeting. Maybe the serum was making her more analytical about what he'd done to her. Instead of anger and resistance, she was able to sort of understand him—she was Elena in private, Helen in formal situations, and Hell in the team. Jed McNeil seemed to relate to her differently at different times. She found that odd and sexy at the same time. It made her feel as if he didn't see her the same as the others.

"I find remote viewing specific only in certain details, Agent Sullivan," she said. "The previous mission gave very obvious clues. Foreign language usage, among other things."

"Perhaps we can only up our remote-viewing percentage with foreign locales," Armando suggested. "Like a worldwide game of hide-and-seek."

"Isn't that what this entire mission has been?" Jed asked. "Everything on our list is spread all over the world and hidden by different hands. I believe you're familiar with how the weapons game's played, Armando, seeing that you moved them around for your family at one time."

Armando smiled humorlessly. "Yes, I'm extremely good at making things disappear."

"Things don't just disappear. They're hidden," Jed countered softly, "but we'll get back to that in a bit."

Helen looked down at her notebook. Armando was in trouble, all right. In spite of what Heath had told her about punishment being for school, she had a feeling Jed had his ways of reining in those around him.

"Let me just start from the beginning," she said. She gave a brief account of the first place, the bars in the windows, and the person curled up on the bed surrounded by the doctor and two other men. She told them that she recognized the man as one of her few rivals during the inter-department contest for SSS. "Since we were looking for my attacker and my bilocation led me to him, it's a fair assumption that this man is being used as a remote viewer by another group to either spy on us or take me down."

"The first attack on Hell in Munich," Flyboy interrupted. "I traced that van to a CIA ID, remember?"

"It's CIA," confirmed Jed. "I'll get more into the details in a few minutes. Go on, Hell."

Helen then described how she and Jed decided to try jumping locations by adopting the other remote viewer's universal agreement. "It seems that his handlers are more ambitious because I kept bilocating from one place to another instead of returning to Hade...Jed back in the Portal." She paused. "I know it all sounds like bad science fiction, all this jumping from one location to another. I didn't even know it could be done. During training, my CIA monitor told me that multiple universal agreements weren't conducive to operations because most viewers become spatially confused. In other words, the more times one bilocates during a session, the more the brain is deceived that what the viewer is going through is real."

"That's why your vitals were fluctuating so wildly," Shahrukh said. "Even after the one time when you stopped breathing, your readings were never truly stable. The only reason Dr. Kirkland never shut it down was because Jed's remained steady after that one incident."

Helen shrugged. "Well, my monitor wasn't having his brain served with a side of Twilight Zone crazy."

They chuckled at her attempt at nonchalance. She couldn't tell, from a quick glance at Jed's direction, whether he found that amusing too.

"When I bilocated that second time, I landed in total darkness. Normally, I'm not afraid of the dark, but this was also in a confined space and it took...ah...a little adjustment, shall I say, before I realized that I was inside a crate, or rather, my bilocated self was. My brain was totally deceived and Jed had to help me out of my initial panic. It was a very uncomfortable feeling, to sum it mildly. Even though physically you aren't there, bilocation is so real to the brain that you feel the tight confines of being in a crate. I had to keep reminding myself that I wasn't really there, that I could do physically impossible things."

"Yeah, I can relate," Flyboy said. "The newest experiments with virtual reality in flight simulation are so real that some pilots got air sick when they tried top warp speed."

"That's exactly how it affects me in the Portal," Jed agreed. "What Helen was seeing and experiencing in her remote viewing, I was able to experience as if I was going through a virtual reality simulation, except that, with our form of deep immersion techniques, Hell and I have found a way to communicate while she's doing her thing. And yes, I felt the trapped feeling of being locked in a small space, just as she did."

The others were intently listening.

"But why did you both stop breathing at the same time?" T. asked. "I know training should have prevented you from panicking so quickly in the dark or being locked up. That's just so not like you, darling."

"Maybe I have agoraphobia," Jed said, amusement creeping into his voice.

"Do you?" T. challenged. "Did that make you lose control?"

"Our brainwaves are in sync during immersive RV, remember," Helen said, not sure why she felt the need to defend Jed. "My believing that I was being buried alive triggered the panic attack, which then brought on a similar experience for him. Jed realized quickly what was happening and brought me out of it."

"So you both sensed each other's feelings too. How incredibly interesting," T. observed. She looked pleased, as if she'd finally gotten an answer to some question.

Helen could see her operation chief's mind racing with obvious questions. What other things did Jed and she share? The others had the same expressions she'd seen on their faces a time or two—disbelief, discomfort, intrigue, paranoia.

"It's not a constant thing. It was just this one-time experience, probably because it was totally unexpected." She looked around. "RV isn't about reading minds, even though I teased you guys about it. It isn't as simple as that. As humans, I believe we automatically block our thoughts off from each other anyway, but during an unguarded moment, certain safeguards get knocked out temporarily."

"Like a psychic crash," Armando said suddenly, leaning forward. "Listen to this theory. In the hallway yesterday, if indeed there was a remote viewer and somehow we both became aware of his presence, and if it was that man you saw on the bed, he first crashed into you in Munich, but this time, I crashed into him."

"Well, actually, you crashed into me," Hell reminded him, pointing down at her leg.

"Yes, but I had to run into—okay, through him first—before crashing into you." He frowned. "All I know is the pain in my head was suddenly unbearable and then—" he gestured with his hand, as if he was performing a magic act, "—run, run, run, my mind said. Before I knew it, I was running to where you and Jed were standing. I knew something was there. I don't know how, but I did."

"Good theory," Jed said. "We have many questions about that incident which we can't answer now. We have certain weapons that need to be located first. Sieve these questions through the back of your mind while we work on our more immediate concerns.

"One, why did they send their remote viewer here? Was it to attack Hell again, or for something else? Two, why was it part of his universal agreement if he was also looking for weapons? It's the third question that is most relevant to the motivation behind all this. That certain elements in the CIA are involved isn't in doubt here, but if they were the same people who stole the weapons from right under the government's nose in the first place, how come they don't know where they are now? Why are they racing us to get to each item?"

Helen jotted down the questions. Jed in computational mode was formidable to behold. She couldn't help but admire how he could take each clue and work it into the big picture. The conference/debriefing could have descended into a long discussion about science fiction, remote viewing and psychic attacks, but with a few questions, Jed had led it all back to the mission. It was true, whether there was anything woo-woo going on or not, certain CIA rogue operatives were after the same specific weapons that were on the list.

"There is an endgame to this. We need to focus on how these weapons are connected. The decoder card is nothing without other weapons. The people at Deutsche International were trying to break its code for a reason." Jed clicked his remote, enlarging each item as he mentioned them. "The explosive device trigger was in that crate because Hell saw Croatian words on the side of it. We already know this, though, because that was the last out-shipment the CIA dropped while Gorman was in charge. Gorman knew it was there, so why not these CIA moles?"

"I wish there was a more definitive way to confirm all this," Sullivan growled. His large hand curled around his mug. "Much as I don't want to spoil our confidence in this remote-viewing shit, a crate with Croatian words on the outside doesn't mean it was in Croatia or Macedonia or wherever else they speak that language."

"I would have been very surprised if you didn't question my certainty about this," Jed said. His light eyes had the spark of a man who was certain about his facts. "Last night, I double checked with Eight Ball and confirmed that the numbers I saw on the side of the crate belonged to the same shipment number sent out in the drone as relief aid. Also, there's another very important piece of proof Hell can produce herself."

Helen blinked. That was the first she heard of any proof. She cocked her head at Jed.

"Tell them what you heard before you bilocated again."

Realization dawned. "I heard a woman's voice. She was barely discernible, but I think she was calling a name. Cameron?"

T.'s startled reaction caught Helen's attention. "A woman?" T. asked, exchanging glances with Jed. "As in Patty and Cam?"

"You know a Cameron? And the woman too?" Helen questioned. She bit her lower lip. "She was locked in the crate and someone was beating the heck at the side of it. It's...Jed, I told you he was talking like an American...was that this Cam?"

Jed nodded. "Some of you were at that vault fire at the CIA HQ not long ago, helping then Task Force II O.C., Rick Harden, to rescue our Nikki. Cameron Candelaro and Patty Ostler, who worked under him, disappeared that night. Word was, their bodies were dumped into two of the crates being shipped out that night. Sullivan, Hell has never met either Cam or Patty Ostler and doesn't know the back story."

He knew, and hadn't said a word.

Sullivan scratched the back of his ear. "Wow," was all he said. He then gave a male shrug, as if that was good enough for now.

"But that was months ago. If she were still in the crate, she'd be dead by now. How do you explain that?"

Hell frowned. "Months ago? She was definitely alive during my RV session." She thought for a moment. A mental snap. "The second universal agreement. It was where the weapons were dropped, not where they are now, so what I saw was at the point in time those weapons arrived at their location."

"So not necessarily the current location," Shahrukh said.

Jed nodded, his expression thoughtful. "But we're close to the trigger. Since our SEAL contact is working on retrieving that item, we'll wait till I talk to him. Next, we have the location of the missing Stealth. Shahrukh, you're going to retrieve what's left of it. It may not be at the same location, but a Stealth isn't difficult to trace when we have a general location."

"Wait a minute—" Flyboy sat up, an indignant look on his face. "The Stealth's mine."

"It's in Kurd country. And he might have to travel through Pakistan to retrieve it. Shahrukh would be able to go in and out of those places better than a blond blue-eyed hotshot, Flyboy."

"There's always another way," Flyboy objected heatedly. "No one's playing with a Stealth without me."

"Stealth parts, Flyboy," Shahrukh corrected. "There wouldn't be much left of it for you to fly."

"I don't—"

"You two can discuss this later," Jed interrupted, "although I'd prefer that you handle Project X-S Bot, Number Five. It's flight simulation and nano-technology, something you're familiar with."

Flyboy scowled. "Give me the file. But that doesn't mean I'm dropping the Stealth discussion, Rukh. Even if I have to fight you with a sword for it."

"That'd be a stupid bet," Shahrukh said, white teeth showing.

Helen couldn't help grinning. Testosterone overload was so fun to watch.

T. winked at her and rolled her eyes.

"Alex, I know your plate's already full with Maximillian Shoggi. I think we need to talk about setting him up with the decoder. Thanks to us, he's already lost out on several important weapon bids. He's a very hungry arms dealer at the moment."

Alex's eyes glittered. "That'd be a pleasure." He turned to T. "Time to get back into your Tasha skin, isn't it? Mad Max thinks you're his link to me."

T. tapped her fingers on the table before turning to Jed. "Evil." She examined her nails. "I think I should be the one going after the Stealth parts."

Helen watched with growing amusement when both Alex and Jed didn't spare her a glance, as if the whole thing was settled. That was so not the way to get T. to cooperate.

"Armando," Jed said, his gaze catching Helen's. She saw the knowing gleam there. "You're going to go undercover at the same place where that remote viewer is. It's a place called Stratter's Pointe."

"What, a quest for which no one will fight me?" Armando asked sardonically.

His mask of bored attentiveness was back in place. Helen hid her smirk. That earlier outburst, though, had already betrayed him. Armando was more eager than he let on. His explanation about the pain disappearing made her question her own reaction to "crashing" into the remote viewer. She'd like to ask him later if he'd felt the odd sensation when it'd happened. Another question occurred. How were Armando's bouts with pain connected to her own unique reaction? Using the chemical imbalance theory, she'd been sexually deprived the last few years, and her body overcompensated, so what was Armando's "chemical" problem?

When no one answered him, Armando continued, in a faux accent, "No send the Asian to no exotic places? No illusion with simulation? No rescuing the maiden in a locked box? I get...a prison ward?"

"It's not just any prison ward. A section of Stratter's Pointe is for political prisoners, which your background would suit nicely. If they check, they'll see that you're connected to the Triads. The other section of Stratter's is actually something you'll find interesting." Jed pushed a file toward his direction. "I was once there, a long time ago, and I met a few people who helped give me some direction. Read up on this place and we'll talk about your next assignment."

Smooth. So smooth. Helen knew exactly what he was doing. It was NOPAIN at its best, manipulation without force. She recalled Jed saying something about him convalescing at that place, but the old photograph on the wall showed him so young. What could he have been recovering from at that age? Stratter's Pointe didn't look like a hospital, although it felt like a medical place in that new wing. Another reason to get to talk to Armando privately. She wanted to look at that file sitting in front of him.

"Political prisoners—like someone who was a captured operative?" Helen asked. She wanted to draw T.'s attention to it. There was so much about this man she didn't know and she didn't think he was going to volunteer more information than necessary. She wanted more from him. "What did you do when you were there?"

There was one of those pauses before he answered. She could feel him withdrawing into himself. He was a hard man to read, with that impassive expression honed, no doubt, from years of sidestepping and evading direct questions.

"Stratter's Pointe was actually my first U.S. home," Jed finally said. "I was at a military hospital healing from some wounds before that and was brought to Stratter's for the rest of my therapy. It was a state medical facility for those injured during active duty who needed a place to disappear to after emergency hospitalization. It still is, but I suppose it's expanded its use. Since Armando has been using the SYMBIOS 2 serum, he's somewhat familiar with the drug. I'm suspecting they're experimenting with similar serums with their remote viewers, and putting our own man inside can find out more." He turned, the intensity in those silver eyes pinning. "You and Armando have bouts of pain. This man too. I think it's all connected. Once we figure out why, we can understand more about these 'psychic crashes', Armando called them."

It was disconcerting how he echoed her own thoughts. Every time she tried to corner him, get him defensive, he'd surprise her by giving in to her. She really hated that.

"Then not send me in there?" Helen asked, knowing the answer, but she was spoiling for a fight. "What will I be doing?"

The way he kept looking at her made her feel like one of those caught butterflies about to be put in a relaxing jar. Couldn't fly away. Going to be pinned. Her heart was thudding even though she knew nothing was showing on her face. At least, she hoped not.

"You're coming with me to the summit, of course, supersoldier-spy. But only if you take the mandatory rest after an RV session. That means no strenuous activity, Hell, for the next two days while prep work's being done. Go home."

Those were fighting words. If she weren't feeling ridiculously pleased with having one-upped him by attending the debriefing, she'd have blown a gasket. But he'd given her some answers, even handed her the reins for a little while, and dammit, she was actually beginning to get why he was acting this way.

It was Jed McNeil's way of saying he was sorry for what he did last night.

"Okay. But I think I should be the one to retrieve the Stealth parts, boys. Pakistan and Kurds? I bet they're into female commandos."

Quiet chuckles rumbled around the table. She'd surprised all the men with her apparent meekness. After all, they all had big assignments, and she was given nothing. She batted her eyes innocently. She doubted they were buying her act.

"Prepare for the Summit in Skopje with Number Eight. Something's going down there, and of course, I'd want a well-rested supersoldier-spy there with me as my companion."

Did every woman react to him like she did? Because that sounded very sexy to her ears. And she wasn't going *off* the damn serum yet, so why was she suddenly turned on at the thought of being with him as a stupid companion?

Chapter Seventeen

Lake Matka, Macedonia

Jed hadn't kept in touch, wanting to give Elena space, while he looked over the last-minute details of the trip to Macedonia. He'd told Dr. Kirkland to hold the brainwave experiments for the next few days.

He already knew she'd reported another migraine two days ago, after she went home. Dr. Kirkland had talked to her via videophone. She didn't want any painkillers. He didn't blame her; he wouldn't want any more drugs in his system either. Even while he made several phone calls, his mind had been on her, wondering whether she was truly resting, or not. He knew that Flyboy had asked her out to dinner. Jed'd had to fly ahead to Europe and didn't know whether she'd accepted the date.

Why would it bother him if she did? From watching their interactions—with their in-jokes and flirtations—Jed had an idea how well the two of them got along. It was only logical; Flyboy was closer to Helen's age than he was, and no doubt, more fun to be around.

He impatiently waved at nothing in particular. He couldn't let his mind wander away every time something reminded him of her. She would be here soon enough. By his side. Where she belonged.

That last sentence slithered into Jed's consciousness and sat there a half-second, like a deadly snake watching its prey before it struck. *Where she belonged.* It was a clichéd statement, one that came naturally with the claim before it. It was something he didn't think he'd ever uttered, even to himself. The shock of it made him pause in the middle of tying the shoelaces on his hiking boots.

He had practically grown up alone. Having someone by his side had never been an option, not even when he'd found his daughter and brought her into his life. He protected those he loved and cared for with the knowledge that distance—physical and emotional—was the best policy.

What he was, what he did for a living, wasn't exactly conducive to open relationships. His daughter was the only person who had the innate ability to understand this, who had given him what he asked for and no more. He hadn't hidden what he was ever since she was old enough to ask questions. Grace was different, anyhow. Running around with her mother for a couple years had robbed her of any sweet innocence. By the time they'd met, his little girl had already developed an instinct honed from having spent too much time around danger and dangerous people. He'd recognized it immediately because he still remembered what it was like growing up in Dublin.

He finished tying the laces and straightened up. Through the years, emotional distance had cost him relationships, some of which he regretted ending. But one couldn't take a life one night and talk about normal things the next. Unlike his daughter, much as his companions knew this as part of his job, in the end, they were unable to live with it. He'd accepted it. He wasn't in a position to change, not without causing major havoc. A part of him also acknowledged that as an excuse.

And here he was, wanting a woman by his side, during a mission that was usually a one-man operation. Where was the total focus, the absolute separation from all things emotional? Intimate words like "where she belonged" didn't exist at a time like this.

"Elena Ekaterina Rostova," he rolled her name—the one he preferred—off his tongue softly, "you've invaded my waking life too, it seems."

The hike up the side of the steep path helped his concentration. Half an hour away from Skopje, Lake Matka was the perfect spot for a private meeting during the week, when visitors were few. And if an accidental death did occur, it wouldn't make the news as one might if it happened in Skopje, where the international media was starting to gather.

The old monastery was deserted at this hour. He turned left, and then another left, heading toward the furthest window, which was so old and stained, one couldn't look outside. He sat on the bench under the old tapestry, waiting in the shadows.

Fifteen minutes passed before he heard footsteps. He'd begun to wonder whether anyone would show up. Sometimes they didn't come. Sometimes they ran away. He sat, waited, and watched the man skulking down the passageway, coming toward the opaquely lit area. He sat on the other side of the bench.

"I do not like being kept waiting," Jed said, affecting the slight accent Europeans had when they spoke English.

"Hiking in the early morning is not easy for me," the man said, rubbing his hands hard. "Are you sure we're alone?"

"We are safe," Jed said. "Do you have the package, Dimitri?"

Dimitri put his hand inside his long coat, then became very still when he realized Jed was already standing behind him, one warning hand on his shoulder.

"No, no gun, Stefan. I have the package inside my coat pocket. Feel it yourself."

"Take it out slowly and hand it over your shoulder." When he complied, Jed took it with his free hand. His hand didn't leave the other man's shoulder. "Do you know why your boss sent you to pass this information to me?"

He could feel Dimitri trembling. The man wasn't a fool. He knew.

"I'm his most trusted man," Dimitri said, his voice a little high pitched.

"I almost believe you," Jed murmured. "Do you know, though, he has a habit of sending me people he wants to get rid of? It's a business arrangement. He gives me what I want, and I dispense with what he does not want."

"If I believed that, I would not be here, would I?" Dimitri asked, this time unable to hide his nervousness. "I did not run. I came here, just as I was told, and delivered the package."

"Yes. A trained mouse follows the maze over and over, looking for its reward. You knew they would find you anyway, so you did everything exactly as you were told to get a reprieve."

"I also have the hope that you want some useful answers, Stefan."

"And there is that." Jed counted a beat of two. "Tell me, Dimitri, I'm assuming that you are a clever curious mouse. What is in the package?"

"Deutsche International's contact that gave them the SEED decoder. The minutes of the last private meeting. I assure you, D.I. just wants world peace. Why do you think we have so many famous politicians and people funding it?"

The last bit was delivered with sarcasm. Deutsche International's front as a world forum to find answers to political strife had drawn quite a unique following consisting of some of the wealthiest and most well-known people in the world—one happy union of politicians, rock stars, peaceniks, intellectuals, geniuses, actors. A think-tank for change. But underneath it all, a market place, as all such places usually became.

"Now tell me," Jed said, "what is not in the package?"

"They are in contact with a man named Gunther. I don't know who he is but I do know he wields a lot of power behind the old guard."

"The old guard," Jed repeated slowly. "As in the Old Guard from the Soviet system?"

"There is only one old guard. Gunther promised D.I. the support of many noted politicians for a new peace movement if his terms were met." There was a pause. "One of these terms has to do with the coming Skopje Summit."

"Something is about to happen," Jed said. "What?"

"That I do not know, but there is an agreement, that D.I. will not unleash its usual verbal attack and crowd disorders, at least not in a meaningful way, once it is over."

"I want something more substantial than that, Dimitri," Jed said icily. "It is your life, after all. Vagueness does not please me."

Jed felt Dimitri tremble again at the quiet menace in his voice as the latter tried to decide whether to talk more or bargain. The man's breathing was erratic and Jed knew the outcome even before he spoke. It wasn't unexpected. Fear for one's life was always conducive to loosen a stubborn tongue.

"I really do not know." Dimitri squeaked as Jed applied slight pressure on his shoulder. The words came out faster. "It is big. The politicians will be affected. Stefan, I have been kept out of their loop in this matter. Please. All I know is...it has to do with the summit itself, the agenda, and D.I. will somehow benefit afterwards. You have everything I know—Gunther and D.I.'s involvement. Please!"

It was time to finish his end of the bargain. The silence stretched as Dimitri sat there, seemingly frozen in fear. He had nowhere to run to anyway. He had known, coming here, that this was his last courier stop.

Jed looked up. Morning light was filtering into the monastery.

"What did you do?" he finally asked. He'd never asked before. It complicated matters to get personal.

"It was stupid, okay? I slept with the boss's wife. And then one day, he came home early with someone I shouldn't have seen."

Jed blinked. Wasn't he just thinking about emotional distance? That the inability to do so led to one's downfall?

"Was it worth it? The sex?" he mused aloud.

Dimitri shrugged. "She was a lonely woman. Look, I was not thinking. Are you going to kill me or not? It is not right, sitting here in a place like this, talking calmly about sex and women when my life is at stake."

Jed cracked a smile at that bit of bravado. He looked down at the top of the man's head. From where he stood, it would be a simple matter to break his neck, a swift and relatively clean way to cancel a life.

He dropped his hand. "Go," he ordered quietly.

Dimitri stiffened. He jumped to his feet and whirled around to stare at Jed.

"Just like that? Do you not want to know who I saw?"

Jed studied the shadowy face, the panic receding just a little. "Keep something for a later bargain with me, Dimitri. I might not feel so generous in the future." He cocked a brow. "Now, before I change my mind..."

The man didn't need a second prompting. Without another word, he turned, stumbled, then ran.

Helen took in a deep breath. The chilly air helped clear her head. She took a long look at the lone figure standing at the edge of the cliff, the magnificent scenery of the morning sunlight dappling the wintry mountainside and the ice-tipped lake emphasizing his dangerous aloofness. He had his back to her, seemingly absorbed in the view, but she knew better. He was certainly as aware of her presence here as he had been back at the monastery.

He looked terribly alone, like an ancient conqueror surveying his land. A ridiculous thought, since Jed McNeil was in faded jeans and battered jacket. *But that was beside the point, wasn't it, Hell?* Jed McNeil in any kind of clothing, speaking in that emotionless tone of voice, was the scariest thing she'd seen and heard in a long time.

He turned. And gestured imperiously. Helen approached cautiously. One did that at the sight of a hungry predator.

He stood as still as the waters below as she studied him. It dawned on her that he was waiting for her to make the first move, to show her reaction.

After all, he'd looked directly at her in the darkened monastery, a piercing stare that had jolted her out of the mesmerizing sight of Number Nine in action.

As usual, her foolhardiness took over. "Should I curtsey? Your Lordship commanded my presence at Lake Matka a day early and here I am."

The corner of his lips lifted. His silver eyes, though, still held that disquieting menace. "You didn't come at the specified time."

Helen canted her brows. "No pleasing Your Lordship, is there?" She thumbed toward the trail from which she'd just came. "Back there, you complained about a man being late, and here, you aren't happy that I'm early." When he didn't say anything, just stood there looking at her, she sighed, and added, "Okay, you said noon. Perhaps you didn't want me around when you were doing your job, but I didn't know you had an assignment this early. I would have sat in there waiting for noon but seeing that you knew I was already hiding in there, I figured you wouldn't mind me interrupting your morning walk."

She hadn't actually come out immediately. A man on the verge of violence was better left alone for as long as possible. But damn, it was cold sitting in that monastery, not doing anything.

Jed turned from her again. The view appeared more interesting to him than her presence. Her instincts were telling her that this man was literally at the very edge, that if she wasn't careful, he might turn and devour her. Yet, she didn't feel afraid of him at all. She took the last few steps so she could stand beside him.

"Tell me, Number Nine," she began casually, trying to push away the image of herself putting her head inside a lion's mouth, "why didn't you finish the job?"

He slanted a glance in her direction, the lightness in his eyes catching the sunlight—a flash of silver heat—and then he looked away again.

"I know what your job entails," Helen continued, ignoring another mental image of herself offering honey to a hungry bear. What could she say? She was curious. "Back there, I know what you were going to do. Yet you didn't. You looked straight up where I was and I felt you changing your mind. You gave that man a reprieve, something I'd bet my entire hat collection that you seldom, if ever, do. Why, Jed?"

There. If he turned and growled at her, she would retreat and leave him alone. The silence went on for so long, she began to wonder whether he was just going to ignore her till noon.

"I didn't want to start our day with your seeing me take a life." He turned and met her shocked eyes. "I didn't want our first date to begin with death."

Helen put her hand on her chest. The world just stopped spinning. "Our. First. Date?"

"Yes, our first date," Jed reiterated calmly. "It was supposed to start here at noon. Not at the monastery where you were hiding, spying on me. You were thinking of catching a glimpse of the real me. Are you sure you did?"

"Our first date?" Helen asked again, ignoring the rest of what he said. "I thought I was here to be part of the team casing the summit."

"In Skopje," Jed affirmed. "You're here at Lake Matka to be with me."

"You didn't ask, so it isn't a date," she declared.

Jed laughed. She stood there in amazement as she watched him throw back his head and real, teeth-baring, amusement-filled male laughter echoed around her. It was a low, attractive sound, the kind that made a woman feel all glowy and appreciated inside. That murderous glint in his eyes had disappeared, replaced by an intent that was pretty blatant in its meaning, at least, from where she was standing. She realized he had dropped that mantle of aloofness behind which he always hid.

"Would you like to spend today with me?" he asked, with a smile that made her toes curl in her boots and made her notice the deep dimple in his chin. Her gaze moved up and was captured by the look in his eyes—so very arrogantly sure. "It's just you and me. No virtual reality, Elena. No simulated scenery. No one monitoring our vitals. We won't be in the ether or playing mind games today. If you like, our date starts right here, right now."

Dammit. How could a girl refuse that? He had deliberately engineered a free day in his busy schedule to be with her. He had backed away from doing his job because he didn't want to start their date with a death. He had, once again, managed to take her by surprise.

"Okay," she said, and put her hand in his. "But only because you asked so nicely, instead of ordering me around."

She knew that the commandos were trained seducers. Lord, if he used that smile as part of his seduction repertoire, the women had no hope.

"So now we'll start it right," he said, pulling her into the circle of his arms.

His dark head descended and his lips parted hers. He kissed with a thoroughness that had her clinging to him, pulling his head lower. His heat took away all the chill in the air.

He had kissed her before, but not like this. His tongue danced across hers, a possessive entanglement that he controlled, pulling away and making her mindlessly chase after, wanting more, needing more. He tilted her head back for better access, his thumb stroking her quickening pulse, as his tongue lazily invaded and explored.

She was heady with his scent, a delicious mix of man, cologne and lust. She felt his hand under her jacket, seeking and pulling at her sweater, and then she was lost in the feel of his hand cupping her breast.

When he lifted his lips from her, she gave a soft mewl of protest. Not yet. She wanted more.

"Was that real enough for you?" he asked.

As if her ragged breathing wasn't indicative enough? She closed her eyes as teasing fingers massaged and caressed sensitive flesh. "It seems real," she said, feigning a nonchalance that was betrayed by a moan. "But then, you can turn me on without VR, remember?"

That he'd planted a sexual trigger inside her head would always be between them. She wasn't stupid. The man was just going to embed it deeper in her consciousness, especially if she was willing. And she was pitifully aware that she was very willing indeed at that moment.

His hand stilled, but he continued to cup her breast possessively. "That's why we're going to do a bit of sightseeing today," he mocked. "Just so you know it's not all about sex."

"Oh yeah? And what do you propose we do this early? Hiking is so unromantic, Jed."

"We can take a boat out on the lake. Check out the dam. Talk."

She considered for a few moments. A date with Jed McNeil. She had wanted to get to know the man better, hadn't she? No file in any agency could give her a better insight than the real thing. She grinned and pulled his hand from under her sweater.

"Okay," she agreed. "Bet you can't keep up with me."

She was sure he'd been there before, but he let her set the pace, following her down the steep path toward the dam. The canyon was just breathtaking to look at and she wished she'd brought a camera. There was a mountain hut near the gorge and they ate a simple breakfast there before hiring a row boat.

The sun, the lake, the quiet bobbing of the boat set the mood. She felt absolutely comfortable with him, just talking, exchanging jokes. This was a side of him she doubted many people saw, and she wondered privately why he was allowing her in.

They crossed the lake and explored the seventeenth century church built on the plateau. At one point, he held her hand as they examined the faded frescos, his fingers lightly playing with the fleshy mound under her thumb, while he pointed out little details of the painted scene. He compared them with other similar frescos he'd seen in other cathedrals. Again, he surprised her with his knowledge about art. That he was well traveled didn't come as a surprise, but she hadn't thought he would be the artsy-fartsy type. She found herself enjoying this man very much.

They drove to Lake Ohrid in the afternoon. Feeling the effects of jetlag, Helen nodded off. When she opened her eyes, they were outside a hotel.

"We're Mr. and Mrs. Jones, if you need to sign anything to the room," Jed said.

He was giving her that look again and her heart was waking up before she did. "Can't you be a bit more imaginative?" she complained. "Mr. and Mrs. Jones?"

He looked more relaxed than she'd ever seen as he pulled out a small travel bag from the trunk. His hair was tousled. He had tied a scarf loosely around his neck. She suddenly wanted to kiss him again. Except for holding hands, he hadn't touched her all day, making a point, and building a slow fire inside her with his long looks and smiles.

"American tourists, Elena, unless you prefer Frau and Herr Schnitzel."

Helen laughed, following him inside. It didn't take long before they were alone in a beautiful and tastefully decorated little room. She was glad it wasn't impersonal, like most luxury hotel rooms. Jed had certainly planned this to the last detail, making everything memorable.

"Hungry?" he asked.

She shook her head. "Later."

She backed away teasingly, wagging a finger at him. He followed leisurely.

"Room service, then," he said, pulling off his sweater. "You know, we've never done that before."

"What?"

"Eat after making love."

She caught her breath. Coughed. He just didn't do subtle, did he?

"Are you nervous?" he asked, amused. He came closer, his hands on his belt. "I promise I won't use it."

There, he'd brought it up, the thing that hung between them. She watched him pull the belt, and her mouth went dry when he reached for the top button of his jeans.

"But as long as you have the power, I won't always be totally comfortable," she pointed out. "Or totally trust you."

He nodded. "I know."

"But you aren't going to remove it, are you?"

"No. I can only promise I won't use it tonight."

"Why?" How could she be sure he wasn't just playing a game, using her attraction for him, just to deepen the trigger?

"Because I want to prove what you're feeling for me isn't my doing. It's more than that. I want you for yourself too."

He wasn't an easy man to deal with one-on-one. Up close and personal, in an intimate setting, she felt the full sensual force of his masculine determination. The sexual charge of a man desiring a woman, taking his clothes off slowly, teasingly, using everything in his power to seduce—everything he'd cloaked from her in public had dropped away. The sound of his zipper brought her attention lower. He was so sure of getting his way with everything.

"You...you like to negotiate." Helen licked her dry lips. "What I want is total control of you this time. You manipulate me enough in VR and RV, Jed. Let me take back some of that power in real life. What do you say?"

For a heartbeat she thought he was going to refuse. Then his hand dropped to his sides. His silver eyes were brilliant gems in his tanned face. He nodded.

"You don't have to use NOPAIN, Elena. I'm all yours."

Helen smiled slowly. She was so going to enjoy making him pay for all those past torments.

Chapter Eighteen

Helen eyed the man standing in front of her approvingly. He really looked good in jeans, especially shirtless. She walked around him slowly, drinking in the sight of a man perfectly conditioned by years of discipline, the tan skin marked with nicks and scars.

He didn't say anything as she circled, just as she'd done in virtual reality the first time they'd met. Except this time, she was checking out the real person behind the programmed avatar.

She frowned at the sight of the mesh of criss-crossed patterns on his back. They held a story of their own. Reaching out, she tenderly touched the scars. They were very old, muted shades, mere marks that hinted of the violence that had left them there.

"These aren't recent." Her voice was hushed. "How did you get them?"

"From a whip," he replied, giving the obvious answer.

So, he wasn't ready to tell her. She didn't push. She understood that he'd lived a life of violence and didn't like sharing the details. It didn't stop her from feeling angry at whomever it was that had scarred him so permanently.

She leaned forward and kissed him between the shoulder-blades, smiling at the slight betrayal of tensing muscles under her lips. She used the tip of her tongue to trace down his spine, tasting him, her palms moving down the length of his strong back as she lowered herself.

"Take them off," he said, when she reached the top of his jeans that were slung low and tempting on his hips.

Helen shook her head. "Quit giving me orders," she reprimanded, even as she tugged.

"I wasn't ordering. I was just suggesting."

The man had an awesome ass. She stepped back and naughtily gave a wolf whistle. Okay, she liked him out of those jeans too. She retraced her steps and he just stood there, letting her take her time.

God-in-jeans naked. All golden skinned and lean taut muscles. She couldn't resist the temptation any longer. Reaching out, she shaped the wide shoulders, palmed the hard biceps and chest, smoothed over one plum-colored nipple, and finally reached the rippling abs. He was hot to the touch, all hard muscle over powerful bone structure. Her fingers trailed the line of dark hair that arrowed lower and then boldly, she circled the waiting erection.

She looked up teasingly. "Alas, Hades, it's not as big as I'd imagined."

His dimple was entrancing this close. His eyes smiled back, even as his expression betrayed none of the eagerness of the hard flesh in her hand. How had she ever missed those incredible lashes? But then, she'd always been mesmerized by the light color of his eyes and never really looked closely at them.

"I won't disappoint." His voice, she noted with satisfaction, sounded husky.

"So sure?"

"Yes."

"How long can you last, I wonder?"

There was nothing modest about his slow, answering smile at all. She could feel herself getting wet. A challenge lurked in his eyes, daring her to continue. Oh, she dared. She had his word that he'd remain passive.

Batting her eyes, she backed toward the bed. "Let's see you on your back, with your hands over your head. You can't move, just like when I couldn't when I took those damn pills of yours."

"But I'm perfectly willing to lie still for your ministrations," he pointed out, as he did as she instructed. "Now take off your clothes and torture me with your naked body."

That made Helen laugh. He was purposely mocking her with simple NOPAIN. He was too damn good at this game.

The sweater was too hot anyhow. He lay there watching her as she did a provocative striptease, enjoying the way he looked at her with undisguised desire. Usually, during a first time with a new lover, she'd feel awkward and unsure of what her partner wanted from her. But after all these months, knowing that he'd watched her naked, having shared his sexual dreams, she felt extremely comfortable with Jed. She knew a lot about what turned him on and wasn't shy about using it. He'd certainly done everything he could to make her want him. She didn't see why he shouldn't get a taste of his own medicine.

She twirled her panties in the air before flicking them over one shoulder. She knew he had a thing for her breasts and she deliberately arched her body to show them to their advantage, slowly running her fingers over the sensitive nipples. His eyes glittered as he watched and her excitement grew, even as she tempted him. Finally, she crawled onto the bed, slowly climbing over his prone body, while still deliberately not touching him.

"You gave me a massage. And did such clever things with your tongue," she whispered. "I think it's my turn to do that to you."

"I promise to hate it as much as you did," he whispered back.

She stuck her tongue at him. "Insolent," she said. "I wish I had a cock ring. Then I could put it around your balls so you couldn't come while you stay hard as I play with you."

He smiled sensually at her. "I'll get you one next time. In fact, I'll get one that vibrates so it'll torture me even more."

She frowned. "This is so not fair when you're being cooperative," she scolded him. "You're supposed to hate the idea of not being able to come."

His chest rumbled with suppressed laughter. "Okay."

Because words obviously weren't doing anything to torture her love slave, Helen dipped down and took the head of his penis into her mouth. He went still. That reaction was much better.

His penis had a slight curve to it and she had to change position to make it easier to taste all of him. She angled her head, slowly taking him inside her mouth, leaning her weight down onto his thigh.

The scent and taste of tangy male desire tantalized her. She used her free hand to run up and down the length of him as her tongue swirled the underside of his penis, then, as she felt his thigh muscles tighten with pleasure, she took the whole length of him deep in her mouth. She repeated this several times, intermittently peeking back at him, enjoying the way his stomach muscles tightened as she timed how close she could get him to coming before slowing and stopping. His eyes were hooded, languorous. His nose flared now and then when she used her teeth to punish, but through it all, he didn't move a muscle.

"How does it feel now?" she taunted.

"It feels very good," he told her huskily, "but this is not a good enough torture. I've been trained not to come that easily."

Helen frowned. "So you aren't feeling tortured at all?" she asked, a little disappointed.

"It's torture, because I want to fuck you, but I can let you suck me all night and still won't come."

She glared at him owlishly. "I'm not sucking you all night just to prove you wrong."

He grinned. "You should torture me by showing me how wet you are, then you should sit on top of me and fuck me anyway you want. Every time I'm close to coming, you can stop and watch me suffer."

She continued glaring at him. "You're giving me orders again, Jed."

He shook his head. "Merely suggesting, dear Elena. I've been good. My hands are still above my head."

"It's not torture when the torturee is making suggestions, you know," Helen pointed out wryly.

"As torturer, you should feel even better than the torturee, right? You should pleasure yourself by using me over and over," he told her solemnly. "It's the first rule of the book. Take pleasure out of the act of torturing."

Helen positioned herself over the stiff erection, teasing him, but not using any pressure.

"That feels so good," Jed whispered. "You're so wet and I want to be inside you. Torture me more, Elena. Take me inside you."

"Okay, and then I'm going to sit so still you're going to beg for me to move," she teased.

She pushed down slowly. He slid in easily, her slickness betraying her state of arousal. She closed her eyes as pressure built. She inhaled as she pushed down more. Her eyes opened involuntarily at the feel of him.

"It's even more torturous if you don't let me in all the way," he instructed. "Light shallow strokes build an urgent need in a man to turn over and fuck hard."

Curious with where he was going with this, Helen followed his suggestion. His gaze was heated as he watched where they were joined.

This was not virtual reality playing tricks with her fantasy. She knew it wasn't. The feel of him was different, a tight sensation that felt, not unfamiliar, because they had done this before, but now, with her on top, she understood. Especially when he started flexing inside her.

"I...it's...you're..." She couldn't continue. She hadn't known it in the dark, and he hadn't done it that night, but at this angle, his erection was pushing against a very sensitive spot in there, prodding and insistent. She could feel him rubbing inside, creating an urgent need to reciprocate, to get it to stroke *that* spot. She leaned forward, putting her weight on his shoulders. He shifted his legs, pushing his body lower in the bed so that his erection remained where he'd suggested—only deep enough, but not all the way. The wicked and insistent kneading continued. And it felt so good, Helen couldn't move. "You tricked me!"

"I'm not moving my hands, just as we agreed," he said. "I'm just starting my torture. The more you feel good, the more you will want to reward me by pushing down deep, and the closer I'll get to coming."

"Not going to let you come," she ground out in a half moan, as she clamped his lower body with her thighs, trying not to move. But that only served to heighten her state of arousal as he teased her closer to the edge of maddening orgasm. To get there, she had to move.

"Don't let me stop you from coming. Torture me, Elena."

She couldn't help herself. She started riding him slowly. Every time she pushed down, she felt the thick head of his penis teasing that spot inside, and she groaned as he flexed. Sitting on top like this, she could adjust her position so he'd get there just right. Without thinking, she slid her knees lower, looking for the perfect angle...and she was lost as she started coming hard. She cried as her lower body jerked eagerly, chasing that intimate caress that took her breath away every time it stroked her right *there*.

"I haven't forgotten that you're still in a sensitive state, Elena."

A hand came down on her lower back—he was totally a disobedient torturee, she thought weakly—and held her down fast, not allowing her to get out of position, and then the slight movement of his hips made her cry out again. Her thighs fastened around him like iron as he kept her immobile, just at the angle she'd wanted. He thrust, almost gently, seeking the sweet spot that had given her that deep pleasure. It wasn't a difficult task, since she could hear herself whimper the moment he located it, and she swam in mindless pleasure as the damn man held her peaking, tumbling over, and peaking again, as he seemed perfectly happy to just flex deep inside her forever.

Never let a man locate one's G-spot, she thought, even as she went under yet another time. Willingly. She felt his hand sliding between them and moaned helplessly as he started to build pleasure there too, till she couldn't think any more. She shuddered, coming so hard she screamed against his hard chest.

He finally relented and pushed her back to a sitting position. She teetered. He was deep inside her. She glared down at his unrepentant expression.

"I didn't come. Punish me some more." He didn't even wait. Hands on her hips, he started moving her up and down his hard length and he closed his eyes, savoring the feel of her. "You feel so good, Elena. You're torturing me so well."

"Not fair," she told him weakly, "you knew I didn't want you touching me because I'm still having my problem."

He pushed her tumbled hair out of the way. "I know. You're stubborn. But you wanted to have your cake and eat it too, hmm? Driving me crazy because you knew I'd be driving you crazy once I started."

Helen sniffed. How did he get to understand her crazy logic so well? "I wanted to know for sure that it's not some kind of sexual manipulation you're pulling on me, that's all. There's no getting over the fact that I'm at a disadvantage because I'm turned on by you and that this state isn't going away till I...don't do that!"

He was flexing inside her again, his hands angling her hips this way and that. She could feel the slide of him against her pubic bone and she straightened, trying to get away from that addictive touch.

"Why not? You need to get your body chemistry back to normal. Once you're sated, we'll see whether I can drive you crazy without the help of serum-induced lust."

Her laughter came out in hiccups. "I like your crazy logic." He *was* being his manipulative self, but it felt too damn good to argue right now. "So, let's see. Am I torturing you still?"

"Hmm, of course. I can't come till you're truly satisfied. That's going to be a long torture, I promise."

That sounded more like a threat than a promise, but Helen didn't have time to think about it. He had begun again. She hissed as he pressed gentle fingers just above her pubic bone, searching, even as his other hand on the small of her back pulled her forward with determined insistence, until she reassumed the earlier position. He thrust up, hard, rocking her back and forth while the fingers pressed down. A gasp escaped her lips, telling him that he'd found what he was looking for.

"It's usually easier to find after the first orgasm."

"Jed..." But there was no stopping him from stroking that erogenous spot inside her. The pleasure was molten hot, as if he were building a fire by just rubbing. She groaned as he positioned her on his body, arranging her with unerring knowledge for her to achieve maximum friction. Then his hand was back between them, pressing down on her mons while he flexed his hips upwards.

The sensation made her cry out, her hands grabbing at the bed sheets. Her head thrashed against his body. She took a bite of hard male flesh and tasted the salty sheen of his skin. She had never known that the inner walls of her vagina could become so sensitive, but the more he provoked her inner flesh, the more the pressure built, until she shattered. And still he kept her in position, the iron clamp of his legs making sure the angle was so...damn...fabulously...right.

"Enough?" His voice was polite, as if he wasn't deliberately driving her out of her mind with pleasure.

She bit him again. How long had she been out? "How close are you to coming?" Her own voice had become husky.

"Close, but I can hold it off."

She looked up at him. "You haven't even moved."

He smiled. "But I'm moving." He demonstrated the truth of it by flexing inside her again. "See?"

"It's just not fair," she lamented, pursing her lips downward in fake drama. "Are you sure we aren't in virtual reality and you're just an avatar I've programmed in my head? What else can you do with that magic scimitar of love without actually pushing in and out like a real man?"

His laughter was low and sexy. "My magic scimitar of love?"

Drawing lazy circles around his nipple, she gave him a saucy wink. "Yeah. It's curved. Like this. And that's why it's got magic powers. It's doing it right now, tapping gently against some part of me I didn't know was so...oh...like that. Is that all you learned from commando sex school?"

His amusement grew when she moved her arm exaggeratedly. He stretched under her like a cat. "What, you think I'm just a one-trick pony?"

Helen tried to sit up and frowned when he held her still. "You just don't let anyone be in charge for too long, do you?"

His legs relaxed, freeing her. "Bad habit."

That mollified her a tad. He really was trying, albeit not too successfully. It was hard, though, to sit up when her limbs felt like Jell-O. And he was still hard as a rock inside her. She glanced down at his hand idly twirling at her curls.

"*You're* a bad habit," she told him softly. "I don't know what to do with you."

"I really think you should continue torturing me by coming again. A suggestion, of course. It's really driving me crazy seeing you out of control and not being able to turn you on your back and ride you."

The image of him over her, thrusting deep and hard, stirred her libido. She shook her head. Was she never going to get enough of this man?

"I'm going to ride you," she told him, "but you still can't come."

"All right."

She enjoyed him like she'd enjoyed few men in her life—with open abundance and an impish delight in giving intimate torture. She used him to pleasure herself, sometimes deeply, sometimes shallowly, until she wasn't paying attention to how close he was to coming any more.

His whole body was taut like a drawn bow, slightly damp from the control he was exerting on his will, his eyes half-closed as he watched her sensual journey. She leaned over, her hands on his shoulders. He opened his mouth as she teased him with her breasts but she kept them an inch above his waiting lips.

"Break for me," she whispered. "How close are you?"

"Very close," he whispered back.

"I want you to lose control, Jed."

"Can I come now?"

"No."

"Okay." His hot breath teased her nipples.

"Bastard. You're supposed to beg."

His eyes were the color of a stormy sea. "Please," he said, just like that.

"No," she said. Heartless, that was what she was, but she was enjoying it, oh so much. She continued riding him at a leisurely pace. "I think it's understandable that I want to be in charge of your body for a while. You don't know what you put me through with your constant teasing."

"Of course I do. I had to take a cold shower many a time after a session with you."

"Seriously?" A thought occurred. "No women to take away your discomfort?"

He gave her a lopsided smile. "No, I don't replace my women."

"Oh." Then, arching a brow, she delicately added, "Women?"

She clenched her inner muscles around him, taking delight in the sudden flair of his nostrils and tightening of his shoulders. He wasn't as in control as he pretended to be.

"Tell me about your *women* now," she invited.

"First tell me you don't believe it's the serum making you do such naughty things to my body."

She stopped mid-stroke. She'd totally forgotten about that part of it. "You know damn well it isn't that any more. I've been trying to make you feel pleasure, if you haven't noticed, not wallowing in my own sensations."

"I've noticed. But I want to hear it from your lips."

She sighed, then leaned down closer. "I want you to come. That's an order," she said before planting her lips on his.

His mouth opened and took hers fiercely as he surged up into her again and again. She felt his iron will dissolving as his tongue tangled with hers in a battle for possession. His body shook under hers as he emitted a deep-throated groan, which sounded so sexy it caused her to slip from the edge with him, falling, shuddering, into an orgasmic abyss.

They must have fallen asleep, or at least she did. When she finally opened her eyes, he was on top and moving inside her, his mouth on her breast, ruthlessly teasing her nipple. She reared up at a tiny bite. Done with words, he was now attacking her like a hungry man, with her as his main course and dessert. His teeth pulled at her distended nipple, teasing it to a hard pebble. He rose on his haunches and rubbed his penis against her clitoris until she shivered with helpless arousal. Now that she'd admitted aloud that she wanted him without the influence of the serum, there were no more barriers. He unleashed his passion and she reciprocated with willing eagerness.

She ran her fingers through his thick hair, responding impatiently to his touch. He looked down, his eyes dazzling her with their intensity. She gasped as he thrust deeply.

"My turn," he growled.

"You're waking the magic scimitar of love," Jed wryly said to the darkness. Her slow hand had woken him up in the velvety darkness.

She gave a sleepy chuckle at his using that ridiculous term. "I was curious whether you're as in control when you're asleep."

He smiled. She didn't know how close she had been to breaking him. She hadn't even tried to seduce him. It had been her sense of humor and her ability to make him laugh that did him in every time.

"Despite the rumors, Elena, my dick, like any other man's, has a mind of its own."

"That's good to know. It's a much simpler creature than you are."

He laughed softly. He couldn't remember the last time he'd felt so at ease lying in bed with a woman. Most of the time—not all—sex was a part of his arsenal. It wasn't easy for him to share any part of himself and he knew he was stingy in the emotion department to the point of hurting those about whom he cared.

There weren't many who could breach his wall. One of them was his daughter, who, like Elena, had a mischievous streak. Another was Nikki, whose gentleness had called out to him like no other. Both women had accepted, rather than tried to change, him; both also didn't change themselves for him. Elena, he realized, was the same way. She was more patient than she let on, letting the answers come to her rather than jumping to conclusions. It was the sign of a well-trained operative. And a damn sexy one, at that.

But he was surrounded by well-trained and sexy operatives. What made her different? Why did he feel this need to be with her the more time he spent with her?

Not comfortable with the line of questions on his mind, Jed turned Elena on her side, spooning her, an arm around her middle. His earlier hunger was the result of months and months of mental teasing and stimulation. The past few hours had only sated it a little. His hand wandered lower. Wet heat. She hiccupped as his finger stroked her in a languid caress.

"I'm too tired to move," she husked out. He pushed intimately against her buttocks. "Aren't you supposed to be done for the night after what we did?"

"It seems you aren't the only one suffering from chemical imbalance," Jed observed. "I don't know when we'll have private time like this again, so I plan to enjoy you as many times as I can."

"What, those fantasies of me in tassels and thong aren't good enough?" she teased.

"Aren't enough," he corrected. "Not any more."

He slid inside her easily, this time making love to her slowly, prolonging the pleasure. He liked this position because he could play with her clitoris as he moved inside her. He discovered that she found his shallow thrusts frustrating, keeping her from actually coming, and his fingers masterfully stimulated her till she forgot to breathe from trying to reach her peak. Only then did he allow himself to bury himself deeply inside her. He felt the first contractions and he timed each withdrawal with each stroke of his finger, keeping her at that plateau as long as he could. Each contraction pulled him deeper, massaging his erection until he couldn't stop the oncoming orgasm. She gasped his name as he crushed her to him, his whole being wanting to get inside her, giving into that current of exquisite pleasure that robbed a man of part of his soul. He continued caressing her with his fingers, till her essence wet his hand and his thighs, till she breathed his name over and over.

He kissed the back of her head as she went limp beside him, totally out of it, inhaling the mixture of her scent and their sex. She was breathing deeply. He wanted her again but it wasn't good form to keep waking up a woman just because he couldn't get enough of her.

Maybe let her sleep for an hour. He could easily stay awake by thinking about his schedule tomorrow. Or mentally run over all the details of various operations. It was a habit of his when he wanted to distract himself.

A few minutes passed by and he felt Elena stir. He turned and kissed her cheek.

"I can feel you thinking. What's on your mind?" she asked.

She could? "Just business stuff." He frowned. "Are you awake?"

"Hmm." She took in another deep breath. "What kind of business?"

"I was just thinking about tomorrow. And making a note to contact Hawk to see what he was doing. I need an update from him."

He heard her exhale, a long sigh, like a person falling into deep relaxation. He assumed she had fallen asleep again and didn't say anything else.

"Hawk's in trouble."

Her calm and slightly monotonic voice alerted him immediately that something wasn't right. The room was dark and he couldn't see her face. "Elena?" he prompted. "Why did you say that?"

"I see Hawk. It's got to be him."

Jed kept very still. "Are you remote viewing?" he asked quietly.

"Yes. I can see a man being beaten by a group of people. It's a huge crowd, with many men in uniform. Confusion. Hawk took down a dozen or so men. Fighting very hard." She gasped. "Ow. Someone broke a bottle over his head. He's down. Blood. They're dragging him out the back way. Too many people. I can't see. Screaming. Girls are screaming and running, oh God."

"Checkered flag, Hell. Disengage," Jed ordered.

A short silence followed. "Jed? What just happened?" She sounded more alert now. "I...oh wow, I did it again."

"You did this before." He leaned over so he could turn on the bedside light.

"Ow! Turn it off!"

Jed frowned. Elena groped for the pillow, covering her face. "What's wrong?"

"The light hurts my eyes. My head's started throbbing."

He immediately killed the light. She immediately turned toward him, a gesture that brought out the protective male in him. These headaches worried him. Not being able to do a thing to help her didn't make him feel any better. He stroked the back of her neck, feeling the tensed muscles there.

"I'm okay. It isn't as bad as that killer migraine from the other morning when I spontaneously remote viewed you on the submarine."

Jed's hand went still for a moment. "You RV'ed me with Cummings," he stated, waiting for confirmation.

"It was spontaneous, like tonight. I wasn't able to do that before, so I don't understand what made me do that."

"What were you thinking before it happened each time?"

"Well..." She drifted off in thought for a minute. "Just now, I was very relaxed and thinking about all the things you did to me that first night you came to my quarters. I was plotting on repeating some of the things you did. During that morning, just before I RV'ed you, I was also thinking about the same thing. I had the avatar program on and I was looking at Hades on the screen and trying to imagine him coming into my quarters and then it got mixed up with my memories of that night, and before I knew it, there I was, smelling sea air." She paused, trying to remember, before continuing, "It...felt different that time. I couldn't see you very well. I sensed danger and part of me wanted to run from the scene. Actually, the more I concentrated, the more difficult it became for me to stay there and I remember turning around and running away. I don't know. It was just different."

Jed recalled the strange feeling of being watched that day. "But not this time?" he asked. "Did you feel the same kind of difficulty this time? Maybe spontaneous remote viewing made you feel alone without a monitor and that's why you ran."

She put an arm around him, her voice muffled against his chest. "Massage there again. Ooh, perfect. No, I didn't get that danger signal in my head when I was remote viewing Hawk just now. I felt your presence by my side and you were talking, remember? So, to me, you were playing monitor, asking me what I saw. I just don't know, Jed. The only thing that I can figure out that ties both incidents is that wild sex with you is just out of this world, baby."

Jed shook his head as he continued to quietly massage her neck and head area. Everything about this woman intrigued him, even her crazy sense of humor.

"Stop joking. We've got to get to the bottom of this. Are you feeling better?"

"Would you rather I complain that sex with you gives me a headache?" She turned onto her back, her hand coming up and caressing the side of his face. "Jed, if this headache doesn't go away, I'll need the serum. I need to be one hundred percent for this assassination we're trying to prevent in Skopje."

Chapter Nineteen

"You're fortunate Amber came to get you when she did then," Jed said. "Our observer contacted us and said that they took you down at the brothel."

Hell frowned at Jed but he was looking at the module feeding in the communication link between him and Hawk, the SEAL who was working undercover in Macedonia. She'd been listening quietly as the other man gave a detailed account about his capture and rescue. It seemed that Hawk's cover with the drug lord, Dragan Dilaver, had been found out by a woman named Greta. Jed had immediately glanced at one of their men and he'd taken off as if he had received a silent message. From what she could gather, there was definitely a connection between Greta and the bomb trigger that Hawk was seeking. The SEAL stressed the importance of time management because it seemed Greta was planning to use the bomb at an important place in seven days.

It was definitely strange listening from the point-of-view of the person she'd accidentally remote viewed. She'd seen it happening to him and felt so helpless.

"I suppose an observer can't lift a finger to help out, can they?" Hawk asked.

Well, not this observer, she thought wryly. She looked at Jed again, wondering how he was going to explain about her "presence".

"He was too far away to help, Hawk, and wasn't even sure whether you were alive. He did say you took down fifteen of Dilaver's men before shots were fired. There were several fights happening and he thought he saw someone shoot you. We were hoping it wasn't you but since we had no contact from you for a while, we had to accept the possibility," Jed said, as he attached the module via USB to the laptop. "Tell Amber I'm ready whenever she is."

"She's almost there."

Helen grinned when Jed looked up at her. She gave him the thumbs-up signal and mouthed "good save". He gave her one of those looks that revealed nothing and, needing a reaction, she mirrored an exaggerated version back to him. He didn't even crack a smile. He ought to have that stone face of his patented.

She wondered about this Amber woman who had saved their operative. It was a brave thing to do, running off to battle a drug warlord at his own compound *and* successfully extract an injured SEAL. She would have loved to be there, in the thick of things, helping her out.

"How long before you can get back to me about what Dilaver and this new person, Greta, are planning?" Hawk asked.

"Give us a couple of hours. Probably this evening, before you leave the area."

"Good. Okay, Jed, everything's secured at our end. We're ready to transmit."

"Hang on." Jed sent Heath an enquiring look. Heath held up one finger as he double-checked the firewalls, then he nodded. "Ready to link up here. There we go."

Helen looked at her back-up link. It was split-screen, one side showing the signal coming in and the other a smaller view of Jed's connection. While Heath's task was to make sure the link remained secured, hers was to monitor for outside interference. She winced at the sight of the man on the other side. His face looked as if he'd gone through the meat grinder. One of his eyes and his lips were horribly swollen. He had told Jed earlier that his physical functionality was at seventy percent. If his body looked like his face—no freaking way. Unless, of course, it's a SEAL. Those dudes were tough sons-of-bitches. One of her trainers was a former SEAL and he'd been an inspiration when it came to mental strength.

Hawk squinted back at her—actually, at Jed—since he couldn't see her. "Did we interrupt something important?"

Hell grinned again. Jed wasn't in his usual casual jeans. In fact, he looked quite dashing and resplendent in formal suit, white shirt, and a tie. With his hair combed back and his face all nicely groomed, he looked like a diplomat, especially with the official-looking sash and ribbons that denoted his being part of some entourage. Dressed formally, he somehow looked more dangerous than ever, making the animalistic sensuality that was so much a part of him even more pronounced.

"I always dress up for dinner," Jed replied with a straight face. "You don't look so good, Hawk. Hello, Ambrosia, long time."

"Jed, it has been a while. How have you been?"

Helen blinked. Wow. Was that the woman who rescued Hawk McMillan? She looked like she'd never left a beauty salon. Her voice was low, very sexy, and she spoke Jed's name like she knew him very well. Helen frowned.

"Good. Can you handle this route?"

"It shouldn't be a problem. I'm transmitting the map I've prepared. Hawk's coordinates match a few areas. Time being the key thing here, which of these routes should we head for?"

"We're printing it right now. Hang on."

Jed turned to Helen. She gave a thumbs-up to show that she was receiving the transmit, then clicked on the command key to print. Jed walked from where he was to get the map from her. She thought she saw a ghost of a smile on his lips when she handed it to him, but she wasn't sure because he had turned his attention to the printout almost immediately, returning to his laptop.

"First, I agree that you should abandon the initial plan to destroy every cache of weapons shown here. The most important thing is to get to the target weapon. Once you have it, you can contact me again and I'll send someone to pick it up. Second, we've compared your coordinates with the aid and relief drop-offs by manned and unmanned U.S. aerial vehicles the last six months. Although your physical description of the woman doesn't fit, we have reason to believe that Greta is the same handler that had worked as a secretary to Deputy Director Philip Gorman's task force in the CIA for the past ten years, so we have a paper trail. We're transmitting a file photo. We've computed that the target weapon is in the cache between Elbasan and Tirana at ninety percent.

"The third factor is still an unknown. We're concentrating on all political activities in that part of the world in the next seven to ten days and putting out a code red alert. From what little Dilaver hinted to Ambrosia, the target weapon is to be used after a decoy has been activated. There's an international summit going on in Skopje right now and the main meeting with certain world leaders present in two days. That, however, will be off the seven-day deadline, so we're assuming that either the event or threat is a decoy and there's another target. Keep your cell or your watch close by, Hawk. Someone will contact you. Check for messages whenever you can."

Helen scribbled in her notes. She needed to remember every piece of information when it came to arguing with Jed McNeil.

"Will do," Hawk said.

"Still the same prepared guy, aren't you, Jed?" Amber asked.

That confirmed it right there that Amber and Jed were more than acquaintances. Helen sniffed. She didn't want to think about *that* right now.

"Still trolling for information, Ambrosia?"

"I can't help but notice that little pin on your collar, that's all. You're at this summit already, aren't you?"

"Wait a minute. You're here in Macedonia, Jed?"

Jed's expression remained blank. "It's just a pin. We'll talk soon. Any messages for Admiral Madison, Hawk?"

"Please let him know that I'm standing by and ready for the team."

Jed nodded. "Talk to you soon. Amber, consider your *veza* settled."

A favor. So, there was the history between them. But she still didn't like the smile the beautiful Amber was now giving Jed.

"No more free rides for you, Jed McNeil," Amber told him.

"Don't be too sure, Ambrosia," Jed said, then cut off transmission. He put down the remote and walked to Helen's small table. "How's the headache?"

He had been asking that several times a day now. "It hasn't gone away."

She could start another argument with him but it took too much effort. Besides, it was hard to argue when a headache was interfering with one's thoughts, so she'd taken to jotting down notes so she wouldn't forget to bring up relevant points when they did argue. She knew that this had become a source of private amusement for the watching Heath. It was a war of wills—hers versus Jed's—and those in the know around them were watching with interest.

"You're still upset with me."

Helen looked down at the keyboard. "*You* would use the serum," she said, in a low voice.

"Not as a painkiller."

Okay, he was in the mood for another argument. "You're thinking of Armando," she said. "I'll have you know, I'm supposed to be taking SYMBIOS 2 anyway *so I can perform.*"

She emphasized the last few words to make her point. She didn't need to bring up the fact that the last two days, she hadn't been able to work efficiently, especially in her own assignments. Jed or Heath had covered for her whenever her headache started to worsen.

"The serum was meant to mitigate your RV downtime, Elena."

"So I could do my job. Hello?" Helen waved her notes. "Do you think I can look for decoys with me being all crossed-eye double-checking my notes? Lying down hasn't made it go away, Jed. You and I know this isn't a normal headache and we don't have much time left as the summit highlight event is coming up."

He had to know she was right. They had been looking through the package he'd gotten at Lake Matka, trying to decipher certain notes.

She read her notes again, looking for more fodder to back her argument.

She cracked her stiff neck tentatively, trying to ignore the tightening band that signaled worsening pain. Hoping to distract him, she put on her best Jed imitation. "First, this is no longer a two-day summit operation. We know that something's about to happen, but now it could be just a decoy. Second, according to Hawk McMillan, that explosive trigger meant that there's another target in seven days. We have to look at the schedule of events. You know there's a good chance of me going into remote-viewing mode to try to find our target because Skopje is a busy area right now. Fourth—"

Jed silenced her by laying a finger on her lips. His silver eyes glittered with suppressed emotion. She couldn't tell whether it was anger or something else.

"Heath," he said in that quiet way that made everyone pay attention, "check the schedules for the next seven days. Your headache's worsening, Hell. Go get some rest."

Without another word, he turned and walked away. Helen scowled till he left the room. She snapped her laptop shut in disgust.

"I've never seen him so...agitated," Heath murmured. "Is it possible that you're actually troubling our Number Nine's usually iron rule to finish a job?"

"That cold and uncaring man wouldn't know agitation if it smashed into the side of his oversized head," Helen declared. "He's just being obstinate."

"Look at it from his perspective, Hell. The only other person who used the serum for 'headaches' is our Armando. That isn't a vote of confidence about the serum's stability, is it?"

Helen thought about it for a few seconds. Okay, so the guy cared, even if he showed it in the most chauvinistic manner possible. *No.* That was all he said, each time. Like his saying "no" was everything that mattered.

"Inflexible," she muttered. "Implacable. Moronic. Mutton-headed." She looked up to find Heath studying her strangely. "What?"

"Those were the words he read out loud this morning while thumbing through that dictionary of his."

Helen frowned. She rubbed the sides of her head. "What are you talking about?"

Heath smiled. "Get Dr. Kirkland to talk to him again, Hell. Or, just get the serum into you without Number Nine's permission." His dark eyes taunted her as he reached inside his pocket and took out a small vial. He set it on the table. "He's at a meeting. How's he to know if you have the serum in you before you see him tonight?"

Helen picked up the vial and studied it for a while after Heath left the room. She wasn't at all surprised that he happened to have it on him. Nothing the commandos did surprised her much. She pocketed the vial.

"Change of plans, Stevens. It seems our Greta isn't going to get to the trigger in time. So the order's changed. We're heading to Skopje."

Jonah didn't look away from the Macedonian TV show he had on. He liked this kind of living very much—nice hotel room, entertainment, and the dish he was eating, something called *gyuvech*, some kind of tasty chicken stew. He'd have loved to have some of that wine on the menu too, but his monitor didn't allow that, of course. He really didn't want to leave Velesta. Those *kafenas*...he had soaked in all that energy available there. Full. His stomach and his little cache of treasure. He listened attentively while he flipped to yet another channel.

"What? Greta failed? Five-One here saw her talking with Dilaver."

"They hadn't left for the drop-offs in time. I bet COMCEN has something to do with it. The instructions said that Plan B has been activated and we're to go to Skopje and wait for the Noretski girl."

"Llallana Noretski? Isn't she supposed to be our very own Project Gem baby?"

"Which just tells you that I was right about all this mind control and remote-viewing bullshit, doesn't it? We're supposed to be in control, but look at what happened. We're being ordered to go here and there, and with nothing to show at the end."

His monitor threw his magazine down on the table. "We're always one step behind, that's all. The other side has a remote viewer too and they're getting their hands on the targets first."

"Well, we keep letting them beat us. We had the list before they could even sort out Gorman's damage. We had knowledge of where each shipment went while they were busy going through red tape. We even had a head start with our testing of the serum on the remote viewers, and yet their operative managed to get to the target in Frankfurt. If we don't get to the trigger before they do, we're going to be replaced."

Jonah reached for the soup. *Chorba.* He liked to remember the food items in foreign countries because food was the most important thing after sex. This was a country he would like to visit again. Beautiful young girls. Good food. If he ever escaped these assholes, he definitely would return. But how could he escape when they had what he wanted most?

He was beginning to put the pieces of the puzzle together by just listening to his CIA handlers whenever they had their little arguments. Greta was the double agent in charge at the CIA division in Washington, D.C., before that big recent scandal, when everything went south. He had kept up with it while he was slaving away in his CIA cubicle, feeling envious that his security clearance wasn't that high. And yet here he was, part of a clandestine team, trying to get hold of some important weapon from a double agent. From what he'd read, this Greta, foreign agent that she was, must be a hell of a spy, having managed to work inside the CIA for ten years.

He realized now that he must help these bastards retrieve the device or he was going to lose them. Obviously, there was someone higher than them pulling the strings and if his handlers were taken away, so would his serum. No, he couldn't have that. He didn't want to go back to living in that place, feeling empty, missing the rush of power from the serum. He shivered in anticipation of slipping into the energy of more of those little whores. They must have at least a dozen men a night, the way their energy pulsated and called to him. And in that one *kafena*, with so many of them, he almost felt like he OD'ed, the sexual charge was so powerful. His cock had turned so hard he hurt. And then, he had found out something new.

Jonah smiled. Since they had live sex acts in the *kafena* themselves, he discovered that it wasn't just memories he could record. The sexual charge given out by those people while they were doing it was stronger; to his delight, when he entered into their glow, it wasn't just his feelings that he experienced but theirs too. Every lustful thrust, every dirty fantasy of those men; and every time they came, it was like feeling two orgasms. He recorded them all. He loved every minute those girls felt powerless against him, or rather, the man with them—who the fuck cared—their fear, their drugged states, their having to please, all that made him feel like the most potent male in the world. He took all he wanted while he had spied on Greta for his handlers.

No, he wasn't going to let that other remote viewer win this time. He must find a way to kill her if he saw her in Skopje. He hoped they would send him near a *kafena* in Skopje. Now that he knew that it felt so much better recording live, he was greedy for more.

Helen looked up at the sound of her suite's main door unlocking. She glanced at the clock to verify the lateness of the hour. She heard the low murmur of male voices, the flick of some lights going off, and the sound of people heading off to their respective rooms. She held her breath. Would he come in?

A few seconds later, Jed slipped into her room without knocking. He closed it quietly behind him. His jacket and tie were off. A few buttons of the shirt undone. Her hands curled a little tighter around the magazine she'd been aimlessly flipping. No man should have the right to look so damn tempting and sexy to any woman who had a headache that refused to go away. There was just no denying her acute awareness of him.

He came and sat on one side of her bed. He had a way of making silences linger. She turned her face up as his hands explored gently. His fingers soothed the back of her head; his thumbs worked circles over her brows.

"Have I told you you're good with your hands?"

"A few times," he murmured. With infinite care, he feathered kisses along the side of her face, tracing the soft line of her jaw, and then moving deliciously down the sensitive area of her neck.

"This can't go on, you know," she said. "You can't keep babying me. I had to leave early tonight when my headache became worse."

"Yes," he said against her skin.

"Yes, what?" She wanted him to kiss her lips.

"Yes, if the serum is going to take away that headache, I'll get you some."

Helen pushed against him so she could look into his eyes. His silver eyes seemed to gleam with an inner fire in the soft lighting. Despite the soft caress of his hands, he looked hard and unyielding. She could tell that he'd been spending time debating his decision with himself.

"I know you're worried," she told him, "and yeah, so am I, but I need this headache gone so I can perform."

"I know."

"So what finally made you change your mind?"

He sat up, one hand absently unbuttoning his loose shirt. "I talked to Dr. Kirkland about Armando. After he'd admitted to taking the serum without permission, Armando answered some questions during tests. The serum did help to block the migraines, but they have side effects." He shrugged out of the shirt. "He claimed to hear voices sometimes. Dr. Kirkland is wondering whether our newest commando isn't just bipolar and needs other medication. But the main thing remains that he had used the serum on the side enough times. He was able to finish his assignments, in spite of his hearing and seeing things."

Helen tried hard not to be distracted as he continued to take off his clothes. He was beautiful to look at and she really would prefer to do other things than talk. She pushed the featherbed lower. It was getting warmer under the comfortable downy material.

"Did Dr. K. consult the scientists who gave me those lectures about the serum?"

"You really want to hear scientists getting ecstatic about quantum entanglement and Bell's theorem?"

"Say what?"

Jed's lips quirked. "Let's just say that half an hour of listening about the existence of the physical world according to quantum theory and how you and I are two particles bouncing airwaves at each other didn't explain a thing about why the serum causes headaches. I can give you the boring science or just simply make the excuse that our Number Six is bipolar."

Nuh-uh. She wasn't going to suffer a pounding headache *and* a lecture about quantum tango, or whatever. "Armando isn't bipolar," she said. "The serum works because it's a pain blocker. We already know it works when a fatigued pilot takes it. Prolonged pain can fatigue a person too, so that's why the serum works. No need for a medical background to explain that, Jed."

He shook his head. "You forget. This is a bio-synthetic serum that has been altered not just as a neuro-blocker, but also as an enhancer. I've already seen the way your body chemistry was messed up, Elena, when your mind and body were fatigued. Simply put, it helped enhanced what your body chemistry believed it lacked. I've been thinking about Armando and his interest in illusions. I wonder whether he started getting more into it from the serum's usage. This is the part about the drug that I don't like."

Helen arched an eyebrow. "Are you saying that I'm going to start performing magic tricks with Armando? Can I borrow the bustier for my costume?"

His lips quirked. "You're just determined to make fun of everything serious, aren't you?"

She shrugged. "It's hard not to when everyone around me is always throwing scientific and military stuff at me. Quantum physics? Hypothalamus gone bonkers? Particles tangoing in space? Go on, explain it to yourself. I just do it, thank you very much." Frankly, Jed's slow smile of amusement at her techy talk was a more interesting subject. The man was damn sexy when he was relaxed and smiling, which wasn't often, from what she'd observed. She sighed, adding, "I know it's serious, but that's how I deal with it. You have your own little defensive mechanism, and I have mine."

She swallowed as she watched him step out of his tailored pants. What was she saying again? Defensive mechanism? She had none, none whatsoever, against this man.

"What's my defensive mechanism?" he asked curiously.

Helen rearranged the pillows under her so she could have a better view of him. She hadn't thought he was going to actually stay with her, especially since he'd been sleeping in his own room since their arrival from Lake Matka.

"You hide everything, even from those you care about." She tilted her head. "But I'm getting better at reading you."

"Is that so?"

"Yup. Like, for instance, I know what you have to do next."

He didn't answer her as he walked into the bathroom. She enjoyed the back view. She lay there, waiting, thinking about his decision. He didn't like to see her hurting, she realized that now, even though he did a great job at not showing it. He'd left her alone last night because she'd taken sleeping pills as a final resort.

When he finally joined her in bed, she was almost feverish with anticipation. He was walking around her room as if they had been sleeping together for fifty years. The lurking amusement in his eyes finally told her that he was teasing her with his usual deliberate, calm manner.

"Heath told me he gave you a vial of the serum."

She glared at him. "So? You think I used it?"

"Did you?"

"I still have a headache," she pointed out.

"That could mean that it didn't work without remote viewing. It affects each tester differently."

She glared at him harder, trying to ignore the hardness of his thighs against hers. "It's right there on the bedside table. You'll see that I haven't used it. You should be pissed off at Heath for giving it to me."

He shook his head. His free hand lifted stray strands of her hair from her face. "Why didn't you use the serum?"

"I..." Helen shrugged and grumpily batted his caressing hand away. She closed her eyes, not wanting to acknowledge the reason. She had wanted to; the temptation to ease the headache that ebbed and flowed was strong. But she hadn't been able to do it. She sniffed. "Damn."

"Admit it. You knew it would be against my wishes."

Her eyes flew open. "Do you know what tact is? There are other ways to say things. This isn't a dictatorship. You're making my headache worse, thank you very much. And if everyone's so damn obedient, why the hell did Heath disobey you and give me the vial? I don't see you telling him it was against your wishes."

His lips tightened a fraction. "Heath was being Heath. It's his job to offer temptation, look for weaknesses. He likes to think he can offer alternatives to a problem."

Helen rolled her eyes. "Are any of you guys ever going to stop testing me? Is everyone trying to own me?"

He tugged at her tightly crossed arms till they loosened. "Just me." He snuggled up against her, his breath hot against her ear.

Something about his tone of voice caught her attention. "Are we going to do it now?" she asked softly.

"If you want to."

She put a hand on her chest in pretended shock. "The great Number Nine asking permission to activate a trigger?"

His hand snaked behind her neck and he pulled her in for a leisurely kiss. He tasted of mouthwash and male heat, totally addictive. She wanted more from him and let him know with her hands.

When he lifted his head, his silver eyes searched hers. "I won't have you remote viewing free form without being aware of me. Quantum entanglement theory be damned, if you took off spontaneously without me around, I want to be able to call you back, Elena. And the only way I know how is to activate the trigger between us."

"I know. I was thinking the same thing too." She grinned, and added, "But I don't mind bouncing particles and creating my own physical reality with you while you do it."

Actually, she was a little awed at how far ahead he'd planned this. He'd embedded that trigger inside her anticipating this problem, and as much as she personally loathed the idea of using her attraction for him against her, she had to admit that it was the perfect way to anchor her. He was asking her permission. She leaned into his hand as he caressed her.

"I'm ready."

Besides, maybe she could actually catch the trigger phrase this time. Her expression must have betrayed her thoughts, or he read her mind. In the soft glow of the room, his smile turned devilish.

"Want to take a pill first?" he asked wickedly, his caress turning into a vise.

She realized, much later, how difficult it was to pay careful attention to words when a master seducer was carefully giving her all his attention.

Chapter Twenty

So far so good. Even at half a dosage, Helen could feel a big difference. The pain was gone, or at least, she didn't feel it. Maybe it was from being nagged by a headache for the last few days, but the sudden lack of tension felt incredible. Undistracted by pain, she could think in whole paragraphs again. She didn't need to distract herself by taking notes.

She frowned. Armando and his illusions—was he distracting himself from his headaches that way? She needed to make it A-1 priority to have a one-on-one chat with that man when she returned to Center.

"Hell, status."

The sudden sound of Jed's voice through the earpiece made her shiver with sudden awareness. Thanks to the serum, she'd been crouching in this position for over an hour now without feeling a darn thing—not the discomfort of her position, not the heat that was making her shirt damp, not any normal need to stand up and stretch at all—and he managed to cut through its effect and disrupt her sense of calm watchfulness by just saying her name.

She peered through the binoculars, checking the auditorium below. "On time," she said. "I see the diplomats on the stage. It's heavily guarded."

With the presence of so many important heads of state, the whole place had been swept by sniffing dogs and detectors, double-guarded with metal detectors at checkpoints as well as security cameras at every possible angle, looking for snipers and suspicious-looking packages. The American contingent had brought their own operatives, but had been told to keep out of the way of Macedonian security, which didn't want any interference from outsiders. Nonetheless, Helen was quite sure there were plenty of other "outsiders" from Interpol, Europol, and other outfits walking around here. No one wanted an international incident. Or at least, on the outside.

There was a decoy out there somewhere and the package given to him at Lake Matka had convinced Jed there was a connection with Deutsche International. While they were busy going through exit points, Hawk had reported in again. She hadn't been close enough to hear the conversation, but whatever was happening at the SEALs' end was serious enough to warrant Jed making several calls as they walked out of their room to head to their positions.

Just as she'd turned to leave, he'd grabbed her hand in the middle of a call, and said briefly, "It doesn't matter that this is a decoy. It means they're still waiting out there for the real thing. Do you remember those CIA faces we saw?"

She'd immediately understood him and nodded. "I'll keep an eye out for them." He'd squeezed her hand and let it go, but she felt his gaze following her out the door. It was while outside, with the crowd and noise, that she had first noticed something different. Sometimes the people she was observing glowed. That was the best word she could come up with to describe it. It only happened intermittently and the sight usually dissipated after a few seconds.

So taking the serum before she was undergoing remote-viewing downtime caused wonky perception. But that was to be expected, right? She didn't have time to analyze it right now, but when she had some time, she'd sit down and make a list of all the odd reactions she had while using SYMBIOS 2. Dr. Kirkland had wanted to experiment using the serum before an RV session anyway, so this decision to use the serum now should give him an idea. Of course, they hadn't thought of spontaneous remote viewing.

She looked through her binoculars again. Frowned.

"Where's Number Nine going, over?" she asked. Jed hadn't said anything about moving out of position.

"He's going down to the underground parking lot. Weber's meeting him there," Heath replied.

"Weber from Deutsche International?" She remembered the name from the last mission. Weber was one of the top guys at Deutsche International where she'd retrieved the SEED decoder. What was D.I.'s connection with all these missing weapons?

"Yes. He had someone pass a note to Jed. Jed says to give him fifteen minutes and not to move out of position. All eyes on entry and exit points. Stay in position, Hell."

It struck her as strange that Jed would leave when the decoy could strike at any time right now. What was in the note given to him?

"Affirmative," she said.

But something just didn't feel right to her. They'd all agreed that, decoy or not, someone was planning to make a statement against this group of leaders gathering here today. The first shot, the one today, was meant to distract from the bigger target, which they were hoping to avert once Hawk took care of business at his end.

"One thing at a time," Jed had said, as he laid out the initial plans.

Why did he choose to go off to the underground garage without more than furtive instructions to Heath?

"Is his comm. device on?" Hell asked.

"Yes, but he can't listen in here because he's going to be busy talking, Hell. He's switched to using de Clerq for all emergencies and updates. If anything happens here, de Clerq will let him know."

That made sense. This way he wouldn't be distracted by all the communications going on by every sector and if they needed to get hold of him, they could pass the information on quickly to Drew de Clerq, who covered the operations from Center through satellite.

"Something's happening down there," one of the other operatives noted.

She trained her binoculars on the circular stage and saw a flurry of movement at one corner. Some of them had that weird glow that she'd been seeing, and she couldn't quite focus on their facial expressions. She blinked several times.

"What is it?" she asked.

"Hang on. Something coming in from de Clerq."

Due to earlier prep work, de Clerq would be able to tap in on certain peoples' private conversations. This move was to enable them to know the actions of the different groups of security detail taking place around them to lessen the chance of getting into each other's way. Eight Ball, COMCEN's computer, could pretty much give instantaneous translations of several languages and conversations at the same time, thus upping their chances to pick up any anomalies and incidences. COMCEN had no intention of allowing any other agencies to get their hands on the trigger, if it made it to Skopje.

"The Macedonian security just caught a woman strapped with explosives trying to enter," de Clerq reported. "She claimed to be from a separatist arm of the KLA and was after the Kosovo representative here."

"Think she's the decoy?"

"Eight Ball calculated it at eighty-five percent, seeing that Dragan Dilaver is KLA and Greta is probably partly affiliated."

All this seemed to connect with everything the injured Hawk had told them in the earlier uplink that Helen had listened in on. Dilaver was a KLA man and of course, if Greta was sending a decoy ahead, she would use a KLA agent.

"So if this is the decoy, and we have the trigger, is our mission over?" she asked.

"We don't have the trigger yet, Hell," de Clerq replied. "Hawk McMillan recently reported in that he was close but hadn't gotten to the dropped crates yet. Also, he'd been sabotaged, so Jed had sent Number One down to help retrieve the trigger immediately. Stay in position while I report in to Jed."

So that was what Jed had been on the phone about earlier. How many missions was the man taking care of in his head? One foot in Skopje, one hand in Velesta, one eye on her, the other eye on various other targets, one finger in some kind of deal with someone in Deutsche International—he was the walking, talking multitasking robot.

Not last night.

Helen grinned. Okay, there were moments when he was actually human.

Despite his façade, there was much more to this exasperating man than the cold, ruthless commando that he showed on the outside. She was intrigued by all the things she'd discovered recently, and she planned to find out more. It was strange, how he turned from a make-believe naked avatar into a real live person, and she was comfortable with both. Well, as comfortable as one could get with a man such as Jed. It would never be easy, she realized that now, especially at moments like this, when the thought of him made her...she frowned, lifting one hand...glow. What the hell. She was glowing.

She waved her hand, watching the trail of light that the motion created. She looked at the crowd below. Now that she looked for them, those odd flashes of colors she had seen earlier were more pronounced, but instead of dissipating like before, they hung, like color bubbles, around some of the people.

Was it the serum affecting her perception? She hadn't seen any glow like this that first time she'd used it, but a one-time usage didn't mean anything conclusively. Besides, this time, she was using it before a remote-viewing session, so she wasn't totally exhausted mentally and physically.

She looked down and studied herself. Yes, she was definitely emitting some kind of glow. Now that she was concentrating on it, she could feel some sort of charge. Heat. It didn't feel dangerous. In fact, it felt natural, a part of her. She closed her eyes for a moment, enjoying the sensation. It was enjoyment. Satisfaction. What was giving her these feelings? She projected her senses outward, the way she did when remote viewing, looking from the inside.

Jed in bed with her last night. His body on hers as he took his time pleasuring her. She could feel the orgasm that rocked her, the same powerful surrender, except this feeling was...a memory.

Suddenly, like channels crossing wires, she saw Jed walking with another man toward a waiting limousine. Her senses screamed, warning of danger.

Helen's eyes shot open. She licked her dry lips and listened to the erratic pounding of her heart. That had felt so real, as if she was actually having sex again. She stared at both her hands, then took in the rest of her body. She was glowing even brighter. What. The. Hell?

Grabbing the binoculars, she did another sweep of the crowd, ignoring those odd bursts of light, studying the stage and those on it. Everything appeared normal.

"See anything, Heath?" she asked.

"Negative."

"You don't see anything that's odd at all?" she insisted.

"Negative. What do you see, Hell?"

People that glow. And oh, she was glowing too. Hell shook her head. Something had happened, was happening. Her inner voice had interrupted a...dream? Illusion? Whatever it was, that charge of heat hadn't been spontaneous remote viewing.

"Nothing," she muttered, but her body was still giving little tremors.

Two men walking down below caught her eye. She recognized them from the remote-viewing session; they were the men monitoring that other remote viewer. Or maybe, it was interrupted by a very quick flash of remote viewing. Jed at his private meeting in the VIP garage. *Danger.*

"Shit. Heath. Three o'clock. Two men in black tie and suits. I know they're up to no good. I'm going to follow them. Can you track them while I get down there so I don't lose them?"

"Affirmative."

So good. So drunk.

He was so alive.

Of course he would be okay alone in this room, were they kidding? Go, go, go, leave him here. Yes, yes, he would track that girl bringing the bomb from Velesta—what's her name again, Llallana—yes, Llallana with the pretty black eyes. But she just got into the car after making some silly side trips; she wasn't going to be here in Skopje for hours.

He wasn't going to tell them about that last little bit, though. Yes, let them wander out there doing whatever it was their boss had ordered. He, Jonah Samson, Five-One, was going to roam free from their monitoring. Free to slide inside any of these people to take and record his fill. The streets were filled with wild women here and they gave him what he needed and more, so much more. All fresh sexual memories, as much as he wanted. He'd never experienced so many kinky things—threesomes and foursomes, even orgies between women. Oh, how he liked that. He could tell some of these women didn't want to do the sex acts he was recording but since he was at the receiving end of their services, he didn't care. It felt good to "feel" the sexual power over them, almost as good as really having their pretty little mouths sucking on him. No, better. Because this way, with the serum enhancing his abilities, every part of him felt stronger. And why not use his talents to achieve the kind of orgasm people would kill to have? The absolute power of harvesting someone's sexual pleasure for his own private mental recording, replayed with his body experiencing every detail. Oh, this new collection was going to keep him happy for many, many nights to come. He smirked at his own pun.

He flitted into the male customers' energy glow too, just enough to pick up their sensations of how it felt to be in those girls. He was careful not to go too deep into those bubbles. He'd discovered that some of these guys actually felt guilty while doing it, even if they didn't admit it, but the feeling was there, and he definitely didn't want that marring his enjoyment of his recording. Shame, pain, all those feelings weren't for him; he had enough pain of his own to deal with.

He remembered slamming into that other operative at COMCEN, the one who'd leapt through him when he'd opened all his channels to record. He still had that guy's darkness hanging inside him, like an icicle of acid, dripping once in a while to torment him. He shuddered. *No, don't think about that, Jonah, or you'll attract that kind of bad energy. We don't want bad and sad. We want this!*

This was a young lady entering the place where his monitors had recently gone into. He recognized it from the flags hanging outside. Lots of security. They were waiting for some bad things to happen.

Jonah smiled. Well, there were the decoys, but the really bad thing wouldn't arrive till much later. Mentally, he quickly checked Llallana's location. Still in the car driving, of course. He shrugged. He had lots of play time.

That lady he wanted was hanging onto the arm of her man. They'd just done it this morning. He could tell from how brightly their energies glowed. He liked them young and sexually open because their energies were the easiest to taste and take for his own. They had less negative shit in them too. He slipped inside the bubble, his channels open, looking for the source of the glow and sucking greedily. It was good not to care. Except for an earphone in case they needed to communicate, no one was monitoring him. He didn't have to hide his hard on; in fact, he was probably moaning his pleasure out loud back in the room, but there was no one there. He sighed in satisfaction. Alone. And this one was so good with her hands. His head felt like he was going to explode from the pleasure. This was interactive media at its best.

Because he felt like it, he let out a maniacal laugh as he stumbled out. He hadn't taken any alcohol, but he felt drunk. He looked around him. There were so many more to choose from...

"de Clerq, pass on to Jed that I'm going down to where he is the back way. Tell him the two CIA agents from Stratter's are heading there too. He'll know who I mean. I'm not sure what they're up to." Helen adjusted her hidden weapon, and added, "Tell him to be careful."

"Ten-four."

The access to her cubby hole was a ledge above one of the auditoriums. It took her a few minutes before she got off it and onto the closest floor. She ran toward the exit.

"Heath?" she snapped as she took the stairs.

"They're eight minutes ahead of you and they took the elevator."

"Dammit. Why am I always running down the stairs? Where are the elevators around here?"

"People on the lower floors are using them. It'll take too long for you to wait. Didn't you read the fine print in your contract? Running up and down stairs is SOP for most closed environment hostile operations."

Helen made a rude noise. Heath Cliffe with a sense of humor? She must really be hallucinating. "Easiest access point to the garage then?"

"According to schematics, there's a side door out the front. Take that. Service elevator to Level Two. That's where the VIPs go to take the private elevator that leads to behind the stage."

She didn't care any more that she might be catching someone's attention with her running. Jed was in danger. She knew this with every fiber of her being.

"Not enough time. Tell de Clerq to instruct Number Nine not to get into the car. Repeat. Not to get into any vehicle whatsoever."

"This is de Clerq." The quiet voice of the operative chief at Command came over her ear mic. "How do you know this, Hell? Try not to catch the attention of the group round the corner. Not a good idea."

Helen slowed down. When she turned the corner, she went down on one knee to tie her shoelace. A group of five men walked past, talking quietly. They looked normal enough, but their shoes, she noticed, were new and the same brand. She straightened up and continued down the sloped walkway.

"I passed on your message, Hell," de Clerq said. "He just signaled an acknowledgment. But how do you know about the vehicle, Hell?"

"Too complicated to explain," Helen said. "Just that I have this feeling that it'll be dangerous once Jed enters the vehicle. Trust me on this."

Please. She knew that going out of position on a flimsy reason wasn't going to make it past many of the other operatives listening in.

"Look," she added, "don't move the others. They can stay in their current positions. Just let me check this one out alone. It's a sudden off-site meeting involving a suspicious character from our last operation, de Clerq. We're also waiting for the arrival of a certain explosive device without knowing the timeframe. If you ask Eight Ball, he'll give you a pretty high percentage calculation on something wacky happening in the garage area."

There was a few moment's silence.

"Okay, Hell. This is your call."

"This is Eight. I'll back her up from behind," Heath's voice interrupted.

"Ten-four. Hell?"

"I'm almost there."

Jumping off the banister onto the walkway below, Helen started sprinting.

Jed blinked, betraying nothing as he listened to Weber. That prickle of awareness, light as a feather stroke. He'd had that sensation before, not too long ago, in fact. *Elena.*

"I need to show you certain files but it has to be done in my limousine, away from any cameras. My man's bringing it around over there, far from arrivals." Weber told him. "We don't have much time before the official ceremonies begin."

Jed nodded. He had dealt with Weber before. A hard-nosed bureaucrat who had been one of the original founders of Deutsche International, he was also one of the few inside the think tank today who was aware that its involvement in international politics wasn't all black and white. Weber and his group would have to have a very good reason to involve Deutsche International in the business of buying weapons, though, what with the think tank's mission statement being world peace and disarmament. From the last operation with Helen, it didn't look like they were disarming the decoder for world unity.

That Deutsche International had been invited as one of the VIP visitors today illustrated its influence within the political circles. A conference filled with the emerging powers of Eastern European countries slowly coming out from the umbrella of the former Soviet Union and their internal strife, watched by the media of the world community, was the perfect place for D.I. to find financiers and supporters for its main cause. But of course, as Jed very well knew and understood, there were covert political deals being haggled by different powers even as the front was a united coalition. There were many different kinds of warfare. He just needed to find the connection that would click the whole puzzle into place.

According to Weber, there was something more than business treaties afoot at this convention and it was something that was troubling enough that he approached Jed, of whom he seldom had direct contact. They had an understanding, the kind that allowed covert information to be exchanged without too many questions.

"Surely you can tell me who you want disposed without showing files? You have never needed to give me the background so thoroughly," Jed mused, speaking in German.

Weber furtively looked around. There were no late arrivals. "This is not for me. It is for the foundation and its future." He paused, nodding to his bodyguard to walk ahead toward the waiting car. He added, lowering his voice, "Stefan, there are only two copies of what I am going to show you, one in that car, and the other in a special security box in a Swiss bank. It will be worth a fortune in the market if it is released by the right person."

Jed lifted his brows. "And what's the catch?" he asked cynically.

"You'll understand once you see what I have."

"Number Nine," de Clerq's voice came over Jed's micro-earpiece. "Hell instructs not to enter any vehicle. Repeat. Code Red. Stay away from vehicle. She's heading your way, right behind two men. She said to tell you they're from Stratter's, that you'll understand."

Jed didn't miss a step as he walked alongside Weber toward the limousine, his gaze measuring the distance between him and the vehicle. His word for today had been providence. Indeed, it looked like he needed some quick intervention right now.

Helen heard a crash and, pulling out a weapon, ran even faster toward its direction. Curses, men barking orders at each other. A thin high cry from further left, beyond a wall that acted as a buffer for VIPs arriving or leaving in their vehicles. That didn't sound like Jed.

Since it was already late, there were no moving cars in the vicinity. Everyone who had to be in the auditorium should already be there, ready for the treaty speech. Everyone but Jed and those who had tricked him to come down here.

"Jed signaled. We created a short power outage, elevators included. You have twelve minutes to get Jed out before Macedonian security reach you, over," de Clerq instructed.

"Ten-four," Helen acknowledged, peering around the corner. Semi-darkness.

It was silent now. From memory, she retraced the underground parking schematics in her head. Buffer wall. That meant the elevator was ten feet from her, closer to her than that first yelp of pain.

She stepped into the darkness that was illuminated by the strips of emergency lights here and there on the walls. *Danger.* She sensed rather than saw the movement behind her and reflex kicked in as she bent forward and moved sideways. Air whooshed where her head had been. She heard the snick of a weapon being cocked. Making a rapid judgment call, she turned, and fired hers. Its silencer emitted a quiet "pop" and the dark shadow before her crumpled to the ground. Helen crouched behind a column.

One down. There was at least one more close by. Where the hell was Jed? She couldn't just shoot at every moving shadow, not without knowing his location.

In answer, a familiar shape dropped down next to her. It would have startled her if she hadn't trusted the instincts that usually warned her of danger. She smiled grimly in the darkness. Easy. She thought of Jed, and he just appeared, silent as death itself. He leaned forward, his lips brushing her ear.

"Weber's driver sold him out. Shot the bodyguard. He's out of the vehicle, looking for Weber. Possibly two hostiles without yours."

Okay, so Weber wasn't one of the bad guys. Helen moved closer and whispered back, "I shot one of mine. Pretty sure it's one of the CIA operatives. One more."

His hand touched the nape of her neck briefly. "I have to get to Weber. They want him as well. We need him alive. Cover me."

He didn't wait for an answer, standing and disappearing into the darkness in seconds. Helen frowned. How was she supposed to cover him? She didn't know where he was heading and it was too dark to tell one shape from another.

She blinked, realization dawning. Of course. Today was the day for decoys. She stood and started to run noisily toward the elevator, making scraping sounds with her shoes. Almost immediately, footsteps came from behind her. She ducked behind another post, pulled out a piece of metal and flipped it at the wall across from her. It hit, thudding loudly. She repeated this, each time aiming a little further, as if "she" were going that direction. Bait.

The man tracking her followed in that direction too, but he was dodging behind vehicles and columns, just as she had been. He wasn't taking the bait that easily. He suddenly turned and started shooting in her direction, sweeping a wide path of bullets that bounced and rained around her.

Helen crouched lower, trying to make herself as small as possible. *That* was no small firearm. It was something a lot bigger, probably an AK-47 machine gun, and a two-and-a-half-foot cement column wasn't going to be much protection, especially if she betrayed her location. Obviously, her hostile had decided that the darkness meant he hadn't the time to play cat and mouse, deducing that Security would be on the way down here soon. But heck, Jed wanted her to cover him, didn't he? She hoped he got to Weber because she didn't think Security was going to be fooled by a short-circuited blackout any more, not with this racket.

She took a deep breath and started running to the back wall, rolling and tumbling, still using the columns for protection, as sprays of gunfire followed her. He was coming after her in earnest, the staccato rat-tat-tat stopping and starting as he searched for her moving shadow.

Bait. She had only a few minutes left before the authorities showed up. He was right behind her now, confident because she wouldn't have anywhere else to run once she reached the back wall. Her timing had to be just right. The main radiators to heat the building should be right ahead. She needed him to aim in that direction.

One more column. Her hostile would think that this was it, and he'd move in for the kill. Helen darted right, then cut left. Bullets hit the pipes and sparks flew, burning her arms as she launched into the air, across the hood of one vehicle, and slid under.

Metallic pops reverberated as the damaged radiators exploded from the gunfire. She heard the powerful whoosh of compressed steam and hot water gushing out. A horrific scream echoed in the darkness. She scrunched her face at the sound. That couldn't have felt good.

"Elena."

She rolled out the other side of the car, her body hitting a pair of shoes. She found herself pulled onto her feet. The roar of rushing steam drowned out Jed's words. He started running, her hand still in his, so she had no choice but to follow. She didn't have time to look back at the man who had been targeting her.

They reached the elevator just as the lights started to come back on. Elena blinked, trying to focus. The elevator doors opened and she found herself pushed gently inside.

"Up, follow de Clerq's instructions, and back to the hotel," Jed ordered.

Helen looked at him. His nice suit was torn and dirty, as if he'd been rolling on a bit of floor himself. There was blood on his hands. The look in his eyes made her shiver—cold and aloof. Unemotional. The eyes of a killer.

She nodded. "Weber?"

"He's okay. But he and I have some explaining to do. I don't want to explain right now. I'll see you back at the hotel soon."

She could hear shouts heading down the walkway where she'd come from. "I'm okay," she answered his unspoken question as she ran her hand lightly up one bloodied arm. "Scrapes."

There was no outward response at all from Jed. "Good decoy. Too much noise," he said, pressed the button for the second floor and stepped back, letting the doors close.

"Wait a minute! That wasn't me—" the doors cut off the rest of her sentence "—using a machine gun!" she finished, and stamped her foot. "Damn it, he always gets the last word."

Later, back at the hotel, Helen watched him giving directives to operatives left and right as he changed back into his jeans and shirt. After making sure she wasn't really injured, he hadn't exchanged more than a few words with her before being swarmed by calls from different agencies. She watched, fascinated as he morphed seamlessly from the cold assassin she'd seen in the underground garage to negotiator, and then to the voice of authority, telling someone somewhere what to do with some kind of information the head of Deutsche International had passed on to Jed. Through it all, his silver eyes watched her like a hawk, following her as she walked around the room. She knew she was acting a tad bit too restless, but she couldn't stop herself. He was emanating the most beautiful glow and if she didn't move around, she would be unable to resist the sudden urge to touch him, to feel all that energy calling to her. What were these bubbly things she kept seeing when she concentrated on a person? Was it the serum? If so, besides overriding her pain and exhaustion, what was it enhancing? And why did she herself glow too?

"Jed, vid-feed from Diamond. He's with Hawk McMillan."

"Be right there." Jed turned to her and said, "If Diamond has secured the trigger, we'll fly back to Center immediately. I want you examined by Dr. Kirkland ASAP."

Helen cocked her head. He was just too serious. "Won't you prefer another day near Lake Matka?" she teased. "I'm not sleepy at all, so the brain entrainment machine's going to be useless. I can think of other ways to use up all this serum-enhanced energy."

The corner of his lips lifted slightly but his light eyes were still watchful. "I'll find a way to tire you out." He caressed her face with the back of his hand. "Food. Drink."

She gave a mock salute and watched him go. Damn, but she loved watching his ass in those faded jeans.

Nooo! The bitch had killed his monitors! They were his only connection to the serum! He hadn't ever considered the danger of his job, that he or his handlers might die. What would become of him?

Jonah hadn't dared go closer to the dead body. He never liked the energy that still clung to the recently deceased. He followed one man, then another, trying to figure what to do next.

Despair raged through him. He didn't even know how to get back to the States. Alone. In the darkness. *No serum.* The thought of being left all by himself brought him into near panic. He willed himself to calm down. There was nobody monitoring his physical body back in the room and he couldn't afford a cardiac arrest right now.

He heard English. American English. Turning, he saw two men conversing in low voices. Definitely American. Following them was easy, of course, and listening in made his blood boil. It was that bitch from COMCEN again, interfering with his life. He continued following them till they reached a hotel room, knowing he would find her there.

The sight of her made him angrier than ever. She was looking down, studying something in her hand, a small frown crinkling her forehead. She held it up to the light and it was a vial, the kind of medical glass container that held drugs to be drawn out through a syringe. He was very familiar with them because his handlers had carried them for his second dosages.

Jonah glared with hatred at the source of all his trouble. The bitch caused this. If he were to be stranded out here, with no serum, so should she. She was going down too.

He wasn't sure what he was doing but he understood his abilities a lot better now. It all made sense. Remote viewers gauged sights and sounds, recording them in an objective way, but he'd managed to cross the invisible line with his special talents. He could see more than that when he remote viewed. Somehow he'd found a way to "record" energy. He recalled the one whose "painful" energy he'd inadvertently taken by mistake—what if he crashed into the bitch now and returned that unwanted gift? What if he took everything from her and left her in pain? Could he do that? He didn't know how, but he was even more powerful now, wasn't he? They'd told him that some remote viewers could be trained to kill. He didn't know how, but he would find a way to damage her.

He'd always known he was far better than the other candidates and he could prove it by trying something new on the one person whom they had deemed better than him. And look at all that glorious sexy glow coming from her. What a goldmine.

Jonah rushed at her, his channels open at full strength. He would suck everything from her. He would find a way to hurt her back. He had nothing to lose.

"Dragan Dilaver is no longer an asset," Jed told Hawk McMillan, giving permission to the SEAL to do what he'd been wanting to do with the drug lord before cutting off the video transmission.

Dragan Dilaver had only been useful as long as he was the only one who could give them the coordinates to the missing explosive trigger. But Hawk had found the crates and the trigger was no longer in it. The SEALs' newest information was also worrisome. A sleeper agent, Llallana Noretski, had it, and Jed had a feeling that she was heading to Skopje, and not back to Dilaver, looking to use it at one of the venues where the international visitors and diplomats were congregating.

Dilaver wasn't running this particular show back in Velesta. He wasn't interested in assassinations when there was no profit involved. No, he was just someone who was to keep that particular weapon for a while and now the person had set his or her plan in motion.

It made sense. A decoy to distract from the real target. Not during the most obvious day—today, with its significant treaty-signing and speeches—but on one that was less suspicious, when a few of the more influential VIPs would be gathered. Like a photo-op during an art exhibit, for instance, that was coming up in a few days. Everyone would be more relaxed because they'd be thinking that the main danger had been taken care of, and with the treaty already signed, the danger was passed.

A sleeper cell program connected to the CIA, ran by rogue operatives for the last ten years, activated. Jesus, Mary, and Joseph. They could activate any number of cells to do their bidding, especially now when the traitors were on the run. They'd had ten years to set up a complex system in D.C., invading the very heart of the CIA HQ, before they were caught. And Jed and his team had—what—these four months to play catch up with just a fucking list of the missing weapons.

Providence had brought Elena to them. Jed could guess how much time she'd saved COMCEN. She, her skills, and the COMCEN Total Immersive VR program had come together at exactly the right time.

He pulled out his cell phone. So many more details to take care of now. He couldn't possibly leave; he had a sleeper cell to take care of. Elena was going to fight tooth and nail to stay, but he was going to send her back to Center. Her headaches and spontaneous remote viewing worried him. And now there were flashes of colors, she'd said. He frowned. He remembered her talking about some beautiful colors in the last RV session they had together, when he had trouble getting her attention to return from the ether. He wasn't liking all these incidents one bit. Elena needed to be in a controlled environment, under the watchful eye of her doctors and COMCEN scientists. He wanted to be with her, but he had a bomb to stop. He'd be back at Center immediately after he'd done his job.

He paused outside the connecting door, mentally getting ready for a fight. It was just a matter of compartmentalizing his desire to be with her, that was all. He was under no illusion that she would figure out immediately that she was taken off an assignment not because of performance, but because of his personal wish. It wouldn't sit well with her competitive spirit. But it had to be done. If necessary, he'd manipulate her to do what he wanted. She would hate him all over again. Couldn't be helped. He'd just have to make it up to her somehow.

He opened the door. All thought froze.

Elena was on the floor, in a seizure. Her body flopped about helplessly and he could see the white of her eyes and her mouth open, silently screaming.

"Elena!"

Jed rushed to her and fell on his knees. He reached out to hold her but she was violently flailing now and her pants came out in a strange monotonic syllable, like an old vinyl record skipping over a scratch.

"Elena!"

He pulled her into his arms and the shaking died a little. Her eyes came back down and he could feel her struggling for control.

"Elena!"

For once, Jed couldn't pull his thoughts together, couldn't string any sentences. He looked up and found Heath staring from the doorway.

"Get a doctor," he breathed out through his clenched throat, then stood with Helen in his arms. "Get help."

Heath disappeared. A low animalistic growl came from the back of Helen's throat, chilling Jed to the bone. It kept on going, becoming a howl, as if some form of possessed spirit was inhabiting her body. The sound was heart-wrenching, a desperate cry for help. He'd never felt so helpless in his life.

"Elena! It's me, Jed. Hold on. Hold on!"

Her awful howling stopped. Her dull eyes lit up at the sound of his voice.

"Jed!" she gasped.

"Yes, it's me." He pulled her higher in his arms, her head rolling back against his racing heart. "Hang on for me, Elena."

"Something smashed. Into...me. Taking over. Ea...eating...eating my brain." Her hand fisted, hitting him on the shoulder. "Stop it! Stop him! Inside. Jed! I...fighting him..."

Jed leaned forward, trying to catch all her words. Smashed into her? Like the incident in the stairwell? "Get him, then, Elena," he urged. "Don't let him win."

"I can't hear. He...screaming...in my head. Pain."

The rumbling growl started again. Helen's body shook uncontrollably. Where the hell was Heath? His inability to do anything shredded him like a knife. All he could do was rock her, trying to absorb whatever it was that was hurting her.

"Jed!"

"I'm here." She seemed to be fighting herself and something else and he couldn't help her.

"Jed!"

"I'm here, baby."

His reassurances reached her and her trembling became less violent again.

"He...it...in pain, Jed. He can't...control...he...wants out. Can't." Her breathing grew labored. "My head's exploding. Can't...see." Her eyes rolled back again. "Going with it...him. I know...it's him...Stratter's. Colors. His pain...I can't take it."

"No, you aren't fucking taking her with you to see colors," Jed roared, wanting to shake whatever it was out of her. He held her even tighter. Must control himself. *Think, Jed.* She was still connected to him through the trigger. This was the unexpected event he'd been anticipating, wasn't it? He was going to keep her safe through sheer will alone. "Elena Ekaterina Rostova, do you hear me? You aren't leaving me. Checkered flag, damn you, listen to me. Checkered flag! You'll not leave me, Elena."

He pulled her face close to his, crooning over and over into her ear so she could hear him The trigger was already activated but right now, repeating it was the only hold he had on her. Her eyes widened, registering it, and for a moment he thought she was winning her battle within her.

"Something's terrifying him," she gasped out. "He wants to...use me...to escape. F...fight...must...fighh..."

Helen's fisted hand slowly uncurled as her whole body went terrifyingly still.

"Nooo!" Jed shook her. Swung her higher in his arms, burying his face in her neck. Panic like he'd never felt before enveloped him. He couldn't lose her. He hadn't told her how much she meant to him. Despair punched a hole in his gut. He shook her again, willing her to open her eyes.

Nothing.

"Nooo!"

Complement

From Jed's dictionary: ~verb (used with object), to complete, form an addition to, supplement to make a complete whole

INTERMUNDIA

Latin, meaning the space between worlds. The past shapes the future and explains the present. A story within a story makes a more complete picture.

Dublin, Ireland

Full moon in Dublin. Conor didn't look at it long. It was too bright and he was too hungry. He was growing out of his clothes again, so he'd better stop eating and growing some more or get some money to buy a new pair of pants. The last option, in his opinion, was doable.

Of course, right now the tightness of his jeans was more because of the administration of a certain pretty female's hand. He was hungry for food. His body was hungry for women too, but when one was jobless and homeless, there wasn't much one could do about either. And when there were plenty of food and a pretty female... Conor narrowed his eyes in anticipation as he watched the young Asian woman release his full erection into the open. His hips involuntarily jerked forward at the sight of her pink tongue licking her lips.

"You look like a young man who likes dangerous women, honey," she said to him. "Yes?"

"I don't know," Conor replied. *Just put your mouth on me.* "Why do you say that?"

"You don't rob an IRA stash and then wait around in one of their houses to get laid by one of their women, sweet thing."

She had a point. But then, he bet most thieves didn't go looking for food in the fridge and then have a half-naked attractive lass serving him when he had trouble pulling out food when he'd trouble holding on to his gun. And then she hadn't protested when he'd leaned in and kissed her.

"You convinced me," he told her boldly.

"How old are you?"

"Why do you care?"

"Honey, as a rule, I don't sleep with boys." She was a beautiful woman, with big eyes and a ripe mouth. She looked at him up and down before adding softly, "But I think I might break that rule tonight. It's been a while since I've had me an inexperienced boy."

"I'm not a virgin," Conor told her arrogantly. "If I fuck you, lady, you're going to beg for me all night, and I don't have time. Your man's gonna be back soon."

"And if you take that whole big sack of weapons with you, he'll hunt you down and kill you," she warned.

Was that supposed to scare him? "He can stand in line," he said scornfully. Lots of men were after his blood.

He'd been on his own for a while now. He considered himself old enough to take care of himself. After all, when one had been kicked out of the house enough times because his ma happened to be taking care of a customer, when one's da was hiding somewhere in a drunken stupor, and when one's older brother had spat at the door the day he'd left for good, one had to grow up really quickly.

It hadn't taken long, and he'd already learned how to live on the dangerous side of life. Stealing had become an art. Just stay out of the gangs; they would kill anyone who was in their territory. He possessed two guns and knew how to use them. He had a knife in his pant leg because sometimes guns made too much noise. He knew what the smell of blood on the hands was like, the way the red could stain one's hands for hours if one didn't wash it off immediately.

"And he can try," Conor continued. But he told himself to hurry because the lady'd said IRA stash. That meant trouble. And yeah, she was a dangerous female to mess around with. He flashed his trademark grin, a wicked devil-may-care smile he knew worked with lots of lasses. "So if he's gonna be mad anyway, ya better come here and let me ravish you a bit, eh?"

Ain't no tellin' when he was going to get laid again. And if he were to be on the run from the IRA, might as well have a good fuck to go.

The woman kneeled down in front of him, putting her hands on his hips. Conor continued chewing on the drumstick, watching her, making sure she didn't have a knife or something. You never know with these bitches. One moment they said they wanted your dick and then the next, they had a knife at your throat asking for your wallet. He wasn't a stupid and starving boy on the street any more. Not even for...he almost choked on the chicken when she took his penis into her mouth. It took several seconds before he could actually focus again.

She paused, looking up. "How old are you?" she repeated her question, running a long index finger under his cock. "I'm debating about turning child molester."

He didn't want to talk. He wanted her to continue doing what she'd been doing, but adults were weird because they always wanted a reason to do something bad. Obviously, the lady needed his permission or something.

He rubbed his sticky fingers on his rain-soaked tee shirt. "I'm eighteen," he lied, then lunged forward, pushing her onto the floor as he quickly parted her legs. He didn't need his jeans off; he was more than ready.

He put his hand between her legs. She didn't have any underwear on and was wet. That was good. The girls he'd been with told him they became wet when they got excited, and he'd discovered that they got wetter if he played with them a bit. He ran his fingers lightly over the woman's pussy. A year ago, he'd never have thought that he would be having sex with a stranger in somebody else's kitchen. A year ago he'd never have thought about checking a woman for weapons either.

The woman squirmed under him. "Oh my," she breathed. "You have clever fingers for a young boy."

"I have more than clever fingers," Conor said brashly, feeling more confident than he actually was. "And I'm gonna show you I'm a man."

She laughed. "You do that."

The woman looked to be in her mid-twenties and was undoubtedly more experienced; he'd better make it last. He hoped he could hold off coming for...he slid into her slickness and bit back a groan. Shit, no way was he going to last more than a minute. Why did a woman feel so good when he was inside her? He clenched his jaw, trying to make it last.

The woman wrapped her legs around his waist, moving her hips up to meet his in unison, going faster and faster. He felt a bit intimidated at how eager she was, at how she took charge of him. The other lasses mostly just lay there.

Maybe if he didn't give her what she was asking. Maybe if he slowed down a bit.

His eyes crossed as he forced himself to move slower, to take his time. He used his strength to keep her swiveling hips in place, his thighs forcing her parted legs down as he buried himself deep and hard, then pulled out slowly. He did it again. The woman started moaning, asking him to go faster. He could feel her getting wetter. Oh yeah, she liked this, all right.

Not. Giving. Her what. She. Wants. He gritted his teeth and repeated, battling the need to come with the need to show her he was a man. Her moans became groans, long and drawn out, and he felt her insides spasming around him. The feeling was incredible. He paused at the wonder of it.

"No...!"

Her shriek took him aback. "No?" he asked, confused, thinking he'd done something wrong.

"Don't stop! Don't stop!" Her voice was urgent and her nails scored his shoulders.

Conor looked down at her, realization dawning for the first time. She wasn't in control any more. *He was.* He liked the feeling very much.

"So you like that, hmm?" he asked. He moved. She shuddered, urging him to go faster. Curiosity had calmed him enough so that he kept his speed nice and steady. She shuddered again, her insides milking him. So, women felt pleasure deep inside and the longer he lasted, the more they came. Could they come indefinitely? Lucky creatures. He could only come once and that was it.

He jerked up, suddenly tense. He'd left the kitchen window open after he'd entered, for a quick exit. He thought he heard a car pulling up outside the building. The sound of doors slamming. The woman under him was suddenly tense too.

"That's my boyfriend, Seamus," she said, her eyes wide. "Get up!"

Three long flights of stairs. Conor cocked his head. "No, I gotta come first, lady."

"What? Are you crazy? Have you no idea what the IRA is?" She started to push him off.

He did, but suddenly, he didn't care. He just wanted to feel her squeezing him again, enjoying him and him enjoying her. Walk from car. Unlock the stairway gate. Three long flights of stairs. He could do it. He grabbed her hands and leaned forward, trapping them against the floor, spreading her legs further apart. He thrust inside her, hard and fast.

"Come again for me," he whispered.

He pushed in all the way and heard her gasp. This time his pace was relentless as he let himself go, concentrating on her heat. Her breathing grew uneven again, like before. Just for the hell of it, he took a deep breath and slowed down. It felt like his whole head was going to explode from the roar inside his brain. He heard the woman cry out and felt her coming all around him. He plunged in deep and his orgasm was like nothing he'd ever felt before. His hips moved like pistons as he kept coming and coming.

His breathing was ragged even as he pulled out of her and quickly jumped to his feet, tucking his sensitive dick back inside his pants. The woman just lay there, her eyes half-closed, her breasts bobbing up and down as she panted.

Her parted legs were lax and he could see exactly where he'd been.

"Got to go," Conor said, feeling cocky. He'd just made this older lady come three times. "I told you I'd leave you begging for more."

He grabbed the sack with the stash of weapons he'd gathered from the other rooms. He had one leg out the window when he heard the front door opening.

"Kitty?"

The woman continued to lie there, her mouth half-opened, watching him. Then she smiled sleepily and blew him a kiss.

Conor grinned. So that was what dangerous women were like. He disappeared into the night.

One month later

Conor stared at the bright moon, with what looked like its twins on each side. Someone told him that was called a blue moon. He'd never actually seen anything like it.

The world had so many things he would like to see. He heard the pyramids in Egypt were bigger than the tallest building. Could one climb up a pyramid? And wouldn't that be cool, he, Jed Conor McNeil, on top of a pyramid with the blue moon shining over it?

He'd get to Egypt some day. He didn't want to remain here, always hiding from one thing or another. Of course, he wouldn't have to hide if the IRA guys weren't so pissed at him for taking off with their stash of weapons. He didn't think he'd committed that big a crime. They were the IRA; one would think they had more weapons than that.

But they were pissed, all right. There was word on the street for the kid with gray eyes. That would be him, cursed with eyes everyone remembered.

"They ain't gray either," Conor said aloud. His eyes were distinctive because they were light, the color of a shiny silver florin, his ma used to say.

And the boy's worthless like a florin too.

Conor grimaced. That line was his da's tag whenever his ma brought up the florin comparison. It hurt. He didn't show it to his father but it hurt to be told he was worthless.

Well, he was worth something on the streets, apparently, because there was a price for any information on him. No one knew his name because he didn't make friends that easily. That was a good thing too, or the IRA bastards would have gotten hold of him by now.

Conor grinned. He had their loot, that was why. He hadn't known they would be this angry this long; he'd heard the IRA had a lot of important things to do, fighting and bombing buildings in one country or another. I guess they had some time to play hide-and-seek with him.

The only person who'd seen him that night was the woman named Kitty, so she must have given a description of him to her boyfriend, Seamus. He wondered whether Seamus found her the way he had last seen her—on the floor, with her legs parted suggestively. If he'd money, he'd bet that Kitty did just that and got that boyfriend of hers so angry that he was using all his time and energy to come after him.

Stupid. Conor lifted his head at the moon again and resisted the temptation to howl. Stupid because everything was about something else other than what was important. He was wasting time here, hiding, when he should just dump the weapons at the guy's front door and then leave town. Maybe they would let him off and wouldn't come after him any more.

But he was stupid too. He wanted to keep the weapons and play hide-and-seek. He wanted to see how angry he could make Seamus and his thugs. The longer they kept the word out on the street that they wanted him caught, the more obstinate he became.

Besides, he'd never seen so many new guns and weaponry in his life. He was very careful when he handled them—didn't want any sudden explosions. He thought of all the men who would be using them. Why did they do what they do? He understood hunger and homelessness, so maybe they did it to provide themselves with a place to stay and lots of food. Not to forget, a girlfriend.

He thought of Kitty again. She'd had a funny accent, not quite British or Irish, as if she was a foreigner. He wondered what country she was from and whether he'd know where it was. China? Hong Kong? He really needed to get hold of a world map, so he could memorize all those fancy names.

He chuckled. Like he would have the chance to impress any ladies with his knowledge of the world map any time soon. He had to find out how to sell shiny new stolen weapons without the IRA fellows finding him. Then he had to figure out what to do with the money he'd get from the sale. Definitely wasn't going to stay in Dublin, but where would he go? He could take the train and visit his cousin but what if Seamus got wind of that and sent men after him there? He was learning fast that men like Seamus would waste time and money for revenge. No, he couldn't do that to Killian.

Conor froze at the sound of footsteps below him. His eyes darted into the shadows of the far right corner of the alley below. Very few people came around to this abandoned building and usually his "guests" were mainly noisy and drunk folks, not one with the quiet footfall of a policeman. He moved back against the building wall so that the moonlight was no longer on him, keeping a clear view of the narrow alley below him.

A shadow emerged. The moonlight, slanting off one wall, gave just enough light to show a tall lone male as he paused to light a cigarette. There was a minute's silence as Conor continued watching, the smell of nicotine wafting up to where he was.

"I know you're up there, son," the man suddenly said, his voice calm and conversational. "I want to talk to you."

Conor pressed his back hard against the wall as he quelled his quickening breathing. Shit. They'd found him.

"I'm not Seamus. I know you're aware he and his IRA friends want you badly. I also know you're pretty good at hiding because they haven't been able to find you yet, but if I can find you, others will, son, sooner or later. Your luck will run out. You see, you stole something really important to several groups of people and they're all eager to get it back. I'm here to help you before you get yourself killed."

Conor listened, not saying a word, his heart thudding louder and louder. This man must think him an idiot. What, was he supposed to come forward and be grateful for the offer?

Still, if the man had wanted to scare him, he could have just rushed into this building with some henchmen. Now, that would be what Seamus would have done. So maybe this man was speaking some truth.

The silence stretched as the man waited for him to speak. Conor didn't move or utter a word, watching the lit tip of the cigarette glow brighter and dimmer every time the stranger inhaled from it. Finally, the man tossed the cigarette on the ground and there was darkness again.

"Okay, think about this. How are you going to get rid of the stolen goods? Pawn them? No pawnshops are going to buy them from a young kid, especially when the IRA is looking for missing weapons. You can't stay in this situation, playing adult games. You have no idea what you've gotten yourself into."

Conor spoke up before he changed his mind. "You still haven't told me what you want."

The shadow shifted, looking up, spending a few moments trying to locate him. Plastered against the wall, Conor stood very still.

"There are actually several things I want but I don't know whether you'll be able to carry out all of them. The main thing, of course, is the weapons. Do you still have them, son?"

"I thought you said I couldn't pawn them off," Conor reminded him. He was right, of course. He'd known that no one would touch weapons stolen from the IRA so soon. But something told him that it was more than mere stolen guns. "What is it that you really want, you and Seamus and all the other people looking for me? I'm thinking it can't be just a bag of guns even though they'd cost you a lot of money to have them replaced. What's with these particular guns?"

"An observant young fellow," the man commented. "Or, a fool for bringing that up. Everything points to you being a reckless boy who doesn't care for a future."

Conor cocked his head. This man *was* strange. He'd never met anyone who talked like that, almost as if they were equals. Yet he knew they weren't. Instinct told him that the stranger couldn't be trusted, just that he was *very good* at sounding trustworthy.

"Does that mean you're going to kill me?" he asked brashly. He was afraid but showing his fear was useless. If he were going to die now, he might as well do it without sniveling.

"It'd crossed my mind," the man replied gravely. "At first, we thought you were somebody more dangerous, sent in to sabotage all the work we've put into our operation, but from what I can gather, you're just very young. A petty thief. Fate, as usual, dealt an unexpected hand."

Conor frowned. Adults talked in circles. He'd no idea what the stranger meant, with his talk about sabotage and operation, but he could sense that the man was dangerous and not to be trifled with. "So I'm free to go if I just give you what you want?"

"Eventually."

"Eventually?" That didn't sound very promising.

"Seamus is still after you, as well as several other groups. I know you don't understand what you've done but believe me when I tell you that it's made quite a number of people very angry with you."

Conor shrugged. He didn't care. What was intriguing was the fact that the man still hadn't demanded the weapons, just asked whether he had them. That was very strange.

"Do you know what a show of faith is, son?"

Conor frowned. "Faith? Like faith in God?"

"Something like that. I'm going to walk up these steps toward your voice, with my hands in the air. The moonlight will let you see exactly that. I'm putting my faith in you that you won't shoot or attack me. All right with you?"

"How would I know you won't shoot or attack me?" Conor asked.

"That, son, would be faith on your part. Besides, if I'd wanted to, I'd have aimed my weapon at that wall you're hiding by right now, and believe me, one of the bullets would have hit you."

Conor believed him but that didn't mean he would admit it. "No, sir, there's a chance you might have gotten me with a bullet but you can't know for sure."

The man chuckled. "Are you saying you're faster than bullets too?"

"No, but this is my hideout. I know my voice bounces off the three walls surrounding me, so you'd have one in three chances at choosing the correct one I'm standing against. If you had been wrong the first few shots, I'd be gone by the time you discover that. Is that also what is called faith?"

The chuckle came again. "Arrogant pup too. That's either going to shorten your life or prolong it, depending on what you have between your ears. Now, I'm still going to be walking up these steps. I'm still going to show you good faith. And when I get up there, I want to talk to you man-to-man."

Conor thought of the knives on him. He fought well with them and knew where to hurt someone quickly. He'd never killed anyone before, though. If he agreed to this man coming up and meeting him, there was more than a good chance one of them would end up dead, he was sure of this much.

The man didn't give him time to answer, though, as he started to head slowly up the steps, his shoes making soft thuds as he climbed each one. The moonlight showed him to be a tall well-dressed man in a long jacket of some sort that was open loosely in the front. His hands, as he'd promised, were way up, free of weapons

Conor watched with narrowed eyes, the thudding in his chest getting excruciatingly loud. He took in a few deep breaths, like the way he'd seen wrestlers do when the bell signaled them to get back into the ring. That helped. A little. He gripped the knife in his hand tightly then deliberately relaxed his upper arm. He'd been in street fights before. One didn't win by tensing one's muscles, because it slowed reflexes; he'd learned that the hard way.

The man stopped on the top step and paused. "Are you going to come out from your hiding place?" he asked softly.

Conor arced his hand in one swift motion and released the knife. He heard the whoosh as it flew through the air. To see whether the man was planning to shoot, he'd deliberately aimed it at the opposite side from where the man stood. The diversion would give him time to get his other knife.

However, the tall stranger didn't react by ducking or shooting. He just stood where he was, his hands still in the air. When he spoke again, his voice remained calm, although a little colder.

"Come on out here," he said, the request this time coming out as an order.

Conor hesitated, then slid out of the shadows, carefully threading his way toward the man, who was studying Conor as closely as he did him. He finally came to a stop about five feet away. The moonlight played with the planes on the man's face—clean-cut, stern mouth, watchful eyes. It was so bright that Conor could see the shiny leather shoes on his feet.

"That was a good diversion tactic but too obvious," the man said. "Next time use the weapon to target the body, just enough to nick, just enough to tell your opponent you mean business. Create fear, don't show it, son."

"Next time dress in clothes that I could wear so there's a reason for me to rob you, mister," Conor retorted. "I'm here, man-to-man, now what?"

"Can I put down my hands?"

Conor frowned. Why was the man so damn polite? He was acting as if Conor had power over what he was doing. "Yeah."

The man lowered his hands. "Nice to meet you. Got a name?"

"Depends. If you're not with Seamus, then who are you?"

Conor thought he saw a gleam of teeth, as if his obstinacy amused the man.

"Ever heard of the CIA, son?"

Dublin, Ireland, Six months after blue moon

"You ready for tomorrow, lover?"

Conor turned from the window. "You shouldn't be here, Kitty. Seamus will be having a tantrum again and I don't want any trouble the night before something big."

Kitty sauntered into the room anyway, picking up scattered items draped across the table and the back of the chair, and looking at them before flinging them down onto the bed. She sat down at the foot, crossing her legs as she leaned back to look at him.

"He won't be home for a while," she drawled, her dark eyes half-closed. "He told me he has to pick up something from out of town."

Conor frowned. "Did he tell you what?"

Kitty shrugged. "No."

The rules for their group were few but specific. No one being allowed to leave the building the day before a big event was one of them. Of course, Seamus thought the rules excluded him because he was, at times, given the responsibility of team leader.

They were going to blow up a bank and take somebody important hostage tomorrow. Everyone was to stay in their apartments so they would get last minute instructions if anything important cropped up. Seamus knew better than to sneak out at this juncture of the operation.

"He's going to be in trouble if McGuy finds out," Conor said. He'd better get on the phone and inform McGuy about this, but first he had to deal with Kitty in his room. "What if someone calls in for Seamus? What are you going to say?"

Kitty shrugged again. "I'm not his keeper. Maybe he went to visit another woman. I don't particularly care."

Walking away from the window, Conor approached the woman in his bed. She was beautiful, with long, straight black hair and big sultry dark eyes that made Asians so exotic-looking. He had never met a woman like her—bold, mysterious, independent.

Ever since McGuy had brought him in and firmly introduced him to this particular group of IRA men as his new help, Kitty had visited his small apartment beneath hers often, even climbing down from the fire ladder outside the window one night and breaking into his room. He'd never had a woman so determined to fuck him. And he'd never had such hot sex. The woman was wild in bed and his dick didn't seem to think it needed sleep.

Of course, at the time, McGuy hadn't known that Kitty was interested in Conor that way or he'd never have given him that particular place to stay. Seamus's seething resentment was misread as anger at a thief being included into their mix.

Conor understood Seamus' silence. Of course the man wasn't going to tell his friends that a boy barely out of school had messed around with his girl. Was still messing with, in fact. He would be the butt of jokes among the guys.

Kitty was insatiable and kept things even more tense between Seamus and Conor. Seamus, she told Conor, wasn't her boyfriend. She and he had an "understanding".

Conor wasn't sure what that meant but after staying there and learning his new life, he was aware that Kitty was very useful to the organization. She could handle a gun and make explosives. She was able to hack into bank computers. She did nifty things with timers and electronics. Conor was fascinated by her and her skills, and didn't put up much resistance to spending time with her.

She had naughty hands that sometimes wandered under the table right in front of Seamus, or sitting with Conor in a car in the dark, with Seamus driving, and Conor had to learn to keep his face pretty

Gennita Low

much expressionless as a hand teased the front of his trousers. The danger of being caught excited him even more. One night, out of sheer frustration, he'd pushed her into a small closet during a break from planning, put a hand over her mouth and fucked her hard. He could hear the others wandering around the place, stretching, taking bathroom breaks. But Kitty had wrapped her legs around his waist and squeezed her pelvis so tightly, he'd almost given them away when he grunted from sheer pleasure.

Seamus suspected, but couldn't prove, what they were doing behind his back. He already resented Conor for the theft of the weapons, but McGuy had coolly calmed everyone down, saying that they needed a young man with Conor's skills. Also, Conor's face wasn't on any official files, so no one would recognize a boy loitering around the bank as an IRA lookout.

Then there was the time McGuy had caught Kitty coming behind him, wrapping a hand around and groping him. McGuy had been giving Conor private CIA instructions one night and was standing in the shadows when Kitty came charging into his room. McGuy was supposed to be away at the time so she'd expected Conor to be alone. Conor had turned to stop her but she had caught his lips with hers and passionately kissed him.

"I've been looking at you all day. I've got to have you, man-child, now, quickly," she said, pushing him so he sat on his bed.

When Conor had glanced over by the window, he couldn't even see the man, but he was sure he was there.

"Kitty—"

But it was hard to fight off a woman who already somehow had his cock in her mouth. He sort of remembered cursing and trying to stand up. He'd looked up again and saw McGuy's shadowy form coming closer.

Shit, had he thought he was in trouble then. But Kitty's mouth was a force to be reckoned with. He had two choices. Stop Kitty and risk her feeling McGuy's presence. Keep her distracted so McGuy could leave.

It was embarrassing to be in that position, but he couldn't betray McGuy. Not after the man had taken care of him like he had the last few months. Besides, a part of him had registered that the older man was testing him or he wouldn't be coming so much closer. Any moment now Kitty would be aware of someone else in the room.

So he went by instinct. He distracted Kitty by pushing his dick hard into her willing wet mouth. Her enthusiastic sucking automatically elicited an equally enthusiastic response from his body. He watched McGuy slipping casually out of his room as he blew his load into Kitty's mouth. She never even knew. But Conor understood he'd passed some sort of test that night.

"That's called keeping cool under pressure, boy," McGuy had said later.

Still under the misapprehension that it was all on Kitty's part, he had told Conor that he had to learn to say no to sex sometimes. However, when he started noticing how aggressively Kitty chased after Conor every time Seamus wasn't around, he shook his head in resignation.

"Son, I know you're young and a hot thing like Kitty's going to twist you around her little finger and make you want to get into her panties every time. Do you know how dangerous that is? Do you really want her that bad?" he'd asked one night.

"Yes, sir," Conor had replied truthfully.

McGuy had looked at him, obviously waiting for a second answer, but when Conor had kept quiet, he gave a sigh. "Well, then, you'll never make it in the CIA if you're going to fall for every pretty woman who wants you." Giving Conor one last level look, he'd added, "You do not, I repeat, do not, ever talk to her about me and you, or God help me, son, you'll be dead faster than you can unzip those jeans of yours. She's a dangerous woman, son."

Conor would never forget that look. The man who had brought him into the IRA wasn't a man who lightly made threats.

"And if Seamus comes back, I'll just slip out the back window again," Kitty's voice interrupted his thoughts.

Conor walked over to stand by his bed. Kitty leaned further back, sliding onto her elbows. A smile of anticipation touched her shapely lips.

Six months. He'd been fucking this woman six months and she always had the same effect on him—tantalizing and tempting. She seemed to know that he liked the danger of thinking Seamus might catch them at it.

"Do you want him to kill me, is that it?" Conor asked, cocking his head. He took a step closer. "You know he's waiting for the chance."

"Of course not. I can't help myself. I think I'm in love with you." Kitty stretched back sensuously. She closed her eyes for a moment. "I think about your cock in me all the time, all right? There's something wrong with that."

The thing about Kitty was, she talked to him as if he was a man, not someone eight or ten years younger. He knew she still thought he was over eighteen, but he also suspected if she'd known how young he really was, she'd still let him fuck her. That was how she was—a woman of passion who didn't care about rules or propriety. He liked being with her; she was raw and sexy, totally at ease with her

251

sexuality. He found himself able to do things with her that he'd never done with the other lasses, mostly because they always coyly refused or they weren't experienced enough. Kitty, however, was neither. She never refused him.

Still, he needed her out of his room quickly. Not only was there Seamus to think about. McGuy was staying over tonight and Conor had been trying to show the older man that he was all grown-up and responsible, that he was a good asset for the CIA. McGuy was going to privately go over certain things with him about tomorrow's operation.

The promise of being trained and going to special schools, of traveling to different countries, and of being given knowledge about things he'd always wanted to learn about, was why he'd willingly followed McGuy back here with the sack of weapons. It was cool to know he was part of an undercover operation even though part of him was still suspicious—why would this man want to take him into the CIA? What if he wasn't CIA?

"Are you going to just stand there, lover boy?" Kitty asked, raising one leg and using her toes to caress the bulge on the front of his pants. "Maybe you want me to wrestle you onto the bed and have my way with you, hmm? In that kind of mood?"

Conor grinned. If he let Kitty play with him the way she liked, they would be in bed for hours and he'd really get into trouble with McGuy then. He unbuttoned his fly.

"You know we don't have time for that," he said. When she stuck her tongue out, lewdly showing him what she'd in mind, he felt his cock responding, pushing hard against his pants. He growled out, "Tease."

It was hard to say no to all that womanly enticement spread out on his bed. He really, really wanted to jump on top of her and fuck her. Temptation had never tasted so sweet in his life. But McGuy had warned him that if he thought only with his cock, he'd never make it. If he started on Kitty now, he wouldn't be just risking Seamus's coming back and discovering them; he would be risking the whole operation tomorrow.

His hesitation didn't go unnoticed by Kitty. She nudged him with her toes again. "What's the matter?" She cocked her head, eyes narrowing slightly. "Don't tell me you're afraid."

"Have you ever thought about what will happen if we got caught?" Conor asked. Ignoring the silent urging in his pants, he turned and sat down on the bed by Kitty. "Not just between Seamus and me. There's bad blood there already, anyway, but you know the rest of the group will have to take sides and I'm still the new man here, Kitty. They'll side with Seamus and I'll be out on the streets again."

"Actually, they'll kill you sooner rather than let you loose on the streets again," Kitty said, with a small smile on her lips.

"Not one for sugar-coating the truth, are you?"

"You want to play with the big boys, you have to learn the big boys' ways," Kitty told him. "Right now you're of use to the cause. You've managed to get inside the bank and find out the things we needed to know. You have an excellent memory for spatial layouts and a talent with getting people to talk. It's not Seamus that's pleased with you but our bosses on top, Conor, because you have shown that you're a natural."

"A natural?" Conor repeated.

Kitty stretched and yawned, kicking off her shoes. "A natural. Who found out on his own that the bank president was buying a new car and therefore saved us from making the mistake of looking for a different vehicle tomorrow? Who thought up the idea of spray painting the outside security cameras?"

He did. He remembered McGuy's approving look and Seamus's scowl. He shrugged. "If you want to rob a bank and kidnap the bank president, then timing's the most important detail here," he said.

"That's right, just as the timing of my explosive device is," Kitty said. She tugged at the back of his jeans pocket. "You're always thinking ahead and your mind is always clicking along like a computer, even though you're sitting there calmly cleaning a gun. And that's why I'm in love with you. You turn me on without even trying."

Conor gave in to her tugging, falling on his back onto the bed. She snuggled against him, her mouth to his ear, her hand busy already. "Is that what love is?" he murmured. Love to him was something that happened on television shows, not in real life. "Love is all about getting turned on while watching me clean a gun?"

"No, lover," she whispered. "It's more than that."

A few minutes later, he murmured, with a smile, "Love's all about watching you clean my gun too?"

Kitty climbed on top of him, her lips wet and amusement in her dark eyes. "More than that." A few minutes later, she added, her voice breathy now, "More than this too."

Conor held her hips steady as he rolled over so he would be on top. Since getting a lover, he'd learned to control himself a lot more. Kitty had taught him many ways to please a woman, such as, if he tilted her hips to the right and angled his thrust—like this—he was rewarded by her soft cries, her insides milking him, as she came.

"More than that too?" he teased, as he continued his thrusts, knowing that she would be too sensitive to talk back to him.

She gurgled as he parted her thighs wider so he could drive inside her deeper, keeping her hips tilted to the right. Soon, if he kept the same steady pace, she would come again, violently this time, and, he'd discovered that if he reached down and fingered her clitoris at the right moment, he could keep her in that state longer.

Her nails raked across his back as she spasmed violently. He was glad he still had his tee shirt on. He wondered whether he could prolong her pleasure even more. He'd heard that some women fainted from coming so much but had always thought that was something his older brother made up; being with Kitty had opened his eyes. Women could do things with their bodies men couldn't. He was fascinated by them and by the way they were so responsive to his touches.

Kitty liked to make love for hours and was so good at giving him pleasure that he always complied, letting her climb on top and take charge of the pace. Whatever pleased the lady was fine by him. But this time, his mind was still on McGuy and he wasn't planning on getting in trouble. He'd like to give her the kind of pleasure that his brother talked about, and then he would have killed two birds with one stone—satisfy his lover and take her back to her place before McGuy showed up. He felt himself grow even harder at the thought of her wild and begging for him.

He pulled out of her and flipped her small shapely body around. He tucked an arm under her tummy and pulled her onto her knees.

"What—what are you doing, Conor?" Kitty turned her head, her eyes mirroring the surprise mingled with excitement in her voice.

She gasped as he entered her from behind, pushing in all the way. He moved his hand that was splayed across her tummy lower as he parted her legs wider for more access. Her gasp turned into a throaty scream as he stroked her with his fingers and slammed into her again.

He didn't relent, changing positions each time she came, taking advantage of her weak compliance to pleasure her differently. She went wild under his mouth, trying to buck him off at one point. He easily stopped that by sucking on her sensitive bud, holding her captive with his tongue.

She begged then. He slipped his fingers inside her.

Her begging turned to moans, punctuated with a few "waits".

He ignored her soft plea to catch her breath as he caressed her with his mouth and fingers, carefully building her heat back to a feverish pitch. Her hands pushed hard against his shoulders as she squirmed, her throaty groans growing louder as her release came in violent shudders.

He tasted her with one final lingering lick and climbed on top again, still rock hard, ready to come himself, wondering whether he could hold off his climax for just a few minutes more. He played with her till he felt her arch upwards, on the verge, then he replaced his fingers with his ready erection, sliding in all the way, deep and hard. She was hot and wet, her whole body eagerly meeting his.

The need to come clawed at his brain. It was sweet agony to slide into her slowly at first and just as slowly pull out, then slam in deep and hard. He forced himself to slowly pull out again. Repeat. He named all the saints he knew as he continued the pace, all the blood in his body seemingly bottling up in his aching erection. Kitty was mindlessly mewling underneath him, her hands stroking his chest and arms, her words a mixture of English and her mother tongue. He'd never heard her like that before.

"St. Ex...pe...ditus..." he forced out. "St..."

He was out of saints to name. He slammed into her. Out of control. Hard and fast. His orgasm came like a force of nature, seemingly endless and violent, taking over his body and brain.

There was a long silence afterwards. Conor finally moved, taking his weight off Kitty. He looked down at her. She was just lying there, her eyes closed, her mouth open.

"Kitty?" he called softly.

A soft moan was all he got. She was out like a light.

Conor smiled triumphantly. Hell, he was going to be a sex god from now on.

He heard the phone ring three times. Shit. That was McGuy's signal he would be here in five minutes.

"Kitty! Where the fuck are you?" Seamus's shout suddenly blasted out of the window above his flat.

Conor looked down at Kitty. Now what? He couldn't fuck up tomorrow's job and jeopardize McGuy's work. One thing was sure. Being a sex god was going to get him killed.

Outside Dublin, Ireland

Conor coughed. The taste of blood filled his mouth and he spat it out. He was a dead man. He couldn't last another round of being Seamus's punching bag. The man would have killed him a lot sooner but he had a lot of hate in him because he knew Kitty had been cheating on him with Conor.

Jesus, Mary, and Joseph. He remembered thinking being a sex god was going to kill him. Did he think he was going to live to see past eighteen, the way he was fucking her senseless right under her lover's nose?

McGuy had been absolutely right, but McGuy's warnings were useless to him now. His protector was dead—some kind of assassination during the last job. He suspected Seamus'd had a hand in it, but didn't have any proof.

He hadn't ever thought McGuy might up and die on him and leave him in this mess. His only friend was part of this group of IRA terrorists and yet not. McGuy had been his shield from the likes of Seamus, who hadn't wanted him in. Without the older man, he had seen the little status he had became nothing.

The first thing Seamus had done within days of McGuy's death was trap him with four of his men and had them beat the hell out of him. Then he'd laid McGuy's death at his door, claiming that Conor had sold their IRA leader to the authorities, using video feed of him talking to agents. It was ironic that he'd been caught talking to those men as a messenger for McGuy because his mentor happened to be CIA himself.

Conor coughed again, the pain in his chest burning like fire all the way up to his eyeballs. McGuy was killed by Seamus's people, not the CIA. He supposed he could tell them McGuy *was* CIA, but fuck that. If he was going to die anyhow, he wasn't going to betray the one man who had given him a chance.

He tried to laugh, but it came out like a hoarse, screechy sound. Gave him a chance. Perhaps he was a fool to believe that. He'd seen McGuy at work—that man was as ruthless as Seamus, if not more. He was like the movie spies, a double agent, a man who took lives and lived dangerously. Giving Conor McNeil a chance was probably just another expedient way for him to use a boy as a go-between.

Conor clenched his hands. He would not cry. If nothing else, he would die like a man. McGuy had once told him death was easy, living was harder. He had never really understood all the things McGuy had told him, even though he'd paid attention. Now, after endless days of starvation and pain, he was wondering who would want to live that hard anyhow.

McGuy, you son of a bitch, dying on me like that. You promised me the CIA would let me travel and see the world.

If you survive this, son.

The echo of the dead man's words lay like a ten-ton weight on Conor's chest. All right. He hadn't lied. Only, McGuy hadn't survived this as well, and he'd been like a father to him the past nine or ten months. It hurt to know he was dead. It hurt to think he was going to probably die soon.

"Conor? Are you awake?"

His head jerked toward the sound. Not that he could see much out of his swollen eyes. He'd recognize the accent anywhere. Kitty. She was really going to get into trouble if she got caught. "Is that my angel of Death coming to take me?" he cracked.

The door creaked and he heard the lock turning. "Hush. I don't have much time. Seamus has to meet someone and I bribed Daniel so I can get to talk to you." She was kneeling by his side, her hands hurting his face. "Oh my God, Conor, oh my God."

"The love of your life, remember? Not your god. Unless you plan to worship me after I go to the other side. And if you think Daniel wouldn't betray you, you're a stupid woman, Kitty, my love."

"Don't be stupid yourself. I'm out of here as soon as I leave you. I'm saying goodbye. Seamus has gone fucking crazy where you're concerned, and I'm not going to hang around and let him kill me too. I know you didn't betray McGuy. Half of us didn't think so either, but Seamus has too much power and you're hard to defend among the status-quo, Conor."

Conor listened, and couldn't help smiling, even though any movement felt like someone was ripping the skin off his face. "I like it when you talk sexy," he said. "So this is goodbye, huh, Kitty? I know you got to care a little to risk coming here before slipping away. If you didn't, you'd have just disappeared."

"Shut up! I love you. I told you I do. Our kind of life isn't supposed to be long and boring, you know. I'm a woman who likes trouble and danger, remember? I'll miss you."

"Are you so sure I'm going to die? Maybe I'll live."

"Seamus brought back a whip last night."

"Shit." That didn't sound promising.

"Conor." There was a plea in her voice. "I can't kill you. I don't want you in pain, but I can't kill you. Not like this. And I can't watch him kill you either."

"I understand." What was he supposed to say? Don't leave him here to die alone? "Kitty, you should go."

"I have another reason to get away quickly. I'm pregnant."

Conor blinked, not even sure he heard right. Shock wasn't close to what he was feeling. Pregnant? "Mine?" he asked.

"I think so, but maybe not." He could almost feel her shrug, that casual lift of the shoulder that was so Kitty. "But that's not the point. Seamus will think it's yours and if he thinks it is, he'll do things to me that would make me very, very unhappy about life, and I don't think that suits my style at all."

"Maybe he'll marry you," Conor whispered, still feeling dazed.

"And would you want your child brought up by Seamus?"

"Fuck. No. Fuck. I can't be a father. I'm not old enough!"

"Now he thinks sperm understands age and timing," Kitty said dryly. "On his deathbed no less. Conor, I know you're very young, but you aren't stupid, even if Seamus might have beaten your brains to molasses. I love you and I'm keeping this baby in case it's yours, so I have to go. Do you understand that?"

"But where will you go?" He didn't want to die now. Kitty was pregnant. Who was going to feed the baby? The poor thing would start life like him, without a loving father. Let's face it, Kitty wasn't exactly loving mother material. "You've got to get me out of here so we can get married so the baby has a name."

He heard her little gasp of shock, as if his words were totally unexpected. "Conor, be realistic. You're half-dead right now. We can't run off without getting ourselves killed the moment we step out of this room together. Daniel will be knocking on the door soon anyway. Look, I just didn't want you to die not knowing I love you and that maybe you're going to be a father."

"Kitty, your brand of charm does wonders to a dying man," he told her. In his own way, he did love this woman and wanted her to get out of this alive. In another, it pained him that she would just give up on him so easily. He was only half-dead, after all. "Well, if you must go, marry me here. We'll just say the words with God as our witness, so the baby will grow up having a nice last name like McNeil."

"You're...not kidding, are you?"

"No."

"Okay."

That was his Kitty. Always quick with decisions. Always liking anything that bordered on crazy.

He couldn't remember the correct wording of the marriage vows. He made most of them up, and she helped him with her version. She held his hand tightly as she repeated after him.

"Honor, obey...well, protect is out..."

"Just repeat it, Kitty love."

"Protect," she said. "I love you. I'll protect our baby."

"And now we're man and wife till death do us part." He was messing up the lines but the "death do us part" bit was coming soon anyway. "Where will you take our baby?"

"To live with my mother."

"Seamus?"

"Won't know. I'm not from Ireland, you know. And the Irish business is too busy to look in a small village in Malaysia."

"All right. But do me a favor after you leave."

"What?"

Could he trust Kitty? He had to take the chance. "Call a number and leave a message for me."

"What message?"

"After the recording, just say, 'Conor's alive' and the date." It was probably too late to do what McGuy told him he must do in the event plans didn't go smoothly. With their inside man dead, why would the CIA care about a boy like him? And how would they know where to find him? And would they even be on time? But a dying man had few choices and one chance. "Leave the location too, Kitty."

There was a pause. "You are CIA!"

Conor lifted one shoulder. "Nah. But like you, I have contacts too. It'd be nice to think I might come out of this alive so I can find you, Kitty. I won't—" a wracking cough interrupted him, "—abandon my child."

She kissed him. Softly, so as not to hurt him.

"You're a really sweet boy. And with a noble streak that's not quite real. I can take care of myself, you know, but I'll do this. If this is your only chance, I'll give it to you. Knowing that I've tried to save you will make it less painful for me."

"Getting romantic, are we?" Conor asked. Kitty would always be Kitty, no matter what. There wasn't an ounce of sappiness in that lass. He whispered the number in her ear. "Did you get that?"

She repeated it back softly in his. "Right?"

"Right. Say it again."

When she was gone, Conor stared up at the darkness. Jesus, Mary and Joseph. He was a father. For the first time in a long time, he prayed to live to see the baby.

The front door exploded. Everyone ran for cover.

Everyone except him, of course, because he was hung with his face flattened against the wall. He could barely turn his head to see what was happening; it hurt too much. He smelled fire and heard the gunshots and shouts all around him. Several holes punctured the wall against which he was leaning and he felt bits of plaster splattering him.

A body slammed against the wall right next to him. It was Seamus, blood gushing from a wound in his neck. His head turned and his startled eyes stared into Conor's.

An hour ago, those eyes had been glinting with malevolent satisfaction. He had pulled Conor up by the hair so he could look into his swollen eyes before telling him, "Today, boy, I'll see you dead."

Conor met the wild terror of the man who had whipped him to an inch of his life. He was making gurgling noises, hand grasping at his bloody throat.

"Not if I see you dead first." Conor forced those words out, grunting more than speaking.

And then the gunfire stopped. There were people walking about but he couldn't see anything from his position. Maybe they thought he was dead. Maybe they were leaving without him. He forced his head to move, so he could look behind him. A horrendous groan came out of him as excruciating pain burned his whole back. He dug his nails into the wall, continuing to turn his head.

The first thing he saw must have been a hallucination. Or maybe he had died after all.

"McGuy," Conor croaked out. The man standing behind him looked exceptionally healthy for an assassinated man. If he were dead, he should look like hell too since he was gunned down and firebombed to pieces. He added, unnecessarily, "You're not dead."

The man shook his head. His hands reached up to cut the ropes binding Conor to the wall. Everything went black.

Someone was moaning. He didn't want anyone to touch his back.

All at once Conor realized that he was the one making that horrible racket. He couldn't struggle against the strong hands hurting him, carrying him away. Everywhere they touched felt like a brand of fire.

"Son, I don't know how you lived through this. I'm here. You're safe. We're going to give you a shot to put you to sleep because you're not in any condition to travel without any drugs. Okay?"

"Kitty—"

"We got the message. She's a bright girl, is our Kitty. She's gone and is okay."

"Where—"

"We'll talk later. On the plane. We're taking you to the States."

Conor felt the drug working and welcomed the release from the pain.

"Promise me you'll take care of her, McGuy. She's pregnant. I...must...find... make sure...find where...my kid...I don't want to die..."

"Hush now."

Conor reached out blindly and found a hand holding his own swollen one. "Promise. My child," he mumbled. He couldn't really form any coherent thoughts. All he knew was that he had something important to do. He must find something. Finally, he gave in to the drug. "My father hated me."

Before he passed out, he heard McGuy say, "I promise. We'll do all we can to find her, Conor." A sigh. "Poor damn kid. Look at what that fucking monster did to his back."

About the Author

Gennita Low is known as the rooferauthor whose bestselling novels feature sexy spies and action-packed military espionage. She can kill six hundred different ways with a nail gun. She's been known to run a job, yell at men, throw bundles of shingles around AND edit a manuscript all at the same time. A three-time RWA Golden Heart finalist and winner of numerous writing awards, Gennita was a translator in a former life, enabling her to scold her workers in Malay, Chinese and German. She's also the beloved prisoner of her four mutant Pomeranians. *Virtually Hers* is her eighth published title.

Blood ties run deepest—and deadliest.

Proof of Life
© 2009 Misty Evans
Super Agent Series, book 3

No matter how many times he patches the holes in the wall, CIA Deputy Director Michael Stone can't forget the night a terrorist took him hostage in his own home. Or the mistakes that transformed him into an overwhelming force to keep his country safe. And now that his niece, the daughter of the Republican candidate for President, has been kidnapped just days from the election, Michael vows to do whatever it takes to get her back.

Dr. Brigit Kent, a consultant for the Department of Homeland Security, knows this particular kidnapper well. Exposing him, however, will reveal her sister's secret ties to a terrorist group. The only way to keep her sister safe is to blackmail the sexy, rock-solid deputy director. A move that puts her directly in his line of fire.

Brigit is undeniably beautiful, brilliant, cunning. But is she friend or foe? The answer to that question could break Michael's personal code of honor—and his heart.

Warning: Bullets and blackmail, good luck and laughter. Surprises and secrets and love ever after...

Available now in ebook and print from Samhain Publishing.

GREAT
cheap
fun

Discover eBooks!

THE FASTEST WAY TO GET THE HOTTEST NAMES

Get your favorite authors on your favorite reader, long before they're out in print! Ebooks from Samhain go wherever you go, and work with whatever you carry—Palm, PDF, Mobi, and more.

Samhain
publishing ltd

WWW.SAMHAINPUBLISHING.COM

CPSIA information can be obtained at www.ICGtesting.com
Printed in the USA
BVOW07s1251250713

326956BV00002B/150/P